## About the Author

At home in Surrey, JULIET ASHTON writes all day in her small study while her two dogs stare at her. The rest of her house, which is full of music and books and comfy places to sit, she shares with her twelve-year-old daughter and her husband, who's a composer (hence the music). She believes wholeheartedly in the power of books to improve lives, increase understanding and while away happy hours.

## Praise for Juliet Ashton:

'Funny, original and wise' Katie Fforde

'Cecelia Ahern fans will love this poignant yet witty romance' *Sunday Mirror*

'You'll laugh and cry your way through this original and touching love story' *Closer*

'It's a gorgeous ride with a hell of a final shock' *Star Magazine*

'A fast paced story with a most unexpected twist' *Image Magazine*

Also by Juliet Ashton

*The Valentine's Card*

# These Days of Ours

## JULIET ASHTON

**SIMON &
SCHUSTER**

London · New York · Sydney · Toronto · New Delhi

A CBS COMPANY

First published in Great Britain by Simon & Schuster UK Ltd, 2016
A CBS company

1 3 5 7 9 10 8 6 4 2

Simon & Schuster UK Ltd
1st Floor
222 Gray's Inn Road
London WC1X 8HB

www.simonandschuster.co.uk

Simon & Schuster Australia, Sydney
Simon & Schuster India, New Delhi

A CIP catalogue record for this book is available from the British Library

Paperback ISBN: 978-1-4711-5505-5
eBook ISBN: 978-1-4711-5506-2

Typeset by Hewer Text UK Ltd, Edinburgh
Printed and bound in Great Britain by CPI Group
(UK) Ltd, Croydon, CR0 4YY

Simon & Schuster UK Ltd are committed to sourcing paper that is made
from wood grown in sustainable forests and support the Forest Stewardship
Council, the leading international forest certification organisation. Our
books displaying the FSC logo are printed on FSC certified paper.

*This book is for*
*Kate Furnivall*

*Please Come to Kate's 5th Birthday Party!*

Date: 29th July, 1981
Time: 2pm–5pm
Address: 36 Lambrook Terrace
R.S.V.P. 01 736 4534

The crumpled invitation had somehow survived thirty-five years and numerous house moves, its words still legible, though faded:

Kate tucked it into the corner of the dressing table mirror as she leaned in, eyeing her reflection sideways, as if trying to take it unawares. 'Not bad. Not *good*. But not bad. Happy Birthday, me!'

The invitation slipped a little and caught her eye. Kate had shared her fifth birthday party with Princess Diana's wedding day. She was ambushed by peachy nostalgia: the whole nation had been so in love with Lady Di. She remembered the mums around the TV set, ooh-ing at the new princess's dress.

*And then Becca broke my new Action Man.* Kate sighed. *Typical.* Her cousin had been unable to comprehend why a

1

girl would want an Action Man, but their classmate Charlie had understood.

Kate conjured him up. Slightly whiffy and very scruffy. The other kids gave Charlie Garland a wide berth because he was different. Kate had overlooked the nits because he was also *good*-different; quiet but not boring, Charlie didn't tease the girls just for being girls.

A sudden noise jerked Kate back to the present. It sounded just like the idiosyncratic yawn of the front door scraping open. She listened hard, but heard only the silence of an empty house, a silence that is actually a gentle soundtrack of ticks and creaks.

Turning back to the mirror, Kate regarded her tired but merry eyes. *This is what forty looks like.* Kate tapped the underside of her chin in case it harboured any ideas about drooping on the threshold of her – gulp – fifth decade. All in all, her reflection didn't look too bad if she left out her contact lenses.

Standing up, Kate paused at a ghost of a noise, more a *swish* than an actual sound. She wondered at her jumpiness. *God knows, I've had enough practice at being alone.* Today, as on every other day, her house curled around her, snug and calm.

And empty. For many, forty was the perfect excuse for a party but Kate had opted out; a lifelong party goer/giver, she'd let the usual suspects know that this milestone would pass with no birthday 'do'.

Reaching into the wardrobe, Kate's hand found the dress immediately. She marvelled again at the weight of it. Pale satin, with the milky sheen of pearls, the dress was cut with a devastating simplicity that echoed more elegant times. Kate could testify to its waist-shrinking, arm-flattering superpowers.

Heavy layers of satin and tulle swooned against Kate as she held the frock against her dressing gown, holding it like a lover. The dress made her feel like Audrey Hepburn. A lumpy Audrey, admittedly, with a few more miles on the clock, but a very happy Audrey all the same. Waltzing dreamily, Kate withstood the urge to reflect and ruminate on this landmark birthday. She wouldn't dwell on the missed chances, the fluffed catches, the absentees she missed so deeply . . .

But sometimes the past pushes in without asking. Suddenly Kate was five again, blowing out the candles on her cake. Charlie had sidled up to her, to stand very close and say 'I like your dress', low and urgently, like a small spy passing on classified information. Kate remembered snapping 'What?' She'd been suspicious of compliments, mistrusting them as much as Becca craved them.

Charlie's hands had gripped his paper plate so hard it trembled. 'I love you,' he'd whispered.

Kate hadn't hesitated; she'd pushed Charlie's face into the iced sponge.

Now, Kate replaced the dress in the wardrobe, where it effortlessly outranked its denim and cotton peers. She stroked it regretfully, as if it was an exotic pet that had to be put down. *Pity I'll never get to wear you.* Kate shut the door on the wonderful confection, its skirt puffing out and resisting. Even if she dyed it or took up the hem, a dress like that could never be anything but a wedding dress, which rendered it quite useless to Kate.

She wheeled at the unmistakable sound of a foot on the stairs. Kate crossed to the door. 'Who's there?' she called, certain now that she was not alone.

Becca's parties were legendary.

This one was particularly well attended thanks to Becca's promise that her parents would be out for the whole evening. With a wink, she'd guaranteed, 'It'll be the best party in the history of the known world.'

A couple of hours in, and on her second glass of suspiciously strong punch, Kate agreed. Not because of the Everest of cocktail sausages she'd helped build, nor the plastic bin filled with ice and beer, nor the fairy lights that transformed the ground floor of Aunty Marjorie and Uncle Hugh's over-tasteful sitting room into a magical grotto alive with possibility.

Tonight would be memorable – downright historic – because, for Kate, tonight was *the* night.

She would *do it*. She would shrug off her pesky virginity. She would have sex. That phrase made Kate wince so she amended it speedily to Make Love, awarding it capitals because, as all the magazines said, as her 'experienced' friends declared, it was a giant step in a girl's life.

Or maybe that should be A Giant Step.

Downstairs, *Things Can Only Get Better*, a constant on Kate's pink Walkman, blared out. Her friends, head to toe in trendiest black, bellowed the anthemic chorus, leaping up and down on Aunty Marjorie's cherished Persian rugs. Everybody Kate knew dressed in black all the time. Polo necks. Tights. It was as if there was no other colour available in the shops; as if all teenagers were constantly en route to a funeral.

Up in the spare bedroom, the music was muffled to a thumping pulse in the darkness. Kate sat on the pile of coats on the bed and regarded her boyfriend of six months, who was kissing distance away. Charlie was taller than her. She liked how she had to stand on tiptoes to kiss him, and she liked the concave spot just below his shoulder where her head fitted when they wound their arms about each other. There were things she didn't like about him – his tendency to get stuck into a tedious conversation with her dad when Kate was ready to leave the house, or his ambivalence towards Becca – but they didn't seem to matter.

'Why not?' Kate was asking. 'Seriously, though,' she said, seriously. 'We're mad about each other, aren't we?'

'Yes.' Charlie's dark eyebrows descended, as if he was in pain. 'Of course we are. Well,' he added, those eyebrows on the up again. '*I'm* mad about *you*.'

Kate punched him. Rather hard. 'Sorry,' she laughed when he flinched. 'So . . . we're crazy about each other and we have a bedroom to ourselves with no parents popping in without knocking . . . so why don't we . . .' Kate had been practising her sultry look but suspected it was more duck than siren.

'It's not very romantic, is it?' Charlie looked around the sparsely furnished spare room with its magnolia woodchip walls and its fitted wardrobes. In a corner stood an exercise bike, with drying underwear – sturdy enough to suggest it was Aunty Marjorie's rather than Becca's – draped over its handlebars. A half-built model aeroplane sat marooned on the beige carpet. 'And I can't think of a single epic love poem about the coat pile.' He squirmed on the shifting hillock of cardigans and jackets.

'Write one, then.' Kate poked him. This time she didn't say sorry. 'Take some time off from writing the greatest novel the world has ever read.'

'You call it that,' said Charlie. 'Not me.' Kate knew if she patted the back pocket of Charlie's punky pinstripe trousers (that wasn't a bad idea; she was keen on Charlie's bottom) she'd encounter a tiny notepad and a stub of pencil. 'You say your novel is about love. Real love. Raw important love. Small, beautiful love.' Kate ducked to maintain eye contact as he dipped his head, wincing as she quoted him back at himself. 'Think of it as research!'

Edging closer, trusting proximity and pheromones to be her most persuasive allies, Kate placed a hand on Charlie's thigh. 'Come here,' she said in a low voice. They kissed and she moved nearer still, so they were entwined, his strong arms like straitjacket sleeves around her.

'Kate, no,' he murmured.

'But why?' she murmured back. Kate knew of Charlie's sexual adventures with his ex. Everybody knew. His ex was not a discreet girl. Kate froze, mid-kiss, as an unwelcome thought coughed and made itself known. 'Christ, Charlie!' She pulled away, popping their bubble of intimacy. 'Did you fancy Natalie more than me?' She jumped up as he laughed. 'Don't laugh at me! Answer the question.'

Spreading his hands in a gesture of surrender, Charlie said, 'I laughed because that's dumb, Kate. I fancy you more than I've ever fancied anybody. I fancy you more than . . .' He cast about desperately for some goddess that any sensible male of his age would lust after. 'More than Demi Moore!' he shouted, triumphant.

'Yeah, right.' Kate knew what she was and what she wasn't. She was five feet and a little bit, with legs that were more reliable than elegant, and a witty face peeping out from a fringe that was never quite straight. She prowled, arms folded, as the moody rumble of Oasis seeped up through the floorboards.

'Don't you get it?' pleaded Charlie. 'I don't just fancy you, Kate. That's only part of it. I love you.'

That wasn't the first time Charlie had said that since Kate's fifth birthday party, but it was still in single digits. Kate stared at him, his straight nose and full lips outlined in the silver moonlight that struggled through Aunty Marjorie's neurotically ironed net curtains. His jumpers were no longer stained and he was now the parent to his feckless mother, but Charlie's basic raw material was unchanged since 1981. He'd been certain then and he was certain now, but how could he be so sure this was love? Kate's friends bandied the word, using it about one boy one week, and another lad the next. Kate was cautious about the four letters, wary of their power, sure of their magic.

Charlie reached out from the bed and took each of her hands in his, unfolding her arms, unlocking her mood a little. 'You never seem to believe me when I say it,' he whispered. In the dark his body was almost invisible in its *de rigueur* black, his disembodied face an anxious oval above his polo neck, his hair wilting a little, despite the gel he lavished on it.

'I do believe you.' Kate looked down at him, benign again. How speedily her moods shifted around Charlie. 'I do,' she repeated sadly. 'So why can't we . . .?'

'I've never done it before.' Charlie's lips clamped shut over his admission, as if daring her to comment.

'Yes you have!' Kate realised how ridiculous it was to insist Charlie was wrong about his own virginity, or lack thereof. 'Haven't you?'

'Believe it or not, sometimes you girls get the facts wrong when you huddle in the loos and swap stories.' Charlie dropped her hands and stood up. Over by the window his slender body took shape in the mercury light. 'I don't know why Natalie said we had sex. We just kissed, really, and fooled around a bit.' He half smiled over his shoulder. 'Sorry. I know you don't like me talking about her.'

'Now I know she's a lying nutcase I don't mind so much.' Kate sat heavily on the end of the bed. 'I really thought . . .'

'I wanted to tell you. But it's embarrassing.' His head sank. 'All the other guys have done it.' Charlie cleared his throat, said casually, 'Guess this is when you chuck me, yeah?'

'What if the other boys only *say* they've done it?' Kate stretched out one leg, inky as a spider in its opaque hosiery, ending in a clumpy black shoe. 'You're right, Charlie. This isn't the right time or place for our first time. We can wait.' Marvelling at his assumption she'd dump him over something so trivial, Kate pretended not to notice how his whole body sighed with relief. 'Fancy a dance?'

'No.' Charlie closed the distance between them with one stride, laying Kate back among the coats and covering her body with his. 'I fancy *you*.' He kissed her, his hair flopping into her eyes. They almost slid to the floor, but righted themselves, refusing to let their lips lose contact.

'You've changed your mind, then?' giggled Kate against his teeth as she tugged at his jumper and he fumbled, chimp-like, with the buttons of her shirt.

'We don't need romance,' breathed Charlie, leaning away just long enough to tear his jumper over his head and toss it away. 'We *are* romance.'

Suddenly the music grew louder. A wedge of gold appeared on the floor. The door had opened, just a sliver.

Kate dived under the coats.

'*Shit!*' Charlie followed her, hurriedly pulling windcheaters and denim jackets and second-hand raincoats over them both. By the time the triangle of light grew large enough to illuminate the bed, they'd burrowed down deep and were invisible to the incomers.

Nose to nose in their murky tent, Kate mouthed *Becca!* to Charlie as she heard her cousin say, 'Julian! Listen! This is important,' in the special voice she used to house-train boyfriends, nine parts candy floss to one part napalm.

'And so is this.'

Kate and Charlie stifled their giggles, their faces beetroot, as smoochy noises travelled through the layers of coats. *Urgh!*

mimed Kate, who had no wish to eavesdrop on Becca's romantic interlude.

'No!' said Becca. 'If I don't get what I want, then neither do you.'

'Oh come here.' Six foot four of British upper class male entitlement, gift wrapped in corduroy and tweed, Julian was accustomed to getting his own way. He and Becca illustrated the well-known paradox *irresistible force meets immovable object*. The pair of them were both irresistible *and* immovable, but Kate knew who she'd back in any battle of wills.

The music from downstairs turned up a notch. Bon Jovi yodelled loud enough to rattle the shelving. There would be complaints from the neighbours but Becca, Kate knew, would visit with flowers and wine and girlish remorse, and all would be forgiven. Good at making a mess, Becca was even better at clearing it up. Countless times, Becca had got Kate out of trouble. Almost as many times as she'd got her *into* trouble.

'God, you're gorgeous,' breathed Julian, as Charlie pretended to vomit.

'Kate helped me choose this.' Becca twirled for Julian in her burgundy micro mini. 'I borrowed her choker.'

'It looks better on you.'

Kate pulled an outraged face in the dark, but had to agree with Julian's ungentlemanly comment. Everything looked better on Becca. Anointed as the family 'Pretty One', she lived up to her title, with expensively tended blonde streaks and a diet-honed body.

Strangers always sensed the girls were related, even though one cousin was leggy and va-va-voom, and the other was shorter, darker and generally huddled over a book (the 'Clever One'). It was the eyes; both Kate and Becca saw the world through china blue peepers that hinted at their shared Irish heritage. Through the coats she heard her cousin defend her.

'Don't you say a bad word about my Kate. She's the best friend I could ever have.'

'I don't know why she puts up with you,' said Julian.

'She loves me,' said Becca, serene, certain. 'Like I love her. I'd give her my last penny.'

'But you'd borrow it back.' Julian risked moving closer. 'Never mind mousey little Kate . . .'

'No you don't!' Becca slapped away Julian's hands. 'Kate's no mouse. Leave her out of this. We need to talk.'

Julian exhaled loudly, his passion efficiently doused. 'I know what it means when girls say that. What have I done now?' He hung his blond head and bit his lip.

'It's what you *haven't* done.'

'Oh Christ.' Julian slapped his forehead. 'That's a big subject. We'll be here all night, woman. Can't we narrow it down?'

'How long have we been going out?'

13

'Six glorious months, beloved.' Julian snaked his arms around her waist.

'Same as us,' whispered Charlie.

'I'll never forget,' said Julian, nuzzling Becca's ear, 'how astonished I was to discover that good Catholic girls do it on the first date.'

Kate's eyes widened and she determined to take that up with Becca at another time; the sly little beast claimed she'd made Julian wait for weeks. *As if*, she thought, *sex is a treat to reward good behaviour, like throwing a chew toy to an obedient labrador.*

'Get *off*.' Becca shoved Julian. She was built along Valkyrie lines; he stumbled backwards on the model aeroplane and fell against the exercise bike.

'Steady on.'

Kate could tell from Julian's patrician tone that Becca had gone slightly too far. Unlike Kate's relationship with Charlie – which just pootled merrily along – her cousin's love affair was a series of strategic skirmishes. They'd met when Becca had applied to be a receptionist at Julian's property firm. He'd declared her 'far too distracting' to work with, and suggested dinner instead. They'd tussled for the upper hand ever since; Kate suspected that Julian underestimated his opponent.

A typical battle had been waged over Aunty Marjorie's Sunday lunch table just a few weeks ago, the balance of power passing from Becca to Julian and back again over the roast potatoes.

'We'd begun to wonder if we were ever going to meet Becca's chap,' said Aunty Marjorie, passing Julian a plate loaded with enough food to feed a greedy family of four.

'Hmm,' mused Becca archly. 'It's almost as if he didn't want to meet my family.' Her look stapled Julian to his chair. 'Almost as if he didn't want me to think we're getting serious.'

Julian laughed uncomfortably.

'So you *are* serious about Becca?' Kate's mum had asked, gravy on her chin.

'Of course he's serious about her,' said Aunty Marjorie. 'Aren't you, Julian? A well brought up chap like you would never lead my daughter up the garden path.'

'Well?' Becca had actually fluttered her eyelashes at Julian, who looked as if he wanted to throw down his cutlery and throttle her.

'I have very strong feelings for your daughter,' said Julian finally.

Aunty Marjorie nudged her husband and Uncle Hugh came to; he often drifted off into his secret dreamworld of golf and silent women.

'Go on,' hissed his wife.

Uncle Hugh looked at Julian with regret in his eyes, the way a vet might look at a gerbil he was about to euthanise. 'Are your intentions honourable, Julian?'

'Do people really still ask that?' Kate had been unable to keep quiet any longer.

'In this house they do.' Becca kicked her under the table.

Kate kicked her back and they both stifled a laugh, regressing yet again to their shared giggly childhood. This private universe, theirs to visit at will, was a place of joy and nonsense. When puzzled friends wondered at Kate's fondness for her cousin, she found it hard to explain why she was so attached to troublesome, all-guns-blazing Becca but it was to do with the way Becca made her *feel*. Around Becca, Kate felt brave. And a little reckless. For one of life's prefects, this was heady stuff.

'My intentions,' said Julian, snatching back the power by being as straight faced and cool as a statesman, 'are entirely honourable. I love your daughter, Mr and Mrs Neely, and I'd never hurt her.'

'Call me Marjorie!' quacked Becca's mother, HRT pulsing through her system like heroin.

As Julian helped Becca stack the dishwasher, there was a murmured conversation at the table.

'Such lovely manners.' Kate's mum was won over by Julian's breeding.

'And that voice . . .' Aunty Marjorie shuddered with pleasure.

'A lovely decent chap,' said Kate's mum, unaware that the decent chap was decanting her niece from her knickers in the utility room as she spoke.

Later, during the inevitable phone review of the day with Kate, Becca admitted, 'Julian was so mad at me. I thought for a minute I'd gone too far.'

'You always go too far. *Too far* is where you live.' Being related to somebody who kicked down boundaries meant Kate could live vicariously through Becca's antics.

'My mum's whistling the Bridal March.' Becca snorted. 'She reckons it's a done deal.'

'And is it?' Kate knew that Becca's ambition was of the berserk variety; she believed nothing was beyond her powers when it came to men.

'More or less.'

'Don't force him into anything.' Kate had a pang of sympathy for Julian, as if he were a wounded lion and Becca a big game hunter. She could almost hear the inward smile from the other end of the phone. The pincer movement had begun.

Now, in the spare room, Kate was privy to its climax.

'You love me, don't you, honeybear?' murmured Becca.

'You know I do,' said Julian. 'I'm nuts about you, sugarlips.'

Kate and Charlie daren't look at each other in their tent of coats. *Honeybear. Sugarlips.* This was too much.

'Why not show me how much?'

'That's what I'm trying to— ow!' Julian felt his cheek where it smarted from Becca's playful slap. 'Take it easy, babe.'

This tense interaction was familiar to Kate and Charlie from the two couples' regular double dates. At some point in the evening, Becca and Julian would inflate a minor disagreement into an all-out row. Passionate, demonstrative, the couple unnerved Charlie, who begged to see less of them.

'But it's Becca . . .' Kate would say. As an only child, she'd appreciated the proximity of a readymade friend. At times the girls referred to each other as almost-sisters. She'd stopped judging Becca years ago, but Charlie had no such history to call upon; from time to time he suggested that Kate should be less passive, that she should say no to Becca occasionally.

In answer, Kate would ruffle his hair. 'You're just annoyed because she bosses you around like a little brother.'

Then Charlie would shrug and they would kiss because he'd always known that Kate'n'Becca were a job lot; if he wanted one, he must put up with the other. The young women's childhood closeness had endured when they spread their wings because each of them felt understood when they were together. Becca knew all Kate's dark corners and sharp angles yet was relentlessly partisan, always on her side, always shoulder to shoulder with her cuz.

'That's just Becca being Becca,' Kate would smile when Becca forced them all to go to the movie only she wanted to see. But she could tell when Becca went too far with Julian, when she tested his goodwill a smidgeon too much. Perhaps pushing him across the spare room when he tried to kiss her would turn out to be one of those times; the pincer movement might be in danger of collapse.

'This is important, Julian, and all you want to do is snog!'

'You put it so poetically.'

In the dark, Kate wrinkled her nose. That edge to Julian's voice only appeared after a drink or three, when he would criticise Becca for her lack of 'culture' and suggest *Can't you be more like Kate? She reads actual books instead of fashion mags.* Kate was flattered that Julian took her seriously, singling her out for conversations while ignoring Kate's (it had to be admitted) fluffy girl chums, but she loathed his relish at taking Becca down a peg or two. And she told him so. Which was one of the many reasons she suspected Julian didn't like her much.

Becca either ignored or didn't catch the sneering tone and ploughed on. This ability to filter out what she didn't want to hear was one of the keys to her success with the opposite sex. 'Think, Julian. What would make my eighteenth birthday party totally utterly completely unforgettable?'

'A murder?' Julian laughed. He seemed oblivious to the gravity of his situation; Kate knew he was ambling into a mantrap. 'Stop asking me riddles, Becca. I'm a bit drunk and I've had too much of your mother's weird quiche, so tell me, gorgeous, what do you want? Because it's yours. You know I'd do anything for you.'

'Anything?' Becca almost purred.

Kate couldn't quite pin down the reason, but she had never endorsed Julian and Becca's union.

It wasn't because he found their crowd juvenile; it was natural that a bunch of teens must seem childish to a successful guy in his mid-twenties. Nor did she hold his haughty manner against him; unlike some of their friends, Kate was amused by Julian's insistence on fine wines and his unshakeable belief that a man without a tie is only half a man. It was something else, something in his eyes when he looked at Becca. Something was missing and that something was love.

Kate knew what a man in love looked like. Charlie had taught her that. With a sudden swelling of her heart for the strange, silly, gorgeous boy at her side, Kate kissed him hard on the lips and he jumped.

Engrossed in their head-to-head, Becca and Julian didn't notice the coat pile move.

'Think. What does a man do when he falls in love with a woman?' Becca's voice was sugary enough to cause dental cavities. 'Mmm?'

'He buys her lots of nice things,' said Julian, lifting her hand and kissing her wrist right by the gold charm bracelet she'd unwrapped an hour earlier. 'And he puts up with her mother. And he gives her lifts here, there and everywhere, even when he's busy with work. And he tells her she's beautiful on the hour every hour. I already do all that, darling.'

'No, I mean what does he *ask* her?'

'Dunno.' Julian pretended to think. 'How was it for you?' He ducked her swipe and said, long suffering, 'Get to the point so we can have a shag, Becca, yeah?'

*Charming.* Kate knew what Becca was angling for.

Some saw the disintegration of Princess Diana's story book marriage as a perfect illustration of why grown-ups no longer believe in fairy tales. Others – such as seventeen-year-old thoughtful Kate – saw it as a feminist fable about a virgin sacrifice to the patriarchy. Becca simply saw a vacancy for a princess. She'd been planning her wedding dress since she was old enough to hold a crayon and now the groom of her dreams was in her sights.

'He gets down on one knee,' said Becca slowly, clearly, so there could be no doubt about what she was suggesting. 'And he asks her to be his—'

'Becca, darling, I love you to bits but—' Julian's incontinent protest was stopped by Becca's finger on his lip.

'He asks her to be his wife,' she whispered.

The room was still. Beneath the coats, Kate and Charlie held their breath. The party seemed to have been muted. *Becca's played this so wrong!* Kate braced herself for the whirlwind of tears that would follow Julian's refusal to co-operate. *She can't hypnotise a man like him into marriage!*

'You are the most insufferable, troublesome, spoilt little madam I've ever come across,' said Julian. 'Will you marry me?'

21

'Yes!' screamed Becca. She jumped into his embrace, almost knocking him over again. 'Yes yes yes! Oh God, where's Kate! She'll die!' She obliterated Julian's face with kisses. 'I must ring my mum!' She kissed Julian again, more slowly this time. 'Do you want beef or chicken at the reception?' she said against his lips.

'You little monster,' said Julian indulgently.

'Can we tell everybody? Right now?'

'Hang on, hang on.' Julian put his hands on her shoulders. 'We need to do things properly. I should call your dad to make sure he approves.'

'He approves, he approves,' gabbled Becca. 'Mum won't let him disapprove.'

*Nobody*, thought Kate, *has mentioned love*. She felt a sense of foreboding that didn't suit the occasion. She snuggled into Charlie, needing his warmth, his solidity. She feared for her cousin, so insanely joyous, so wrong-headed. This empathy, this desire to protect a woman who didn't seem to need protecting, was a vital strand in the ties that bound Kate to Becca.

As Becca burbled, Julian shepherded her out of the room, trying and failing to dampen her stratospheric enthusiasm.

The door closed behind the newly engaged couple. Kate and Charlie crawled tentatively out from their bolt hole like startled woodland creatures.

'Bloody hell,' said Kate.

'That,' said Charlie, 'was a terrible proposal.'

'To be fair, all proposals are terrible to you.' Charlie was infamously anti-marriage.

'Yeah, but, if I *had* to propose,' said Charlie, his quiff in disarray, 'I'd do better than that. It was so unromantic. It was like a joke.'

'Julian wouldn't dare joke about weddings with Becca.' Kate giggled, not with mirth but with a nameless anxiety. 'They've messed up, Charlie. Really badly. I don't think he loves her.'

'I don't think she loves him,' said Charlie.

'Oh shit!' Kate put her hand to her mouth. 'She'll make me be bridesmaid!'

'Ha!' Charlie seemed delighted. 'Chiffon! Ballerina pumps! And a big flowery thing on your head!'

'Should we, you know, go downstairs?' Kate gestured half-heartedly towards the closed door, unsure if she could cope with the levels of excitement Becca would reach during her announcement. Sometimes, if she was honest, the strain of being a walk-on player in Becca's set pieces got to Kate.

'Suppose we should, really,' said Charlie.

They stood, irresolute, both reluctant but neither wanting to be the bad guy.

'I'm so glad you're *you*,' said Kate. 'And not Julian.'

'Um, good,' said Charlie uncertainly. 'Just for the record, I've *never* been Julian.'

'You're so . . .' said Kate, holding up one hand. 'And he's so . . .' She held up the other.

'Thanks for explaining so fully.'

'You know what I mean.'

'The stupid thing is,' said Charlie, 'I do know what you mean.'

On paper, Julian was the perfect catch. His looks and wealth and bearing ticked all the standard boxes.

Shabby Charlie, always bent over a notepad, prone to giggling until tears came out of his creased eyes, doodler of doodles, writer of love limericks, partner in crime, ticked the boxes Kate had drawn for herself.

'I'm glad I found you, Charlie.'

They took a long hard look at each other. 'And I'm glad I found you,' said Charlie.

Propelled into each other's arms, they dropped to the bed, pulling at buttons, grabbing at straps. Giggling, groaning, they flailed about, arms and legs thrashing, a growing excitement driving them forward.

'We need a . . .' Kate sat up, her hair across her face, her bra absent.

'A . . . yeah, we do.'

Neither of them seemed able to say *condom*.

'I, um, I do have one, actually.' Kate bit her lip.

'You wanton woman you,' said Charlie.

It was a slippery little so-and-so, that one precious condom Kate had acquired.

'Whoops!' It flew across the room. 'Ow!' It caught her in the eye. Finally, it collaborated and Kate lay back and Charlie's face came so near it swam out of focus.

'I love you,' he said.

'I love you,' she said.

Their mouths, their bodies and their eager hearts met. Kate had expected sharp pain but there was none, only a furious and compelling excitement surging up from the centre of her. When it seemed to peak she found there was still more, until finally she and Charlie were limp and clinging to each other.

'Did I make loads of noise?' she whispered against his damp hair.

'Just a bit.' He was breathless.

A huge cheer erupted from downstairs and for a horrible moment they thought their amateurish lovemaking was being applauded.

Kate realised. 'Becca's made the big announcement.'

They didn't move for some time. Kate gave up dissecting how she felt about what they'd done and just *was*. When they stood up, her legs seemed to be boneless. 'I'm a bit wobbly,' she said, bumping elbows and knees with Charlie as they pulled on their underwear amid the avalanche of coats that had slid to the floor. Despite the very adult nature of the last fifteen minutes, she felt juvenile and giddy. As Kate tackled the buttons on her shirt,

Juliet Ashton

Charlie said, 'If I believed in marriage, I'd ask you to marry me.'

'If I believed in marriage,' said Kate, 'I'd say yes.' She pulled up the zip on his trousers. 'But we don't believe in marriage, so . . .' She kissed him. It felt different to the 'before' kisses. Something had changed. They were in deeper. She shivered, partly from the thrill of it but also from a fear of the vast adult universe she glimpsed from this new vantage point. 'Something's bugging me, Charlie,' she admitted.

'What?' he asked, stricken.

'You thought I'd chuck you.'

'Oh, *that*.' Charlie downsized her misgiving, taken aback by her frown. 'I panicked. I knew you wouldn't. I know we're strong. We are, aren't we? We're good.'

'Look, we don't want ever to get married, but can we say we'll never chuck each other? How does that sound?'

Charlie put his hand on his heart and said, solemnly, 'I hereby swear never to chuck you.'

'And I swear never to chuck *you*.' Arms around each other, they mooched out, loved-up Siamese twins.

## Love Is ...

Mr & Mrs Hugh Neely
&
Mr & Mrs John Minelli

request the honour of your presence
at the marriage of their daughters

*Rebecca Charlotte Neely & Catherine Rose Minelli*
*to*
*Mr Julian Ames & Mr Charles Garland*

on Saturday thirtieth of August 1997
at three pm

Roman Catholic Church of St Thomas of Canterbury
Rylston Road, Fulham
RSVP

Kate leaned back against the Tampax machine and caught her breath. The powder room's fussy blinds and gilt mirrors were a respite from the frenzy of the ballroom. The people who'd warned that her wedding day would fly by were wrong; it seemed to have been going on for half a century.

The service had been overwhelming, a tsunami of emotion. Repeating her vows in the festive shadows of stained glass felt significant in a way that very little else ever had.

Since then she'd shaken countless hands, eaten a vast meal without tasting a thing, smiled through speech after speech, taken the microphone to thank her parents, danced, drunk, eaten again, made nice with the youngest bridesmaids, and posed for snaps with relatives she'd assumed long-dead. All while wearing a veil.

Spotting herself in the mirror she wondered who was that drag queen in white. Her lips were blood red. Her eyelids were three different shades of bronze. The make-up artist had said airily *Lots of my brides ask for 'natural' but they're glad I didn't listen when they see the photographs*. Although her dress was simpler by far than Becca's corseted extravaganza, Kate felt as if the white satin was wearing *her*. The train stalked her, the headdress bit into her scalp, and the lacing crushed her ribs like a murderous lover. She wanted to tear everything off and flee through the cutesy latticed window in her undies.

'Jesus!' Becca appeared and backed against the door as if a lynch mob was after her. Her streaked hair high and wide, she gleamed and glinted, every inch of her tanned or glossed or studded with diamante. 'I need a ciggie, Kate.'

She clambered via a sink on to the high window ledge. It was a curiously un-bride-like thing to do but Kate had discovered that almost anything, apart from standing still and beaming angelically, looked inappropriate in a wedding dress. It was the least practical item of clothing she could imagine and that, she supposed, was its point.

Puffing smoke out of the window, Becca gasped, 'Granddad's drunk. He's doing the twist. At least I hope it's the twist. Maybe he's having a series of strokes. Mum's desperately engaging Father Gerry in conversation so he doesn't notice.'

'Father Gerry,' said Kate, 'is drunker than Granddad. And Charlie's mum is drunker than both of them put together.' She'd tried to steer the elder Mrs Garland away from the bar but it was beyond her; Kate's new mother-in-law had last been seen propositioning one of the best men.

'Isn't it time you told your mother and your . . . husband that you smoke?'

They both pulled a face at 'husband', as if it was a forbidden phrase they suddenly had licence to use.

'I don't smoke. Not really.' Becca blew a perfect 'O'. 'Just the odd one now and then.' She flung the cigarette out into the dark and slithered down, shedding sequins. 'God, you look stunning, cuz.'

'It's just expensive fancy dress.'

'I never want to take mine off.' Becca pirouetted, almost toppling over in her platform heels. The brief she'd given the designer had been precise: *imagine Jennifer Aniston was a*

*Spice Girl*. 'It's past 1am. It's nearly over. Isn't it extra spesh,' she said, taking Kate's hands, 'that we did this together?'

'That was lovely, what you said in your speech.'

'About you?' Becca pouted in the mirror and checked out her cleavage. 'I meant every word.'

'I could tell.' Kate knew it was heartfelt because Becca hadn't cried.

'And to think,' said Becca, catching Kate's eye in the glass, 'you and Charlie always said you didn't believe in marriage.'

A knock at the door, and Kate's dad peered sheepishly in. 'Mum's on her way,' he said, unaware that his top hat had left a ridge in his greying curls. 'She's a bit upset, so . . .' He darted out of the way as the womenfolk bowled in past him, jabbering.

'She might be OK for all we know.' Aunty Marjorie shredded a tissue between her fingers.

'They said *he's* dead.' Mum wailed, 'Dead, Marjorie!', as if this was her sister's fault.

'Who?' Kate and Becca straightened up, alert.

'Di.' Mum's voice shook.

'Di . . .?' Kate couldn't recall even a third cousin called Di.

'*Princess* Di?' Becca comprehended and her hands flew to her face.

'There's been a car crash in Paris.' Dad looked at his wife as if she was a suspicious package which might blow up at any moment. 'Princess Diana's in hospital and her young man was killed.'

'She's cursed, John!' Like all Irish women of her vintage, Mum both loved and feared a curse. 'I was only thirty when she married that auld two-timer Charles, and you girls have grown up with her, and now . . .'

'There's hope, Mum,' said Kate. It would be easy to mock the middle-aged suburban woman's devotion to an aristocrat but Mum had aped every flicky hairstyle, every cumbersome hat, every patent court shoe her beloved princess wore.

'Who,' keened Mum, 'will look after the Aids patients if my Di goes?'

'Princess Di can't die.' Becca was brisk, no-nonsense. 'She just can't.'

'She can.' Aunty Marjorie was fatalistic.

'Let's say a prayer and trust in Him upstairs.' Kate knew her mum's bunions were suffering in her new satin shoes and, judging by the older woman's face, her control tights were misbehaving. 'Our Father, who art—'

A loud banging on the door interrupted the pious scene. 'Open up!' shouted a deep voice.

'No way!' Becca ran to the door, surprisingly fleet for a woman whose dress weighed the same as a small car. 'Grooms aren't allowed, Julian! Brides only!'

'Too many bloody brides at this wedding,' laughed Julian from the other side of the door. 'Charlie, mate,' he shouted. 'Give me a hand here.'

Squealing, enjoying herself, Becca tried to hold the door against the intruders but she gave in and the grooms half fell into the powder room, both miraculously holding aloft an unspilled tumbler of whisky.

'So, wifey,' said Julian, straightening up, his cheeks a little red, his blond hair a little tousled, 'how does it feel to be the new Mrs Ames?'

'It feels great.' Kate bent backwards as Julian threw an arm about her waist and pulled her to him, kissing her hard. 'Whisky breath.' She crinkled her nose.

'You love it,' he said.

'I do.' Julian was manly in all the textbook ways and Kate was constantly surprised by how much it turned her on. Throughout her teens she'd mooned over fey boys, boys who read poetry and looked into the middle distance thinking big thoughts. Boys like, well, Charlie, who was now submitting to having his cravat straightened by his new wife. Julian's swagger, his hunger for life and his blithe expectation that things would go his way were an exotic cocktail after a lifetime of tea drinking.

'Ow.' Even though, at times, he could go a little far. 'You're squeezing my whalebones,' complained Kate, feeling small against Julian's expanse of waistcoated chest.

'Sorry. You smell bloody divine.' Julian kissed her hair, her immovable hair which Kate couldn't wait to comb out.

Standing back to survey her cravat handiwork, Becca seemed satisfied. 'God, Charlie, I fancy you in tails.'

'I look like an idiot.' Charlie had been anti-top hat, anti-cravat, anti-fuss throughout the wedding planning tornado.

'No, you look nice,' said Kate shyly, as if they'd just been introduced. The road back to something akin to friendship was long and full of potholes; much of what they said to each other came out awkwardly.

'It's not a wedding without top hats,' said Becca, a variation on a theme. *It's not a wedding without a floral arch/a harpist/an eight tier cake.* To avoid tantrums, the others had, separately and collectively, given in. Even so, the mistake on the invitations – only noticed *after* all one hundred and fifty had been mailed – sparked a fit. *It looks as if I'm marrying Julian and Kate's marrying Charlie!* Becca had raged. *As if we've all gone back in time!*

As if they'd gone back two years, to be precise, to the fatal row that hindsight pinpointed as the moment when the music changed.

The argument that ended the Kate and Charlie show had seemed trivial, little more than a tiff. During one of their long, meandering phone calls, Kate had prodded her boyfriend about his decision not to come home that weekend from Keele University.

Like most arguments, that wasn't what they were really fighting about.

'I have to catch up. I'm really behind.'

Kate pictured Charlie's digs on campus, a rectangular box made cosy with Pulp posters and collages of photographs. She imagined him lying on his ethnic bedcover, surrounded by books and stained mugs and CDs as he said, with patience that was somehow patronising, 'Staffordshire's a long way from London, darling. I come home a lot, you know. This weekend I have to buckle down.'

Usually, Kate was understanding. She knew Charlie's shambolic home life had given him a thirst to make his own way. If he studied hard he could expect a First, the key to unlock his literary ambitions. That evening, however, Kate was less concerned with his literary ambitions than she was with the collage on the cork pinboard above his head.

Each time she visited a few more photographs had been added. Snap after snap of 'mega' nights out, of Charlie huddled over a bottle-strewn table with his new best friends all caught mid-guffaw by the camera's flash. Kate was glad – sincerely glad – that the decision to study so far from home had worked out, that her boyfriend was making friends and having fun.

But.

As Charlie would ruefully say, 'There's *always* a but.'

But . . . did all these new friends have to be girls? Girls with shampoo-advert swingy hair, an endless wardrobe of strappy tops and a complete ignorance of bras?

The pinboard had been on Kate's mind as she went in and out to work. Her desire to leave sixth form and find a job had astonished Charlie. He saw higher education as an opportunity it was rude to refuse but Kate was impatient to launch herself on what she thought of as the real world.

Working in retail ('You mean you're a shop girl, pet,' Mum would correct her) was frustrating and rewarding and hard graft. Kate, despite her family's misgivings about 'missing out' on a degree, was playing a long game. She had a head for business: surely the best way to develop it was in a hands-on environment, learning something practical every day.

The real world turned out to be banal. Early starts. Clocking on and clocking off. Naively, Kate had assumed that working in a party supplies shop would be 'fun' but retail was retail: it certainly didn't merit a collage of party snaps, like Charlie's work hard/play hard life on campus.

'How's the book coming along?' She changed the subject.

'Slowly.'

'Maybe it'd go faster and you'd have time to come home if you didn't party so much.'

Charlie's answering 'OK, Grandma!' would usually make Kate laugh but that night her insecurity called the shots. The thought of his lissom new friends with their girly names

– each one an Emma or a Sophie – made her feel like a care-worn character from a Victorian novel: *Poor Kate, the Humble Shopgirl who dies of consumption in an attic.*

Instead of laughing, Kate banged down the phone.

Dismayed at herself, and wishing she hadn't done something so, well, *Becca*, Kate stared hard at the phone, then jumped when it rang.

'Hi,' she said, sweetly and full of trepidation, relieved that Charlie had diffused the situation.

The relief vanished when her gentle, peaceable Charlie spat, 'So, let me get this right. I do what I'm told, yeah?'

'No, listen,' began Kate. She closed her eyes as the curdled conversation slipped away from her. 'I just—'

'I'm not a poodle, Kate. I don't come when you click your fingers.'

'I know that!' Kate took a deep breath. Slamming the phone down was what Charlie's mother did when he called home to check she was all right. To check she was *alive*. She should have foreseen the traumatic connections it would spark. 'I didn't mean to—' She stopped. 'Hang on. Who's there with you?' she asked, as a female voice murmured in the background.

'Nobody,' said Charlie.

Kate assumed she'd heard a stray snatch of radio until Charlie amended his answer to, 'Well, just Ellie.'

*Just* Ellie. Just a glossy haired, big eyed model-in-training. 'And you think it's OK to have a private conversation with *just Ellie* in the room? I'm talking to *you*, Charlie, not some silly tart I've never even met.'

The silence was thick, like soup. 'Actually,' said Charlie, 'you're on speakerphone.'

It was the girlish giggle that did it. Down went Kate's phone for the second and final time. *He let me embarrass myself. He aired our dirty linen in front of a stranger. He doesn't care how I feel.* A thought that had been gestating for a while rose up fully formed. *Charlie's changed since he went away.*

In the white heat of her annoyance, Kate felt like a glorious martyr, a latter day Joan of Arc. *I've been supportive. I helped him move in to his digs. I never moan about how much I miss him.*

When he rang back, she'd let him have it right between the eyes. Or she'd cry. Kate folded her arms and waited; her Charlie wouldn't hold out for long.

Kate fell asleep with her bedroom door open so she could hear the phone in the hallway, and woke up to its sulky silence in the morning.

Despite her confidence in him, a day passed.

Then two.

Foolishly, Kate allowed herself to believe that Charlie had a cheeky plan to show up at the weekend. For forty-eight hours she watched the front door like an abandoned dog. Becca, an expert in Kate behaviour, guessed something was up, but her 'all men are pigs' rants made Kate feel worse.

Not all men were pigs. Charlie in particular was lovely. After the first rush of fury, Kate beatified him: St Charlie, patron saint of Good Boyfriends. He was kind, he was thoughtful, he was easy-going. But was he still hers?

The silence set, like concrete. Kate didn't call because Charlie didn't call. Possibly, up in Staffordshire, Charlie didn't call because Kate didn't call. Shock set in that Charlie could turn on her so thoroughly, over something so petty.

Becca was airily certain it would all come good. 'You *can't* split up,' she said. 'You're KateandCharlie! All one word!'

'I think we're separate words now,' said Kate, changing TV channels willy nilly, unable to settle.

'Fight for him,' advised Becca. 'Before some Emmy or Lucy nabs him.'

'We're not like that,' said Kate, miserably aware that the 'we' might be past its sell-by date. She needed Charlie to prove to her that the one hundred and sixty miles separating them didn't matter. *Am I part of Charlie's present or his past?* Kate worried that she was fast becoming a dot on the horizon in Charlie's rear-view mirror.

'Glam yourself up,' said Becca. 'Jump on a train. Shag your romance back to life.'

'Has that worked with Julian?'

Kate felt cruel when Becca's eyes flickered. She picked up the remote and they sank into the sofa for another consoling episode of *Pride and Prejudice*. Her cousin had been fragile since Julian bowed out of her life, saying, 'The magic's gone.'

'The magic's gone?' squawked Becca out of the blue over one of Darcy's speeches. 'What does that even bloody mean?' She did that a lot, suddenly referencing the break-up halfway through a conversation about something quite different. Kate had come to realise that Becca scrolled constantly through those last heartbreaking conversations with Julian.

Kate could have recited the dying weeks of Becca's engagement along with her. She knew all the quotes by heart, all the barbs Becca and Julian had slung at each other, knee deep in the wreckage of their relationship. It had finally foundered on the night Julian, backed into a corner, had shouted *Ever since we got engaged I've felt as if there's a noose around my neck.*

'I was the best thing that ever happened to him,' said Becca.

'By quite some way,' agreed Kate, muting *Pride and Prejudice*. This was the only possible response, but the truth was that Kate had grown fond of Julian. She'd seen the breach coming, clocked his fading interest in the prospect of a wedding. He'd surprised Kate by confiding in her, exposing a depth to him she'd never suspected. Guiltily, she'd realised that she'd always treated Julian as some sort of shop mannequin; well dressed but lacking feelings. To make up for her lack of empathy, Kate had tuned into him, trying hard to repair the holes that had appeared in his relationship with Becca. It had done no good, and now that he was gone she felt as if she'd lost a friend. 'You could nab another bloke just like that.' Kate clicked her fingers and Becca's face drooped. 'Sorry.' Kate put her hand over Becca's. 'I know you only want Julian.'

'But he doesn't want me,' said Becca. 'The bastard.'

Kate envied Becca's organic approach to man trouble. She did whatever occurred to her, whether it be wallowing in candlelit baths sobbing along to 'their' songs or blitzing Julian's answerphone with messages alternately demonising him and begging him to take her back.

With no skills in this area – new to heartbreak, Kate had never experienced anything half as painful as Charlie's loaded silence – her unhappiness made her a better employee. First in, last out, Kate was diligent, welcoming every tedious task as a respite from the spin-dryer of morbid thoughts in her head. The shop was immaculate, the rudest of customers treated with exquisite courtesy; Kate appreciated the distractions of the working day.

The phone on the counter at Party Games received the same treatment as the phone in her parents' hall. Kate stared at it, jumped whenever it rang, drooping when she realised the caller wasn't Him. Twice a day she held the receiver to her ear to check it was working. In the right mood, Kate laughed at this behaviour, but that mood was increasingly elusive.

Her cousin was a different animal; 'I can't face going in,' whined Becca, two days out of every five. The reception desk she manned at a Soho media company was damp with tears and she was prone to putting callers through to the wrong pony-tailed executive, so keen was she on relating her tale of woe to her colleagues.

Charlie's number danced teasingly in her head, but Kate went resolutely cold turkey. She loved him too much to call him; that's how she sold her stubbornness to herself. Their relationship was honest, straightforward, like a clean page in one of Charlie's journals. They used to watch, baffled, as Becca and Julian tore chunks out of each other like warring T-rexes, and felt grateful for their own uncomplicated rapport.

No, Kate would keep her page clean. She'd honour their way of loving each other. If Charlie wanted her, he'd call; she was, after all, the aggrieved party. If he didn't want her, if he took this breach as an opportunity to end their relationship, then there was nothing she could do to change his mind. She couldn't bear imposing herself where she'd once been desired.

Kate wanted Charlie, but that was pointless unless he wanted her back.

A month in to the cold new landscape, Kate had an epiphany.

*We've broken up.*

Kate Minelli was now just another human to Charlie Garland. An ex. She couldn't rely on him in that special way any more. She must carry on alone.

Mistrustful of melodrama, she examined that feeling. *Of course I'm not alone*, Kate rebuked herself.

It felt like loneliness, though.

'How do I get through this?' she asked her father, red eyed late one evening at the kitchen table when she couldn't sleep and he supplied hot chocolate and a shoulder to cry on.

Dad sighed. 'It's not what it was,' he said. 'It's not what it could be. It is what it is, darling.'

'Mum's philosophy is more basic,' said Kate. She impersonated her mother's dismissal of her daughter's distress. *You can do better than that Garland boy!*

Quietly – Mum might be listening in – Dad contributed his own impression of one of his wife's favourite sayings. 'There's plenty more fish in the sea!'

'But my fishing rod's broken.' Kate sipped her chocolate, tasting the care Dad had put into making it.

'Mum's doing her best,' said Dad, recognising the soft look in Kate's eyes as hurt. 'We named you after her, but there the resemblance ends, love. She's in one of her strops because of this trip to China I'm planning.'

All roads led not to Rome but to Charlie; mention of Dad's much discussed (and argued over) desire to visit China reminded her of how well her two favourite men had got along.

Unanimous for once, Kate's parents had despaired of Charlie's chaotic upbringing, but whereas Mum muttered darkly about the revolving door on Mrs Garland's bedroom, Dad never disparaged Charlie's mother. Instead, he forged a friendship with the boy, one that enriched them both.

Unaccustomed to paternal input, Charlie was flattered when Kate's dad sought him out. They would sit and talk while Kate got ready to go out, usually about Dad's pet topic, Yulan House.

Kate and her mother tended to tune out when Dad brought up the Chinese orphanage he sponsored in a modest way, sending them a few pounds each month. He'd heard about it from an intrepid colleague who'd volunteered at Yulan House a few years earlier. Inspired to send a little money with a brief note, Dad was charmed to receive a handwritten reply in quaintly perfect English. It was the start of a correspondence between himself and the lyrically named Jia Tang, an indomitable woman who dedicated her life to Beijing's abandoned babies.

Dad and Charlie would pore over the latest newsletter from the orphanage, both of them expert in the building, the facilities, the newly planted vegetable plot.

'I suppose,' said Kate, 'you and Charlie won't run the London Marathon in aid of the orphanage now.'

'No, probably not.' Dad blew out his cheeks. 'Charlie understood,' he said quietly.

'I know.' Kate screwed up her face, damming the tears, sick of crying. It had been easy to love a boy who passionately believed that one day her dad would achieve his dream of visiting Yulan House, no matter how much her mother grumbled that the money would be better spent on a new microwave, an extension, a hot tub. The trinkets, in other words, that her sister Marjorie boasted about. 'Dad, don't let Mum stop you booking your tickets to Beijing.'

'Trouble is,' said Dad, 'your mum's right. We can't really afford it.'

'What does that matter?' Kate was vehement. *One* member of this family should be getting what they wanted out of life. 'You go, Dad. I'll handle Mum.'

'Ah, the optimism of youth. If your mother could be handled, don't you think I'd have the knack by now?'

'You do . . . love Mum, don't you?' Kate felt impertinent, as if she'd pushed at a door better left locked.

'What makes you ask that?'

'Just that . . .' Kate had taken off without knowing where she would land. Sadness was mangling her thought processes. 'Sometimes it seems as if you don't have much in common.'

'We have you.'

'Am I enough?'

'You're more than enough, love.' Dad exhaled, frowning, shaking his head, trying to explain. 'Me and your mum, we rub along. We get by. She's a complicated woman and I'm a . . .' He groped for the right word. 'I'm a bit of a dead loss, I suppose.'

'What?' Kate almost forgot her dejection. 'You're the best dad ever.'

'But husband?' Dad looked down at the table, an introverted expression on his face as if looking into his own heart. 'I'm not sure how many marks out of ten your mother would give me.'

The phone rang, shrieking in the quiet house, and Kate ran to it, heart bouncing.

'Is that St Hilda's church?' asked a frail voice.

Next day, as Kate and Becca browsed shoes in a high street shop, Kate told Becca about the late night wrong number. She turned it into a wry anecdote, editing out the part where she kept Dad up until midnight, sobbing. Her cousin didn't smile. 'Hello! Earth to planet Becca!'

'Listen. Don't shout at me, but . . .'

'What?' Kate narrowed her eyes, looking up from the shoes she was trying on, a variant of the chunky black pair she'd worn into the shop. *You always buy the same shoe!* Charlie used to say. After four weeks of silence, he'd drifted into the past tense. *Who*, thought Kate with exquisite self-pity, *will tease me about my Groundhog Day shoe purchasing habits now?*

'I spoke to Charlie.' Becca flinched as if awaiting a blow. 'Well, say something.'

'About me?'

'What else would we talk about?'

Suspended between hope and dread in an icy limbo, Kate managed to say, 'And?'

'We met up, actually. For a coffee.' Becca picked up an ankle boot, studying the plain grey footwear with a fascination it didn't deserve. 'Are you annoyed?'

The question rang the tiniest of alarm bells. 'Of course not.' *Why would I be?* The only reason Charlie would contact Becca would be to reach out to Kate; he was ambivalent, to say the least, towards her cousin. And yet, Kate had a complex reaction to this development. Foolish, but it stung to think of them ordering cappuccinos and settling down at a table without her. She hadn't even known he was back from Keele. It was still term time. She wondered, her heart stuttering, if he'd come home to fix their tattered togetherness.

'Good.' Becca put down the oh-so-fascinating boot. 'Good.' She seemed to be at a loss for words, which was out of character.

'How did he seem?' Kate wasn't sure what she wanted to hear. She loved Charlie – still – but a wretched part of her longed for news of hollow eyes, stubble, a new drinking habit.

'He's had his hair cut.'

'No!' It was absurd to feel so betrayed. 'What else?'

There was a pregnant aspect to the silence as Kate waited, one shoe on, one shoe off. Eventually Becca said, 'He asked me to give you this.'

Kate recognised the envelope, small and cream, as the sort that used to arrive every other day, stuffed with quirky drawings, jokes, declarations.

'Take it,' said Becca when Kate hesitated.

Kate wanted to swear and knock all the shoes off the glass shelves but was too well brought up to do either. She turned her head and shut her eyes, blocking out the innocuous envelope.

'Take it.' Becca was soft, pleading. 'Please.'

Kate accepted the envelope. It was light as a feather. Whatever Charlie had to say, he'd used very few words.

'You have to read it,' urged Becca. 'It's better to know.'

'Later.' Kate stuffed the envelope into her bag, pushing it deep down among the strata of receipts and gum and stray lipsticks. 'So?' She held out her foot, made a slow circle with her ankle. 'Shall I buy them?'

'Go home,' said Becca, her tone heavy. 'And read the letter.'

Obediently, Kate put back the shoes and did as she was told. At home she circled the note, putting it off until finally it could be put off no longer. Curled on her bed like a foetus, she ripped open the envelope. One reading and the contents were fixed on her consciousness forever.

*Kate*
   *This split is for the best. Not everything that looks like love is love. You're free and so am I. I hope you'll be happy.*
      *C*

*I'm dismissed*, thought Kate. Not needed. Unfit for purpose. Surplus to requirements. The note's coldness took her off guard, as did the doorbell. *Becca!* she thought, grateful, leaping off the bed.

She almost didn't recognise him, partly because he was the last person she expected to see on her doorstep and partly because the expression on his face utterly altered him. Julian looked, for once, apprehensive. 'Am I . . .' he said. 'Is this OK?'

'It's, um . . .' It was awful, but Kate's manners overruled her distress. 'Come in.' Julian was so big and so male and he made her regret her bare feet and the wrinkled grey pyjama trousers her mother despaired of.

'How's Becca?' said Julian as Kate filled the kettle. 'The crazy calls have stopped so I'm a bit worried about her. In case she's, you know, done something . . .'

'Becca's not the sort to kill herself.'

'True.' Julian in casual wear of jeans and cricket jumper was more groomed than Charlie had been for his university interview in his sole suit. The kneejerk comparison startled her: Charlie was no longer Kate's business.

The kettle danced to a boil against a backdrop of reverent silence, as if the cramped kitchen was a church. She and Julian had never been alone before. Through her dazed heartbreak Kate found herself wondering what on earth he was doing in her house.

As if he'd heard her question, Julian said, 'I'm not really here to talk about Becca.' He swallowed audibly. 'I heard. About you and Charlie.'

Kate nodded. They were a news item.

'I thought you two were for ever.'

'So did I.' Kate began to cry. 'Sorry.' She tore off some kitchen roll. 'Ignore me. I'm being daft.'

'No. You're not.' Julian made the tea, which felt vaguely embarrassing. Mum's Pyrex mugs in his big hands. 'Milk? Sugar?' He was clumsy, but Kate was touched. She found herself talking. About Charlie, about how she felt, about how just moments ago she'd come slap bang up against the brick wall of his indifference.

'I'm boring you,' she said.

'You couldn't,' he said.

Kate looked at him questioningly and he didn't look away. She felt the need to mention her cousin. 'Becca's been so distraught about you . . .' Even as she said it, Kate realised something. For the past few days Becca had been different. Upbeat, even.

'I know,' said Julian gently, considering his words, head bowed. 'But she'll recover. She'll be OK. I was a project, wasn't I? I didn't break Becca's heart. I took a hammer to her pride, sure, but her heart is intact.'

'No,' said Kate, instinctively loyal. 'She adored you.' She amended the tense. '*Adores* you.' This day was whirling by, pushing everything into the past.

'Things have their time. Then they're over.'

'So why,' said Kate, 'did you ask her to marry you?'

'It seemed like the right thing to do. She's quite a girl.'

'*Woman*,' said Kate, warningly.

'Woman.' Julian altered his language with a courtly dip of his head. 'It was exciting. But it was a mistake. I hurt her, even though I promised never to do that. I don't intend to hurt anybody else if I can help it.'

Sensing hidden meanings smuggled in his language, Kate did her best to ignore them. Sitting at the table, she invited Julian to do the same. Over Mum's home-made shortbread, she asked him about his work, noticing how he became animated.

'What about your job?' he said. 'How's that working out?'

'OK, I think.' Kate reconsidered. 'Actually, I love it. It's just that it's hard to love anything at the moment.' She wondered how long it would take her to surface.

'Do you think you'll end up buying a shop?'

'What?' Kate laughed with shock. 'I'm just a shop assistant, Julian.'

'You're not *just* anything.'

Kate looked at him and he looked back. Something happened. Something flexed its muscles and came to life between them. It was Kate who broke the spell, standing up, fussing with the biscuits. She was seeing Julian as a person for the first time. Not as Becca's trophy boyfriend. The fact that she was flattered shamed her, but shame couldn't quench the quiet fire he'd lit.

As Julian left, he made a speech. That's how it felt, as Kate stood on the swirly hall carpet and Julian spoke at her. He seemed nervous: another first.

'What you need is peace and quiet and time to heal. Maybe a relaxed meal out somewhere nice, with somebody you know, would be good. Somebody who won't expect you to be chirpy, who won't expect anything more than a peck on the cheek at the end of the night.' He paused.

'This somebody,' said Kate. 'Would it be you?'

'It would.'

She smiled and her face seemed to creak. 'Julian . . .' She sighed. 'You know I can't say yes.'

'Becca . . .'

'Exactly.' Kate admitted at last that she found Julian attractive. *It's because he's forbidden fruit*, she thought. Nothing to do with his bearing, his tigerish eyes, the fact that he'd laid himself bare by coming to her like this.

Julian became more bold, more his usual self. 'I'll book a table at eight o'clock, one week from tonight, at Zilli's. Come in your dressing gown if you're still miserable. If you don't turn up I won't harass you. I won't even call.' Julian stepped outside, into a sharp, bright, heartless afternoon. 'But I'll be terribly disappointed.'

'Thank you,' said Kate mechanically as she shut the door.

Humbly, respectfully, he'd handed her all the power, running the risk of looking foolish, for the chance of dinner with her.

Try as she might, Kate couldn't picture it.

A carefully laid table. Soft lighting. Julian holding a menu. And herself, washed, tamed, face brightened with make-up and body inserted into some form of outfit. She recoiled. The notion confounded her.

What perplexed her more was when Becca asked, a day or two later, 'Now that you and Charlie are well and truly finished, would it be OK if I had a drink with him now and then, kept in touch?'

'It would be very very far from bloody O bloody K!' screamed Kate. 'Are you kidding? Why would you . . .' She ran out of steam, her chest rising and falling. 'Are you *interested* in Charlie?' Kate couldn't find a facial expression that did justice to her sudden conjecture.

'God, no.' Becca was distressed. 'I just don't want to lose him. As a mate.'

'But you've never been mates,' said Kate.

Later, Kate picked up the phone and dialled Becca's number. 'Sorry,' she said, twisting to check out the back view of the red seductively clingy dress she'd just bought. 'I overreacted. After all, like you said, Charlie and me are over.'

'Are you sure?' Becca sounded doubtful even though she'd been the one to open this awkward dialogue. 'I mean, I have to see him at least once, to hand back his note.' Kate had given Becca the single page, folded back into its original creases, to return to Charlie. She'd added nothing to it; he'd said it all. 'But if it makes you unhappy I won't see him again after that.'

'Becca, I don't have the right to be possessive about Charlie.' Kate took a deep breath. 'And while we're on the subject of exes there's something I have to tell *you*.' Kate sensed how Becca struggled to conceal her surprise at her news.

'Good!' said Becca, over-loud. 'Why not, eh?'

'Yeah, why not?' said Kate.

Their 'Goodnights' were stilted, like actresses in a bad play.

The dress was too racy. Kate dashed up to her bedroom, where she tore it off and reached for her old faithful over-sized white shirt. *I'll probably spill pasta all down it*, she thought.

'I like the shirt,' said Julian, later. 'Even with bolognese sauce all down it.'

Over the next few months, Becca insisted on double dates. 'The sooner we all get used to our new arrangement,' she said, 'the better.' And she was right. The tension eased. The awkwardness dissipated. Before long Becca and Julian were casually indifferent to each other.

For Kate and Charlie it took a little longer to reboot.

The first time Julian had proprietorially thrown his arm around her in a pub she'd jumped. Charlie hadn't turned a hair. Just moments later Charlie had kissed Becca with enthusiasm, with – goddammit – *gusto*.

That was the night Kate first held Julian to her, returning his desire with her own, cementing their string of dates into something more profound. He'd been committed from the start, careful never to bully or nudge, until Kate had to agree, against all the odds, they were a good fit. In retrospect, her two years with Charlie looked like a naive first stab at love.

After the blow of Charlie's desertion, it was a revelation that somebody could love her. The somebody turned out to be quite a catch. Not because Julian was a property mogul in the thick of a housing boom, but because he was steadfast and loyal, employing none of the cat and mouse tactics he'd used with Becca. Kate would look up from a book and find his hooded blue eyes on her, studying her, as if revising to sit an exam in Kate Minelli.

'What do you see in me?' Kate asked, genuinely curious, when he took her to meet the folks and she was cowed by the manor house, his father's drawled vowels, his mother's assertive way with a pashmina.

'I see my future wife,' Julian answered.

Not long after that, Becca had sought her out, blurted, 'Charlie and me are getting married! Say you're happy for me or I'll call it off I swear, honest to God.'

'Of course I'm happy for you.'

Kate's new life fitted seamlessly over the old and when she accepted Julian's ring (an heirloom emerald the size of an egg) so soon after her cousin announced her engagement to Charlie, it was coincidence.

'*Sheer* coincidence,' Kate insisted to her worried father as they celebrated the good news. 'He'll look after me, Dad.'

'I brought you up to look after yourself, young woman,' said Dad. 'But if you're happy, I'm happy.'

'And I'm happy!' Kate told him.

In the powder room it was the dregs of the wedding day. Kate fantasised about the moment she could unlace her corset. Becca was tweaking her headdress in the mirror, peering critically at her front teeth as if they might have changed since she got married. Charlie watched his new wife with a mixture of wariness and excitement, like a child let loose in a sweet shop.

*She's shaken him up*, thought Kate. *He looks like all his birthdays have come at once*. Charlie had never experienced the full glare of Becca's headlights until they began dating. She'd paid him scant attention when he was just her cousin's fella; now that he was her property Charlie was lavished with attention, the happy object of her saucy affections. He was breathless, like a child who keeps going back, time and again, for one more ride on the rollercoaster.

It wasn't jealousy that Kate felt. That wasn't the right word for it. A year of double dating had seen her swim upstream through jealousy, resentment, disbelief and anger until she reached acceptance. Now all she felt, when she saw their heads together, one dark, one fair, was a twinge of irritation that Charlie hadn't cast his net just that tiny bit wider.

Knowing it was hypocritical didn't diminish the feeling.

'Could somebody explain,' said Dad, hovering by the door with Uncle Hugh at his side, interlopers among the girlish trappings of the ladies' loo, 'why Hugh and I paid for a reception when everybody's in the toilets?'

'The ladies have minds of their own, John,' said Julian.

'That's hardly news.' Dad had an arm's length accord with the newest recruit to the family. Kate's heart went out to her sweet, doing-his-best father, whose Chinese trip had been postponed yet again to make Becca's deranged matrimonial dreams come true. Kate would have preferred a registry office and a long lunch, but Julian had been keen to 'do it properly', so Becca got her way.

'Any news?' asked Aunty Marjorie.

'No.' Uncle Hugh was solemn; he tailored his demeanour to his wife's needs at all times. 'Not yet. I'm sure Di will pull through.'

'And are you a doctor?' barked Aunty Marjorie.

'Well, no,' admitted Uncle Hugh, who was a financial advisor. 'I just have a feeling, dear.' He smiled bravely, his stiff upper lip coming in handy as it so often did when dealing with the women in his life. Kate felt, as she often felt, that she wanted to put an arm around her uncle, who put up with so much yet always seemed happy. As if he was exactly where he wanted to be. *That's what a happy marriage – however odd – does for you!*

A tipsy guest bowled in, singing, and made for a cubicle. From the ballroom they heard a sing song break out to *Danny Boy*. Kate hoped against hope her new parents-in-law, who were snobbish enough to sneer at the Queen, had left.

'How's the new job going?' Kate's mum rarely addressed Charlie and he jumped.

'Great, fine, good.'

'He's a *natural*,' said Becca. 'The radio station love him, don't they, darling?'

'Oh they do,' repeated Charlie, sardonic.

*So they should*, thought Kate. A would-be novelist with Charlie's flair was wasted churning out jingles and adverts. Their new roles didn't allow for intimacy – like two shy vicars, it had taken months for Kate and Charlie to get beyond innocuous small talk – so they'd never discussed his new career. Unless Charlie had changed completely, he would *hate* such work.

Then again, Charlie *had* changed completely: he was married to a woman he'd disliked, after all. The biddable man-child welded to Becca's side was nothing like the sweet and bolshy boy Kate had loved. Maybe alien bodysnatchers had come in the night, swapping Charlie for an advertising copywriter.

Like a formally dressed kidnapper, Julian edged nearer, eager to whisk her away. He trailed his fingers down her lace sleeve and Kate's arm shivered with excitement.

Whispering in her ear, his breath tickling, Julian said, 'Are you happy, darling?'

'Very,' she whispered back, seeing only him in the midst of the crowd.

The pivot of the past few years – more significant than Kate and Charlie's schism or Julian's appearance at Kate's front door – was Becca's pregnancy.

By the time the blue line firmed up, Charlie had dropped out of university and the wedding date was nailed down, a year ahead of the original timing.

A wedding planner was enlisted. White frocks were tried and found wanting: 'Just because I'm pregnant doesn't mean I have to *look* pregnant!' Caterers were tormented, florists publicly flogged. All for this one day, a day which had worn Kate out.

'We did it, cuz.' Becca extracted Kate from Julian's grasp, taking her firmly by the shoulders. 'We really did it.' Her gaze, even under false eyelashes, whisked Kate back to childhood, or rather to some formless ageless state where it was just the two of them, sharing perfect understanding.

Which was not the same as perfect happiness, but was profound all the same.

'We did it,' agreed Kate, suddenly tearful. She hesitated, then folded Becca down to her level, finding her ear to whisper, 'You can try again.'

Becca squeezed Kate brutally tight. 'Oh Kate,' she whispered.

Kate had been holding Becca's hand when the sonographer couldn't find a heartbeat.

'Come, wife!' Julian asserted himself with a kingly shout.

Becca pulled away, apparently recovered. 'Time to drag my Charlie to the bridal suite.'

Even after the hymns and the speeches and enough quiche to sink a battleship, that 'my' sounded all wrong.

In the taxi, her ears ringing, Kate turned to Julian. 'As weddings go,' she said, 'it was a brilliant wedding. But,' she leaned in, found his lips, 'I'm so glad we don't have to do it ever again.'

Kate & Julian Ames
The Penthouse, Royal Quay,
Chelsea Harbour, London, SW10 1QT

20.11.99

Hi Guys,

Do you want to come to us for Millennium Eve?
I'll do sushi.
That's an offer you can't refuse. Get here about 8pm
and be prepared to stay up late.

K and J xxx

'I don't believe in the millennium bug,' shouted Kate to Julian, as he moved about the living area, setting out glasses, tipping ice noisily into a chrome bucket.

'That's because you're a wise woman, darling.' Julian dimmed the lights. 'It's crazy to think planes will fall out of the sky and all our emails will go haywire just because computers can't recognise the date 2000.'

'I read somewhere that all hospitals will have power cuts on the stroke of midnight.' Kate confronted the slab of tuna with a feeling of doom completely unrelated to the millennium bug. 'And radio alarm clocks will rise up and take over the world.'

'I like this part of entertaining best.' Julian moved into the kitchen area of their open plan apartment and handed her a perfect martini. 'When it's just us before the guests arrive. In fact, let's call and cancel, so I can ravish you among the raw fish.'

'That's a tempting offer.' Kate shimmied out of the scope of his arms. 'But I have *loads* to do, Julian. What made me say I'd make sushi?'

'We should have bought in.'

Sometimes Kate forgot they were well off. She waited for buses in the rain as taxis raced by. She bought economy mince for Julian's beloved shepherd's pie. When he airily booked first class air fares or ordered the most venerable claret on the wine list her tummy contracted. 'Home-made's nicer.'

'Not sure that applies to sushi.' Julian eyed the lumpen California rolls lying like casualties of war on the marble worktop. He was a veteran of Kate's cooking fads, manfully trying her goulash and her sea bass and her stir fries. 'Can we cancel? I want you to myself tonight. It feels historic.'

'That's why we've invited Becca and Charlie. That's why I'm going to smell of fish tomorrow.'

'Just one phone call and it'll be you, me, a movie.' Julian held up a California roll. 'And a takeaway.'

Kate poked out her tongue. 'It's too late to cancel. Especially on such a special night. Behave, man.'

'You're right,' said Julian. 'And besides, Becca would hunt us down and kill us.'

'We haven't had much . . . *us* time this Christmas,' said Kate. 'Maybe we should do a mini-break somewhere?' She envisaged chintz, open fires, brocade sofas; the antithesis of her own home. 'I could arrange cover for the shops and—'

'Darling, I can barely draw breath at the moment. Take Becca and go somewhere hot and ludicrously indulgent. My treat.'

'I'm not married to Becca,' muttered Kate, as she rinsed an orange lozenge of salmon.

'Darling, don't mutter, *please*.' Julian played with a remote, and stiff white drapes slithered tither and yon until he was satisfied.

If the apocalypse really was due in five hours' time, somebody had forgotten to tell the good people of the Chelsea Harbour development. The view from the kitchen was the same as ever: the white modern blocks flanking a marina were glamorous enough for a five star holiday vista yet she saw it every day through the wrap-around glass walls. Kate shivered and reached for the angora bolero Julian had bought her for Christmas.

As lights came on in windows the complex glittered against the dark winter sky like an outpost on some distant, wealthy planet. Chelsea, enduringly chic and moneyed since its famous King's Road kick-started the swinging sixties, was self-assured, never deigning to notice unemployment figures or natural disasters.

Much like Julian, who surfed the housing market, never getting wet, always ahead of the wave.

'Wish I'd done a roast.' Kate flung a ruined batch of rice in the bin. When she'd scribbled the invitation sushi had felt celebratory, and 'right' for their lifestyle.

Kate had caught that word from Julian: she teased him *people don't have lifestyles, matey, they have lives!* but nobody could deny their apartment was stylish. Lifestylish.

Initially, she'd baulked at the openness, the glossy pale surfaces, the hard edges, disappointing Julian, who had expected his wife to jump with joy at the mammoth her hunter gatherer hubby had laid at her feet.

They'd compromised. Julian got his Bang & Olufsen sound system and Kate got her colourful rugs. Julian was fond of pointing out how she softened his minimalism with her books and vintage china. *We're the perfect team*, he'd say.

One day she'd win her battle to have actual handles on the kitchen cupboard doors. One day he'd manage to stop her leaving make-up smears on the glass shelves in the arctic white bathroom.

This was marriage. Love in action. Julian didn't know about Kate's rainy day account, where she stashed a hundred quid here, fifty there. One day, if Julian ever fell off his surf-board, they might be glad of it.

At the sound of the doorbell, Julian threw open the enormous veneered front door. Kate hastily civilised the chaos on the worktop as Becca's effusive *hello*s argued with the Gypsy Kings CD Julian had chosen.

'God I LOVE this place!' Becca stalked across the apartment in her sky high shoes, her beaded black dress an excellent match for the surrounding monochrome. She looked around, noticing everything. 'New Buddha statue!' She pointed at a silvered ornament then threw her arms around Kate. 'Happy New Year! Love the blouse. You're brave doing sushi.'

Kate looked down at her white satin shirt. A Rorschach blot of soy had blossomed on a lapel, like a dirty rose.

A cork popped. Becca threw open the door to the terrace and stepped out among the dejected ficus trees in their hand-made pots.

'Hi.' Charlie held out flowers and wine, the customary offering to the god of dinner parties.

'Ta.' Kate took the gifts. 'I love . . . um, actually, what are they?' She frowned at the blooms.

'No idea,' said Charlie.

As Kate sought out a vase, she felt him looking at her hair. The boyish cut, an impulsive decision, was meant to be chic but she worried it gave her the look of a prison warder.

'What happened to your hair?' said Charlie.

'It fell off,' said Kate.

A beat, then he laughed. She laughed too. They laughed more than the feeble joke merited.

'Julian likes it,' said Kate. 'I'm not sure.'

'Julian's got taste.' Charlie gestured around the flat. 'He must be right.'

Kicking off her shoes, Becca dragged Julian in from the terrace and shouted, 'Turn up the music, Kate!'

'Give me a mo.' Kate hovered over the control panel. She turned a random dial and the lighting went from 'candle-light' to 'extra bright'.

'Argh!' Becca cowered like a vampire struck by the sun until Julian reached over Kate and conjured up a flattering twilight.

By the time they took their seats for dinner, Julian was a little fuzzy around the edges. He swiped a handful of edamame, dropping some so they lay like jade beads on the black grain of the table. Kate fancied him tipsy, when he pawed her like a lion, but it was early for him to be this squiffy.

'Lay into the starters, everybody.' Kate wondered if she'd sweated her foundation off. 'Try the yakitori chicken thing.'

'Why aren't they on paper plates from your shops?' asked Charlie. 'Those nice fish patterned ones.'

Too frazzled to put a diplomatic spin on Julian's plea that she not bring her own products home, Kate shrugged. *Paper plates are not really* us, he'd say.

'You've gone to so much trouble,' said Becca. 'I'm crap around the house, aren't I, babe?'

'Yes,' said Charlie. His hair was super short above the collar of his dark blue velvet jacket. Kate wondered how he'd smuggled such an obviously second-hand garment past his wife, who was violently anti-charity shop. 'I expected your mum and dad to be here tonight, Kate,' he said.

'God no,' said Julian, a touch too fast. 'I mean, we saw plenty of them over Christmas,' he added.

'By plenty,' said Kate, 'he means too much.' She sympathised; she too had longed to escape from the small, hot kitchen where her mother had incinerated a turkey on Christmas Day. A need to impress the son-in-law had culminated in a panic attack over the lumpy gravy. 'Dad's a bit down at the moment.'

'Why?' asked Charlie.

'Why'd you think?' Becca was wry. 'He's put off his trip to that stupid orphanage again.'

'But he lives for Yulan House,' protested Charlie. 'The Christmas card he sent us had a picture of all the kids on the front.'

Julian nodded. 'John's fascinating on the subject.' He didn't listen when Kate's dad spoke about Yulan House but made sure to look interested.

'Mum says they can't afford for Dad to travel all that way. She says it's enough for him to sponsor an orphan. *Charity begins at home*, apparently.' Kate stirred her miso with a chopstick. 'They're buying a caravan instead.'

The glance Becca threw at Kate was empathetic: she knew how Julian must have scoffed at such a plebeian purchase.

'I love caravans,' said Charlie, wistfully.

'We're looking at a time share in Ibiza,' said Becca.

'That we can't afford,' said Charlie.

'That you pretend we can't afford,' said Becca, adding a 'babe', as if the endearment would make up for annoyance in her voice. 'We can't keep borrowing Kate and Julian's villa, can we?'

'We don't mind,' said Kate, knowing that Julian did mind a little. When Becca took up residence in the Tuscan square stone house she was harder to evict than bedbugs.

Relieved that the starters were well received, Kate returned to her showroom kitchen. Truly on show, feeling that the eyes of the residents opposite were trained on her, Kate rolled, and sliced, and cursed her culinary ambition. Julian had drunk too many of his own cocktails to understand the subtle marital distress signals whizzing his way. She heard him, over at the mile long sofa, ask Charlie about work.

'He's been poached!' Becca answered for her other half in her excitement. 'He's starting at a new ad agency in February. BBH or something.'

'Bartle Bogle Hegarty?' Julian knew a little about every area of business. 'Very prestigious. Congrats, Charlie. A fully blown media dickhead at last.'

Charlie raised his glass in a toast. 'To me! And all the media dickheads in the land.'

'It's a good job,' said Becca. 'Good money.'

'Can't argue with that,' said Julian. 'Well done, mate.'

'Yeah, well done,' called Kate as she hacked at spring onions.

She couldn't claim to know Charlie any more. The space he took up had become emotionally blank, the past pixilated. The old Charlie would have cut off his leg before writing adverts for a living; he'd changed as much as she had.

'May I,' asked Becca, 'see your new bidet?'

There was no aspect of the flat's interior design she didn't covet.

'Your rather strange wish,' said Julian, 'is my command.' He ushered her to the en-suite.

'You look as if you're struggling.' Charlie materialised by the raw fish. 'Need a hand?'

'God, yes.' Gratified somebody had noticed, Kate gestured at a platter. 'Could you arrange my attempts at maki rolls so they look appetising?'

'I'll try.'

They didn't catch each other's eye as they worked, but, like the easy laughter over her regrettable new haircut, this silent collaboration was a step forward.

The new millennium was a time not only of superstition but of hope. Kate and Charlie couldn't avoid each other – Becca would never allow that – but perhaps they were on the brink of a new era when they could be friendly and savour each other's company again.

'Is that OK?' Charlie stood back from his handiwork.

'It doesn't look like the picture in the book.'

'As long as it tastes nice.'

'True.'

Such politeness.

They'd never discussed the second miscarriage. She mourned the lost little soul but lacked the vocabulary to empathise with Charlie about his bereavement. She'd spent long hours with Becca, whose uncharacteristic withdrawal into herself had worried the family. From their conversations, Kate knew Charlie had insisted they refrain from 'trying again' too soon.

'He wants time for us to heal,' Becca told Kate. 'He says no need to rush. He thinks we should travel, have some adventures together.'

Becca's acquiescence was atypical: *she must really love him*, thought Kate.

This tendency to doubt the calibre of her cousin's marriage was a habit Kate was trying to break. It was her new year – a new millennium! – resolution, along with a vow to be more grateful for her own luck in love and life.

'So,' said Charlie, 'I hear you own three shops now.'

'I don't own them,' said Kate. 'I manage them.' She over-saw every aspect of 'her' shops – as she thought of them – bringing to bear a pernickety perfectionism lacking in other areas of her life. No two working days were the same. Like a truffle hound, Kate nosed out emerging trends and was ruthless when vetting prospective staff members. Only those with a ready smile and a muscular work ethic need apply. Julian believed she spoiled them but Kate believed that everybody deserved to be rewarded for their input. Her team would do anything for her.

Sometimes, when she stepped back and took in the bigger picture, Kate smiled at how seriously she took her job. *As if I'm the leader of a nation and not the manager of a handful of shops.*

Julian and Becca emerged from the adoration of the bidet. 'Don't get her started on those shops,' he said. 'She can talk all night about them.' He launched into a high pitched impression of Kate that he only did when sloshed. '*Oh I'm so tired. Oh I need to be up early to open up the Blackheath branch.*'

'That sounds just like you!' Becca clapped.

'So then I say to her,' said Julian, '*Leave! Be a proper wifey.*' He put his arms around Kate and buried his face in the back of her neck, severely cramping her sushi-making style. 'It's not like we need the money.'

'I like working.' Kate struggled to cut up a radish with six foot four of bloke leaning on her.

'I noticed. You're always at bloody work.' Julian straightened up.

'So are you!'

'It's not the same thing.'

When Julian had first shown an interest in Kate's work, she'd assumed he understood her ambition, but it transpired

71

Julian thought her need to work would blow over, like a head cold.

'Now, now.' Becca put her hands on her hips. 'No fighting, you two. You can't start a new millennium on a row.'

'We're not fighting,' said Kate.

'We never do,' said Julian.

After years of ducking as Mum chucked china at Dad over minor transgressions it was soothing to live with somebody so easy-going. When the cumulative civility got too much she simply rang her mum and provoked her.

Julian's penitent face made a silent apology and Kate leaned over and stroked his cheek. In the midst of the dinner party they forged a moment of togetherness, before his eyes slid from hers.

'Let's eat!' Kate resolved to limit Julian's alcohol intake.

The dining zone (Kate cringed when Julian referred to it that way) was black panelled, with black glossy floor tiles. A black table floated amid black chairs; it was like eating down an elegant mine and made Kate feel as if she'd been shoved forward in time, becoming an older, more poised version of herself. The sophistication of her life was like a gorgeous coat she'd spotted in a shop window, and never dreamed she might own. Yet here she was, wearing it and trying to look as if it was comfortable.

Even presented on the best wedding-present crockery, Kate's sushi spoiled the photo-shoot perfection of the setting, as if a child had scribbled on an old master.

Becca was fulsome in her praise: 'Wow! This is dee-licious!'

Kate winked at her, grateful.

When talk turned to mortgage rates, Kate poured herself a hefty glass of wine. Becca regarded Julian as a property guru, and was always keen to pump him for insider tips.

'I keep telling Charlie we need to flip a property,' said Becca, pound signs almost visible in her blue eyes.

'I keep telling you we can't afford it,' said Charlie.

'You should listen to Becca,' said Julian. He turned to his disciple. 'Why not consider buying off-plan and selling on without even taking possession?'

The collusive eye roll Kate and Charlie shared was the first in more than two years, since the wedding. They both looked away, as if caught stealing.

'The key word,' said Julian, 'is liquidity.'

Slipping away to change her shoes, Kate sat on the bed and removed her shoes, rubbing the arch of her foot. *Madness*, she thought, *to wear high heels in your own home.* She found her slippers and pushed her toes into their fluffy innards.

She only meant to sit on the edge of the bed for a moment, but she couldn't resist lying back among the pillows. Weaned on fairy tales, she'd always wanted a four poster: Julian had insisted on making this dream come true. In the spirit of compromise, he'd bought a modern version in black tubular steel, with no hangings.

Finding the remote control on the bedside table, Kate pushed a button and ivory silk drapes purred across the glass wall, cutting her off from the nosey parkers celebrating across the way and fading the room gently into darkness. She remembered when the remote had malfunctioned, condemning her and Julian to sleep in a goldfish bowl. She'd had to dress in the bathroom.

'Eh?' Time skipped and suddenly Becca's face was an inch from Kate's.

'You fell asleep, you silly old bag.' Becca hauled her up. 'Come on. It's almost midnight. I promise we've stopped talking about mortgages.' She giggled fruitily. 'Well, me and Julian have stopped. Charlie hasn't said a word since you left the room.'

An early firework spat across the sky. Dinner debris littered the table.

'Don't you dare!' Julian tugged her onto his lap as Kate began to clear away. 'You're off duty now.' He kissed her, his mouth demanding and uninhibited as if he'd forgotten they had company.

Giving in for a moment – Julian was good at many things; kissing was one of them – Kate pulled away, rubbed her nose against his. 'Not quite off duty,' she said. 'I made chocolate roulade for afters.'

'Decadence,' said Julian approvingly, 'after all that wholesome fish and rice bollocks.' He slapped her bottom when she stood up.

'Stop it,' she said, almost annoyed but not quite.

'I'm sorry,' said Julian, quietly so only she could hear. 'About earlier. Slagging off your job like that. Naughty Julian.'

'Five minutes to go!' Becca danced by herself on the rug, reaching out to press gang Kate as she passed en route to the sink. 'Spoilsport!' she called as Kate eluded her.

'Full glasses for the toast,' said Julian, topping up the flutes on the table.

Charlie grabbed gratefully at his, as if it was a life belt, not a glass.

'No, not for me.' Becca nipped over to place her hand ostentatiously over her glass.

A penny dropped. Kate said, 'You haven't drunk a drop of booze all evening, cuz.'

Becca put her hands together as if praying and said to Charlie, 'Can we tell them? I know we said we'd wait but . . .' Without waiting for his response, Becca squealed, 'I'm pregnant!'

'Wow! Congratulations.' Julian enveloped Becca in a hug.

Kate didn't look at Charlie. She waited her turn with the lady of the moment, and squeezed her close. 'This is amazing. Do you feel OK? Any sickness?'

'I feel a million dollars.' Becca was alight with energy, bouncing on the spot. 'It's so exciting!' With visible effort, she cranked down the glee and said, gravely, 'Of course it was a shock at first. We'd decided to wait. But lightning struck!'

If Charlie shared Kate's suspicion about how lightning could strike Becca's ovaries not once but twice he hid it well. Both this pregnancy and her other, lost, baby had taken root in her body at a time when she was, allegedly, taking steps not to conceive.

'We've been dying to tell you, haven't we, Charlie? We can't keep anything from you two.'

'We're delighted for you.' Julian put an arm around Kate, dragging her close. He was good in these situations, knowing the right thing to say. He had none of his wife's double edged misgivings, apparently. Kate felt grubby, bad minded. Babies were good news; so what if Becca had jettisoned her contraception so this one would arrive earlier rather than later.

'I've already handed in my notice,' said Becca.

'Well, you've asked about maternity leave,' said Charlie.

'Oh yes, that's what I meant.' Becca didn't even bother to disguise the panto wink she threw Kate's way. The receptionist job in a luxury spa, the latest in a long line of similar positions, had never struck Kate as very convincing; Becca bounced off to work in full slap and killer heels as if acting the role of a woman with a job. There was no way she was going back after giving birth.

'You'll be an amazing mummy.' Kate felt her eyes fill as she realised the truth of that. Her maddening, passionate, lioness of a cousin would dote on her cub.

'Oh Kate!' Becca beamed, her shoulders hitched up to her ears with the impossibility of semaphoring her emotions. 'You next!'

'Oh, well . . .' That blindsided Kate. She thought she'd given up blushing years ago, along with spots and New Kids on the Block.

'You'd better get cracking! We're not getting any younger!'

'Kate,' said Charlie, 'is twenty-three.'

Now it was Julian who Kate didn't look at. 'Not exactly past it!' she laughed toothily.

'There's plenty of time,' said Julian.

'No time like the present.' Becca, known for her tenacity, chose to pursue the point, despite her hosts' body language.

'We've got a lot on our plate,' said Julian.

'This apartment isn't what you'd call child friendly,' said Kate.

They were still smiling, still entwined.

Kate went on, wondering as she did so why she had to justify herself. 'I want to make a mark at work before I have babies.'

'My wife,' said Julian, 'is too busy to have babies. Sometimes,' he laughed, 'she's too busy for *me*!'

Kate wondered had she imagined it, but no, she hadn't. Julian had infused the joke with meaning, as if sending her a message above the others' heads. Perhaps he'd taken lessons from her mother, who was conversant in the Irish dark arts of subtle scolding. She countered by keeping her own tone light. 'Ooh, I wouldn't say that.'

Their sex life was a subject they returned to often.

*Where's the wild girl I married?* Julian would gripe as they sat up in bed reading, a radio news programme mumbling in the background.

Having explained once, twice, thirty times, Kate would attempt to explain again.

*I get tired because I work hard. And I bloody love it.*

She couldn't find the language to go further without hurting him. To point out that when he got home all he had to do was pull off his tie, pour a drink and gripe about his business deals, in comparison to Kate's race around the supermarket, preparation of dinner, serving of dinner, clearing away of dinner, all the while nodding sympathetically at the aforementioned gripes.

*Is it any wonder I don't feel like performing the Dance of the Seven Veils on demand?* What's more, Julian liked some added value in the bedroom. At the end of a long day, suspenders held no allure for Kate, who longed instead for fleecy pyjamas.

'We'll get around to babies!' she grinned.

'Excuses excuses!' Becca was in full schoolmarm mode. She prodded Julian, as she made her points. 'This little one inside me needs a playmate!' Prod. 'What are you so fright-ened of?' Prod. 'Man up, Julian, and put your lovely wife in the pudding club!' Prod.

'If you must know,' Julian said, shaking off her finger more brusquely than he would ever do sober, 'we've been trying since our wedding night.'

Outside, Chelsea Harbour came alive with the first of Big Ben's midnight chimes sounding from dozens of full volume television sets.

'No joy. Nada. Not even a scare,' said Julian bitterly. 'Happy now, Becca? Never content until you've gone too bloody far, are you?'

The last chime boomed over the silence in the apartment.

Julian wrenched back the sliding doors as the sky erupted in gunpowder flowers of scarlet and gold.

'Happy New Millennium!' Kate grabbed Becca and kissed her cheeks. They clung to each other, whispering *Sorry* and *It's OK*.

Julian and Charlie slapped each other's backs in the tenta-tive, jokey manner patented by Englishmen who can't relate to each other emotionally.

Gratefully relinquishing Charlie, Julian pulled his wife to him as if rescuing her from terrorists. 'Happy new every-thing. I'm an arsehole,' he said into her hair. '2000 will be our year, I promise.'

The moments when Julian opened up to her like this, like a flower whose centre she could suddenly see, still had the power to stir Kate. *If only you'd let me in more often.* She suddenly wanted to be the woman he needed, the lover he craved.

Kate kissed him. Like the wild girl he wanted her to be, her face was wet with tears that she could pass off as New Year sentimentality.

'Don't cry! You'll start me off!' yowled Becca. 'My hormones are all over the place.'

'Happy New Year, Kate,' said Charlie, at her elbow.

She had to kiss him. It would be peculiar not to, especially as Julian was smothering Becca, making sure she knew she was forgiven. Kate leaned forward. Charlie smelled different, *posh*. He used the cologne Becca bought him. 'Happy new thingummybob to you too,' she said.

The affinity they'd felt earlier had nowhere to go. She and Charlie weren't friends but cousins-in-law (if such a thing existed). They had too much history. Too much dead air lay between them.

And empathetic eye rolls weren't fair on Becca or Julian.

Charlie had been right when he wrote *This split is for the best*. She'd been right to hand back his note. They were done.

No planes fell out of the sky. No computers exploded.

But the chocolate roulade slumped.

*Charlie and Becca*

invite you to CELEBRATE
the christening of our beautiful daughter

*Florence Susan*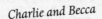

12.30
13th September 2003
St Bernadette's RC Church, Gold Street, Iffham
luncheon to follow
Dragonfly Cottage, 11 Mill Lane, Iffham

RSVP flobigday@gmail.com
Don't forget to reply –
I need to know numbers!!!

'I hate doing this,' said Charlie, to general laughter. 'My wife's much better than me at making speeches. But then she's better than me at most things.'

Becca tried, and very nearly succeeded, in looking humble as the crowd crammed into the conservatory looked her way.

'But, today I have a job to do as daddy to this little lady here.' Charlie bounced Florence Susan in his arms. The blue eyed, chrysanthemum haired Flo giggled, as she did most of the time. 'I want to introduce her to all of the people she's going to love as she grows up.'

*Aww* said almost everybody. Kate nudged Julian; his face didn't fit the occasion. She assumed he was trying not to choke on the shabby chic of Becca's new glass extension. A bunting sceptic, Julian looked uncomfortable among the patchwork cushions, the rattan chairs, and the old trunks repurposed as storage. 'Storage for what?' he'd hissed. 'Yet more dusty old tat?'

'That lady in the corner,' said Charlie, pointing Flo's pudgy forefinger, 'is your godmother, Kate.'

There was a smattering of applause, as if being godmother was a talent, even though so far all Kate had done was buy a silver rattle. She nervously readjusted the enormous hat that would ruin all the photos of this red letter day.

'I suggest you be very very naughty whenever she babysits,' said Charlie. The gentle joke got a huge laugh; this was an easy audience.

'I'll teach her to swear!' called Kate, regretting it when an elderly guest muttered, 'Well really!'

'Thanks!' Becca winked from where she stood behind Charlie, like a presidential candidate's wife. All in red, with a ruffle at the knee, she carried her 'baby weight' with glorious aplomb. Not for Becca the new mum uniform of stained tee shirts: she was hyper groomed, her eyebrows waxed and her lips plumped with collagen. With her new bottom-heavy figure she was a glamorous update of a pagan fertility icon, glowing with life. Around her neck, her name hung in flowing gold letters; Becca modelled herself on Carrie Bradshaw from *Sex and the City* with the doggedness of a cult member. Three years into the new millennium, it was clear that this new century – and motherhood – suited her.

'We don't really care what you're going to be when you grow up.' Charlie lifted Flo to look her in the eye as the Indian summer sun silhouetted them in gold. 'We don't give a monkeys whether you're the Prime Minister or you sweep the streets. We just want you to be happy, little Flo. We want you to know you are loved.'

'Hear hear!' shouted Kate's dad from where he stood sandwiched between a refurbished birdcage and a tailor's dummy wearing an antique nightdress.

More clapping, but Charlie wasn't quite finished. 'Come back, Becca,' he said, as she beetled off to fill glasses and make personal comments. He laid his arm around her shoulders, as if to anchor this vivacious vision to his side. 'Most of you know what we went through before Flo came along.' The atmosphere changed, the smiles turned tender. 'We've had a cot ready since 1997.'

Behind her, Kate felt Julian smother a sigh. Raised in a family of stiff upper lips, he abhorred such sharing. Recently she'd noticed him avoiding Becca; he was, Kate suspected, bored of the constant battle for 'ownership' of Kate that Becca waged. Any minute now he'd start lobbying to go home.

'I always knew my wife was one in a million but I didn't know she was brave and determined and . . .' Charlie smiled. 'I've run out of superlatives. It's all thanks to Becca's refusal to give up that, after losing two dearly wanted babies, we have Flo.' He sounded slightly strangled now, and the room willed him to carry on. 'My wife and my daughter. I'm proud of you both. I'll look after you both. Always.'

Kate wiped her eyes as she clapped with everybody else.

Stooping, Julian said into her ear, 'Becca certainly is one in a bloody million, thank the lord.' He ignored Kate's rebuking elbow in his ribs. As Becca approached them, fielding congratulations and compliments, he whispered, 'I tell you, that baby is *glue*. Flo's holding that marriage together.'

'I don't agree,' murmured Kate as Becca pushed through the throng. The glue was the miscarriages. Both times Becca had been reduced to a wordless lump of suffering, clinging to Charlie, all her vitality gone. The pain caused by the first little life losing its foothold inside Becca just before the wedding had been redoubled when it happened again, just two months after her impulsive disclosure on Millennium Eve. Charlie put aside his own grief to comfort his wife. Having seen her well-hidden fragility, Charlie was bonded to Becca.

'Do you approve of my conservatory, Julian?' Becca was coy, certain of herself. 'Reclaimed brick floor! Green oak frame! I love it when the sun streams through the glass like this. I don't know how you townies cope, living in filthy old London.'

'The same filthy old London,' said Kate, 'you lived in for your whole life until two months ago.'

'I suppose it's different,' said Becca, turning away to adjust an arrangement of driftwood and candles, 'when you're childless.'

Stuck for a response, Kate watched Becca pounce on another knot of guests, checking their champagne levels, beseeching them to make another circuit of the buffet table.

'I'm sure she didn't mean that to sound so . . . harsh,' said Kate as she took off her hat with a great sense of relief and followed Julian into the cottage's quaint kitchen where the booze was laid out.

'There you go again.' Julian rifled through the massed ranks of bottles for the good stuff, the bottle he'd brought. 'Making excuses. Your whole family bends over backwards to accommodate Becca.' He caught sight of his reflection in the window. Kate saw the momentary pause as he checked his hairline. Julian was horribly conscious of its retreat, like a slow tide. Kate told him it suited him and

Julian told Kate she was only saying that to make him feel better. When he checked himself out in shiny surfaces she wanted to take him in her arms, reassure him, but that would mean she'd noticed and Julian would hate that. 'Becca's the only person I know who's simultaneously top dog *and* underdog.'

'You're right,' said Kate, gazing about her at the other female guests and wondering *when did handbags get so gigantic?* The more chic contingent looked as if they'd brought everything they owned to the christening. 'But that's just Becca. I don't mind.'

'See!' Julian was exasperated. Holding the bottle by its neck, he led Kate outside.

The garden – or *gardens* as Aunty Marjorie preferred – clung to its summer glory, a watercolourist's delight of greens and blues and deep pinks. A piñata hung from the gingerbread eaves of a summerhouse. Multicoloured bulbs snaked through the willow branches. When Kate had invited Becca to take what supplies she needed from the shop's stockroom, Becca had filled her car. Spotting her prey, Kate hurried across the grass, self-conscious in her oyster-coloured dress. The saleswoman at Harvey Nichols had assured her that 'nude is so now', but Kate felt as if she was streaking. 'Charlie!'

Charlie turned and smiled, knowing what she wanted. 'Here you go.'

Accepting Flo, Kate marvelled again at the baby's warm denseness, like a bowling ball in a nappy. She loved Flo with fierce simplicity: nothing compromised Kate's feelings of delight and protectiveness. 'When will she start looking like you, Charlie?' she laughed.

'It's only fair she looks like Becca,' said Charlie. 'She did all the hard work, after all.'

'Nice speech.'

'It was a bit icky. But Flo makes me a bit icky.'

'Me too.' Kate nuzzled the pink face, breathing in Flo's baby smell of mingled vanilla, mud and farmyard. 'You look as if she kept you up all night again.'

'Gee thanks.' Charlie rubbed the back of his head, making his dark hair stand up on end. 'You'll spoil me with all these compliments.'

'At least *you* have an excuse for the bags under your eyes.'

'You'll always look seventeen to me,' said Charlie. 'Mind you,' he added, 'you looked really old when you were seventeen.'

'Bloody cheek!'

'Seriously,' said Charlie, 'you haven't changed a bit.'

'That's so sweet. And so untrue.' Kate's features had asserted themselves, as if her real face had arrived after years of regrettable experiments with eyeliner and bronzer. 'We all change.'

A small white ball of animated fur ran past, yapping.

'Jaffa!' shouted Charlie. 'No! Don't—'

'Too late.' The dog had pelted straight into the new pond. 'What *is* Jaffa?' asked Kate. 'I keep forgetting.' Was he a shih tzu crossed with a poodle? Or a poodle crossed with a pekinese?

Monitoring Jaffa's doggy paddle to safety, Charlie sighed. 'I think he's a cross between a lamb and a cushion. The animal's an imbecile.'

'Becca says he's a brilliant guard dog.'

'The only thing he barks at is his own reflection.'

A shout carried across the garden. 'Hey, Chas!' a bumptious guest shouted. 'Is that loo roll ad your latest masterpiece?'

'Yes! That's mine!' shouted Charlie, adding *you pillock* in an undertone. 'I never thought,' he said, 'I'd be writing scripts for puppies playing with toilet paper.'

'It's my favourite commercial. Poodles. Bog roll. It's like a mini Harold Pinter.' Despite – or perhaps because of – Charlie's disdain for advertising he was a success. Headhunted again to a newly formed agency, he was powerful enough to insist on working from home two days a week. The long commute was the only way Charlie could make Becca's dream of a rural idyll workable. He knew, as did Kate, that Becca would have a new dream before long.

'You're allowed to be proud of what you do,' said Kate.

Charlie didn't look convinced.

'How's the book?'

'Coming along, you know.'

'Could I take a peek some time?' Kate hadn't read Charlie's manuscript since what were now the olden days, when they'd gone out together. 'If you don't mind, that is.' It's an intimate thing, to read words when they're fresh, when they're still attached to the writer; until recently Kate wouldn't have dreamed of making such a request.

The loss of the babies had not only bound Kate ever tighter to her cousin but also, inevitably, to Charlie. Gradually, Kate and Charlie rediscovered much of their old affinity. Neither Julian nor Becca protested: Kate had underestimated them.

Now it seemed laughable that once upon a time Kate had held back from such banter with Charlie in case it unsettled their other halves, challenged the status quo.

The status quo was not so easily threatened. After that initial, juvenile partner-swap, they'd all hunkered down for the long haul. It struck Kate that all four of them were 'stayers', made of similar material to her parents, who had never dreamed of leaving each other, despite their ups and downs.

As rooted in his marriage as the willow tree on the edge of the lawn, Charlie wouldn't now recall what he'd written to her in that other life, but his cold turn of phrase was impossible to expunge from her memory; it was as word perfect as the Shakespeare she'd studied at school.

*Not everything that looks like love is love* tripped as easily off her tongue as the *Hear my soul speak* line from *The Tempest*, both quotes as archaic and irrelevant as the other.

'Here, take this starlet to meet her public.' Kate relinquished Flo, who was muttering bubbly sweet nothings to herself. 'Bask in her reflected glory.'

The baby was greeted with exaggerated joy as Charlie strolled around the garden, showing Flo off to all and sundry.

'Look at Charlie.' Kate's mother had been keeping Julian warm for her. 'He's a natural.'

'Why doesn't he just whip out his nipple and breastfeed?' said Julian, shocking his mother-in-law. Some guests had already drifted away. Julian looked pointedly at his watch.

'There's no need,' said Mum, 'for talk of nipples.' Happily stout, she'd embraced midlife wholeheartedly, running towards bad perms and elasticated waists as if they were old friends she'd been expecting. 'Your dad,' she said, 'was like that with you, Kate. Couldn't put you down.'

'Where *is* Dad?' Kate resolutely ignored the desperate, covert signals Julian was sending out that it was time to go.

'Having a sit down,' said Mum, patting her hair, her dress, her garish jacket into place with her endlessly fluttering and fussing fingers. 'He gets so tired.'

'Dad?' Kate baulked. 'He's last to bed and first up.'

'He *was*,' said Mum. 'The years take their toll on all of us.'

Disliking this picture Mum drew, Kate steered the conversation to safer ground. 'Becca's doing wonders with this garden, isn't she?'

Julian let out a discreet sob of boredom.

'It's a credit to her,' said Mum, always ready to praise her niece. 'Why you don't have a garden I can't think, Kate. You and Julian paying all that money for that flat and all you've got is a silly balcony . . .'

That was the trouble with mother/daughter chatter; with Mum there was no safer ground. Contrariness was her default setting. *Especially when it comes to me.*

'Gosh,' said Julian. 'Is that the time?'

'Have you changed your hair?' Mum inspected Kate's fringe, flattened by the regretted hat.

'No. Why?' Kate put a self-conscious hand to her head, steeling herself.

'It looks nice.'

'Oh.' Kate grinned. *A compliment!*

'For once.'

*Count to ten*, Kate advised herself. She and Mum were constantly cracking, yet never broke. She envisaged herself dashing about with sticky tape, endlessly repairing, endlessly making good. It stood to reason that this eternal, rolling dissonance – it never flared into anything more specific – had to be at least fifty per cent her fault. However hard Kate tried, they always ended up in the same place. A place of mild discontent, of petty grievance and pointed words.

With that in mind, Kate felt able to broach a forbidden subject. *I could be as nice as pie all afternoon and she'll still wish I was more like Becca, so I may as well do some work on Dad's behalf.* 'Mum,' she said, hoping her gulp wasn't audible, 'we need to talk about Dad.'

'What do you mean?' Mum's face was all vigour.

'I mean,' said Kate, cowed by that expression, 'why don't you give your blessing to his China trip?'

A small groan escaped Julian: the groan of a man who knew he wouldn't escape any time soon.

Kate was carefully casual. 'Now that you've got your caravan, and Dad's about to retire, you could even go with him. Marriage is about compromise, after all.'

Kate's own marriage was a see-saw: lately she'd sensed or maybe just suspected a pulling away in Julian so she'd made more of an effort. Not just in the bedroom – although she was astounded at the effect a red basque had on Julian's state of mind – but by listening when he talked about the nuts and bolts of the property world. She would nod and ask pertinent questions, watching how his aristocratic face, drawn from a template that stared out of portraits in stately homes, would flush as he talked her through the latest deal. He didn't return the favour but she didn't expect that; Kate's career was small potatoes compared to his. Secretly, Kate preferred the immediacy of her party supplies emporiums, where she satisfied small needs and there was a justice to each transaction quite unlike Julian's massive profits and macho jubilation at having 'won'.

Mum trembled as she said, 'Don't you lecture me, madam. You and Dad might be close but you don't know everything.

Things are different now.' She screwed up her lips, as if trying to keep in something dangerous. 'Very different.' The moment passed and she said, 'Ignore me, love. I'm worn out.'

'That's because you're always down here, helping Becca out.' Kate didn't understand why both her mother and her aunt flew constantly to Becca's side as if she was dealing with quintuplets. 'Maybe if you spent more time with Dad and—'

'Spend time with Dad?' Kate's mother interrupted, insulted. 'Dear God, if you knew the half of it.' She disappeared, pushing brusquely through Flo's fans.

'Right.' Julian rubbed his hands together. 'You managed to upset your mother even more quickly than usual, so we might as well go.'

'Thanks for the support.'

'I'm joking, silly,' said Julian. 'Not about going home. I'm deadly bloody serious about that.'

'Kate!' Becca descended on them, her face flustered. 'There you are!' she said, as if her cousin had been hiding. 'Could you pick up some empty glasses? Put them in the dishwasher?'

Before Kate could answer, Julian said, 'We're guests, not staff.'

'I don't mind,' said Kate.

'But I do,' said Julian, turning away, grabbing a glass from a passing tray. 'Not that it matters.'

Diligent, Kate toured the garden with a growing stack of glasses. Seeing Charlie and her dad confabbing on a garden bench, she put them to one side and played truant.

As she approached, she heard her father say, 'She'd be so proud of you, Charlie.'

'She would,' agreed Kate, perching on the arm of the seat, leaning against Dad. They all looked at Flo, happily playing with Dad's tie, and thought of the grandmother she'd never meet.

It had been a classic alcoholic's death. A year earlier, on a mellow early autumn day like this one, Charlie's mother had slipped on the stairs and plunged to the bottom, lying against the door her son had to force open after two anxious days of getting no response to his calls. He'd half expected such a calamity all his life but that didn't seem to soften the blow. Charlie had sunk into a morass of guilt and anger and, most shamefully and only whispered to Kate, relief.

Becca, embedded so firmly in her own family, the epicentre of a web of relationships, had sympathised with his grief, but found it harder to empathise with the aftermath. Charlie, with no blood relations left, felt himself sticking out in the universe like a sore thumb. Becca seemed grateful for Kate's willingness to talk and talk around the subject with Charlie once she'd exhausted her own compassion.

Maybe because she'd lived through Charlie's youthful realisation that he had to parent his own hapless mother, Kate got it. She understood the ins and outs of Charlie's complex remorse and furthermore she understood how it formed the platform for his love for Flo.

The child was *his*. Flo was tied by blood to her orphan daddy who had never known his own father. When Kate sensed the profundity of that connection, it had been the turning point in the rediscovered harmony with her old friend. It was to Kate that Charlie had whispered, desperately, *Let's hope Death takes some time off, now.*

'Flo reminds me of your mum,' said Kate's dad, taking her on his lap.

They all knew that to be untrue, but Charlie smiled.

The shoulder Kate leaned against was bony. 'When,' asked Kate, 'are you going to resist Mum's diets, Dad?' Kate couldn't allow him to age; she'd been trying not to notice the slackness of his face, the diminishing of his frame. His one good suit hung loose on him. 'Step away from the crispbreads and low fat cheese.'

'I've demolished a few slices of cake today,' said Dad conspiratorially. 'You and Becca were up all night baking, I hear. Whatever happens, you'll always have each other, you girls.'

'That's a bit maudlin, Dad,' said Kate. 'For a christening.'

As talk turned, inevitably, to the Yulan House orphanage, Kate listened patiently and without much real interest to the news of the foundations being laid for the new wing, and the fresh push in fundraising it would need. Kate's mother was unaware that the bright new website, featuring smiling photos of Jia Tang and her growing clutch of charges, had been funded by Dad: for the sake of Minelli harmony, it must stay that way.

The whitewashed compound outside Beijing didn't feel real to Kate. It was so foreign, so *other*, in the sharp sunlit images she saw only on the screen of her Dad's iPod. 'Lovely,' she said, absent mindedly, as Dad showed her yet another shot of yet another squealing child dashing about a dusty yard. Her days and her thoughts were so thoroughly accounted for on this small patch of home turf that she had nothing left over for her father's pet project.

Not so Charlie, it would seem. 'Remember when we ran the marathon together to raise money for the kids?' asked Charlie. 'How much did you raise last year? A grand, wasn't it?'

'Nearer two.'

'How come you didn't run it this year?'

Dad shook his head. 'Those days are gone, son.'

Detecting a morbid edge to Dad's mood, Kate launched into an impassioned case for her father to finally travel to China and shake Jia Tang's hand.

'There are things to sort out at home,' said her father.

'Like what?' Kate was fired up about the injustice. 'Painting Mum's toenails? This is your *dream*, Dad, and it's achievable. One of us should see our dreams come true. I'm working on Mum.'

Dad's *No!* was adamant and he welcomed the change of subject Becca brought with her, as she forced them to budge up on the bench. 'Nobody's *touched* the quiche. I put some on a plate for Julian but he's on his phone doing some property deal.' She nodded approvingly. 'That man's never off duty.'

'Hmm,' said Dad.

'Come on, Charlie.' Becca prodded her husband. 'Time for Flo to do another circuit.'

'Sometimes, Flo has a look of Kate, don't you think?' Dad smiled at Flo's effusive burp. 'Same dreamy eyes.' He carefully passed her to Charlie. 'She's all yours, almost-son-in-law.'

'Ha!' laughed Becca, from halfway across the garden. 'Almost!'

'That was a close shave for all of us,' laughed Charlie. 'Phew!' He wiped his brow as he followed Becca.

'He was joking, love.' Dad's smile faded when he caught the look on Kate's face.

'I know that.' She laughed. It had a tinny sound, like a broken toy. 'I'd better go and find Julian.' She picked up her glass burden once again. 'He's fretting to get home.'

'I know how he feels,' said Dad.

There were people everywhere, all of them in Kate's way, leaning over each other to grab at tiny triangular sandwiches as if famine had broken out. A semi-circle of fawning women surrounded Charlie, who was jiggling Flo and holding forth knowledgeably on formula milk and nappy rash. Uncle Hugh hovered, rocking back and forth on his heels.

Somehow his title had got lost in the mix; Aunty Marjorie was more of a grandmother than Uncle Hugh was a grandfather. The look on his face said different. Kate noticed how he tailed the hiccupping little bundle as the baby was shown to the masses, exuding quiet pride in his miracle of a granddaughter. He jumped out of Kate's way with a *Sorry, love!*

Taking two more laps of the garden, looking for Julian's golden head above the fray, Kate wondered what kind of a daddy he would make. Would he take to it as passionately as Charlie, who had confounded everybody with his enthusiasm for Flo, after he'd begged Becca to wait?

As she entered the house, its cloistered feel was welcome. Kate paused in the quiet passage. Julian was philosophical, never accusing, but she felt his impatience. She felt his suspicion, never uttered, that *she* was the reason they had no children.

Closing her eyes Kate let it wash over her, the feeling that somewhere, circling the stars, drifting through the universe, was a child. Her child. It would come when it was ready; it would come at the perfect time.

There was no way to share this certainty with Julian, a man who believed only in what he could touch and feel.

Suddenly, Aunty Marjorie materialised, and marshalled Kate's help in handing out yet more quiche.

Looking for somewhere to dump the tray – when would Aunty Marjorie learn that her quiche tasted of flip flops?

– Kate skulked by the downstairs loo, eavesdropping on the genteel argument leaking through the door.

'You never think of me, do you? Tell her. Or I will!'

It was, Kate realised, her mother's voice. She pressed her ear to the door.

'Do you think it's easy,' said her father, in a hushed howl, 'to tell your own daughter such a thing? That you're leaving her?'

'But you can leave me easily enough. Is that it?'

The door was yanked open and Kate slid away like a cat burglar as her mother stormed out, making, no doubt, for Aunty Marjorie like a menopausal heat-seeking missile. *Where are you, Julian?* She scanned the party, as a hand caught her arm.

'I've been looking for you,' said her husband, drawing her into the utility room, a temple to white goods that smelled of fabric conditioner.

'I've been looking for *you*.' What she expected Julian to do about her parents, Kate wasn't sure, but he would do something. Julian always took charge. He would straighten out what must be a misunderstanding. Her father was a stayer. Like her. Like Julian. Some things in life you could rely on.

Or so she hoped. 'You first,' she said.

'I've just wound up a ve-ry sweet deal.'

In the new spirit of wifely enthusiasm she asked was it the wharf, or the big old warehouse in Spitalfields or maybe the deconsecrated chapel ripe for conversion?

It was none of those profitable but dull things. 'It's a house. *The* house.' Julian nodded encouragingly until Kate caught up with him.

'What?' She put her hands to her face.

She hadn't made a very compelling case for the house. Scepticism had been writ large all over Julian as Kate guided him through high ceilinged rooms hung with yellowing paper, all reeking of damp and mould and dead people's lives. The reasons she loved the strict, tall, Georgian building were all to do with the heart. The house needed rescuing; she never could resist a sob story.

The house yearned to be loved. True, it was tough love it craved. Walls must be torn down, floorboards pulled up. Out of the rubble a handsome home would emerge, its elegant windows shining and its painted front door ajar, welcoming them into its peachily lit parlours, and bedrooms in the eaves and a kitchen glowing like a furnace of happiness in its belly.

'Just like that?' Kate was giddy. Only this morning the house had been a mere idea.

'Why hang about? I move fast. As you know.'

He was triumphant, a Napoleon in a linen suit. Kate bit her lip, damming up the question that wanted to be asked. *Why didn't you tell me?* She hadn't wanted it dropped at her feet, like an offering. She'd wanted them to negotiate together, plotting and scheming. 'You're amazing,' she said, meaning it, absolving him speedily.

'It's a long time,' said Julian, 'since I felt this excited about a purchase.'

That was what she needed to hear. 'I have so many plans.' Once she started talking about reclaimed fireplaces she might never stop. 'It'll be *ours*.'

Julian's ferocious work ethic had inspired her to build her own mini empire in the image of his enterprise. With the money he loaned her – she insisted it was a loan; he was relaxed about it – Kate had bought the three shops she used to manage. She was proud of that, gave it her all, but the house would be their joint project. A home for them both, not a showhome pad.

And, if Kate was honest with herself – this sometimes happened if the wind was in the right direction – a substitute for the baby that had yet to make an entrance.

'Did you remind them I asked for ten thousand off the asking price?' It had taken nerve to suggest that to the estate agent but she'd wanted to impress Julian with her hard-headed tough-talking ways.

'I knocked fifty grand off the asking price.' Julian ruffled her hair. 'Clever you. Finding a gem. Doing your bit.' He frowned. 'Kate! You're doing it again. Going off somewhere inside your head.' Julian tutted. The delicious spell was broken. 'I want my wife back, please.'

'I was just daydreaming.' Kate offered her face to his on tiptoe. 'About you. Stripped to the waist. Wielding a sledgehammer. Covered in dust.' She kissed him and they were there, knocking down a wall, doing something solid and practical and sexy. She pulled away and they were back at the christening.

'Oh God, Julian, something's happened. It's Mum and Dad.'

Kate explained, and as she knew he would, Julian took charge. 'It'll be some misunderstanding.' Instantly, her fears were scaled down. 'I'll go and find them, sort it out.' He put his hands on her shoulders. 'And *you* stop collecting empties. My wife is no waitress.' He twirled Kate to face the door. 'Join the coven that's taken up residence in the kitchen.'

Grateful, trusting – Julian will get to the bottom of this – Kate held out her arms as Flo was handed into them like a relay baton, by a perspiring distant relative.

'You're hungry, aren't you?' Kate recognised the grizzling noise. 'You want some lovely mushed up banana, don't you?' And a sleep. Flo was badly in need of peace and quiet. *As am I.*

The kitchen was crammed with women trying to be useful and getting in each other's way. Decamping back to the utility room with Flo and a banana, Kate was soon joined by Becca. With a sinking sensation in her stomach she recognised the expression on Becca's face as Needing To Talk.

'What?' she said flatly.

'What do you mean *what*?' said Becca innocently.

'Your mummy,' said Kate to Flo as she spooned mashed fruit into the baby's mouth, 'needs to say something to me but she doesn't know where to start.'

'And your godmother,' said Becca to the baby, 'is a know-all.' She leaned back against the washing machine, arms folded. 'You're right, though, Kate. I'm disappointed.'

'In me?'

'We barely see each other any more.'

Before Kate had time to splutter at that fiction, Becca said, 'Why can't you be happy for me? I didn't have Flo to spite you, you know.' She fumbled with a tissue she plucked from her sleeve. 'I'd give my right arm for you to be a mother. You know that.'

Kate didn't know that, because she'd never discussed babies with Becca. There had never been a right time to do so with a woman either recovering from the loss of one child or high on hope at the conception of another. There had never been anything in Kate's attitude to justify this chin wobbling and nose dabbing. 'Hang on, when have I ever—'

'You don't know what I went through to have Flo.'

Looking down at Flo's domed head, crowned with its fluffy halo of hair, Kate said, 'I think I do, Becca.'

'No,' said Becca darkly. 'You do not.' The tears arrived and Becca burbled through them, opening and slamming drawers like a demented robot. 'If I could wave a magic wand and give you a baby, I would. I wish this was a double christening. Don't hate me because of Flo.'

Aunty Marjorie swung into the utility room, felt the atmosphere and froze, before backing out like a Nissan Micra reversing out of a tight parking space.

'You're being daft.' Kate wiped banana from Flo's chin. 'I see a lot of you. Not as much as when you lived in London, admittedly, because I have a more than full time job and I don't always have the energy to travel out here to the arse end of nowhere. *You're* the one who moved away!'

'You're the boss. You can take time off whenever you like.'

'Being the boss means *longer* hours. It's not like when we used to play shops.' Kate didn't expect Becca to understand: she hadn't worked since she'd left her receptionist job in 2000. She said, more gently, 'You're telling yourself stories, Becca. How could I, of all people, begrudge you this little dumpling?' She handed over the baby and Becca broke down, sobbing over Flo's head. 'Sssh. Please. Whatever you're crying about, it's not us. Can we stop this?' She bent and parted Becca's blonde hair to peer at her face. 'Sorry, cuz, but I don't envy you. Which is a shame, because we both know how much you love being envied.'

A sniffle converted to a giggle. 'It's the hormones,' said Becca.

'Them again,' sighed Kate theatrically. 'This is very *you*, Becca, to move away and then scold me because you feel isolated.'

'I know you all think I'm a drama queen . . .'

'If you're leaving a gap there for me to contradict you, you'll be waiting a long time.'

'Cow.' Becca threw a crumpled tissue at Kate. 'But I *feel* things deeply, you know?'

'So does everybody. We just don't turn every day into a three act opera.' She added, perhaps a little late, 'But it doesn't matter. You're just you.'

'Julian disapproves of me,' said Becca, with an inward, thwarted look. 'I thought we were friends again but . . .'

'Julian loves you.' How easily that tripped off Kate's tongue. A huge word like *love* and she could misuse it just like that.

'He does, doesn't he?' Becca's confidence was a buoyant critter, never on the floor for long. 'You've tamed him, you know.'

'I've never tamed anything in my life.' *Or wanted to*.

'He was kind of bigger and more brash before you came along. Now he's more quiet, easier to handle.'

'You make him sound like a cat I found in an alley.'

'A pedigree cat!' laughed Becca. 'A big pedigree tom cat.' She fixed Kate with a look and Kate stood to attention: that look reminded her of their mothers' way with a glare. 'You've tamed me, too. I'd be worse if you weren't around.'

'Worse? Don't talk about yourself like that.' Kate didn't want to hear such language from Becca. 'You don't need correcting or . . . or *taming*, you twit.' Kate had never suspected Becca of this kind of self-knowledge; she'd believed her profoundly unaware of the effect she had on the family, of the allowances they constantly made for her. 'You're perfect just the way you are.'

'I need you, Kate.' Becca sounded about ten years old.

'And I need you, you idiot.' Kate put her arms around mother and child. It would be difficult to make more time for Becca when she factored in the new house as well as the shops, but she'd do it somehow.

'Trouble is,' said Becca, 'you don't understand how hard it is to juggle a child and a husband and to live a twenty minute drive from the nearest shopping centre. You have it so easy, Kate.'

Calling on years of experience, Kate bit her tongue one more time.

'May I interrupt, ladies?' Julian was stern. Becca responded to his demeanour by widening her eyes at Kate, giving her arm a squeeze and leaving them together.

'Your parents are in the conservatory.' Julian hadn't returned with a ready made solution as Kate had hoped. 'They looked so dour I daren't go in.'

The party had thinned out. Napkins were strewn on the conservatory's tiled floor and paper plates were abandoned on each carefully distressed surface.

Uncomfortable on a twee wrought iron bench, Kate's parents were slumped, puppets whose strings had been cut. When they saw her, they sat up with discernible effort. She wondered how long they'd been doing that, brightening for her sake.

Julian began. Kate, who couldn't find the right words, was grateful that their marital see-saw was in good working order. 'Something is obviously up, folks. Your daughter here is suffering. Can we talk about it? Kate and I might be able to help.'

'Nothing's up.' Dad was there immediately with a rebuttal. 'Like what?'

Mum was doggedly silent. She looked at her lap with savage concentration, emanating energy as if she wanted to leap up and scream.

'Dad . . .' appealed Kate.

'Love, it's the end of a long day,' said her father. 'Let's talk another time.'

'Your daughter,' said Julian, 'overheard something very upsetting and she deserves an explanation.'

Mum snorted. An expressive noise from the soundtrack of Kate's childhood.

'She heard you say something about splitting up.'

The pair on the bench jerked, as if the ironwork was suddenly electrified.

'What?' scowled Mum.

'That doesn't make any sense,' said Dad.

The silence persisted and Kate was at war with herself, wanting it to end but knowing it would end unhappily. 'Please, tell me.'

Mum said, 'Your Father has—'

'No.' Kate's dad held up his hand. It was, Kate noticed, bony and pale. More elegant than before but more grim. 'This is my story. I'll tell it.' He told his daughter about the symptoms that had assailed him almost a year ago. He described the constant nausea, the endless indigestion. 'Mum nagged me to go to the doc.' Instead of sending him home with a prescription, the doctor sent Dad to a specialist. 'I had what's called an endoscopic ultrasound.'

'And?' prompted Kate when he faltered.

'And they diagnosed cancer of the stomach.'

A sensation like snow falling. Like a cold blanket muffling the sunny room. Kate crossed into a different realm. A place where her father was ill. A new and icy place. Julian put his arm around her. Warm and heavy, it couldn't quite cut through the chill.

'Now, let's be honest, everybody panics when they hear the word cancer, don't they?' Dad said, conversationally.

Kate could imagine how her mother had reacted. Cancer was a voodoo word in the family, six letters which, if spoken aloud, might conjure up the ogre that took both Kate's Irish grandparents long before their time. It was the troll whose touch shrivelled, whose breath destroyed.

'My cancer was caught early.' Dad reconsidered. 'Early *ish*. Stage 1B and slow growing. All of which is good news, love. As far as any of this is good news.'

'What are they going to do?' Kate found her voice and a small, reedy voice it was.

'They've already operated.'

Kate leaned back, as if he'd slapped her. 'You had an operation and I didn't know?' This was fantastical.

'Well, we didn't want to worry you.'

'We? I didn't agree to any of this.' Mum was robust. 'I've wanted to tell you from the get-go.'

'The oncologists weren't too alarmed. The main fear with stomach cancer is that it spreads to the liver but the CT scan put their minds at rest.'

*Oncologist*. Such an ugly word. 'So the operation was a success?' Kate wanted to stick her fingers in her ears. She could only bear one answer.

'It was.' Dad nodded and beside him his wife made a deep noise like a growl. 'It *was*,' he insisted. 'I didn't even need chemotherapy.'

The ugly words were coming thick and fast in this cute and stultifying room.

'So, the plan was, I would tell you I'd had a brush with cancer and we'd all have a hug and that would be that.'

'But?' Kate said the word hanging in neon above their heads.

'But, indeed.' Dad seemed to ossify, turning to stone in front of her. He didn't want to say it. Not, she knew, for his own sake but for hers. 'It's come back, love,' he said.

Kate realised that Julian was holding her up.

'I'm so sorry, John,' said Julian. 'I'm so very, very sorry.'

'Are you angry with me, Kate?' asked her father.

'How could I be?' Kate was ashamed. She should have known. One of her people had fallen and not only had she not picked him up, she hadn't even noticed he was on his knees.

Other people entered the room. Words like *prognosis* were bandied. Aunty Marjorie took her sister's hand. Becca began to howl, as if she'd been stabbed. Charlie was bone white. Death, it seemed, was still on duty.

It was Julian who noticed, who realised that Kate needed to be alone with her father. He herded the others back to the sitting room, suggesting strong drinks all round.

Left in the conservatory with Dad, Kate sat alongside him on the hard bench. She took his hand, feeling his long fingers in hers, like when she was tiny. He'd stressed he wasn't in imminent danger, that all this fuss was unnecessary, but Kate felt every moment to be priceless. As if she was already looking back nostalgically at herself and Dad sitting in the lavender dusk, holding hands. As if he had already gone.

'This is why I didn't want to tell you. I don't want to be ill dad. Pathetic dad, in the corner with a blanket over his knees.' Dad squeezed her hand tighter; she felt encouraged by the strength in his grip. 'There's still a long way to go. A lot the doctors can do for me. This is just a blip, that's all. A setback.'

The treatment, they both knew, could be as arduous as the ailment.

'Dad, why don't you come and live with me and Julian? Mum can come too. We've tons of room.'

'What a recipe for disaster. You're my daughter not my nursemaid, Kate. I want to see you *live,* not run around after me like some drudge. Anyway it hasn't got to that stage yet.'

*Yet.* Kate loathed that inoffensive little three letter word.

'When you were born,' said Dad, 'you changed me into a completely different person, different to the one I was before you arrived. Since that day, I've been Kate's dad. That's brought responsibilities. Some big, like keeping you alive. Others small and easy, like picking you up from school. Do you remember me asking you what you did at school? And your answer?'

'*Nothing.*' It was a family joke. It soothed. And stung.

'I don't have to collect you from anywhere any more. The days are gone when you call home in tears because some friend said something nasty and you need to come home right *now*. But, to me, you're still that child. Even though you're a woman with a career and a husband and responsibilities of your own. When I think of you, out there on your own, charging about, doing your thing, I want to throw cotton wool on the ground beneath your shoes. I want to hold your hand, just like I did coming home from school. I want to insulate you against the hard corners of life. And it . . .' Dad's voice went damp, dwindled to nothing. 'It *kills* me,' he said, after finding it again. 'It kills me to think of leaving you. That,' he said quietly, 'is why I didn't tell you. Am I forgiven?'

'There's nothing to forgive.' Kate stood up, to satisfy her restlessness, but sat straight back down again, scrabbling for her father's hand. If she was to cope with this news, and be of some actual use, she had to fight the sensation that every moment could be the last she shared with him. 'This changes everything,' she said, blankly.

'No, not for you.' Dad sounded almost irritated. 'I won't have that, Kate. You're young. You're healthy. This is *my* problem.'

'Wrong, old man.' Kate's near future had changed completely, like a watercolour dropped into a muddy puddle. 'You're stuck with me.'

'You're a little warrior, aren't you, Kate?'

'Me? I just bowl along in Becca's shadow.'

'Not at all.' Dad looked insulted. 'You're the prize, darling. You're the quality. I love Becca, but I'm not blind. She prods you about, positioning you here, there, where she wants you. But you have a mind of your own. At some point you'll rebel.'

*Against what?* 'Becca means well.'

'True. But she's blinkered. You, though, you see all too clearly, although sometimes you hum and look the other way, denying what you know to be true in order to get through the day more easily.'

'We're not meant to be talking about me,' said Kate.

'I'm not well. Indulge me.' Dad scooped up her hand and kissed it. 'Oh come on, love, *laugh*. We'll need our sense of humour to get through this.'

And after they got through it? *I'll be without you.* Kate forced a smile.

'Ye Gods, Kate, is that the best you can do?' Dad's mock outrage prompted a more genuine grin. 'Every day will bring us something good, you'll see.'

'Bloody hell, Dad, you sound like a guru. Let me have a bit of a cry, will you?' Kate leaned against him, shoulder to shoulder. 'I'm still getting acclimatised.'

'So here's a little story while you get acclimatised.'

'Like the ones you used to make up for me at bedtime?' Laying her head on her father's shoulder, Kate closed her eyes, willing herself to be that little girl again. Safe. *Ignorant.*

113

'Like I said, we're never too old to learn something new. It happens every day. Yesterday I learned that your mother doesn't like it if I compare her coffee to soup. Today I learned something even more astonishing.'

He paused, forcing Kate to murmur, eyes still shut, 'Go on.'

'I thought I knew you better than I know myself, but today I learned that you're still in love with Charlie.'

The silence was profound. Kate contemplated letting it stretch and stretch until her blush wore off but she knew how patient her father could be. 'That, Dad, is about the daftest thing I've ever heard you say.'

'Denial, again.'

'Dad, you shouldn't say things like that. I mean, as if!'

'If I remember correctly it was going very well up until a stupid little tiff. If your mother and I had an argument like the one that finished you and Charlie, we wouldn't even notice it.'

'That might be true but doesn't that prove something to you? If Charlie and I were meant to be together we'd have weathered that storm.'

'I didn't say you were meant to be together.' Dad sounded almost sly. 'I said you still love him. Quite a different observation.'

'I don't love him, Dad.' Kate felt her throat thicken at lying to a man in his condition. 'Well, let's just say if I did, what good would it do me?'

As if the birdsong and chatter through the open doors had been stilled, Kate saw a present day where that beastly note had never been written. She saw a poverty stricken pair, struggling and arguing, long past the carefree years of unbridled lust and the belief that life was all potential. That gilded era was all they'd shared: the first sign of trouble and they'd fallen apart.

'We're different people now,' said Kate.

'I should hope so. Only dullards never change.' Dad shifted so that Kate had to sit up. She felt as if she barely existed. She was just a white noise of anxiety. 'Lately . . .' Dad swallowed. 'More than that. For some *years*, I've felt an ache in you, Kate. You look the way your mother looks when she's got one of her heads. As if you're not quite there. Not quite *you*. As if something is wrong, maybe just a small thing I don't know, but it's getting in the way of your happiness. A stone in your shoe.'

'Happiness,' said Kate with a small *pfft*. 'What *is* happiness?'

'There are many downsides to a life-threatening illness.' Dad patted Kate's hand when she mewled. 'But the silver lining is that you see things very clearly, without the clutter. I've been thinking about happiness, whether it exists, how to go about finding it. It's not constant bliss, that's for sure. There's no such thing. It's more a general feeling that all is as it should be. For *you*. Happiness is bespoke.' Becoming more animated than he'd been all day, Dad said, 'It's nothing to do with other people's expectations. Nothing to do with what's best. You need to feel right in your own skin.' He looked directly at his red eyed daughter. 'Sometimes, Kate, you seem as if you're acting instead of feeling real emotion.'

'Don't we all do that to some extent?' Why were they talking about her at a time like this? Kate felt she was being harried, hassled into a tight corner. As if she'd been found out in some misdemeanour.

'Possibly. But that's no reason to relax into it. Chase the real things. Real pleasure. Real pain. Real love.'

'Christ, Dad, cancer's made you deep.' Kate was proud of the way she faced the dreaded word and joked about it. That was how Dad wanted it, so that was the way she'd play it. Blowing her nose hard – plenty of time to cry in the car on the way home – she said, 'There are more important things to think about. Like getting you to China.'

'Too late for that now.'

Deep in her heart, Kate disagreed. She refused to think of her father's life as an egg timer rapidly using up its allotted sand. She would stretch time; it was never too late. 'We'll see,' she said.

From: mrs.sarah.ames@gmail.com
To: jxrames@amespartnersinproperty.com
Subject: Daddy's 80th
18 Aug 2004 13.35.


Darling

Do forgive the email invitation but I'm frightfully busy.

Can you and the divine Kate join us for a small dinner at home to celebrate Daddy's birthday? Nothing fancy. 7 for 7.30 Saturday, 11th September.


Ciao
Mumsy

Marrying into the Ameses had taught Kate two things about toff families. They have dirty kitchens and a high proportion of the men go into the woods to shoot themselves. Feet sticking to the kitchen floor, she'd heard many tales about 'darling Uncle Josh' or 'good old Sir Bernard' who'd done the decent thing and blown off their own heads in a copse.

A third thing joined the list that Saturday night. As Mumsy took their coats – it had taken Kate some years and considerable self-restraint not to giggle when Julian called his mother by that name – Kate realised 'Nothing fancy' meant all lights blazing, rooms thronged with guests and, at the least, four courses of almost cold food.

'Dearest Julian.' Mumsy laid his navy Crombie over her arm. Her cheekbones were worthy of a Cherokee, embedded in an English rose complexion. Offering her face for a kiss, she dazzled in floor length black, her bearing unchanged since her youth spent modelling furs at Harrods.

'And Kate, my angel.' She slipped the Zara special offer duffle from her daughter-in-law's shoulders. 'Always so pretty.' She recovered her startled expression speedily with an 'Oh! Do you, um, have a new job, my dear?'

*My dee-ah.*

Julian spoke for Kate. 'We're going on afterwards. To a fancy dress.'

'I see,' said Mumsy. 'As a nurse. That is too, too funny.' As ever the phrase served instead of a laugh. 'What are you going as, Julian?' Mumsy surveyed her son's tailoring.

'Myself,' said Julian.

'Too funny,' repeated his mother.

A 'girl from the village' mixed them drinks in heavy crystal, as the crush of people in satin and bow ties tried not to stare at the nurse on Julian's arm.

'When you said *nurse*,' murmured Julian, steering Kate towards a grand piano laden with silver-framed photographs,

'I imagined something racy. You know, white mini skirt. White stockings and stilettos.' His gaze travelled sardonically up and down her sky blue tunic and shapeless polyester trousers.

'The invitation says come as your hero. Why would a sexy nurse be my hero?' If you like your heroines compassionate, expert and committed – and Kate *did* – nurses were an obvious choice. Her outfit was perfect, bar one detail: the small velvet shoulder bag: even a busy nurse has to stow her lipstick somewhere.

A harpist struck up. A ripple of applause travelled around the room like a polite Mexican wave.

'I assumed you'd like some time off from hospital paraphernalia. You've spent most of the past year in one NHS waiting room or another with your dad.'

'Or is it you, Julian, who'd like some time off from it?'

'And if I do? Does that make me the villain of the piece?'

Relenting, not wanting another argument, Kate said, 'Of course not.' She checked to ensure there was no dowager in earshot. 'If it helps, I've got no knickers on.'

'Really?' Julian's eyebrows shot up to where his fringe used to be.

'No, you idiot, not really!' As if she'd dine knickerless with her in-laws. Like most men, Julian's libido sometimes got in the way of his brain.

They wandered, scattering a 'How do you do?' here and a 'Good evening' there, to the elegant salon. 'Is this a conservatory?' asked Kate, chewing her fishy hors d'oeuvres beneath a soaring glass ceiling. The room had little in common with Becca's conservatory: the chandeliers were real and it was ten times the size.

'We've always called it the orangery.' Julian checked her out to see if she snorted. 'You must be tired. You'd usually say something like *ooh an orangery, m'lud! I had to make do with a wendy house.*'

'Would I?' Kate didn't like the sound of her usual self; Julian shouldn't apologise for his background any more than she should.

'And you'd be right to mock,' said Julian. 'It's ridiculous for Mumsy and Dad to rattle around this big old wreck on their own.'

It was tacitly accepted that the house would pass to Julian one day. Kate could imagine the speed with which he'd sell it. He'd never understood Mumsy's attachment to a pile of bricks and mortar. As one of the help whisked away her plate, Kate checked her watch.

'Stop worrying, Kate. We'll make it to the fancy dress.'

'I'm not worried,' said Kate, who was worried. This was more like a wedding than a dinner party. 'Is your outfit in the boot?'

'Yes, yes.' Julian was short, as if Kate had asked him this a hundred times.

On reflection, she had probably asked him ninety-nine times.

'I wish you'd tell me who you're coming as.'

'It's a surprise.'

At the head of their table the Brigadier said, 'Shall I tell you all the secret of a long life?' He was tall but stooped, a fairground mirror reflection of his elder son. 'Walk everywhere. Early to bed. Plus a decent single malt every night at nine on the dot!'

A 'Hear hear!' greeted this.

Mumsy found Kate's eye. 'A good wife helps, doesn't it, Kate?'

'And kiddies, of course,' Julian's father continued. 'They keep one young. And then the grandchildren arrive.' He motioned to the four blond and wholesome tots sitting with Julian's brother and their blonde, wholesome mother. Kate assumed her sister-in-law had been manufactured in a factory that churned out suitable wives for the English upper classes. *That* lady knew her fish knife from her butter knife, and had never graced Mumsy's dinner table in an NHS uniform.

'Speaking of which . . .'

*No*, thought Kate. *Don't, please, sir.*

'. . . when are you two getting on with it?'

Kate stared at the plate of roast beef which had been set in front of her. Mumsy, she knew, would save them with one of her perfectly timed interventions.

But Mumsy was distracted by the guest to her right, who'd managed to overturn a glass.

'It's not like you, Julian,' laughed the Brigadier, 'to drag your feet, boy!'

'Sir,' said Julian, 'I wasn't born until you were forty-four, remember.' He was smiling, easy, every inch Mumsy's son.

'Maybe, but— oh, beef! My favourite.'

Thankful for the Brigadier's toddler attention span, Kate relaxed.

'I've heard,' said Julian into her ear, 'that one has to have sex to have babies. Or maybe that's just a rumour.'

Kate wondered if Julian noticed that she said nothing for the rest of the meal. He was assiduously attentive to the elderly lady on his left, displaying all the innate charm and benevolence she so valued in her husband.

Marriage was so intense. She found she could love Julian passionately at 7 am, loathe him by lunchtime, be indifferent to him mid-afternoon and be hopping from foot to foot waiting for him to come home at dinner time.

That scabrous aside had soured her towards him, on a two-party night when they would need all their emotional energy to reach the finishing line.

So Kate swallowed the bad taste, made allowances, saw his side of the story. Sexually, they'd hit a wall. She was always too tired.

'Not too tired,' Julian would snap, 'to run from shop to

shop, to chase after your dad, to drive to and from Becca's house.'

He was right. She must try harder. *Now I sound like a dim witted schoolgirl.*

Dessert was predictably delicious, but Kate barely tasted it. She was eager to be off. 'Come on, Julian,' she said, as her spoon went down. 'Off to Aunty Marjorie's.'

'Oh joy,' said Julian, rising and dabbing his mouth with an heirloom.

After farewells that adhered strictly to the laws of etiquette, Mumsy waved them off from the front door.

'That was the first time I've heard a harp played live,' said Kate, as the car ate the country lanes, nearing the light pollution of the suburbs.

'And the last, let's hope.'

During one of the times they'd talked without armour, Julian had told Kate *You're my family now.* For Kate, their marriage lived in those brief interludes of closeness; the rest of the time it merely survived.

Poking around in the glove compartment for a tissue, Kate found the invitation to the second 'do' of the evening. 'Listen, Julian.' She quoted Aunty Marjorie's distinctive style, somewhat different to Mumsy's careful formality. '*Come as your hero! Or heroine! Mustn't annoy the feminists!*' She laughed, fondly. 'She put three exclamation marks after feminists.' Kate shifted in her seat. Her man-made trousers were itchy and uncomfortable and she longed for her new black jeans. She'd hesitated before buying them, turning round quickly so as to surprise herself in Top Shop's changing room mirror. *Am I too old for a ripped knee?* she'd worried. Two years off thirty, Kate was looking older in subtle ways she couldn't quite place. No wrinkles yet, no crow's feet, but her bloom was fading. Ironically, she'd never known she *had* a bloom until it began to fade.

'Is their place still called Hujorie House?'

'Yup.' Kate surreptitiously eyed Julian to see if he was being stern or indulgent. Sometimes her family amused him; at other times she felt him prickle with a toxic mixture of embarrassment and disdain. 'Tonight let's get up to no good. Just the two of us. After the fancy dress party.' Her hand landed gently on his thigh. She loved the dormant power in Julian's body when it was at rest. He was athletically built for a man who spent his days at desks or on the phone.

'I hate it when you do that.'

'Do what?'

Julian flicked at her hand. 'Diarise it. As if sex is on your to-do list. Defrost freezer: tick. Collect dry cleaning: tick. Screw husband: tick.' He kept his eyes on the white lines disappearing beneath the car. 'Although if we're honest, the freezer gets defrosted with more regularity than we have sex.'

Counting to ten stopped Kate from responding in kind.

Despite how painful it was to talk about it, she'd persevered. So Julian knew why their love life had dwindled. Bit by bit, Kate was able to admit how overwhelmed she sometimes felt. How weary. How worried. After hours of painful to and fro, she'd found the words to satisfy him that it wasn't a problem with her heart, nor her loins, but with her brain.

Julian even conceded that after a day calling the shots at work *and* overseeing the refurbishment of their new house, he was often glad to collapse into bed like a felled redwood.

*Our libidos are out of sync.* Knowing that arguments wouldn't help them rediscover their rhythm, Kate stayed quiet until they pulled up at Aunty Marjorie's gate.

'We needn't stay long.' The usual pre-emptive reassurance.

'I . . .' Julian chewed his lip. 'Look, I'm not coming in.'

'But . . .' Kate was dismayed. Her tunic crinkled as she let go of the door handle and turned to face him. 'So there's no outfit in the boot?' This was a new low. 'We're always straight with each other, Julian.' She sensed both their thoughts hopping to the same branch. 'Well, *I'm* straight with *you*,' she said, meaningfully.

'Not that again, please.' Julian started the engine. 'Work's *fine*, Kate. Got that?' He closed his eyes, as if he was officially the most patient man in the world. 'This is just one party. I usually do my duty. Go in, give your aunt my best, then get a taxi home.'

'How will I explain your no-show?'

'I don't know.' Julian didn't sound as if he much cared. 'Why not say I'm not up for another evening of chit chat about China and cancer?'

When she reached the gravel she heard his shout of *Kate!* but she kept going, past the gnomes, past the fake wishing well, past the garden thermometer shaped like a sunflower. A feral Marilyn Monroe lay, whimpering, in a flowerbed.

Madonna opened the door. To be specific, the 1990 Jean Paul Gaultier version, with high ponytail and golden conical bra, opened the door. 'Where have you been?' said Madonna, in Becca's voice.

The house juddered, its walls alive with midlife energy. Through the sitting room door, Kate glimpsed Sitting Bull shaking his booty.

'Where's Julian?' squawked Princess Diana from the kitchen; Aunty Marjorie's tiara was askew.

'Working on the house.' Kate ignored Becca's sceptical look. It wasn't the first time she'd employed the handy excuse; in truth, she and Julian were not hands-on and the house didn't need them. Kate's daydream of Julian swinging a sledgehammer while she painted skirting boards, her hair in a scarf and an adorable smudge of emulsion on her nose, hadn't come true. Instead workmen and contractors crawled over the Georgian gem like ants. 'Where's Dad?' Always her first question nowadays.

'He's fine,' said Becca firmly. 'Despite that bloody awful outfit you're not actually his nurse. Tonight, matron, you're going to have some *fun*.'

This bossiness would be unacceptable from anybody else, but Kate readily handed the reins to her cousin. Throwing herself around in the fractured light of Aunty Marjorie's glitterball would be just the ticket, rocketing her back to school disco days when Becca would fend off lovestruck, spotty boys and Kate would, well, stare at Charlie, mostly. In Becca's shadow, Kate felt strong and ready, as if the valiant *joie de vivre* rubbed off on her.

There was Dad. In the corner. Not the blanket-over-the-knees invalid of his fears but nonetheless apart from the action.

Together, Kate and Becca danced kookily around him. 'Not another nurse,' he laughed. 'I see enough of them, thanks very much.'

Beneath the Shakespeare wig – bald on top with fetching auburn border – his hair was poker straight and pure white. Chemotherapy was his stylist; his hair had grown back that way. The other side effects – tiredness, nausea, a tingling in his palms – had all receded, as the doctors promised, once the course was over.

Becca sashayed away, and Kate crouched at the Bard's knee, fussing with him, checking he'd taken his 9pm pills. Dad's failure to thrive after the second, far more invasive surgery had disconcerted his multidisciplinary team. Sensing her mother's fatigue, Kate had stepped up. Withstanding Mum's belief that cancer was some form of black magic, Kate researched her father's condition.

She'd gone from having no idea what a lymph node might be to a working knowledge of cancer. The brisk breeze of education blew away the fog of Irish superstition. Scary metaphor was redundant when reality was formidable enough. Tablets for this, tablets for that, tablets to counteract what the first tablets did to Dad's beleaguered constitution.

Her father's moods shifted as he lost his sense of taste, regained it, suffered odd aches in the far reaches of his anatomy. His gums bled. His feet were sore. There was no trick cancer wouldn't play, as it toyed with them.

When Dad fell asleep – he nodded off sporadically, no matter how frenzied his surroundings – Kate kissed his forehead and made for the patio.

The massed lookalikes impeded her progress. As ever, Aunty Marjorie had invited far too many guests. Despite her pretensions, Hujorie House was a fifth the size of the Ames home. Through adult eyes it was not the swanky establishment five-year-old Kate had envied. Reproduction everything allied to terrible artworks and swirly carpet, all of it scrupulously matchy-matchy: Hujorie was everything Kate's new home wouldn't be. Yet she felt perfectly at home there. She loved it despite its faults. Kate hoped people felt the same about her.

The cool of the patio was welcome.

'Jaysus, you nearly gave me a heart attack!' Mum's pale face, draped in voluminous blue, swam in the dark.

'Is the Virgin Mary, Mother of Jesus, supposed to have a sneaky fag in the garden, Mum?'

The back door delivered Aunty Marjorie to them and the cigarette was flicked neatly into the bushes. Even sisters have their secrets.

'It's so *hot*!' Aunty Marjorie fanned her puce face. 'I'm a victim of me own success with these parties.'

Uncle Hugh, whose last minute application of a bed sheet had transformed him into Gandhi, said, 'I hear there are storm clouds gathering in the housing market, Kate. Is hubby worried?'

He was almost knocked off his bare feet by the storm of tutting from his wife and her sister.

Mum was outraged at this slur. 'Julian's a smart cookie.'

Aunty Marjorie said, 'Sure, only the other night wasn't he talking about the grand profit youse'll make on that house you're renovating.'

Uncle Hugh turned to Kate. 'Isn't that meant to be your forever home, as they say?'

'We're keeping an open mind.' Some details of the house were not as Kate had envisaged. Concrete worktops were, Julian assured her, very *now* and would add to the 'sale-ability'. Her campaign for a reading nook off the master bedroom had fallen on deaf ears: family buyers need more bedrooms, and 'the stupid planning officers won't let us extend'.

Secretly grateful to the stupid planning officers, Kate knew that without their veto Julian would have torn off the back of the building and replaced it with a three-storey glass box. He was right: such boldness would 'maximise the profit potential'. But it would also desecrate a fine old house. She planned to hang on to the house forever. Profit meant nothing to her in this instance.

'You're lucky,' said Aunty Marjorie, 'to have a grand fella like that looking after you.'

'He's a good head on his shoulders, all right.' Mum nudged Aunty Marjorie. 'He keeps my little eejit on the straight and narrow!'

As they tittered – Aunty Marjorie surreptitiously sniffing Mum's breath – Kate wondered if they pressed a 'mute' button when she talked of the chain of five shops she'd painstakingly built up. The little eejit contributed half the household expenses, correct to the last penny.

'S'cuse me, folks.' Kate's mobile chirruped and she turned away, into the darkness of the lawn. 'Hi,' she said.

'I'm home,' said Julian. 'How's the party?'

'The usual. Superman's crying in the loo.'

There was a pause.

Julian asked, 'Are you still angry with me?'

Kate sighed. 'I wasn't angry.'

'I was an arse.'

'I was hurt, Julian. But I wasn't angry. If you'd said you didn't want to come right from the beginning I'd have understood.'

'I meant to go. I wanted to support you. I know you don't like seeing your dad on the edge of things.'

'You do support me.'

Another pause. Kate hated having emotional conversations on the phone. She liked to watch Julian's eyes. It felt a waste to touch on such matters, so rarely discussed, while so far apart.

She heard the suck of their fridge door opening as Julian said, 'It's horrible here. The flat feels empty.'

Kate had seen little of the apartment lately. Her life was a hamster wheel of taking Dad to hospital for his myriad appointments and rushing over to Fulham whenever Mum panicked because he'd gone a funny colour or seemed oddly drowsy. She knew Julian had missed her when she'd sat up through the night to keep her restless, unhappy dad company after his chemotherapy sessions.

It was perverse: the power she held over her husband was only illustrated by negatives. By Julian missing her. Kate felt exquisite tenderness at how couples hold each other's happiness in the palms of their hands.

Julian said, 'It's too damn quiet.'

'Wish I could say the same.' Becca had commandeered the karaoke machine.

'Is that, oh, what's that song?' Julian reached for it.

'*Say My Name*. Destiny's Child.' Kate made him laugh by joining in with Becca's screeched *say-my-name-say-my-name*.

She laughed too. When they were daft together, Kate and Julian worked. They made sense. It was when they were both head down, their shoulders tensed, that they were brittle with one another. Some days Kate's life felt like one long exam.

Kate had repaid the money Julian had lent her, yet still felt as if she owed him something. When he bristled because he reached home before her and had to pull together a meal of leftovers, half of her bristled at his male presumption and the other half agreed with it. She would love to please him by flinging open the door and kissing him, the aroma of home-cooked food wafting around them.

*But there's only one of me to go round.* Only one Kate to belt from hospital to shop to hospital to home. Once upon a time Julian would have scoffed that the answer to that conundrum was simple: she must give up the shops. He hadn't said that for a while.

'Don't put your fingers in the light sockets or play with matches, will you?' Did Julian ever notice how she sometimes faked her energy levels around him? He had tumbled to the bottom of her priorities, simply because he was her husband and therefore always *there*. It wasn't fair. 'Most blokes would order a takeaway and watch a brainless action movie where every other cast member gets blown apart by aliens.'

'I'm not most blokes.' Julian would go into his study and knuckle down. 'I'm the bullying bastard you married.'

'Shush. We're over that silly spat now. I'm glad you're not here, to be honest. This party is so different to the one we just left that it might blow your mind.'

If Julian's parents' legs fell off they wouldn't *dream* of bothering their offspring. They asked nothing of their grown children apart from a Christmas card and the occasional dinner. Julian put up with a lot from her close-knit clan.

'Anyway, Julian, support works both ways. If you'd only tell me a little more about—'

'Good God, darling, I'd bore you to death.'

Persevering, Kate leaned on a wonky gazebo and said, 'For example, why not tell me what was said at that meeting with your investors yesterday?'

'How'd you know about that?' Julian couldn't camouflage his irritation.

'Because you wander about the apartment talking very very loudly into your phone, you twit.' She waited. 'So?'

'So, it was the usual panicking, the usual accusations. Things are tough for everybody but they know I'm on top of the situation. Or they should. I told them to back off.'

'You said you've been here before. Where's *here*?' Kate had felt tremors; she needed to know if the aftershock could reach the penthouse.

'I can't discuss serious matters while your cousin's belting out r'n'b in the background, darling.'

'How about when I get home? Please? Will you stay up?'

'Kate, you'll be tipsy and knackered and full of stories about what A said to B and who got off with C. Don't worry that pretty little head, yeah?'

Julian didn't know about Kate's Running Away account. That had to remain safely hidden from the peril she could smell on the wind. She'd stand shoulder to shoulder with Julian, through thick and thin, but nothing could endanger that money.

Processing the thoughts crowding her 'pretty little head', Kate by-passed the heaving epicentre of the party and crept up the stairs. In the spare room, she found what she was after.

On the bed, Flo lay on her back, arms flung out, face tilted and her cherub mouth slightly open. At eighteen months she was a more fully realised version of her baby self. The flossy wisps of hair had settled into a custard-coloured bob and her chubby limbs had lengthened. Kate could look at her all day, every day and never find a single fault.

Coming up behind her, Charlie whispered, 'She's getting big, isn't she?'

'She'll be married soon. Who has she come as?' Kate took in the tiny jeans and a sequin top which was obviously cut down from an adult garment.

'Who do you think Flo's heroine is?' asked Charlie. 'Sorry, I mean who do you think her effing heroine is?' Being Bob Geldof for the night was proving difficult: since his daughter came along Charlie had been careful *not* to swear.

'Ah, I get it!' Kate rocked with laughter. 'It's you!' She pointed at Becca, hovering over the child, rearranging her the way mums do. 'Flo's heroine is her mummy.'

'Flo's mummy was in charge of Flo's costume ergo . . .' Charlie's hair was losing its Geldof disarray. It was tidy hair that wanted to lie in a sleek cap, the way Flo's did.

'Be honest, Kate.' Charlie sat on the rug and Kate joined him. 'Julian just didn't want to come, did he?' All three of them had escaped the action with a bottle of something cold.

'It's obvious.' Becca swatted at the ponytail that seemed constantly in her face. 'They had a row on the way and he wouldn't come in. Now he's pouting at home, grizzling about being neglected.' She wobbled on the stilt heels no self-respecting Madonna clone can be without. 'I know Julian pret-ty well, don't forget.'

Feeling Charlie squirm beside her, Kate wished Becca wouldn't mention their partner-swap so casually. Neither she nor the men ever referred to it.

135

'I don't blame him, not really.' Kate refused to demonise her partner.

'He's doing his best,' said Charlie.

'In what way?' Becca's voice went shrill. 'It's Kate's poor dad who's doing his best, fighting like a hero. We should all have come dressed as Uncle John tonight!'

'That,' said Kate with feeling, 'would make for a very strange fancy dress party. Everybody in fair isles and comfortable slacks.' She'd often heard Becca refer to Dad's 'battle' with cancer: it helped Becca to see it that way, so Kate had never challenged it. Like Mum, Becca never countenanced Dad's death: *death*, they seemed to believe, *happens to other people*.

Charlie was able to follow Kate to that place in her head where she was quietly preparing for both the practical issues and the gaping Dad-shaped hole in their lives. They even managed to joke, gently, about it. It helped her at a time when very little could. Kate said, 'I don't blame Julian getting bored of it all every so often. Illness is repetitive and depressing.'

'Tough! Mind you,' said Becca, 'you might consider not talking so much about the orphanage. That,' she said sagely, '*is* boring.'

Taking that on the chin, Kate warned her it was about to get even more boring. 'Dad doesn't know it yet, but we're running away to China together.' She relished their astonishment.

Spending more time with her father meant helping him

with many tasks; Kate refused to call this *putting his affairs in order* but she knew that was how Dad saw it. One of the jobs she busied herself with – it was imperative that she feel useful – was to collate the correspondence between her father and Jia Tang, the founder of Yulan House.

She'd laid out eleven years of handwritten notes and printed emails in front of her dad. Despite her immunity to the virtues of the orphanage, Kate had found herself becoming engrossed as they sorted them together, quoting lines here and there. She liked the man who wrote those letters; they were thoughtful, philosophical, *smart*.

And Jia Tang was his equal. The warm friendship had risen out of the written word in front of her like a hologram. She'd knelt back on her heels, laughing. 'Maybe you should have married *her*, eh, Dad?'

He hadn't laughed. Instead, Dad had applied the seldom used full version of her name. 'Not everything in life is a joke, Catherine.'

That's when Kate had decided that, come what may, Dad and Jia Tang were going to meet. They were going to clasp hands. *It'll give him something to live for*.

In the here and now of the spare room, Becca and Charlie were silent. Actively silent, as if there was much they could say but they chose not to.

'I've planned the whole trip. It's costing a fortune. We'll travel first class, with help at every stage. I've taken out the most comprehensive insurance imaginable. The lady who runs Yulan House has insisted we stay with her and— what?' She looked from Charlie to Becca, belatedly grasping their disapproval.

'Kate,' said Charlie, 'your dad's not well enough to do all that.' He said it sadly, as if breaking something to her.

'Obviously not at the moment.' Kate smiled at their naivety. 'But he'll brighten up. Look,' she said, as the others passed worried glances, 'I'm not stupid. It's not as if Dad's going to be leaping around like a deer. I know he's changed for good. And I know . . .' She stumbled. However many times she faced this fact it never seemed to diminish. 'I know, realistically, he hasn't got that long left. But he has good periods and bad periods and as soon as he rallies I'm poised to book the flights.'

'Isn't it a tiny bit ambitious?' said Charlie.

'You've gone stark staring mad,' said Becca. *Shtark shtaring*; she was drunker than Kate had thought.

'This is Dad's dream. His *dream*.' Kate emphasised the word. 'He's done so much for Yulan House, put so much energy and imagination and even cash into it over the years. He deserves this.' She was baffled by their reaction. She'd envisaged whooping and hugging. 'I won't let him die without seeing Yulan House. I can't.'

Charlie sent Becca a warning look, accompanied by a slight shake of his shaggy Geldof hair.

Becca said, 'Let's talk about this tomorrow.' She stood, stretched, and adjusted her conical breasts. 'Look after the fruit of my loins, you two. I have to *sing*.' She bounded out of the room and almost fell down the stairs in her keenness to return to the karaoke machine.

On the bed Flo stirred and grumbled. She was a gentle child, happiest in somebody's arms, not an adventurer. A little spoiled perhaps, but when Kate peeked at the strawberries and cream face on the pile of coats she thought *Of course we spoil her: she's adorable.*

When Flo settled down again, Kate and Charlie sat with their backs against the bed in the semi-darkness.

'In a way,' said Charlie, 'I'm glad Julian didn't come tonight.'

'That's not very nice.' Kate butted shoulders with him.

'Don't get me wrong. I'm fond of the guy.' That, Kate knew, wasn't quite true. Charlie and Julian were meshed together, like family: you're not required to like your family. 'But I don't miss the sneering. My parents-in-law and Julian don't agree on what makes a good party.'

'He's working on the sneering thing.' This was a safe place, a circle of trust where both Kate and Charlie could lovingly diss their other halves, in the knowledge that it wouldn't be repeated, or inflated. 'After years of practice, he can confront Mum's musical cake slice without wincing.'

Charlie laughed. He, too, loathed that cake slice.

*All lovers need to let off steam*, thought Kate, feeling a warm buzz of satisfaction at making Charlie hoot. A tendril of guilt crawled over her but she brushed it away. If wives can't whinge a little about their husbands then the pressure builds up until eventually they blow. Becca's tendency to overstate – *Julian said WHAT?* – rendered her useless for gentle grousing. Sane, humane Charlie was perfect. 'What are you working on?'

No point asking about the novel. It had been months since he mentioned it.

'At present I'm penning a campaign for a leading brand of feminine hygiene products.' Charlie remembered his fancy dress costume. 'I mean effing feminine sodding hygiene feckin' products.' He glanced neurotically at his daughter but she was asleep.

'Julian goes all funny if he finds a stray tampon. As if it might bite him.'

'I've got over that. My desk at work is covered in sanitary towels.'

'Nice image.'

'The budget's astronomical. We've got an award winning lighting guy, a top UK art director and the producer's booked a household name to do the voiceover. But, it'll still end up being two birds frolicking on a beach with a kite.'

'You daren't make it realistic.' Kate sketched a scene with her hands. 'Imagine it. A woman, her face pale and her hair greasy, bent double and shouting at her boyfriend.'

'How did we both end up in such dumb jobs?' Charlie ignored Kate's affronted yip. 'I sit up all night writing scripts to make people wander into supermarkets and put a specific product in their baskets. You sell paper hats and party horns and . . . and . . .'

'And Donald Duck masks,' said Kate, helpfully. The truth was more complex than Charlie admitted. They both worked hard and Kate derived a simple, real pleasure from handing over a bag full of trifles. 'Don't knock it. It pays the bills.' She wondered if, deep down, Charlie was proud of his 'silly job' the way she was proud of her shops.

'Has Becca told you her latest scheme?'

'The flat in town? Yup. 'Fraid so.'

'She talks about it as if it's essential. As if everybody has a country house and a *pied à terre*.'

From long phone calls at late hours Kate knew how lonely Becca felt in the cottage when Charlie stayed over in town, burning the midnight oil for some entitled client.

Charlie said, 'She says we can use it for date nights.' He widened his eyes. '*Date nights*. Aren't they something made up by women's magazines?'

'Probably.'

'Becca says she wants to be like you and Julian. Having slap up meals in the hot new restaurants.' Charlie looked sideways at Kate. 'Is that what you do?'

'In a word, no.' Kate was accustomed to Becca's grass-is-greener-on-the-other-side mentality. 'Last night I knocked up cheese on toast for us both.' She'd carefully carved around the jade dots of mould on the cheddar.

Neither of them pointed out it had been Becca's decision to move to the country, just like neither of them had pointed out it was her 'heart's desire' to have a dog when she whined about exercising poor over-bred Jaffa. Kate asked, 'Can you afford to buy another property?'

'Yes,' said Charlie. 'As soon as I grow a money tree out of my bum.'

Her chuckle died on her lips. 'Oh good God. Do you know where we are?'

Puzzled, Charlie said, 'Marjorie's spare room.' Realisation dawned. 'Christ. Is this the bed we—'

'Yup.'

Their shoulders sprang up to their ears as embarrassment and nostalgia fought for supremacy.

'How long ago?' Charlie totted it up. 'Ten years.' He whistled. 'Is that all?'

'I thought it was less.' Kate felt tender towards those two awkward, lusty teens. She remembered the tingling, the breathlessness. It had been a watershed, a night of epic change. Kate felt shy, suddenly. That night she and Charlie had been naked both literally and metaphorically.

'I was very, um, *keen* if I remember rightly,' said Charlie.

'Keen's one way to put it.' Kate couldn't meet his eye. She wondered if she'd gone as pink as she felt. '*Bloody quick* is another.'

'I've improved since then.'

'Oh really?'

'I've got awards and everything.'

This light banter was do-able. Any exploration of the deep emotion they'd felt was not. 'That's not what Becca says.'

Charlie jerked. 'Eh? What's she said?'

Kate barked, a short, sharp delighted laugh. 'Nothing! We don't discuss it, you fool.'

'Well, you never know. You two are close.' Charlie slumped with relief.

'It would be icky,' said Kate. 'We can't talk about . . . you know . . . *before*.'

They were silent.

'Look at us, awkward again,' said Charlie, half serious. 'Shame. We've worked so hard to be *normal* with each other.' He sketched quotation marks in the air.

*Can I take his hand?* Kate didn't allow herself to think too hard. She reached for his fingers and held them. 'No, it's not awkward. Let's not let it be awkward.'

'This is good. *This*.' He squeezed her hand. 'This is good, isn't it?'

'I don't know what I'd do without you, Charlie. I mean, Dad and everything . . .'

'Friendship.' Charlie nodded vehemently. 'It's the most important thing. Not that I'm belittling love. Love is great. But . . .'

'This is so much better. I agree. It really is.' Kate sighed happily. 'Isn't it?'

'It is.'

'We can talk,' said Kate. '*Really* talk. And because we used to . . .' She wasn't sure how to describe it.

'We used to be in love.' Charlie was sure, apparently.

'Yes, exactly, because of that, we know each other well and there are no misunderstandings. Friendship,' she smiled, '*rocks.*'

'I second that.' Charlie repeated himself in an Oirish accent. 'I feckin' second that, you bastard.'

Kate laughed. 'This is nice,' she said. And it was. It just wasn't *enough*.

Letting go of her hand, Charlie pulled out his wallet and rifled through it. 'Look at this.'

'Not another pic of the most photographed child on Earth?'

'Nope.'

It took a moment for Kate to recognise the folded envelope, the 'K' in Charlie's handwriting just visible.

'You gave this back to me once, Kate.'

'I remember.' Kate wondered what Charlie was smiling about. She felt flattened, like a tent peg hammered into the grass, at the sight of the note.

'I want . . .' Charlie sucked in a great breath through his teeth. 'Bear with me, Kate, I didn't plan this. But I want you to have it.'

Kate clambered to her feet. 'No thanks.' She was curt. She glanced at Flo on the bed and the little dot's resemblance to Becca stung. This was not a conversation to have in the same room as such an innocent.

'Hang on.' Charlie leaped up. 'I'm doing this all wrong. Sorry. Can you just humour me?'

'What?' Kate was impatient, confused.

'It wasn't easy writing that letter, you know.'

'It wasn't easy reading it.'

'But it's yours.' Charlie held out the ageing envelope, which seemed to Kate to have doubled in size.

'I don't need it.' Kate closed her eyes. 'I can quote the sodding thing, Charlie.'

'Is this a row?' asked Charlie, amused and dismayed at the same time. 'Are we fighting?'

'Don't be cute.' When he put his head to one side like that it demeaned what she'd been through. On this evidence, the break-up had been radically different for Charlie, a matter of little import. His rejection of her was something he could joke about.

'Can we start again?' Charlie's plea was tinged with annoyance. 'This has gone awry. I didn't mean to . . . Look, take it, Kate. It's addressed to you.'

Snatching the note, Kate said, 'Great. Thanks. Bloody hell, Charlie.'

The party devoured her when she dashed downstairs, whirling relentlessly, a snake eating its own tail, suddenly rearing up when it seemed about to flag. Every other guest was what's known as the wrong side of fifty, but Kate had never known such wild energy at festivities with people her own age.

Grabbing a drink Kate retreated, stuffing the envelope angrily into her bag as she bumped into Becca.

'Ooh. Somebody's cheesed you off.' Becca jumped back as Kate stormed past her. 'It's Julian, isn't it?'

'No. Yes.' Better to make Julian the fall guy than explain to Becca.

Sitting on the doorstep, they shared the drink, as they had in the old days at parties. Behind them a centurion and a policewoman (a sexy one, naturally) did the twist on the hall carpet.

'Shall I ring Julian?' Becca slapped her corset as if searching for her phone. 'Get him to come?'

'Don't be daft.' Kate defended her scapegoat. 'He puts up with a lot from me. Let's give him a night off.'

*Not everything that looks like love is love*, thought Kate, as Becca rampaged on.

'None of what's going on is your fault! Did you make your poor dad ill? No!' Becca crossed herself. She hadn't set foot in a church since Flo's christening but old Catholic habits die hard. 'Should you apologise for being a shit hot business bitch? No!'

*You're free and so am I*, thought Kate.

'He made vows!'

'We all did,' said Kate, half listening. *This split is for the best.*

'In sickness and in health. Well, it didn't specify. He should support you through your dad's sickness too.'

This second rejection by Charlie should be a pale reprise but it hurt as much as the first time. There was only one possible reason: she loved him still.

Charlie was at the head of the stairs, Flo small in his arms. They were a cameo of gentleness, of straightforward love. A feeling of exclusion, of pressing her nose against a toyshop window swept over Kate. She went to find her father. She could hide there, by the side of his armchair. She could lose herself in the dozen little tasks he needed done.

Dad waved her away. 'You go and enjoy yourself, love.' He'd just woken up. Only an invalid, alienated by the slow subjugation of his body, could sleep in the midst of this maelstrom.

'I *am* enjoying myself,' said Kate, counting his meds, refilling his water glass. Inspired to reach out to Julian, she sent a text.

I love you J. Don't worry. We're OK. xxx P.S. Get ready for a thorough check-up from Nurse Kate!!!

Despairing of her inability to sex up her texts, Kate longed to be near Julian. Becca's rant had, perversely, brought him into sharp focus as a good uncomplicated person who had always loved her. *I made vows too*, Kate reminded herself. And if they were to the wrong man, that was Kate's fault, and Julian shouldn't suffer for it.

'Did you see the pics of Yulan House's new driveway?' Dad was groping for his phone.

'Yes, I did.' Just as she was now expert on lymph nodes, Kate was knowledgeable on the pros and cons of tarmac in a hot, damp climate. 'Jia Tang sounds confident about getting that grant to refurbish the smaller dormitory, doesn't she?'

'She's always confident. That's her nature.'

'I guess so.' Kate watched Charlie jiggle Flo on the dancefloor.

'Have you chased up the last few sponsors for your 10k run?'

'Almost.'

Flo had the room delirious with happiness.

'Good. How much did you raise in total, love?'

Charlie wiped his eyes, laughing fit to burst, as Flo strutted her funky toddler stuff.

'Just over three hundred quid. I was ruthless, remember. I roped in everybody I've ever met to sponsor me. Keep sipping at your water, Dad. Keep hydrated.'

Each nugget of Yulan House news, each exhortation to swallow this or take that, was a gift from Kate to her dad. They were tokens of love, just like the countless ones he'd given her by tucking her in at night, kissing her on the forehead when she left for school, scribbling a limerick in her birthday card each year.

Charlie was giving Flo these same gifts. The to and fro of parental love continued. Charlie could never repudiate Flo and therefore could never repudiate Flo's mother. It was Kate who must be denied over and over.

Joining them with the face she reserved for talking to her uncle – as if he had regressed to a slightly deaf childhood – Becca said, slightly too loud, 'How are we feeling? Is the music too much?'

'I'm fine, sweetheart.' Dad was gracious, knowing Kate would limit his exposure to his niece.

'If you want anything, just tell me.' Becca was shouting now, her eyeliner almost gone. 'You're a fighter.' Becca grabbed Dad's arm. 'You won't let it beat you.'

Tears threatened behind the false eyelashes. Becca had a real dread of losing her uncle. Their parents, all four of them, were a sacred quartet who had shaped the lives of Kate and Becca.

Indulgent, Dad patted her hand. When he was in pain or suffering from sleeplessness he could be short tempered, but on the whole he tapped into a newfound serenity. He needed it; people behaved oddly around mortal illness.

'Let's dance, Madonna.' Kate rescued her father.

'Whoo hoo!' Becca cleared a path with her elbows and plucked Flo off the carpet.

The lights laid bare the mess. The sitting room looked as if vindictive, efficient burglars had ransacked it. Princess Di hoovered around Shakespeare asleep on the sofa as the Virgin Mary tied up bin bags. Becca swayed, watching the older women clear up.

Her ears ringing in the sudden calm, Kate stabbed out another text message.

**Leaving in 10 mins! Brace yourself for Nursie's diagnosis! xxx**

Charlie was in charge of collecting glasses; the plastic ones from Kate's shop that looked 'just like the real thing'. 'It's exhausting swearing all the time,' he told Kate, with what felt like exploratory friendliness. 'I don't know how Bob Geldof copes.'

Kate's smile seemed to reassure him there were no hard feelings, but she noticed he studied her for a long moment before leaping out of the way of Aunty Marjorie's drunken vacuum cleaner.

The mulish introverted look on Becca's face presaged a row. Charlie kept a careful ten feet between himself and his wife at all times. Becca usually neglected her other half at parties, but tonight Kate had noticed her cousin watching Charlie and Flo together with a special intensity, as if studying a pair of animals in the wild. When Becca's lips worked like that, furiously writhing against each other, it meant she was trying to keep something in. Something that would break things, shatter stuff. To distract her, Kate handed her a broom but when the same square foot of lino had been swept a dozen times, she said, 'Come with me,' and led her out into the garden.

The bitter cold slapped them in the face. Time to get it over and done with. Kate's breath was fog as she said, 'What's the matter, Bec?'

One of her cone breasts dented, Becca said, 'Nothing. Well. Everything.' She threw up her hands. 'You're always good and I'm always . . . I'm bad, Kate.'

'Nobody's *always* anything.' Kate didn't like the idea of herself as a perennial goodie two shoes.

'You're going to hate me.' She screwed up her face, as if in pain. 'Why oh why . . .' she began.

'*Why oh why* what?'

'Eh?' Becca looked confused at having her train of thought interrupted. 'Let me speak for once, Kate!'

'Go on, then. Just this once.'

'You are definitely one hundred per cent going to hate me. From here.' Becca tapped her wig. 'To here.' She pointed at her feet.

She seemed to mean it. 'I could never hate you,' said Kate. 'Not unless you murdered somebody. And even then it would depend on who you murdered.'

'I hate myself.' No tears. Not one. This was a bad sign. 'I had to do it, Kate. You won't agree. But I did. I had to do it.'

'If you have a confession, madam, get on with it.'

'You have to know, right? And you have to say it's OK. I feel so bad about it. I wake up in the middle of the night.' Becca hugged herself in her outrageous gear, a goose pimpled superstar. 'You have to absolve me.'

'I'm not a priest.' Kate's skin prickled. She felt something heading for her, hard and fast. A comet. 'Why the sudden urge to confess? Can't it wait until you've sobered up?'

Shaking her head as if such a suggestion was madness, Becca glared at her. 'I've waited long enough. It's eating at me. You're the only person I want to tell, the only person I *can* tell.' She closed her eyes, as if blocking out a vile apparition. 'I thought I could bear it, but it keeps raising its head. I'm glad I'm a bit pissed. It's the only way I'll get it out.' She opened her eyes, their expression fierce. 'First, though, promise you won't judge me.'

That was too much to ask, even for somebody accustomed to Becca's outrageous demands. 'All I can promise is that I'll try and understand.'

Eyes wide in smudged mascara, Becca whispered, 'Flo isn't Charlie's.'

'How do you mean?' Kate's brain went smooth; the meaning of the simple sentence simply wouldn't click into place.

Stamping her foot Becca said, 'What do you *think* I mean? Charlie isn't Flo's dad.'

Even though Becca had barely raised her voice those words were grenades. Both women glanced, paranoid, at the domestic tableau framed by the lit kitchen window.

At the sink, Charlie stared out at them. Kate's breath paused until he waved the washing up brush playfully.

'Shit,' croaked Becca. 'I thought he heard. He can't know. Not ever.'

Kate felt burdened, stiff. Becca had dipped her in emotional cement.

'I know what you're thinking.' Becca was defiant. 'But I did it for pure reasons.'

'You don't know what I'm thinking.'

'Charlie can't have a child, Kate! He couldn't give me a healthy baby, then he couldn't give me one at all. This was the only way.' No longer defiant, Becca was pleading.

'Is it . . . are you having an affair?'

'God, no. It was a one night thing.' Becca revised that thought. 'A three night thing. I don't even have the guy's number any more. He has no idea.'

Circles within circles. Another victim of Becca's free-wheeling selfishness.

'And Flo?' asked Kate. 'When are you going to tell her?'

'Flo?' Becca's horror implied she'd never even considered that eventuality. 'Why would I tell Flo?'

Amazed she had to answer such a question, Kate said, 'You mean why does a person have the right to know the identity of their own father?'

'I knew,' spat Becca, 'you'd be mean to me.'

'Then why the hell did you tell me?'

'I wish I hadn't.' Becca was back in her comfort zone, hugging her resentments to her pointy chest, the aggrieved party.

Sensing an eruption of some sort in the air, Kate battled her own feelings to soften her voice. 'It's good that you've got this off your chest.' She was already nostalgic for a minute ago, the time before she Knew All. 'But you can't undo everything just by confessing.' She moved towards Becca. 'Listen—'

'I'm tired of listening.' Becca was, Kate could tell, tormented by her own misdeeds. She thrashed about, trying to evade the spotlight by accusing the nearest person – usually, and this time, Kate – of something equally heinous. 'What makes you so high and mighty, Kate? Some of us screw up! We can't all be perfect like you.'

*This is the whole family's doing*, thought Kate. There was a perpetual amnesty on Becca's countless minor crimes. *We're all Frankenstein and this here is our monster.*

Becca stamped her foot again. 'Nobody understands what it's like to want a baby month after month.'

'Plenty of people understand.'

'But I *needed* a baby!'

'For God's sake . . .' The self-pity was so thick Kate could almost see it lying across Becca's shoulders like a mangy stole. 'So many women – and men – feel the same. They go through hell and high water to conceive. But they don't do something like this.'

'It's all right for you. With your shops and your pots of money and a flat straight out of *Elle Decoration*.'

*But I don't have a baby*. It was on Kate's lips, and there it stayed. It was too personal, too intimate a fact to fling during a row.

'And you have Julian,' said Becca.

'And you have Charlie.' *My* Charlie. The possessive pronoun shocked Kate and she turned away.

'I've made Charlie happy. You see him with Flo.'

That was undeniable.

Becca shook Kate by the shoulders. *As if*, thought Kate miserably, *we're in an eighties soap opera.*

'Please, please, you have to promise you don't hate me. I couldn't bear that. I'd die.'

'No you wouldn't.' Kate was tired of the hyperbole. As if

Becca owned all the strong emotion in the world and could model whichever one took her fancy. For many years, Kate realised, Becca's happiness had been other people's responsibility.

'I would! I'd die. Your opinion of me means more than anybody's.'

Kate hung her head. She had, she realised, a sword in her hand. With that sword, with one sentence, she could end Becca and Charlie's marriage.

Charlie would never forgive such intimate deceit. Becca would disgust him. He would leave her.

Their neat quartet would be lopsided.

There may be a knock-on effect.

Ripples . . .

Adrenaline surged through Kate when she imagined a tomorrow that featured Charlie as a free spirit.

His head was bent over the sink. It jerked up; Dad had entered the kitchen, holding Flo by the hand. Charlie picked her up and both men talked to the child, blowing suds from their fingers to amuse her.

'I couldn't hate you, Becca. But I hate what you've done.' Even though it had resulted in the miracle that was Flo, Kate deplored Becca's tactics, her belief that the end justified the means. She sighed and held out her arms.

'Sorry. Sorry. I'm sorry.' Becca wept in Kate's embrace.

The furrow in Charlie's brow asked a question Kate answered with a wry face, as if to say *Oh it's only Becca being*

*Becca.* Charlie knew his wife could cry that zealously over a broken nail.

'I'm sorry for being unfaithful,' gasped Becca. 'I'm sorry for bringing Flo into the world like this. I'm sorry for telling you.'

'I'm glad you did.' Kate held her tighter. 'I'm a big girl. I can cope.'

A lover of truth, a believer in its power, Kate could see no way to tell Charlie this basic fact about his own life. It would destroy him: she used the word with full knowledge of its weight. Charlie would break into pieces. Flo was one of the building blocks of his existence. To Becca she said, 'No more stunts like this. Promise?'

'Promise.' Becca began immediately to distort the lighting on what she'd done, changing it to a rosy glow. 'It's not all bad. Flo's healthy and happy and we all adore her. Charlie and I didn't have to go through any treatment. We—'

'No! I'm not going through the looking glass to Wonderland with you, Alice. You lied to Charlie and you'll lie to Flo all her life. Don't dress it up.'

'But you forgive me?'

'That's not my job. But I do understand.' Kate also understood that Becca had handed her the magic formula to end her marriage to Charlie.

It could never be used.

The note throbbed in the pocket of her tunic. Rejected twice over by Charlie, she still wanted the best for him.

157

Yulan House
28th January 2007

Dear Kate

Soon we meet you and your father. It is like seeing old friends.

Forgive me but we organise a small party in your honour. The children desire to meet the great English man who never forgets them.

Yours
Jia Tang

The tea had gone cold.

It was a kind thought from a nurse who'd noticed Kate's woebegone face as she watched the curtains of the A&E cubicle whisk around her father, but the tea sat unattended as Kate went outside to make the necessary phone calls.

First on her list was Aunty Marjorie. 'Dash round to Mum's, would you?' Kate had asked. 'So she won't be alone when I ring her.'

'Is he . . .' Aunty Marjorie had said. 'He's not . . .'

'Just a funny turn at the departure gate. They're assessing him now.'

There had been nothing funny about Dad's turn. As Kate pillaged her handbag looking for their boarding passes, Dad had slithered from the plastic fixed seating.

'He's a bad colour,' somebody said in the crowd that gathered.

To Kate's eyes, he had *no* colour. Her father was ghostly as she knelt and rubbed his hands, waiting for the ambulance. Inert, cold, he seemed dead, but Kate could feel the slender thread that tied him to her, a cord deep inside attached somehow to his heart. It was taut.


'I'm coming right now,' said Becca when she'd stopped swearing.

'Nonsense.' Kate was brisk. 'You're too far away. And Flo's at nursery. There's no immediate danger. Just stay there, yeah?'

'You shouldn't be on your own. He's not going to . . . is he?'

'Die?' Kate tried the word for size and didn't like it. It was time to be honest with Becca. 'I really don't know.'

She was more honest with Julian. 'He's dying. This is it.'

'You poor love.' Julian sighed. 'Christ, darling, I'm sorry.'

'He's in a nice room. Very modern. Everybody's being lovely.'

'How are you, though?'

Kate heard the fear. They were approaching the summit that had glowered over their marriage. 'I'm good.'

Kate could cope. Because her dad was still with her. The thread was still tightly drawn. *This bit*, she wanted to say to Julian and the nurses who were treating her like bone china, *is the easy bit*.

It was afterwards, when Dad was gone and Kate still had all this love but nowhere to put it, that would be the problem.

'Go for a walk. Clear your head. This could be a long haul.' Julian hesitated. 'I'm about to leave for my meeting with the bank but I'll cancel if you like. I could come and sit with you.'

The dreaded bank meeting was too important to rearrange. 'You go, darling. Give them hell.'

'When you get home we'll light the fire. A nice quiet evening on the sofa, just the two of us.'

'Sounds perfect.'

The hospital bled all over the local landscape. Escaping it, taking Julian's advice, Kate kept checking her watch as she found a parade of shops.

She knew there'd be no nice night on the sofa. Tonight would be critical. Kate would stay by her father's side. By now she was accustomed to sleeping on a chair.

Julian disapproved. 'How can it help your dad to watch him sleep?' he'd say. 'He needs you fresh and rested, not exhausted.'

She'd tried to explain. It was painful, yes, to see him in a hospital bed. It was also real. She grasped at these last events, the last snatches of togetherness. They gave her something she could never describe as pleasure, but which was a close relation. It felt *right*.

The older Kate got – her twenty-nine years felt twice that today – the more she relinquished the quest for happiness. A quest for harmony, or maybe contentment, made more sense. Just as Dad had said.

Browsing chocolate in a newsagent's, Kate thought how often Julian had recently said *I just want you to be happy*. Like a mantra. That, he'd said, was the reason for keeping his financial woes hidden from her.

*You underestimated me*, she'd told him. If he'd come to her sooner she wouldn't have reacted with such horror to the landslide of final demands. Tackling them, drawing together the knowns and unknowns, whistling up bank statements, analysing data, Kate had noted his amazement at her competence. *Who do you think you've been married to all these years?* she'd laughed. A chain of eight shops across the south of England doesn't build itself.

Julian, it transpired, knew little about the nuts and bolts of the company that bore his name. Kate, who knew every lane and byway of her own set up, drew him a map of the tangled paths that had led him to the brink of ruin. Julian had ignored the day to day processes in order to concentrate on the bottom line. Profit was all.

On their first night in the new house, sitting by an open fire, glorying in the three empty floors of severe Georgian beauty, he'd confessed, 'I thought you'd leave me when you saw the mess my affairs are in.'

'Idiot.' She'd kissed him. They'd made quiet love on the reconditioned floorboards.

A shop further down the street caught Kate's eye. A laugh came unbidden. She could barely believe it. According to the sign on the door, it was five minutes to closing time. Kate finished her Bounty with one bite and pushed at the door.


Watching her father through the window, Kate stood on the paving slabs outside his room. Her phone to her ear she coughed, rehearsing what to say when the other party picked up.

Dad's hands were so white they were blue. The veins stood out like cord pushing through his shrivelled skin. He was asleep, although that didn't seem the correct way to describe his limbo-like state. She felt that he was levitating, between one state of being and the next.

Her call went to voicemail.

'Charlie, hi. You've heard by now, Dad's been taken ill. Nothing drastic. Well, not yet ... I have this feeling, though ... Don't tell Becca but I think this is it ... Anyway ... um, that's all, I guess, so, well, bye.'

The carefully nurtured reconnection was important to her. Charlie's company was a haven where she was her best and worst self, where the giggling spiralled out of control and where she could off-load dark thoughts.

Watching him with Flo had been an enduring pleasure. Now it felt like a brightly coloured snapshot that had fallen in the fire and was cracked and burned around the edges. Kate felt no temptation to enlighten him about Flo's conception: it wasn't her job. Flo was cared for, loved: as the saying went, it wasn't broke, so Kate need not fix it.

But still it rankled. If Charlie knew something so fundamental about Kate's life, she would expect him to tell her.

When they were teenagers, Becca had soundly mocked Kate for scribbling 'KM 4 CG together 4 eva' on a school book. Becca had been right to roll her eyes; KM and CG couldn't even sustain a friendship. Kate missed Charlie even when he was right there in front of her.

Returning to the room, Kate heard Dad say, 'Could you ...?' He gestured at his pillow with a hand so crooked his wrist might have been broken.

Deftly, efficiently, Kate plumped the pillow and made him comfortable.

'Where's Mum?' He was crabby. He'd asked the same question five minutes earlier.

'On her way.'

Kate chattered a banal soliloquy. No point in bringing Dad up to date with the news; her serious minded father, who'd always had a philosophical take on world events, had lost his taste for politics, for anything that happened beyond the family. Sickness had shrunk him; Kate knew that it took most of his energy to maintain his poise. He'd barely registered the terrorist bombs that had ravaged London six months earlier, and had no comment to make on David Cameron, newly elected to lead the Tories and widely tipped to be the next Prime Minister.

So Kate told her father that Mum had been to the cinema to see *The Queen*. 'She didn't think much of Helen Mirren. Far too attractive to play Her Majesty, apparently. Of course, Mum's never forgiven the Queen for being offish with Princess Di.' She updated him on Flo. 'According to Becca, she's gifted. According to Charlie, she can bang out *Three Blind Mice* on the xylophone.' She leaned closer to hear what he said and agreed. 'Yes, she *is* the prettiest little thing in the world.'

'Book?' croaked Dad.

'There's trouble at t'mill about the book, Dad. And it's all your fault.' Dad's ill health had affected them all. For Charlie it had shed a sideways light on life's certainties: it had shown him that there are no such things. Inspired, he'd handed in his notice and reapplied himself to his novel. 'I think it hits Becca anew each morning that she's no longer the wife of a jetsetting media hot shot. She can't deny that Charlie's in seventh heaven, sitting up in the loft, wearing an ancient jumper and writing his heart out, but she's scared the money's running out.' Kate did her bit, jollying her out of her moods, asking *Are you down to your last pair of Louboutins yet, Little Orphan Annie?* There was never any question of Becca searching out a part time position around Flo's nursery hours; such a suggestion would spark a glare that had been known to kill.

A commotion in the corridor announced Mum and Aunty Marjorie who were unable to arrive anywhere without knocking things over and shouting.

Kate could tell her mother had carefully arranged her features before entering the room. It was to no avail: at the sight of her husband, Mum began to weep.

As she hung over him, dripping tears onto his pyjama top, he patted her with his oddly straight hand. He couldn't quite turn his neck to take her in properly. Kate felt as if he was leaving them bit by bit, his solidity ebbing with each small physical change.

Collecting herself, Mum stared about the room. 'What the feck have you done in here, Kate?'

'Party,' said Dad. He'd run out of sentences, apparently. Solo words were all he had left.

A paper dragon, its concertina folds the brightest of yellows, cavorted across the wall opposite Dad's bed. Chinese paper lanterns, their tassels still in the heatwave hospital atmosphere, hung above his head, and on the bed Kate had strewn fringed shawls blazing with lush embroidered flowers.

'And what are you wearing?' Mum took a step back from her daughter. 'Is it a Chinese thing?'

'It's called a cheongsam.' Kate twirled, not easy to do in the form fitting crossover satin dress. A size too small, she'd paid over the odds for the display purposes only outfit in the window of the tiny Chinese emporium that sat miraculously between a dry cleaner's and an estate agent in this beige suburb. 'As we couldn't make it to Jia Tang's party, we're having one of our own.'

Kate could tell Mum was doing her best to be annoyed, but she couldn't manage it. 'Him and his Yulan House,' she tutted.

'Wife,' was all Dad said as Mum sat, rending tissue after tissue, spouting nuggets of gossip. Dad hadn't given a toss about the woman next door's exploits when he was healthy; Kate assumed Dad gave even less of a toss now that he was sick. It helped Mum, though, so they all listened dutifully to her rhetoric.

The debate about whether or not Mum should stay the night raged until late. Aunty Marjorie prevailed, finally, and took Mum by the arm.

Bending over her husband to say goodnight – not goodbye, never goodbye when he was in a hospital bed – Mum recoiled when Dad said, 'All that lives must die.'

'Oh Jesus, he's going!' cried Mum. 'Kate, he's going!'

'It's a quote, Mum. From *Hamlet*. It's just Dad being Dad.'

After Mum had gone, when the room was quiet again, Kate said, 'I know what you mean, Dad.'

*This is ordinary*, he was saying. *This is just part of life.*

The festive colours of the decorations glowed as the night crept on, as beyond the windows turned to black pricked with points of artificial light. Still in her cheongsam, even though it was uncomfortable, Kate appreciated the antiseptic NHS room's attempt to be cosy and beautiful.

The email from Jia Tang had made her cry. 'We hold your father in our hearts. He is a good man.' Kate believed Dad had smiled when she said, 'She's not wrong, Pops.'

When Charlie called she didn't pick up. His message sounded confused, like somebody trying to put furniture together without instructions. 'But . . . you were going to China today . . . so what did . . . I mean . . .?'

Charlie had been against the trip. And he'd been right. It had been an act of hubris, and the gods had cut Dad down.

Kate wouldn't be able to bear any reproach; it would break her and Kate needed to run a little longer on the scant petrol in her tank.

*Did I wilfully ignore how frail Dad's become in case it jeopardised the trip?* Kate retraced the past couple of weeks. She'd kept checking with her father to ensure he was still keen to make their epic journey.

*Perhaps I gave him no choice.* Dad, after all, was ill not stupid; he knew the expense and effort Kate had gone to.

*Or maybe he was acting.* That was the most painful option, Dad pretending to be more vigorous, less depleted than he really was rather than disappoint his only child. Desperate to hear his voice, she took Julian's call outside in the cold.

'So. What's happening?'

'The same. No real change.'

'Should I come? I can if you like.'

If just once Julian would forgo the *if you like*, she'd beg him to get there as soon as possible. The three words, so ambiguous, forced her to say, as usual, 'No, stay put. I'm OK.'

'It's probably another false alarm.'

'Probably.' It wasn't. Cancer had cried wolf so often Kate knew the difference. She was impatient to get back inside to where Dad made barely a dent in the bed. The thread was sagging.

'By the way, it was pretty tough at the bank.'

'Sorry, darling. I forgot to ask: did they extend the loan?'

'Not exactly.' Julian sighed and Kate imagined him dragging his hand heavily down his features. 'By which I mean they laughed me out of the room. I've put a fortune through that bank but the minute I ask for a little wiggle room . . .'

'We have plan B.'

'Hmm.'

'We talked about this.' Ames Partners in Property was springing leaks faster than Julian could plug them up. 'We have to act fast, darling.' Raising money on the Party Games shops was the obvious next move, but Julian's reluctance to admit that his wife was now the breadwinner held them back. This change in their circumstances had altered Julian profoundly. No longer a *My way or the highway* chap, he deferred to Kate with a wary mindfulness, as if he was the ringmaster and she a lion who'd somehow wangled the whip into her paws. It was, Kate knew, the only reason he hadn't insisted they put the house on the market to save the company. He would never admit it, but they were living in it because she, the boss, wanted them to.

For Kate, Julian's crisis was another example of the rises and dips of the marital see-saw: she conceded that it was easy to see it that way when you were up in the air and not down in the mud. She longed for them to be a partnership, to be in harmony. She longed for him to turn up at the hospital, without asking if he was needed there.

Had Julian believed her when Kate said she'd willingly sell the house if they had to? For now, she appreciated her private front door and a garden on terra firma.

'Let's not talk about this now,' said Julian. The ice in his whisky on the rocks clinked as he upended the glass. 'Concentrate on your dad. Call me if anything changes.'

Her hand was on his. There was no such thing as time any more, just an endless now.

'Love,' said Dad about midnight, setting Kate's heart racing in case it was a farewell.

He slept a little. Mainly he kept his eyes on his daughter. Whether he could hear she didn't know. 'How about we remember ten brilliant things we did together?' She got as far as two; when she recalled how he'd saved the day at her fifth birthday party by insisting she received the Action Man she wanted instead of the Princess Barbie Mum had chosen, she found herself crying. 'Silly old me,' she grumbled. 'Crying is Mum's job.'

Cups of tea. A form filled in and signed. Murmured voices beyond the door. An hour. Another hour. Just the two of them, suspended in space.

'He's a tough nut,' whispered a nurse, dressed just as Kate had been at Mumsy's party. Poor Mumsy, her beauty blighted by a stroke, she now favoured coquettish veiled hats, and continued to throw small dinners for a hundred people.

Another nurse, an older lady and one of those natural healers whose presence was balm, stole in, smiling when she saw the lanterns. Touching Dad's forehead, she frowned and took up his papery wrist.

'It's close, dear,' she said.

Kate wanted to say, 'No,' in every language she could muster. She wanted to semaphore to whoever was in charge of the universe that she couldn't do without her dad just yet, thank you very much.

'You can cry, dear.' The nurse's hand on Kate's shoulder, so capable and compassionate, unleashed something.

Tears dribbled onto the thin bedcover, so neatly folded back. Kate kissed Dad's cheek, and drank him in. Beneath the pharmaceutical top notes he still smelled of himself.

He was falling away from her.

'Daddy.' Kate never called him that. *Don't go.* She mustn't say that. He'd told her that the hardest part of this whole undertaking was knowing he must leave her. Kate must put him first, just as he'd done with her since she was born.

The nurse left them together.

The thread snapped.

Out in the car park, in the dirty pool of yellow light around a street lamp, Kate jabbed at her mobile, her fingers fat and clumsy.

Every time she thought she'd finished crying, she began again.

Sniffing, she composed herself as she heard the sound of a phone ringing in a distant room.

'Hello? Kate?'

'He's . . .'

'I'll be there before you know it.'

Charlie found her in the visitors' lounge, a room that resembled a dull chapel, with low padded seats and dried flower arrangements, static and dead, on every polished surface.

'I can't stop crying!' Kate despaired of herself, as Charlie folded her to his shoulder, her head against the niche she remembered from long ago.

She still fitted.

The insomniac hospital never went quite to sleep. Now the streets around it woke up, the first buses chugging past, lit up against the still-dark dawn.

On a bench, legs stuck out in front of them, sat Kate and Charlie, drinking foul coffee.

'Julian should be here by now.' The troops had been rallied. Julian was on his way to the hospital. Becca was bundling up Flo for the drive to her parents' house, where Aunty Marjorie was preparing for them all. There was talk of quiche.

'He was almost a dad to me,' said Charlie.

'I know. He liked that. He was so chuffed when you stopped work to go back to your book.'

'That chat he had with Becca about letting me write probably saved my marriage.'

'He had a chat with Becca?' Kate hadn't known. 'Is that Julian?' Kate sat up, then slumped again. 'Nope.'

'That was a genius touch, decorating the room. If John can't go to China, then China must come to John!'

'That reminds me. I must let Jia Tang know.' Kate had already had to say 'He's gone' five times over to the family. The list of people to inform grew each time she thought of it. She might delegate: Julian would do it if she asked him. 'And, God, the funeral . . .'

'Plenty of time for that,' said Charlie.

But time was relentless. Kate was already hours into the new post-Dad era.

A clock chimed five as her phone cheeped to remind Kate it was time for Dad's first tablet of the day. She thought of his watch, still on the table beside his empty bed. It had been weeks since he'd been able to wear it. It chafed his skin, he said.

'Charlie,' said Kate, 'was I selfish? Did I ask too much of him?'

Catching on immediately, Charlie said, 'No. Planning the trip to China kept him alive, I think.' He twisted to face her miserable profile, laying his arm along the back of the bench. 'Gave him something to live for. You did the right thing.'

'Mum thought it was a stupid idea. So did Aunty Marjorie. He was sick, Charlie, and there I was, pushing and pulling him to get him to the airport.'

'The only person whose approval you need is your dad's. And he understood what you were doing.'

'He did,' said Kate. 'Dad got me.' Past tense already.

'You were trying to make his lifelong dream come true. You almost bloody did it.'

'Until Dad went and spoiled it. Self-centred sod.' Kate tried to laugh but her face buckled and she was a child again. A child who wanted her daddy.

'Come here.' Charlie's arms went tight around her. She felt his tears in her hair.

Struggling against his arms, Kate brought her face up, close to his. 'Thank you, Charlie,' she whispered. Some people make things better just by being there.

'Shush, it's OK.' Charlie closed his eyes and chastely kissed her on the forehead, through her matted fringe.

His lips stayed there. He breathed against her.

At the same moment, they curved in to each other, as if obeying a high pitched instruction inaudible to other human ears.

Charlie's mouth travelled down her face, imparting tiny kisses as it went.

Kate's mouth was ready when he reached it. She parted her lips and felt Charlie inhabit her, familiar and exotic.

A car horn sounded harshly and they sprang apart, as if scalded.

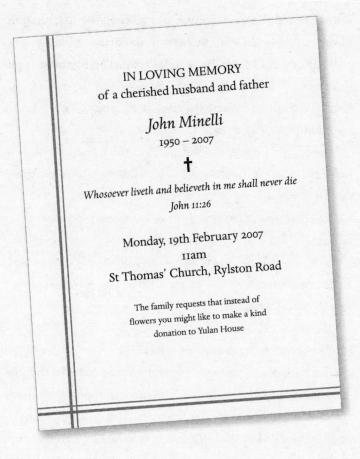

IN LOVING MEMORY
of a cherished husband and father

*John Minelli*
1950 – 2007

✝

*Whosoever liveth and believeth in me shall never die*
John 11:26

Monday, 19th February 2007
11am
St Thomas' Church, Rylston Road

The family requests that instead of
flowers you might like to make a kind
donation to Yulan House

'First of all, thank you everybody for coming today. It's a real honour to give the eulogy for my father.'

The pulpit was higher up than Kate had anticipated. Nearly ten years ago she'd knelt at this altar and the same priest now coughing behind her had blessed her marriage.

Kate adjusted the microphone and ignored the sombre bulk of the coffin, laden with flowers, in the corner of her vision.

'I know Dad would be grateful to you for coming.' *And don't think I didn't notice the disapproving looks at my red coat.* Kate and Dad had discussed this: 'I've always liked you in bright colours,' he'd said.

The family pew was divided. The older half head to toe in black; Becca, Charlie and Flo in rainbow plumage. At the end of the bench sat Julian in grey.

'As you know, Dad was born only three streets away from here.'

That struck Kate in a way it hadn't when she'd rehearsed. A man with his head full of the Orient had travelled only a few hundred yards.

'He was a quiet man.'

*He couldn't get a word in edgeways.*

'But he loved to talk about the things that mattered to him.'

Kate paused, grasping for the next thought. Her sleep patterns were haywire. Bereavement had made her physically ill, blocked up and shivering, as if she had a cold. There was the occasional miraculous hour when she would freewheel, absorbed in some task, but then the smell of a jacket or the pitch of a stranger's laugh would remind her and she would plummet to the basement again, mired in grief.

'Many of you are aware of Dad's chief passion.'

Heads nodded fondly.

'He never tired of raising funds for Yulan House. Later, if you come back to the house with us, I'll play you the beautiful video message the children sent.'

*I won't watch, though.*

It was too much to ask. The children's sweetly expressed sympathy was unbearable.

Watching television or listening to the news on the radio were just two of the ordinary activities that had become endurance tasks; Kate felt that her father's death should be in the headlines. Other people going about their humdrum days astonished and affronted her. How could they all just carry on as if nothing had happened?

'Dad was a devoted family man, a good friend and neighbour, a loving son and an upstanding member of his community.'

Mum had insisted on that bit. Dad couldn't stand the neighbours and 'upstanding' was the sort of pompous language that made him itch. The gospel quote below his name in the order of service was also a Mum touch. Kate had lobbied for Shakespeare but Mum had stood firm: no husband of hers was going into the ground a heathen.

*She didn't let him have his way about going to China and now she won't let him have his way about his own funeral.*

The red nosed priest's pious way with a prayer used to make Dad giggle. Kate was grateful her father wouldn't have to endure the funeral tea: quiche as far as the eye could see.

'Dad would be deeply moved by the way you've all reached out to comfort us at this terrible time.'

*Terrible time.*

Such platitudes. It described it, yes, but barely scratched the surface. Mum was tight lipped. She wouldn't talk about him, and said helplessly *Don't cry, love* whenever Kate was overcome.

At those moments, Kate was grateful for Becca. Her cousin's own mourning was, inevitably, over-egged but Becca's taste for high drama meant she was at ease with Kate's deep emotion. She allowed Kate to talk incessantly about the man they'd lost, one minute nostalgic, the next weeping, before returning to baffled anger that such tragedy was permitted to happen.

'Come and stay,' Becca had wheedled. 'I want to look after you.'

'I'd love to.' That was true. 'But I'm too busy with work and the funeral and everything.' That wasn't. She couldn't stay at Becca's house because of Charlie. Because of that kiss.

'Mum has asked me to personally thank all the family for their kindness. They're all here today. My husband, Julian. Aunty Marjorie and Uncle Hugh. Becca. And we mustn't forget Flo. And Charlie.'

The metallic yowl of feedback ripped through the church. Kate jumped. She couldn't remember what came next.

*We kissed.*

Uninvited, the memory barged in and made itself comfortable.

'Um . . .' Kate dug into her small shoulder bag, looking for her notes as she remembered the warmth of Charlie's lips against her own. The pleasing clash of their faces.

'Err . . .' Kate blinked away the unbidden sensual memory. Out of place, wildly inappropriate, it stopped her in her tracks. She took a deep breath, desperate to compose herself when the folded paper leaped into her hand. 'Ah. Here we are. Sorry. Bear with me.'

In the ten days since she lost her dad – *only ten?* – Julian had been carefully kind to Kate, wary of her as if she was a fragile, valued object. Kate didn't like to admit it but the calamity had shone such a searing light on her life that she could be in no doubt about her priorities.

Julian was a distinct and clear entity, on his own, near the edge of her mind. Surely, as her husband, he should be centre-front. He should loom large.

Kate matched Julian's reserve with her own. There were no cross words, no confrontations but the no man's land between them had grown darker and wider.

Bereavement could tear couples apart: that hadn't happened. But neither had it brought them closer. Instead they'd retreated into caricatures of themselves.

Desperately unfolding the piece of paper, Kate wondered at its blankness. It wasn't her notes, it was the envelope Charlie had handed back to her. Somebody in the congregation cleared their throat as she stared at the untidy handwritten *Kate*.

'I made some notes, but I'm just going to speak from the heart.'

Charlie's head was bowed over Flo, who sat in his lap, subdued by all the sad faces around her. The depth of his grief surprised everybody except Kate.

Indulgent and protective with Kate, Becca was impatient with Charlie. 'He needs,' she'd said, 'to stop moping and get back to writing his bestseller.'

Charlie never described his novel in those terms.

'It's easy to speak from the heart, as my heart is very full.'

The angry car horn that had prised Kate and Charlie apart on the hospital bench hadn't been Julian's. Kate had almost fainted with relief.

Charlie's face had stayed close to hers. Intent, transformed, made urgent.

In her head, clear as a bell, she'd heard a line that he'd written. *Not everything that looks like love is love.*

Poised and still, they'd regarded each other.

*Don't speak first*, Kate had counselled herself.

'Sorry.' Charlie had seemed to snap out of a trance. He'd looked away and Kate was lonely without him: she'd felt suspended and supported by his gaze.

'No, *I'm* sorry,' she'd said, passing a hand over her face.

'What was I thinking? I mean your dad's just . . .' Charlie

had stood up, then sat heavily down again. Close to her but very deliberately not touching her, he'd stared at his lap, unable to say any more.

Eventually, on a sigh, Kate had said, 'Becca . . .'

His face contorting, Charlie had let out an agonised huff, then nodded.

Loyalty can be a rare commodity but with Kate it was a strong, twisting, blood red thing. She couldn't betray Becca and she couldn't behave in a way that was incompatible with the fierce protectiveness she felt towards Flo.

There they had sat, prim, until Julian turned up.

Kate hadn't felt prim. Despite the cataclysmic nature of the night's events, despite her churning sadness, she'd wanted to claw Charlie's clothes from his body and feel his skin against her skin, cooking that special lovers' alchemy.

Accustomed to regarding her sexuality as a sleepy, querulous creature, she had barely recognised the all consuming lust that took hold of her and shook her, from her hairline to her shoes.

A church pulpit is not the most appropriate place for such memories.

'My wonderful dad took a long time to die. I've heard some of you say that he was brave and that's certainly true. But he was often frightened. Children don't usually get to be around their parents' fear. Because they love us, they keep it from us. It was a privilege for me to know Dad well enough for him to share his fears with me before he went. Sitting with him, watching him sleep, I used to wonder where I'd put the love after he went. Now I know.'

Kate paused.

'I can put it in the same place. In many ways Dad's still here. I was so close to him, and our communication was so crystalline that I can hear what he'd say in most situations. So I still badger the poor man for advice.'

The congregation laughed at that, a small, relieved explosion.

Mum laughed along with them. Kate noticed her hat was askew. A beam of sunshine, stained gold by the stained glass, spotlit Mum. Kate saw her in stark relief.

And she was just a person. A woman trying to get by like the rest of us. More than that, she was a woman who must surely have coveted the easy affinity between her husband and her daughter.

Undoubtedly, it was chilly to be the odd one out in a set of three, never getting the joke, pulling in a different direction. It must have been as chilly as this chapel.

In the midst of Kate's epiphany, a hypothesis intruded. It would be harder to lose Mum than Dad. *Because I don't know her.* Not in the profound meaning of the word. A meaning Kate now appreciated.

*Have I grown up at long last?*

Kate promised herself to hug her mother later, no matter how much the all-elbows woman protested. What if Mum's refusal to talk about Dad was not because she would not, but because she *could* not?

The black coat didn't quite fit. Mum stealthily undid a button. She was a woman who was misunderstood by her partner, a woman mired in a mismatch of a marriage.

If Kate was honest – the surroundings demanded it – she could relate to that.

'Dad believed in me. Which is a big deal for a girl child. He encouraged and supported me. Not only me. There are other people who'll miss his loyalty.'

Missed calls from Charlie were piled up in Kate's phone. She had let them ring out, needing to absorb and digest what had happened between the two of them before she could face him. Bent out of shape by the loss of her father, Kate didn't know whether or not to trust the serpent hiss of her subconscious that his kiss had been fuelled by pity.

Her toes curled in her red boots.

'*Love* was the last thing Dad said. I've thought a lot about love since that night. It's not a decision you make. It doesn't have to be logical. It's often inconvenient and messy and unapologetic about what it asks of you.'

Unsure where she was going with this, Kate sensed puzzlement from the older funeral guests at this departure from standard eulogy fare.

Kate couldn't look at Charlie. She wouldn't look at Julian. She felt them both resonate, like tuning forks.

'Searching for the meaning of life has become a cliché, but Dad contemplated life deeply during his final months. He could no longer bear artifice. He said, more than once, that I needed to work out what I truly wanted in order to live honestly.'

Kate found Julian's eye. He stood and slipped away, head down, out into the cold morning.

Nobody noticed him leave. All eyes were on Kate, waiting for her to carry on.

*I'm sick of loss.*

Kate had lost Charlie, her dad, and now Julian had been swallowed up by the bitter brightness outside. She'd been aware as she spoke how he would interpret her words. The night before, she and Julian had talked more bluntly, more freely than ever before. Her sadness had stripped her so she couldn't pretend any more; he had matched her, truth for truth. They'd faced what they had and, more crucially, what they lacked.

It felt correct for Julian to leave, but that didn't stop her wanting to tear after him, to gabble that they could fix things. She stayed silent until the feeling receded. Not completely. Just enough for her to carry on.

'A little late I'm taking his advice. I'm working out what I really want. Thank you, Dad.'

*Thank you. And goodbye.*

**Shhh!**

You are invited to a surprise
**Divorce Party**
for

# KATE

Let's raise the roof
and celebrate
Kate's freedom!

22.2.08
Ludwig House
186 Ismay Road, SE5
RSVP: bonkersbeccaoopboopadoop
@gmail.com
7pm

Be on time so we can surprise her!

**Girrrrrl Power!**

The plastic carrier bags bit into Kate's fingers as she emerged from the tube station into the rat-coloured evening.

Glad that Becca was staying over after one of her intermittent assaults on London's boutiques, Kate foresaw a muted evening of food and wine and conversation. Weighing down the bags were two bottles of what a magazine article had assured her was a 'cheeky lovable red' and some toothsome treats. The Atkins Diet was working wonders on her behind but wreaking havoc with her head; Kate would have happily sold her body on a street corner for a bowl of spaghetti. Tonight there would be lasagne and cake and, hopefully, recovery from the hour she'd spent pelting around the gym with her personal trainer.

She'd have to fend off Becca's insinuations. 'But *everybody*,' Becca had insisted, 'has an affair with their personal trainer. It's the law.'

Already anticipating the shower's rain on her sore limbs, Kate called out 'Becca!' as she kicked shut the front door. The panelled hallway was painted in a duck egg tone it had taken Kate an age to source. The air was soft, like talc. It was always tranquil in Ludwig House.

'Where are you?' Kate pushed at the drawing room door and her home exploded into light and colour and shouts of 'Surprise!' Cameras flashed. Women catcalled. Emerging from the melee, Becca yelled 'Happy divorce!' and stripped Kate of her plastic bags, replacing them with a champagne flute.

*I Am What I Am* struck up on the CD player and the women began to dance with pagan abandon.

Kate joined in. She had no choice. The quiet evening she'd planned had dissolved with the shout of 'Surprise!' At first she was doing her duty, but as one defiant heartbreak anthem followed another, Kate was swept up by the music. By the time they were all caterwauling along to *These Boots Are Made for Walkin'* she was just a swaying body disconnected from its fretful mind.

Suddenly, she slumped. As if somebody had pulled out her plug, Kate sagged against the fridge. She watched the seething mass of wrap dresses and up-dos, wondering where they got their energy. It was easy to slip out unnoticed and climb the stairs.

Kate sat on the side of the freestanding bath and plonked her glass on the basin. The prosecco had made her head swim. Mild nausea swirled in the pit of her empty stomach.

Pretty and orderly, blue and white delft tiles stood in rows above the basin. Kate remembered Julian's overexcited text from a second-hand shop.

Wait till you see what I've found! Love you xxx

Two floors above the music, Kate couldn't hear the party goers. This house wasn't a party house. It was too grand. She'd tried to cosy it up when they moved in, lighting fires, rearranging the furniture; living in it alone she'd given up. The grand symmetry defied her. Ludwig House was a mausoleum. A beautiful one, carefully restored, with hope in the grouting between the tiles.

'Hurry up!' The door shivered as it was banged from the other side. 'I'm bursting!'

Becca, in a complicated gold dress, tore in and perched on the toilet, weeing ecstatically as Kate retouched her make-up at the mirror.

'Thank God,' said Kate, 'for eyeliner.' A sweep of brown and her weary eyes woke up. At her feet, Jaffa snuffled and grumbled, nose to the floor. 'Why is Jaffa here?' She'd already tripped over the dim animal a couple of times.

'Jaffa loves a good boogie.'

This was disingenuous. Jaffa, thanks to his habit of leaving small tidy poos as calling cards, was welcome nowhere, but Becca secretly harboured a hope that people talked of her as *that glamorous woman who brings her little dog everywhere.*

'Kate, change into something sexy. You're back on the market.'

'No I'm not.' Kate was happy in her black silk shirt. 'And even if I was, it's all women at this party.'

'So you're saying you only make an effort around men?' Becca loved taking pot shots at what she called Kate's 'so-called feminism'. 'Those women are your homies. They're your crew.'

'Actually, they're my book club.'

Pulling up her thong, Becca said earnestly, 'We're all there for you, hun.'

'One hundred and ten per cent?' Kate anointed her wan cheeks with cream blush. She appreciated the gaggle of women currently conga-ing down her hall. Her friends were a broad church; the twelve party guests included her new assistant, a young woman riddled with piercings, and a standard issue mum of two Kate had met at the gym. They all, in their individual ways, helped her muddle through the current challenging era but, unlike Becca, Kate had never cultivated a gang. Kate needed only a small band around her. The band had shrunk when Dad was picked off by fate's sniper.

And then Julian went.

Kate had expected distance to lend perspective but no, her relationship with Julian still mystified her.

*I still don't know who let who down. Or if either of us did.*

'Giddy up, doll face.' Becca slapped her cousin on the bottom. 'You're not hiding up here all night.'

'I'm not hiding,' said Kate. 'I'm gathering myself.'

'Whatever,' laughed Becca, shoving her out of the (reconditioned) door and back to the raucous charm of the party.

'I will survive!' Cometh the hour, cometh the pop anthem. Gloria Gaynor defined the theme of Becca's party, and the women drowned out the original majestic vocals as they belted out the defiant, optimistic lyrics.

This time of night Kate would normally be stirring a risotto or settling down to ponder the week's accounts. The banks of fairy lights Becca had strung up softened the room in the same way as Kate's preferred candles, but with more wattage, more oomph: should Becca ever become Queen of Everything she would illuminate the entire world with fairy lights.

Not convinced that the island's worktop would withstand dancing heels, Kate left Becca up there: this time next week the house's new owners would gut the entire building.

A text arrived.

I assume it's safe to ask if you've already had your surprise?

Kate replied:

The joint is jumping!

The response landed immediately.

Are you drunk yet?

Kate typed:

Funny you should ask – I'm the only one who isn't!

As Kate waited for another text the phone rang and she took it into the drawing room. Seating herself on a packing crate, she put the mobile to her ear.

'Silly to keep texting,' said Charlie. 'Seriously, do you hate the party?'

'No,' laughed Kate. 'I love parties. Why would I hate it?'

'Maybe because a divorce party is the worst idea I've ever heard.'

On the dancefloor, Becca had shouted over the music, telling Kate how she'd ignored Charlie's attempts to talk her out of organising a surprise party.

'Becca means well.'

'I know that. But opening bottles of bubbly because you and Julian have broken up seems, well, flippant.'

'I can do flippant.' Although she was grateful for Charlie's concern, she didn't like the person it described. As if Kate was an old lady, too sweet and vulnerable for the hurly burly of society.

'You're exceptionally good at flippant. But a divorce party . . .' Charlie let out a frustrated growl. 'I said to Becca, not *everything* is an excuse for a bash.'

'I love my divorce party. So there.'

'Fibber.'

Kate *wanted* to love it. She wanted to be the Kate she once was, the fresh-out-of-the-box version, who couldn't hear music without getting on down with her bad self. She sighed, half laughing. 'I just want to go to bed.'

'Me too.' Charlie gave a short laugh. 'Not with you. That came out wrong.'

Laughing along with him – what choice did she have? – Kate found the idea of going to bed and finding Charlie in it rather lovely. 'You know I'm travelling back with your missus tomorrow? Unless you're sick of me.'

'Never. We can take Flo horse riding again if your bottom's up to it.'

Kate closed her eyes and heard the rhythmic complaint of the saddle, the plod of hooves, Charlie's involuntary fearful exclamations when his sleepy steed tossed its head, all to a backdrop of non-stop commentary from five-year-old Flo: 'Look a little bird hello birdy she's flying about and now she's gone.'

Miraculously, Flo resembled Charlie. As if he loved her enough to make her long straight hair grow darker, and her eyebrows arrange themselves as two orderly brushstrokes. 'I can't think of anything nicer.'

'I'll let you get back to your posse,' laughed Charlie. 'I don't really know what to say. Happy divorce?'

'That's a lovely sentiment.' *I wish you were here*, Kate added silently, as if hoping he would develop telepathic powers.

'It's going to be fine, Kate, really.' Charlie changed the tone. 'I believe you've done the right thing.'

Returning to the dancefloor, Kate welcomed the music and the movement and the ribald singing. They offered her some camouflage, a noisy place where she didn't have to wonder about whether she was doing the right thing or the wrong thing. *I did the only thing I could.*

A couple of hours later, with some of the 'crew' departed, the diehards kicked off their shoes and arranged themselves around the kitchen table.

'To girl power!' Becca lifted her glass in a toast.

'To old bag power!' Mum of Two lifted her glass; Kate liked her more and more.

The prosecco that seemed to spring spontaneously from rocks in Becca's wake had mellowed Kate. *This*, she thought, *is what this kitchen is for: people coming together.*

Her assistant read a text on her BlackBerry that made her shoulders droop. Only messages from her feckless boyfriend had that effect on her. 'Men are gits,' she said.

'True.' Becca turned to Kate. 'Don't make that face. They are. All of them have the potential for git-like behaviour. Even your perfect Charlie.'

'*My* perfect Charlie?' As Kate spoke, she buried her face in her glass, hoping her pinkness could be attributed to the wine.

'St Charlie, who puts up so patiently with his loony wife. He has his moments.' Becca folded her arms, a stance approved by the women in their family when complaining about the men in their family.

Before Becca could go on, Kate's assistant took down a framed photograph from a shelf and asked, 'Who are these lovely people?' Skilled at protecting Kate from tricky customers in the shops, she was now doing the same thing at home.

*I must sort her out a pay rise*, thought Kate, saying, 'That's the staff and children of Yulan House. That jeep they're standing around was paid for with funds I raised in memory of my dad.'

Feminine exclamations of sympathetic delight showered down on Kate. *Women*, she thought, *are such a good audience.*

'They do amazing work there. Life changing things are routine. Some of the children they take in are abandoned because they have disabilities, or because of the Chinese one child law that doesn't allow families to have more than one baby. No matter what the reason, however ill the child is, Yulan House never turns anybody away.'

'That's so beautiful.' Mum of Two was touched.

'What's even more beautiful,' said Kate, 'is the way the staff treat the kids. My dad got to know the owner quite well. From afar, obviously. Jia Tang makes sure emotional needs are met, not just practical ones. So the children are safe and fed and warm and educated and, well, *loved*. She started the place thirty years ago and she's still there every day, devoting herself to them.'

'*That's* girl power,' murmured Kate's assistant.

Becca said, 'Uncle John would be so proud of you.'

'While he was alive I didn't appreciate Jia Tang, how

extraordinary her work is. I just went along with it because it made Dad happy. Now it's part of my life. I'm helping them scrape together the dosh for a new play area.'

'I'll help!' said Mum of Two.

Becca said, 'Kate, you've done enough. They can't expect any more from you.'

'They don't expect a thing.' Like Mum, Becca distrusted Kate's commitment to the orphanage, believing it to be an unhealthy manifestation of mourning. 'How often can you feel like you're making a genuine difference? When you see disaster and poverty and pain on the news, don't you wish you could reach out and help in some small way? To say *You're not alone; I care?*'

'Calm down, cuz. You're not saving the planet!'

When Kate's assistant bridled, Kate quelled her with a look. Kate and Becca were as close as sisters, which meant that sometimes they were as rude as sisters.

Perversely (that could be Becca's middle name) Becca had chosen to echo Mum's attitude, treating Jia Tang as a rival, as if the love and care Kate showed Yulan House detracted somehow from what she gave to those closer to hand.

The promise Kate had made during the funeral, to hold Mum tight, had been kept. She was a dutiful daughter, calling her mother every day, visiting often, sharing the heavy lifting as Mum adjusted to life as a widow. Beyond a casual mention, they didn't talk about Dad.

For proper, in-depth nostalgia, Kate went to Charlie, who was always ready to reminisce. The subject he avoided, with even more diligence than Mum avoided the subject of Dad, was the kiss.

The push-me-pull-you embrace on the bench outside the hospital had un-happened. They never mentioned it. It was the elephant in the room with them; it was the elephant that went horse riding with them.

During their cousinly heart-to-hearts, Becca would sometimes say, 'I always expected Julian to cheat on you. I would have killed him with my bare hands if he did.'

There seemed to be a tacit agreement underpinning these chats that Charlie would never do anything so low as betray his wife. He was, apparently, above suspicion. Kate had turned that over in her mind as Becca castigated Julian. At times over the past year, Charlie had seemed ready to make a pronouncement, as if he was working himself up to proclaim something.

*Spit it out!* she'd silently beg. Tired of translating signals, of dissecting that one outbreak of physical action, Kate needed words from Charlie. Something to chew on. The naked truth without the dos and don'ts forced on them by their situation.

With the pathetic crumbs she had to go on, Kate veered from blushing at schoolgirlish notions that he could ever desire her to certainty that he loved her.

The obvious solution – to stop turning it over in her mind, to step away – was not open to her.

*Speak to me, Charlie*, she pleaded, even as he was speaking to her. *I'm not fragile. I won't break.*

No declaration had been made. Charlie was the faithful man his wife believed him to be, and Kate admired him for that. That she wanted him, at some deep level that was impervious to common sense, was true; what was also true was that Kate needed all her loved ones to be safe and content. Or as much of either as is possible. She couldn't build her own happiness on the broken backs of Becca and Flo. And neither could Charlie.

This was one of the many reasons Kate loved him.

Perversely was also *her* middle name.


The music was over. The house was dark, apart from the fairy lights doggedly sparkling in the kitchen. Having waved off her last guest, Kate returned to the kitchen table and Becca.

The leftovers of the party food looked irresistible, as leftovers do. 'Mmm, salami,' purred Kate, dropping a fat coin into her mouth.

'It's about babies really, isn't it?'

'What is?' Kate reached for a gobbet of brie. '*Star Trek*? Algebra?'

Refusing to be deflected, Becca assumed her most sage expression and pointed at Kate with her glass. 'Your obsession with Yulan House is about babies.'

'I wouldn't call it an obsession.' Kate chased the last olive around the platter.

'Babies. Babies. Babies.' Becca leaned forward. 'Be honest with me.'

'I always am.' 99.9 per cent of the time Kate was straight with Becca. Only one dark little closet was closed to her cousin, the one where she kept her feelings for Charlie. They were resilient little buggers, these feelings; locking them up hadn't killed them off. They thrived on a starvation diet.

'If you had a child of your own you wouldn't have this urge to save the kiddiwinks of the world. You'd have more than enough to do, believe me.' Becca made motherhood sound like endless toil, as if she was a sweatshop factory worker and not an indulged yummy mummy with a hands-on husband. 'There are ways to have them on your own. You don't need a man any more.'

'So you're saying I can't attract a bloke?' Kate savoured Becca's consternation: to Becca this was the vilest of slurs. Kate measured her self-worth in other ways. *Just as well, as I'm fairly certain I* can't *attract a bloke.* Her equipment was rusty.

'You know that's not what I meant. Any man would be lucky to have you,' said Becca. 'Especially now you've lost a bit of weight. But why would you want a man? We've agreed they're all pigs.'

'Have we? I don't remember that vote.'

'You're telling me Julian isn't a knob?'

'I am telling you, hand on heart, that my husband is not a knob.'

'Ex-husband.' Becca pointed to the decree nisi she'd taped to the wall.

'Nobody behaves well in a divorce. The process is too adversarial.'

'Your divorce was more adversari-whatsit than most.'

'This is old ground,' said Kate.

'Julian was greedy and nasty and he almost ruined you.'

It wasn't Becca's trademark hyperbole; trapped in the burning rubble of Ames Partners in Property, Julian had staked a claim on what he'd previously insisted was Kate's money. Staring bankruptcy in the face, he clawed at Kate, exacting pound after pound of flesh. He'd been so determined, so brutal, so unlike his former incarnation that she entertained a dark suspicion that the serpentine deals collapsing all around him were less than lilywhite: the cash was desperately needed to plug up the holes and keep Julian out of jail.

She had never ring-fenced her income. The money was a by-product of Kate's zeal, theirs to share. She'd offered it to Julian many times in the past, to bail them out before the debts became unwieldy.

The lawyer had called this 'naive'. Kate called it . . . she had no word for it; it was simply what couples *did*, surely?

'He'll come for you like a rottweiler,' said the lawyer.

'We were married,' Kate had said, wondering what had happened to the lawyer to make him so cynical. 'It's only money.'

The cynical lawyer had been proved right. Kate felt as if she'd been mugged. The girl in the dated wedding photographs was a foreigner.

*Did I really believe it was forever?*

Standing to put glasses in the dishwasher, Becca said, 'This stunning house . . . I could weep.'

'It's not as if I'm homeless.' Kate had politely declined Becca's repeated offers to move into Dragonfly Cottage. The offers had been so frequent and so impassioned they'd begun to sound like threats. A bland rental round the corner had been secured. The furniture was headed for storage. Kate would miss her books.

'Your new flat's a shit hole. Julian has a lot to answer for.'

'The divorce is finally over. That's the main thing.'

When Becca, Mum and Aunty Marjorie got together they cackled like Macbeth's witches, casting spells of female disgust and calling down calamitous revenge on Julian's head.

'I hope the rest of his stupid hair falls out,' said Becca, aiming an empty bottle at the swing topped bin.

'Don't!' Kate never joined in with the witchy bitchery. Julian's monstrous behaviour had only started after his attempts to haggle a trial reunion. His actions thereafter had been fuelled by pain. Kate had broken his heart, just as surely as Becca had wrenched off Action Man's head. The tortuous divorce was one long scream of *Why don't you love me?*

As an aficionado of how it feels to love the wrong person, Kate couldn't hate Julian for what he'd done.

'If he was even half a man,' said Becca, 'he'd have just walked away.' Chin down, she was muttering like Kate remembered her doing when some kid at school had upset her. 'They're all vampires, every one of them, sucking the life out of us. Leave it long enough and they all betray us in the end.' Becca sniffed. 'The funny thing is, I'm not even angry about it.'

'About what?' Kate stacked the plates.

'I keep thinking I'm angry, but I'm not. I'm scared.'

'Of what?' Kate looked up, engaged. Becca rarely admitted to fear.

Becca lifted her eyes to Kate's. 'My husband's in love with somebody else.'

Kate felt the floor tilt. 'What?' she said stupidly. 'Charlie wouldn't . . .'

'He bloody would and he bloody has.'

Later it would feel laughable that for a split second Kate thought Becca was referring to her. 'How do you know? You do jump to conclusions, Becca.'

'They've been at it like rabbits. There's an email trail. Spare me the lecture about reading other people's emails,

Kate. If Charlie doesn't want me to pry he shouldn't have the dog's name as his password.'

'It's a real affair?'

'A real affair, with sex and hotels and quickies in the back of the car.' Becca pulled a disgusted face. '*Our* car. The car I use to take Flo to soft play!'

'Who is she?'

'She's the biggest slut in West Sussex. They met on a creative writing retreat. I told you that book was trouble! He starts every email with *To my dark lady*. So she's got black hair, I guess. I haven't seen a photo.'

'That's from Shakespeare.'

'Him again,' sighed Becca, as if Shakespeare was a nosey neighbour who kept popping in for a cup of tea.

'Shakespeare dedicated his sonnets to the dark lady.' Kate could quote the sonnets only because of eavesdropping on Charlie and Dad. 'It's not to do with the colour of her hair.' Kate went no further. Becca wouldn't want to hear that the dark lady was a complex, mysterious figure whose allure was powerful enough to enmesh poor Will even though he knew it was wrong to love her.

'It's a stupid name,' said Becca, petulant.

'Yeah.' Kate thought it wildly romantic. She was sad, very sad, that she would live and die without a man ever calling her his dark lady. 'Julian used to call me Boobalicious.'

Laughter broke over them like a wave. Heads back, cackling brazenly, they slapped the table.

'Oh . . . oh,' gasped Becca as they came down.

Wiping her eyes, Kate said, 'What are you going to do?'

'I'm going to kill him.'

'No, really, what are you going to do?'

'I'm really going to kill him.'

They laughed again, but without the same abandon.

'I don't have to do anything,' said Becca. 'According to the emails he's going to leave me. Us. Me and Flo. Charlie doesn't want us any more.'

Back to back in the big sleigh bed, Kate and Becca slept together as they had done so many times in their history.

'It'll all work out.' Kate whispered the ever useful shibboleth as she turned out the lamp.

In her dream she walked down an endless corridor. She woke before it was light and watched the patterns made on the ceiling by the headlights of the occasional passing car.

That pregnant feeling, the sense that Charlie had something to divulge: Kate had been right about that. Her certainty that he was unable to betray his little family had been misplaced.

Plainly, Charlie was perfectly capable of loving another woman. He just wasn't capable of loving Kate.

The shop, on the intersection of two narrow roads, was the
cornerstone of Kate's empire. Her first, her favourite, she'd
come through its door as a Saturday girl in her early teens.
The old shop had been chaotic and gloomy, with a stockroom that defied her efforts to streamline it. The day she
bought it Kate had begun the process of ripping everything
out, commissioning box shelving and painting everything a
celestial white.

Called in at short notice to cover for her flu-stricken
manager, Kate was enjoying a day behind the counter. Like

the fond husband of a plastic surgery devotee, she remembered the shop's original, more homely looks with fondness.

'No, those don't go there!' Her temporary assistant was hopeless. Too short to reach the shelves and prone to tearing open whatever took her fancy. 'Come and help me test these whistles, Flo!'

Flo's emphatic advice was useful when customers dithered in Fancy Dress Corner. 'Don't be a princess,' she said. 'Princesses are sissies.' In combat trews and a camouflage tee, Flo defied her mother's attempts to pretty her up. Often mistaken for a boy, she liked her dark hair kept short, glossy as a surfacing seal.

The night before, Becca had come to Kate's for supper, a weekly staple in their diaries. In between over the top compliments – 'Kate, that lipstick gives you a mouth like Marilyn Monroe' – and her usual carping – 'When are you going to leave this blah rental and buy a proper home?' – Becca had touched on a subject she returned to from time to time.

'I'm going to tell him.' She'd cut into her steak with gusto. 'I am. I'm going to tell my sodding ex that Flo isn't his.'

'No, you're not. You only say that after a few vinos.'

'He should know. It's only right.'

This high and mighty reasoning had been absent when Flo was conceived. 'Today you had another row with

Charlie, so you want to lash out. You know the person you'd hurt most is Flo, so you're not going to do it.' Kate had popped a chip into her mouth. 'So let's change the subject. Who's in love with you this week?'

A fan of internet dating, Becca was evangelical about its delights. Not for Becca a toe in the water: she immersed herself up to her neck, seducing whoever took her fancy.

Such promiscuousness had gone down badly with the older generation. Kate's mother declared it 'a cry for help', but Kate couldn't perceive any sadness in Becca's stream-of-consciousness tales of rumpy pumpy. It was obvious to Kate that Becca would return to Charlie in the blink of an eye, but her cousin was canny enough to accept that when such a mild mannered man reached the end of his generous tether there was no going back. So, instead, Becca went through *males/25–50/gsoh* like a hot knife through butter. Careful to keep her hectic love life from Flo, there were no gentlemen callers at home: Flo's stability was a priority for both parents throughout and after the divorce.

'I think I've found somebody,' Becca had beamed. 'He's a cameraman. Works on some news programme, I think. I wasn't listening. Too busy working out when to pounce. He's nuts about me.'

'Who isn't?'

Becca assumed that birds sang in her honour. *Perhaps,* Kate had thought, *they do.*

Having both gone through the mill of divorce, the women's recovery times differed. Kate had floundered longer in the initial stages of self-doubt, which included a conviction that cats (cats she did not yet own) would one day feast on her undiscovered corpse.

The emotional loneliness they both faced had nothing to do with the number of friends they could call on. The pursuit of love, of connection with a special 'other' was keenly felt even by Kate, who spelled romance with a small 'r'.

The cameraman beau would be history next week. Entirely male in her approach to love and sex, Becca moved on speedily once she'd made a conquest.

By comparison, Kate was not merely female but Victorian female: she had at first regarded dating websites with spin-sterish horror.

'Charlie and Julian are sorted.' Becca had typed in Kate's profile, hands flying like a dressage pony's hooves. 'High time us girls were fixed up.'

Intentionally ignorant of any details about Julian's new girlfriend, Kate was disconcerted by how much his newfound *amour* dented her pride.

From a new flame's point of view, Julian was a keeper. Even during the divorce, when Kate could have papered her walls with legal demands, she'd never shaken the suspicion that life had handed her a diamond and she'd treated it like a rhinestone. If another woman could love Julian without wanting him to be somebody else entirely, he was indeed a gem.

Like Mum's icon, the sad princess, there had been three people in Kate's marriage.

Sometimes, when out shopping with Becca, or standing in line at the cinema, Kate fantasised about turning to her cousin and saying, 'My enduring love for your ex-husband has blighted my life.'

In the here and now, the cheerful *ding!* of the shop door delivered a flustered Charlie. 'Am I late?' Full of sorries, he explained that his consultancy session had run on, and bent to catch his breath just as Flo launched herself at him.

Kate asked, 'Did you leave your skateboard outside?'

'Ha and also ha.' Charlie grabbed his daughter and blew raspberries on her cheek. He had built up an immunity to Kate's digs about his 'second teen-hood'. The boyish blazer one size too small, the spotless trainers and the choppy hair-cut were red rags to a bull.

'Where were you, Daddy?'

'I was out working, sweetiepops.'

'How was it?' Kate picked up streamers and confetti that Flo had 'tidied'. 'Grim?'

'I can't complain. It pays the bills while I vomit out my book.' Forced into media consultancy work by the demands of supporting two households, Charlie's euphoria at nabbing a literary agent had been tempered by the flock of rejection letters. 'Sometimes I don't know if I'm a novelist who writes ads on the side, or an advertising consultant who writes novels on the side.'

'Compromise makes the world go round.' Kate had *compromise* tattooed on her soul.

'I made my own bed,' said Charlie, setting down Flo. 'Now I'm lying on it.' He frowned. 'Thanks for babysitting. Again. Have I made you late? I know it's a big night tonight.'

Kate looked at her watch. 'Keep me company while I get ready.' She signalled to Flo, and the child, with great ceremony, carried out her special job of turning over the sign on the door to read 'Closed'.

Brewing coffee, Charlie talked through the changing room curtain as Kate slipped out of her work wear. 'The shop looks brilliant. I love the sweets in bowls on the counter.'

'They're the ones I stock for party bags. If people try them they're more likely to buy.'

'Sound business sense allied to a feel-good vibe. The Pastel Tycoon strikes again.'

Kate liked it when he called her that.

'Can you take Flo same time next week? These guys want me back.'

'I'd love to, but I'm in Manchester for a trade fair. You know I'd cancel if I could but—'

'Don't be daft. We rely on you too much as it is. I'll see if Becca can change her plans.' Charlie lowered his voice so Flo, absorbed in an ant she'd met, couldn't hear. 'It'll only be a date with some jerk she's met on the internet.'

Shucking off her jeans, Kate asked, 'Is that the green-eyed monster I hear, Mr Garland?'

'You know it's not.' Much to Becca's chagrin, Charlie was resolutely unjealous. She'd prophesied he'd fall apart without her: he'd lost half a stone and visited Cuba. 'I just wish she'd ease up a bit.'

'Plus you worry about her.' Kate knew that Becca was under strict instructions to call Charlie when she reached home after each assignation.

'You hear stories. Just because we're not married any more doesn't mean I want her dumped in a ditch by some psycho.'

Kate jumped at the movement of the curtain as Charlie handed in a mug.

'Don't panic, Kate. I'm averting my eyes.'

The way Charlie treated her as a 'mate' sometimes irked Kate. The new bra – a purchase overseen by Becca – did its job expertly: her breasts were twin lacy lifeboats. Charlie had been the first male to see her in her undies; now it was forbidden, or a joke. Maybe both.

'Is this the second or third date with Walter?'

'*Warren*. Fifth.' Kate pulled up the zip on the black column dress and neatened the sheer sleeves. Tucking a diamante pin in her hasty up-do, she agreed with Becca: that last little touch made all the difference. She allowed the woman in the mirror a brief burst of virtual applause. At the ripe old age of thirty-three she'd forgotten she could still pull it out of the bag when called upon.

'Fifth?' Charlie whistled. 'Getting serious. When do I get to meet him? Give him the *if you ever hurt her I'll break every bone in your body* speech?'

'You're as bad as Becca. Five dates equals three restaurant meals, one blockbuster movie and a picnic. How can that be serious?' Kate and Warren worked well on email and in flirty texts but less well face to face. She knew the reserve was all on her side.

'What does he do for a living?'

Kate let out a small cry when she couldn't find her fancy shoes in her overnight bag. Locating a heel with her fingers, she relaxed and said, 'He's a talent agent. Represents actors.'

'Anybody famous?'

'That's what everybody asks.' Kate stepped out in her finery.

'Wow!' said Charlie.

'You look like a thuperthar!' yelled Flo.

'This William's a lucky guy.'

'*Warren*.' Whatever his name, the guy was about to get very lucky indeed.

Becca had torn through Kate's tissue-thin reason for not committing to anything, be it man or flat. 'You can't *keep* blaming overwork for being in this faceless flat a year on, or for being so single your downstairs has healed over. You've lost your mojo.' She'd waved a finger at Kate. 'It's only sex!'

Tonight, Kate had invited her mojo along.

Sitting on the counter, looking younger than his years, Charlie asked, 'Where's he taking you dressed like *that*?'

'To a country house weekend party.'

'Like *Gosford Park*?'

'I hope not. It's a gang of close friends. Every so often they get together and hire a mansion for the weekend. There's a chef. Organised games. Long walks.'

'Sounds . . .' Charlie wrinkled his nose. '. . . awful.'

'Warren's a nice guy. I'm looking forward to it.'

'I know that face. It's your *I'd rather be curled up with a good book* face. Sharing a room?'

'None of your biz.'

'That means you are.'

Kate waited for him to say something that hinted at envy. She waited in vain.

'It'll give me a chance,' she said, 'to get to know him better.' Much better. With no clothes on.

Well built and rugged, Warren towered over Kate. The kisses they'd shared were delicious; the memory of them played a tune down her backbone. It was time to 'go exclusive' as Becca put it: after tonight Kate would cancel her one outstanding internet date with another prospective suitor. She would open up to the possibility of something real happening by allowing the laid back but self-assured Warren to fling her about a bed.

The shrill innocence of an urgent question from Flo shut down this nascent sensual daydream.

'How many sicks have you done in your whole life?' Without waiting for an answer, Flo scuttled to her favourite spot, a niche under the counter where she played a rolling, complex game nobody else understood.

'So,' said Charlie. 'How many sicks *have* you done?' He tailed Kate as she tucked in the shop for the night, locking away the cash float, righting the shelves.

'Are you attempting a beard?' she asked.

'I prefer the word *grow*.'

'Please don't.'

'Get with it, Grandma. All the dudes are into facial hair.'

'Exactly.'

'Are you inferring I'm not a dude? I have to do my best. As you and Becca constantly point out, I have a much, much, much younger girlfriend to impress.'

'I don't think we use three muches.'

The ten year difference in age, not a particularly startling gap, moved Becca to refer to Charlie's lover as 'your school friend'. Editorial assistant for a fashion magazine, Lucy was actually garlanded with degrees and qualifications.

'Are you and Lucy on an even keel again?'

'Yeah. It was just a blip, like you said.'

The autopsy of Charlie's big row with Lucy had kept a yawning Kate up half the night. A throwaway comment he'd made about one of her friends had started it all. 'But, Kate,' Charlie had said in his own defence, 'the guy wears a *sarong*!' She'd heard fear in his voice; he'd thought he was losing Lucy.

'Thanks for lending me your shoulder to cry on. Can't believe it'll be two years in November. Lucy and me, I mean.'

'I can believe it.'

'I thought she was just a catalyst, giving me the courage to stand up to Becca.' Charlie glanced at his daughter but she was lost in her make believe. 'And yes, I know how self-ish that sounds, but I didn't think I was capable of jumping feet first into another full-on romantic situation. I thought I needed time to regroup, and heal.'

At one point Kate would have stored away that nugget, translating it as the reason Charlie hadn't turned to her when his marriage crumbled, but she'd stopped combing his conversation for clues. 'I knew it was something special. When it all came out, when you talked about your dark lady, I could see it in your eyes.'

'Really?' Charlie smiled inwardly at that. 'Becca still thinks it's a pervy thing. Cos of Lucy's age.'

'A man like you would never leave his wife and child for a pair of perky boobs.'

'Ouch. Don't put it like that. I didn't leave Flo. She's a few feet away, playing houses. I can imagine what your dad would have to say.' He looked at his feet, shifty suddenly.

'So can I.' Kate heaved a box of *Keep Calm and Party On* napkins onto a high ledge, before wiping dust from her evening dress. 'He'd say you should follow your heart.' Charlie's face told Kate he couldn't let her get away with such hokum. 'He'd also say you're a damn silly bugger.'

Still a constant in Kate's life, her image of her dad had grown vague. Sometimes she woke up in a panic, unable to picture his face. When she composed herself and shut her eyes, he always returned, bringing relief and a yearning so deep it felt like a physical pain. 'Look at this photo I unearthed at Mum's.'

'He was a handsome sod when he was young.' Charlie grinned at the faded snap, one corner of it torn. 'Look at you!'

Younger than Flo, a chubby kneed Kate and her father were caught in the midst of a fit of giggles. Every over-saturated detail was dated, from the frenetic wallpaper to the long collar on her mustachioed dad's paisley shirt. She saw everything she missed in his face. His depth and his soul and his lightness of touch. 'This is my favourite photo of him.'

'Even then he had a thing about China.' Charlie pointed to the coffee table in the picture. 'Look. A Chinese teapot.'

'I hadn't noticed that.' Kate peered at the distinctive squat pottery shape. 'I must scan it and send it to Jia Tang.'

Now in monthly email touch, Kate and Jia Tang lived different lifestyles but had much in common. Or so Kate hoped: she aspired to Jia Tang's strength of character.

'He'd be chuffed about what you do for Yulan House,' said Charlie, still studying the picture. He, too, could get nostalgic about the past and the people who'd been airbrushed from their present.

'I suppose he would.' That wasn't why Kate did it. She was no Chinese themed Miss Havisham, walled up with dead dreams. 'But it's not a memorial to him. That'd be creepy. I love the orphanage.' Yulan House gave Kate far more than she put in. 'When I look back,' said Kate, 'I was possibly the only ten year old in our neighbourhood who was an expert in China's one child policy.' The plight of ordinary people being fined for having more than one baby had touched her father deeply. He'd told Kate about the punishments meted out, about homes being seized, about 'unregistered' children being ineligible for school. Ten-year-old Kate had thought that sounded like a bonus but Dad had put her straight. 'He wanted me to have empathy. To care,' she said.

The shop door opened.

'Sorry!' shouted Kate. 'We're closed!'

It was Lucy. Definitely not a dark lady, more a sunny lady. No stereotype younger hottie, she had a pixie cut and men's shoes, but was still demonstrably young and lovely enough to validate the teasing of Charlie.

'Hi! Hi hi hi!' Lucy's arrival was noisy. Kate had noticed this in younger people, the tendency to arrive with maximum cheek kissing and hugging and extravagant welcomes. As she bent to accept Lucy's embrace she made a mental note to stop lumping herself with the older generation. Around Lucy, so effortlessly trendy, it was easy to think of herself as a dinosaur.

'You look *amazing*!' Lucy's lavish praise – it came with clasped hands and gasps – was also typical of her age group.

'Lu-cee!' Flo threw herself at the girl. 'Come to the wee-wees with me!'

'Yay!' Lucy let herself be led by the hand to the bathroom at the back of the shop.

No kiss for Charlie: the couple were careful to rope off demonstrations of affection until Flo was out of the way.

'She's so good with Flo,' said Kate. Taking Flo to the toilet was something even her besotted godmother dreaded. It was a long affair, entailing rambling stories about Flo's imaginary friend, wet pants, and toilet roll all over the floor, culminating in a standoff when Flo refused to wash her hands.

It would be obvious to hate Lucy but Kate wasn't up to the job. Lucy was not to blame for the end of a marriage that had been riddled with dry rot from the beginning. Just as she was not to blame for her chic hair, her bottom that managed to be both small but insistent, and the ten year head start that made Kate look like The Thing from the Crypt when they were photographed together. It was impossible to dislike a woman (Kate knew Lucy was more than a 'girl') so outgoing, so kind.

Lucy had admitted her terror at meeting Kate, and not only because Kate was the devastated wife's cousin and best friend. 'I could tell how important you are to Charlie. If you hadn't approved, it would have been curtains.'

Kate *had* approved. So much so that she and Lucy had a friendship of their own. She saw what Charlie saw in Lucy. Sweetness and strength. And somebody to look after. 'Two years?' she said as Charlie washed up their mugs. 'If Lucy was more pushy she'd wonder why you're not living together.'

Very quickly, treading on the heels of her sentence, Charlie said, 'She knows I'm never getting married again. Things are good the way they are.'

Charlie wasn't the sort to dabble in love. Kate waited for him to speak and he did. 'Flo's had more than enough upheaval in her little life.'

'Flo's fine. And she loves Lucy.' Or *My Lucy* as Flo referred to her.

'Lucy loves her,' said Charlie tenderly.

Shrewdly, Lucy had accepted Charlie and Flo as a unit. Loving a divorcee who shared access with a capricious

ex-wife meant their affair was compromised by his obliga-
tions from the beginning. He was often unavailable to her,
but she'd never questioned Flo's status in the pecking order,
or gone head to head with Becca. *To go through all that*,
thought Kate, *Lucy must love Charlie a lot.*

Charlie dried the mug, badly, and put it back in the wrong
place. 'What if she's a symptom of my . . . what did you call
it?'

'Your early onset midlife crisis? I was only teasing. You
make it too easy for me, with your soft top car and your new
six pack and—'

'A gorgeous bird on my arm?'

That was very un-Charlie language. 'We all know Lucy's
much more than that. Just relax and let it fall into place. Face
it, mate, you love being in love.'

'I do.' Charlie held up his hands as if under arrest.

'Love suits you. I can't imagine you playing the field.'

'I'm not sure I know where the field is.'

Kate found the field chilly.

Flo burst out of the bathroom, leading Lucy by the hand.

'I should get going,' said Kate, casting about for her evening bag.

'Hang on.' Lucy dug in her own tote. 'I borrowed these
from the shoot today.' She slapped Charlie when he frowned.
'OK, I *stole* them.' She handed over a pair of enamelled ear-
rings, chrome chimes hanging from them.

'Perfect.' Kate clipped them to her lobes, noting how Lucy pecked Charlie on the cheek as Flo danced about their legs. How long could this puritanical reserve last? Could it, *should* it, last forever? Kate wondered if Lucy wanted babies of her own.

Turning away, Kate loathed her unwanted insider knowledge. Neither Charlie nor Lucy were aware that Charlie was incapable of giving her a baby. They could waste years trying before turning to alternative methods. Was it right or wrong not to tell them? Kate had consulted her oracle, Dad, and decided to cross that bridge when they all came to it.

'Do you approve of my bag?' Kate held it against her, glad to have a fashion maven on tap. Disloyally, Kate welcomed Lucy's input more than Becca's; the latter tended towards the low-cut and the high-hemmed, her only criteria whether or not it rendered the wearer 'hot'.

'I love it. Very nineties. I have sooo much retro in my evening bag collection.'

*Retro?* The bag, which constituted Kate's entire evening bag collection, had been a present from Charlie back in 1995. She'd dug it out from the back of a drawer and dusted it off, glad to see it again after a long absence in fashion Siberia. It rarely went out; its last excursion had been to Dad's funeral. Tonight it would enter a whole different world; the bag was on its way to its very first country house weekend party.

★    ★    ★

The table, like the room, referenced the glamour and formality of a bygone age. Kate, who'd worried she might be over-dressed, now felt a little dressed down.

Under cover of the tablecloth, Warren's hand was on her thigh. He seemed to have intuited her intentions: maybe they were better suited than she realised. Amid the clamour of conversation, Warren whispered just behind her ear so that his breath tickled.

Touching the nape of her neck, bared by her pinned-up hair, he said, 'Sexy. I like it.'

Kate looked into his eyes, emboldened. He'd never been so frank before.

Their hostess, Helen, orchestrated the table with an archness that seemed very studied to Kate. She interrupted them now, with a tap on her glass. 'Now now, you two. At least finish dinner before you get to grips with one another.'

*She's got history with Warren*, thought Kate, looking up to find Helen's sparkling, calculating eyes on her. She took another forkful of delicious food: it was ambrosial, but there wasn't enough of it. Everything else on the table was super-abundant: heavy blossoms spilled from oversized vases; the wine sat like blood in crystal decanters; fat candles dripped wax from many-armed candelabra. The green and gold edges of the opulent room were dark, but Kate and the other guests were well, if favourably, lit by the candles.

Different tonight, Warren was revved up, intent. The other guests, all smart and professional types with perfect manners and ready conversation, seemed to share this electric feeling. Kate giggled at the jokes, even if they were a little heavy on the double entendres for her taste.

'You've got, like, incredible eyes.' The woman opposite, a frail thing in couture, spoke suddenly to Kate. 'Hasn't she?' With jerky movements, she gestured at the others to appraise Kate.

*She's high*, thought Kate.

'Kate's a peach,' said Warren. His smile was wolfish. Kate, who hadn't been devoured for quite some time, thought of bedtime and smiled back at him.

'Before dessert, a little fun.' Helen stood up and handed something to the man to her left, then continued around the table, giving each diner a bejewelled mask, the Venetian design that sits on the nose and disguises just the upper half of the face.

Kate took hers.

'Blue,' said Helen. 'For our novitiate's beautiful eyes.' She took Kate's hand and kissed it.

Glad she'd been able to suppress her snort, Kate looked forward to telling Becca about the weirdo mistress of ceremonies.

'Dessert,' said Warren, 'is always something special here.' Behind his coal black mask his eyes glittered.

'There'd better be custard,' whispered Kate. 'Or I'll complain.'

'If that's what you want, Helen will arrange it.' He didn't seem to get the joke: Kate wouldn't dream of asking for custard at such a table. He kissed her suddenly, and hard.

As her neck bent back, Kate felt the force of his mouth against hers, and swooned pleasurably. She pulled away, unwilling to kiss too passionately in company. 'Later.' She squeezed his leg.

He gave a little growl, more lupine than ever, and Kate felt something drop away deep inside her. A dessert lover, she would happily forgo custard to be alone with Warren. He was going to be *wild* when they finally escaped these peculiar friends he liked so much.

'I must powder my nose.' Kate stood. The twee language felt appropriate for the *fin de siècle* splendour of the house.

'Hurry back!' called her stoned admirer from across the table, her tiger-striped mask pushed back into her hair.

Nose powdered, Kate explored.

Mostly unlit, the house was a dark Pandora's Box of jewel-like rooms with gilded cornices overhead and plush rugs underfoot. A door led to another door and another until Kate was on the terrace at the back of the house, grateful for the sweet fresh air she hadn't realised she needed.

No light punctured the darkness in the grounds that wrapped around the house. Kate had driven through a tight tangle of lanes to reach it; it stood at the centre of its domain. She remembered how keen Warren had been to collect her in his sporty car. *I like to get to places under my own steam*, she'd insisted. He was an assertive man; he'd pushed. When Kate had pushed back, he'd liked it.

'You're an independent little thing, aren't you?' he'd said.

Kate didn't know any other way to be. And she'd corrected him: 'I'm not little.'

He'd liked that as well.

*The others will be wondering where I am.* Kate turned, but her feet were reluctant to leave the terrace. On the brink of a form of commitment to Warren, she was rooted to the spot. Drawn to the virile, attractive man, Kate also felt a repulsion she couldn't explain.

Out of step with many – Becca for one – Kate took sex seriously. It was an emotional contract for her, some-thing profound. She desired Warren; it wasn't prudery that got in her way. It was something else. A subliminal Stop sign.

*Kate*, she told herself. *Get back in there and jump on him.* She needed to climb out of her rut. She was a mindless hamster in a cage, working all hours, breaking off only to babysit a goddaughter or visit a mother who picked a fight every time.

*I need somebody to call my own.* A man she didn't have to share. One who returned her desire.

Such a man was only feet away. Stirred, back on course, Kate rooted in her bag for a breath mint as she hurried back across the terrace. Her fingers found paper.

Kate was heartily sick of that note. During the funeral she'd resolved to tear it into tiny pieces and throw it away, but in the vortex of grief and grim practicalities she'd forgotten. The damn thing certainly chose its moments to jump out at her.

*But this is a new era.*

Charlie, despite his feeble protests to the contrary, had settled down. The note was out of date. For all Kate knew, Warren would send her notes that would overwrite the wording of this frigid little rejection.

*I'll burn it!* At the table, she would hold it to one of the candles. It would be just the sort of behaviour to amuse this kooky entourage.

Ferreting out the envelope, Kate was nonplussed by how it felt. Taking it from Charlie at the fancy dress party, she'd stuffed it into her bag without noticing; at the funeral she was in no state to realise, but now she saw that the envelope was thick, heftier than the flimsy note she'd returned to sender.

Opening it, Kate extracted two creamy sheets of water-marked paper, tattooed with lines and lines of Charlie's distinctive handwriting.

Kate scanned the pages, concentrating hard.

Heat began to build in her stomach. She needed action, violence even. She needed to run. Kicking away her shoes, Kate took off, trying to outrun old news she'd just read for the very first time.

Tearing through the house, Kate took a wrong turn or two as she tried desperately to locate the party, to find Warren. He held a promise of something different to the unhappiness snapping at her heels.

Bursting through ornate double doors, Kate stopped at the sight of the table, lit in the centre of the shadowy room like a stage. All the players turned at the noise, their foxy masks giving them the look of startled animals.

Helen, still at the head of the company, appeared to be doling out dessert, smearing thick cream on the breasts of the flaky young woman who was stretched out, naked, among the overturned vases and sticky pools of spilled wine.

Bent over the woman, his lips to her body, Warren wore only his shirt.

Kate noticed, in the same second, the red weals on his buttocks and the whip wielded by a portly man who'd bored her earlier with anecdotes of his stamp collection. Both men's erections rivalled the whip for rigidity.

'Kate,' said Warren. 'Join us, gorgeous.'

The sacrificial offering on the table began to laugh, wildly.

Helen's mask was white and feathered. 'Kate's shy,' she said.

'Trust me, Kate. It'll be fun,' said Warren. He took off his mask, tucked in his chin. It was the look Kate gave Flo when the child refused to eat her greens. 'Oh dearie me. Have I misjudged you? I thought you were special.' He held out his hand, as if all was forgiven. 'Come on. We don't bite.'

Like Cinderella, Kate fled shoeless down the dark sweeping staircase, not knowing if Warren gave chase. When the venerable front door refused to give she yipped in panic and tore at the latch.

Hearing her name, Kate turned.

At the top of the stairs, Warren held up a candlestick. 'Don't go. Please. Let's talk, yeah?'

Kate pulled harder. The latch co-operated. The gravel was sharp underfoot.

In a moonlit lay-by, Kate turned off the ignition, crossed her arms over the wheel, and laid her head on them. She cried like a child, untrammelled and noisy.

Taking their natural course, the tears eventually receded, like the tide, leaving flotsam and jetsam in its wake. Kate folded out the creases in the paper.

*Dear Kate,*

*I'm trying to make sense of this silence.*

*Becca has suggested I write to you and tell you how*

I feel, and that she'll deliver the letter to you. She's been brilliant.

Why have you stopped trusting me? I've always had friends who are girls. Whether you're around the corner or on another planet it doesn't make any difference to how I behave with them. I'm your boyfriend. Or I hope I am.

I love being your boyfriend. It's great. I don't want to stop being your boyfriend but I don't want to hassle you either. I've been waiting and waiting for you to call or write or something but there's nothing. You seem to have moved on. I knew you'd outgrow me one day but I didn't think it would be this soon.

So it's up to you. Because I know I still love you and you must know that too. A light that bright doesn't just go out. But I don't know how you feel. You have a proper job, you're earning money and I know how ambitious you are. I nearly didn't accept my place at Keele in case you got bored of having a layabout student as a boyfriend. Is that how you feel? Do you want to move on?

For the record, here's how I feel. I can't even think of loving any other girl. You're everything to me. I think of you when I wake up and before I go to sleep. I want to know you and love you forever. When we're old I want to shuffle around supermarkets with you, complaining

231

*about prices. I want to go through all the good stuff and all the bad stuff at your side. I want to make love to you every day. I want to sleep beside you every night. I want to make babies with you. I want the lot. You make me greedy. You make me confident.*

*But if I don't do the same for you, I understand. I don't like it, I HATE it, but I'd never pin you down.*

*What I'm trying to say is, I love you, Kate.*

*Cx*

Kate's past was in a foreign language and she'd been working from a poor translation. Like the freaky party she'd just fled, her history was not as it seemed.

1995 was as vivid to her – no, *more* vivid – than yesterday. Kate could see herself and Becca in that shoe shop. She inhabited her younger point of view as nineties Kate stared down at her foot, the ankle skinny as a stem in the heavy lace-up under consideration. Kate's body remembered its physicality. Lighter, with a higher centre of gravity.

Becca, her bob falling over her face, had asked the question so tremulously. Did Kate mind that she'd met Charlie for a coffee?

No wonder Becca had been tremulous. Present day Kate closed her eyes and punched the steering wheel.

*I reassured her, said of course I didn't mind.*

The ravenous way Becca insisted she open the note Charlie had sent, that she read it right there and then had looked like concern.

*It was fear*, thought Kate. *Fear that her scheme would fall apart.*

The scrawled message Becca handed over in the shoe shop was a short and pithy dissolution of their relationship. Writing it, Charlie believed that Kate had already read his longer letter.

*He thought I ignored this beautiful cry from the heart.*

Their go-between, far from 'brilliant', had fooled them both, withholding the initial letter and only delivering the second, brutal one.

Time travelling again, Kate was at Aunty Marjorie's fancy dress party, as Charlie handed her this declaration of his feelings, for what he assumed was the second time. Charlie, unaware that she thought it was his crushing rejection all over again, must have been astonished by the violence of her reaction.

*I snarled at him.*

Kate shook her head, rearranging her thoughts in the light of this new evidence. From now on she must stop referring to Charlie's note – his second note – as a rejection. It was instead an acquiescence. Charlie's surrender to the inevitable.

*He thought I didn't love him any more.*

It was too late. The words, so carefully chosen, so very Charlie, had been robbed of their power by the passing years. By the time he finally put it into her hands at the fancy dress party it was no more than a poem.

The motorway was a black carpet, rolling towards London. Kate was desperate to get back to her flat and close the door behind her. Tomorrow she'd email Warren and bow out of his erotic fantasy world; tonight there was no space in her head for anything but the evil prank Becca had pulled so long ago.

In slow motion, as if her past was a cheesy TV movie, Kate saw young Becca handing over the momentous note to young Kate. *I was unformed, embryonic.* Kate had been unable to countenance a life without Charlie squarely at the centre of it.

Taking her exit from the motorway, the tick-tick of the indicator filling the car, Kate considered the flimsy nature of Becca's plot.

One phone call would have blown it out of the water. A chance meeting on the street. Charlie casually recalling two notes instead of one. Kate recalled how she'd stared and stared at the phone, pride and doubt conspiring to stop her dialling Charlie's number.

*It couldn't happen now.* People were so interconnected with texts and Tweets: all it would have taken was one late night, drunken *I love you come back* and there would have been a frantic reunion.

But none of these tiny, ordinary things had happened. Becca's gossamer structure, so typical of her hubris, was as sturdy as a castle. *She didn't even try to keep us apart!* Kate was stupefied by Becca's insistence that they remain a tight-knit trio. *She was so sure of herself.*

At each step of the way, Kate had colluded unwittingly with her cousin, reinforcing the bars of her own cage, making sure Becca's deceit stayed hidden.

Finding their way back to cordiality, Kate and Charlie had played into Becca's hands, roping off certain areas with the emotional equivalent of crime scene tape. When Charlie had finally broken through and handed her the original letter, she'd refused to read it.

*Was he declaring himself to me afresh? Was he reaching out?*

Anger glowed bright and hard within Kate, turning her heart to concrete. She felt white hot contempt for Becca, the flipside of which was pain. A horrible pain, such as Kate had never felt before; the product of a beloved confidante setting out to hurt her in cold blood.

If Kate had burned it, as planned, she could have gone to her grave without knowing.

*But what* do *I know?*

Streets shaped up through the windscreen. Kate was back to the stop/start traffic of town.

All she really knew for sure was that Charlie had loved her a long time ago.

Wrapped up in the past, at first Kate didn't hear the phone. Stationary at a red light, she looked at the image taking up the screen. Charlie, Lucy and Flo sitting at a bistro table; Flo wearing Lucy's on-trend sunglasses; Charlie waving; Lucy laughing so hard her eyes are slits. Flo looked thrilled to be out so late with the grown-ups.

Hope u r having fun with Wilhelm! Big kisses from us all but specially Flo xxx

The contrast between the wholesome scene and the debauchery Kate had left behind wasn't lost on her. A pattern was emerging: an independent woman, more than capable of making sensible decisions, sleepwalks into situations because it's easier to conform with the Greek chorus around her than listen to her gut.

Beyond the surface sexual attraction, Warren hadn't interested her. He was, she could now admit, a bore. If he went missing Kate could tell the police only his approximate height and hair colour; she was unsure about his eyes. Blue? Brown? They could be tartan: Kate had never looked that hard.

*Although after tonight I could tell the cops he was a swinger.*

The commonplace lust Warren had inspired fell away the moment she saw him creepily play-acting over the spread-eagled body of that disturbed young woman, laid out like a buffet.

Kate didn't want Warren any more than she wanted the other men she'd whistled up from the ether of the internet. Kate would, as planned, cancel the one date pencilled in for next week: not because she was 'going exclusive' but because, it was clear, love was not to be found online.

Or anywhere.

Love was not for Kate. It seemed simple for others. She knew people who had to fend off love, disentangling themselves from one liaison in order to dive, head first, into the next one.

*For me*, thought Kate, *love is a pair of heels disappearing around the corner.*

As the drivers behind her beeped their annoyance at Kate's failure to notice that the lights had changed, alternative realities reared before her eyes.

A youthful Kate and Charlie making up. Falling back into step. Drifting, entwined, through their twenties. A low-key wedding on the spur of the moment. Perhaps no wedding at all. An adopted little chap underfoot. Sharing the cooking and bickering about whose turn it was to take out the bin.

It was a far more cosy scenario than sitting shoeless and tear-stained in a getaway car, the memory of Warren's breath on her neck burning like a brand.

The cacophony of car horns brought Kate to her senses. With a karate chop, she changed the indicator and took a sharp right, in the opposite direction to her house.

Love eluded Kate for one simple reason: she already had the only love she'd ever need. Charlie was a mountain, one she could not go over, round or through. He blocked out all the light.

Charlie had moved on, no longer the boy who wrote that note; he'd got over Kate because he had to.

Cold facts insisted she face them. Whatever Charlie meant by handing her the note at the party, when he finally left Becca, he hadn't turned to Kate; he'd found somebody new.

Scrabbling for a tissue, Kate blew her nose. She coughed and shook her shoulders as the car passed familiar scenery. *If love is not for me*, she thought, *I'll stick to what I can see and touch and understand.*

Kate had to grapple her life into a shape that made sense to her, not to her Greek chorus. She would focus on something simple and clean; a possibility emerged from her fog of dark thoughts immediately.

Untainted by crossed wires, Yulan House provided her with challenges and joy. It was mutually beneficial: Kate saw how her own efforts impacted on the children and staff. No potential for betrayal there, just a pure transaction based on respect.

Yulan House needed help. Kate needed purpose. *What if I borrowed Dad's dream?* Her own boss in all senses of the word, with no partner or child, Kate was in a privileged position. She could make sweeping changes without seeking anybody's permission. She could grab her tawdry, monochrome life by the scruff of the neck and shake it. Light-headed at the thought of paring down her business life and ramping up her charity work, Kate murmured 'Come *on*,' under her breath as she waited for the car in front to join a roundabout.

Before a new chapter could begin, before Kate could draw the dividing line between the day she knew nothing and the day she knew *everything*, there was a task to be taken care of. She champed at the bit, ready to expend her hectic intensity on this detail.

Slowing outside Becca's gate, Kate looked up at the cottage's lit windows.

*I won't knock.* She would bang on the front door, like a bailiff. *I'll tell her I know.*

Kate's bare feet made no noise on the path. She stood at the door, devising several grisly modes of murder. The bloodier the better.

All that was vengeful fantasy; more realistic was the justice Kate would mete out.

*I'll out her.* Everybody would hear of Becca's cruelty. The whole family. Charlie. Even Flo would know one day what a witch she had for a mother.

*I'll take back all my love. I'll rescind the protectiveness. I'll spit on the shared memories.*

And then Kate would drive home and never speak to her cousin again.

*A light that bright doesn't just go out.*

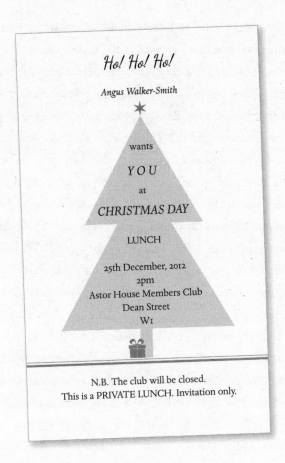

*Ho! Ho! Ho!*

*Angus Walker-Smith*

wants

*Y O U*

at

*CHRISTMAS DAY*

LUNCH

25th December, 2012
2pm
Astor House Members Club
Dean Street
W1

N.B. The club will be closed.
This is a PRIVATE LUNCH. Invitation only.

The setting was perfect, as if somebody had bottled Christmas and sprinkled it over the room.

Beyond the shuttered window, the empty street was sharply drawn in cold grey light. Even Soho's naughty teeming thoroughfares are quiet on Christmas Day.

Within, the Grade II listed panelling and the leaping fire made the salon feel like a private sitting room, although the bar at the back of the long double room debunked that illusion. Dressed up, holding a sherry and feeling festive, Kate was glad of the locked front door. Today the club was not a public place. Today its comforts and delights were for invited guests only.

A tousled head bobbed up from behind the bar. 'Where oh where is the sodding decanter?' There was no heat in his bad language: Angus adored Christmas. *Angus* is *Christmas!* thought Kate, watching him drop things and exclaim and help himself to a sneaky sip. Tall, wide, with an extravagant belly, he could have been a shop-soiled Santa were it not for his hair.

The absurd halo of white blond hair (quite natural, despite its detractors' claims) was impossible to domesticate. It exploded constantly, a nuclear fission on his head. As befits such a Dickensian character, Angus's clothes were not recognisably modern. The tweed and velvet, flecked with ash and riddled with rips, could have been filched from a country house wardrobe at any stage during the past century.

'Why,' roared Angus, 'won't it snow?' He was speaking to nobody and to everybody. Kate didn't feel obliged to answer. Astor House was a success only partly because of the noble bones of the building. The real secret of its enduring popularity was Angus.

Like him, the club was louche but inoffensive. Grand but jolly. It welcomed all-comers, but booted out the rude and the snobbish. High jinks of all sorts were indulged; a member could be blacklisted for sexually harassing a woman but applauded if he started a food fight.

'Door!' bellowed Angus at the sound of the bell. 'Get that, somebody!'

Kilian O'Brien was shown in by a mohawk-haired member of staff, one of three on duty and earning triple rate. An ebullient girl, she was unusually quiet.

Kate understood. Although Angus was no star-chaser – he routinely turned down boorish celebrities' requests for membership – his hospitality attracted many well-known folk and Kilian's star shone brighter than most. The daintily built actor unwound a long long scarf and surrendered to a bear hug from Angus.

'You came!'

'Of course,' smiled Kilian. He was dark, neat, and pulsing with the charisma that is the natural atmosphere of idols. 'Who in their right mind turns down an invitation to one of your infamous Christmas lunches?'

'You've met my girlfriend, Kate?'

'Yes.' Kilian turned his green eyes to Kate. They were like jewels. He recalled they'd discussed China. 'Merry Christmas,' he said in a dancing Irish accent, and kissed her, shyly, on the cheek.

It had surprised Kate the last time they met that Kilian was so low-key, so diffident. Her heart had been fluttering so hard she'd wondered if he'd heard it. *Daft, but I expect actors to be like the parts they play.*

They talked about Kilian's chickens as Angus poured more sherry. The man had never mentioned a significant other; Kate wondered if he was gay. As an actor specialising in romantic leads, coming out might be tricky.

Maybe that was the reason for his invitation. There was always a reason. Angus flattered people, begging them to come, saying it wouldn't be the same without them, but the truth was he had divined they would be alone on the most convivial day of the year and he wanted to right that wrong.

As Kilian detailed his fowls' various ailments, Kate sneaked a look at Angus, who was laying out tiddly widdly canapés on paper plates from her new range. Illogical to be staring at Angus when she had the sole attention of a heart throb. Angus had not been meant to happen. He was just the final internet assignation after the orgy, one she'd tried to cancel, but felt obliged to honour when her date sounded so disappointed.

The mohawk waitress ushered in Charlie. Not at all awed by this guest, she barked, 'Charlie's 'ere,' and abandoned him.

'Charles!' Angus was upon him and Charlie quailed as if being greeted by an exuberant dog. Angus's bulk diminished Charlie's stature, even though the hours spent at the gym (another by-product of Charlie's mourning for Lost Youth that amused Kate) had turned the lanky boy of yore into a well-built, broad shouldered man of substance. Angus was blunt about his own body: 'No other word for this but *fat*!' he would say, rubbing his tummy, but his rotundity was so obviously due to a surfeit of good food and great wine that he delighted in it. This delight was infectious; even if Angus had been skinny he would seem large, thanks to his voice and manner, his expansive gestures, the way he remembered and used everybody's name. Early on Kate had noticed that children and dogs adored him; they are *never* wrong.

Charlie's attempt to stay cool when confronted with Kilian was an early Christmas present for Kate, who accepted his tissue-wrapped package and kissed him on his cold cheek.

'Contessa!' shouted Angus.

'Ah, Mum's here,' said Kate, breaking away from her clique to welcome her mother, who'd been wafted to the club in a chauffeur driven car, courtesy of Angus.

This gesture, plus her aristocratic nickname, was one of many reasons Mum was pro-Angus, to the point of lobbying Kate to make an honest man of him. Not close to his own family – Kate had never been introduced to a single relative in their three years together – he delighted in Kate's Irish clan. 'My friends are my family,' he was wont to say. He collected people the way Jaffa collected fleas: effortlessly.

With the arrival of Aunty Marjorie and Uncle Hugh, overdressed and chattering like parakeets, Angus said, 'Nearly all assembled!'

*London café society would kill to be here*, thought Kate. *And there's my aunty accepting a Baileys with an 'Ooh I shouldn't really!'* Kate sat beside her mother on a Chesterfield.

'I don't like what you've done to your hair, Kate.'

'I haven't done anything to my hair, Mum.'

'Well, you should.'

Kate's hair, longer these days, was casually drawn up into a ponytail. When she let it down, it was just for her and Angus. She caught one of his staccato bursts of laughter from the bar. Angus could pin down the moment he fell for Kate: eight minutes into their first date.

'When I knocked over your wine and it went all over your trousers.' Angus liked to reminisce. 'You just dabbed at the stain with your napkin and told me to go on with whatever bloody anecdote I was boring you with.'

He was not to know that Kate hadn't cared about her patterned harem pants, that she'd cared about very little. Kate had been going through the motions, not just of the date but of her life. She washed her hair, prepared her food, did thirty lengths of the local pool every morning like an automaton. Everything had had to form an orderly queue because at the forefront of her mind was Charlie's letter.

How often she'd wished she could forget the callous wording of the other note, not knowing that the sincere yearning in the original letter would hurt her even more.

Charlie clinked glasses with her. 'Bottoms up,' he laughed.

The doorbell rang again, and delivered a bespectacled woman to the gathering.

'Is that . . .' Charlie asked.

'It is.' Kate nodded. 'Rosie Smith.'

'Where have her . . .'

'Boobs gone?' Kate wondered how many more of Charlie's sentences she would have to finish for him. Rosie had that effect on the opposite sex. 'She's taken out her implants and started wearing glasses because she is now a serious actress.' Kate tapped him on the nose. 'Put your tongue back in. Unbridled lust is not a good look on you.'

Disapproval emanated from Mum and Aunty Marjorie, who looked on, lips as tight as a hen's bottom, as Angus fell upon Rosie, showering her with the compliments she needed and introducing her to her fellow revellers. They had all seen the topless photo shoots; the bluestocking make-over didn't fool anybody, especially as the woman persisted with clingy dresses and tottering heels. Kate noticed how Charlie, the very model of a modern liberal chap who decried women dressing to please men, cleared his throat and passed a hand through his hair. Angus was immune. Women like Rosie – who Kate secretly thought of as *poor old Rosie* – were the reason he'd turned to internet dating.

His blurred profile pic had given little away. Not that Angus could ever lead with his looks. Emailing Kate out of the blue, he wrote that he'd noticed from her photograph that she had freckles on her nose: 'And in my long experience you can rely on nose-freckled folk.'

On meeting him, Kate had recognised him. Back in his decadent advertising days, Charlie had been a member of Astor House; Kate had met him there for drinks and seen Angus roaming the rooms. Since then, she'd seen him in the gossip columns, always raffish and rowdy looking, with tossed hair and messy clothes.

Towards the end of their obligation date, strolling along the South Bank primly apart (Kate now appreciated how hard that had been for the tactile Angus), Kate had asked why such a famed bon viveur, surrounded by celebrated sexpots, was on a dating site.

Aware she would never see him again, it was an idle question, a prelude to a farewell as Kate geared up to return to the Kate-shaped niche she'd carved.

Thinking before he spoke, Angus hadn't responded in kind to the throwaway enquiry. 'Because,' he said, pausing by the hulk of the National Theatre, 'people run through my fingers like sand. I'm in my world, but not *of* it. Sex is currency. The shallowness dismays me. Women I've dated have berated me for not introducing them to movie stars.' He had, he told her, acquired x-ray vision. 'I see who's on the make. I see who's floundering. It's easy to lose your footing in Soho. I know who's desperately hanging around until the cocaine comes out, and who should be tucked up in bed with a mug of cocoa instead of dancing on the tables. You,' he'd said, turning to her, 'interest me.' He smiled. 'You really have the most lovely face, Kate Minelli.'

Unaccustomed to compliments – Charlie's were too antique to carry any weight, Julian had been miserly with them and Warren's were ones she'd rather forget – it had taken a while for Kate to realise that Angus meant every word. She came to recognise the difference between the air kissing, the 'Darling you look *gorgeous!*' to the hoi polloi at Astor House, and the whispered 'You have such soul' he dropped in her ear at unexpected moments.

When Angus hailed a taxi for her that first night, he hadn't lunged. He'd taken her hand and said, 'I'll hold you in my heart until I see you again.' The feeling of well being, of being thought about, that flooded through careworn Kate was one she hadn't experienced since the death of her father. A layer of grief had simply peeled off and flown away, flapping in the air over the South Bank. Without realising it, Kate had settled into a bizarrely premature old age; wincing when she knocked into things and treading carefully as if she might slip. Angus's attentions had coaxed her back to her thirties.

'I'll get it.' When the doorbell cut once more through the festive babble, Kate escaped Rosie's me-me-me small talk (Charlie was helpless in the woman's tractor beam) and went to the front door.

'Happy Christmas!' said Becca, on the doorstep.

★　　★　　★

A different doorstep, three years earlier. Kate banged and knocked and rang in the darkness.

A tremulous 'Who is it?'

Kate answered with a vigorous 'Me!'

There was no need to name herself. The power of history, blood and love opened the door in a trice, even though enough dark energy coursed through Kate for her to kick it down. Fists balled, expletives gathering on her lips, she quivered as bolts were drawn.

The door opened, and there was sleep soiled, bedraggled Becca, her greatest friend, her almost-sister, her most barbarous adversary.

All Kate's ire disappeared. She held out the letter. 'Why?' She hadn't meant to sound so weak; she'd meant to be a fury.

Becca's face folded in on itself. No fight in her either; she recognised the piece of paper.

'How could you?' Kate was high pitched. 'How could you do this to us?' She had meant to say 'to me'.

'I've been waiting for this to happen,' said Becca.

Inside the house, they sat in the pool of light thrown by the low-hanging shade above the circular kitchen table. Kate eschewed the soft chairs; she wanted hard seats and hard facts. They came out slowly, in a non-linear fashion.

'It's almost a relief,' said Becca.

Jaffa snored at Kate's feet. The kettle, the fridge, the

cherry-patterned blind were all the same. She was changed, however. She no longer felt at home here.

Before they got to the 'how' Becca had a lot to say about the 'why'.

'I've always been jealous of you.' Planted when they were both children, Becca's resentments had been watered until they grew vigorous. And dangerous.

It was all news to Kate.

'You and your dad got on so well. When I went round your house it was alive and warm, with the fire going, and your books all over the rug.' Her own parents, said Becca, were 'joiners', always out and about, playing golf, sailing their boat, dragging her to grown-up parties where she'd get overtired and vomit down her new dress.

Sensing Becca was working herself up, Kate got in early with her rebuttals. 'Hang on a minute. We had a fire because our house was unmodernised and freezing cold.' She remembered her mother comparing their house to her sister's 'palace'. 'We'd have killed for a boat!' From Kate's point of view, Becca's childhood had been glamorous.

'But,' said Becca, 'did you ever envy me?'

'Never. But that's about my temperament, not whether or not your life was enviable.'

'I was spoiled,' said Becca, pulling her dressing gown tighter, 'but I was ignored.' She was more familiar with the back pages of her father's newspapers than with his face. 'And, Christ, the pressure from Mum. She's always expected so much from me. You're lucky. You could withstand your mum.'

'Lucky?' Kate drummed her fingers on the pine. 'Everybody's lucky in your version of events. Except, crucially, *you*.'

'Exactly!' Becca, never expert at spotting irony, seemed glad of the empathy. 'You had your dad. He was always *there*, always ready with a cuddle if your mum was on the warpath.' Becca had nobody. 'My mum and dad threw all your exam results in my face. I grew up knowing they thought I was stupid. I couldn't be successful on my own terms. I had to nab a husband, and a house, and have babies.' All liberally sprinkled with sanitising money. 'Otherwise I'd be a failure.'

'So far, so self-pitying.'

'Then I bagged Julian. Mum was pleased at last. He wasn't like the other boys. I was dazzled.' Her initial I-can't-believe-my-luck reaction never had the chance to settle down into anything approaching love. 'I guessed early on that he had a soft spot for you.'

'I don't believe you.' Kate sat back. 'I would've noticed.'

'Why would a man that sophisticated and worldly be interested in me?'

Kate had never heard Becca disparage herself. 'Because . . . because of a million reasons. All the guys were after you.' She remembered it well; wallflowers have long memories. 'You were catnip.'

'I was candy floss. You were clever and funny and had all

these opinions on things I hadn't even heard of. Looks fade, Kate. Brains don't.'

Becca wiped at her wet cheeks with a savage hand. Kate didn't leap up and hold her, coo it all better as she'd always done in the past. Their friendship had finally come of age, fifteen minutes – or thereabouts, Kate wasn't certain when she would stand up and leave – before it ended. Becca said, 'We were given our roles. Pretty One. Clever One. We swallowed it whole without question.'

Their family were neither psychologists nor evil geniuses. None of the parents could have foreseen what would happen. Carefully, the girls had taken pains never to overlap. The Pretty One could never be interested in topics other than herself; the Clever One believed herself unattractive.

It struck Kate forcefully that she loathed confronting her appearance in the slab of mirror at the hairdresser's, or happening upon her reflection in a shop window. She looked down at her hands, at the unvarnished nails kept short; even though she'd dressed up for the country house party she hadn't contemplated painting them a showy red. The Clever One, Kate had no confidence in her own femininity.

The roles assigned to Kate and Becca in childhood had fused to their skin.

Becca said, 'It wasn't fair that Julian liked you. You already had the perfect boyfriend.'

'Hardly! You thought Charlie was a chump.'

'I mean he was perfect for *you*.'

'Do you want me to apologise for being in love?' Kate leaned forward. 'I'm not the one in the wrong, Becca.'

'Sorry. I just . . . I need you to understand.' Becca dried her eyes, shook her head like a pony refusing its bridle, as if to discourage any more tears. 'It's important.'

Kate could see that it was *too* important. The hot-house nature of their kinship had blurred boundaries.

'When Julian dumped me, I was all over the place.' Becca blew out her cheeks. 'But, to be honest, I knew I'd get over it.' Becca grimaced. 'Just being me wasn't enough for a man like Julian, that was clear.'

When Becca heard that Kate and Charlie had suddenly split, although she felt terrible for her, self-interest had bobbed to the surface, like a cork. 'It was comforting having you to suffer with.'

'Glad to be of help.'

'Don't.' Becca said it half-heartedly, as if she knew she had no right. 'So. Charlie sought me out. He wanted to know how you felt, but he swore me to secrecy. I agreed, cos I wanted to keep the lines of communication open.'

'Plus,' said Kate, remorseless, 'it gave you the upper hand, keeping something from me.'

'No.' Becca looked sorrowful.

Kate wasn't buying it. 'Carry on, for God's sake. Let's get this over with.'

'Charlie wasn't like the Charlie I knew. He was pissed off with you for prolonging the argument.'

Ten years of backdated umbrage made Kate growl.

'I put him right,' said Becca, glad to be on the side of the angels, if only momentarily. 'I said, *Charlie, it's not just Kate's fault.*' She nodded, pleased with herself. 'I did my best for you.'

'At this point.' Kate could imagine Becca's ambition to be a combination of fairy godmother and Nelson Mandela, an acclaimed peacemaker who would part-own Kate and Charlie's romance from then on.

'His pride was hurt.' Becca understood what was going on in Charlie's mind. 'Your silence freaked him out. He was afraid to bare his soul in case you'd changed your mind about him.' Over watery cappuccinos he'd asked Becca, *What if we manage to glue everything back together but it just falls apart again at the next silly row?* 'All the change worried him. Him at uni, you at work, with miles and miles between you.'

During their second or third session – Becca couldn't remember which – she suggested he write it all down.

'Why didn't you tell him to pick up the phone? You knew I would have taken him back on the spot.'

'I did!' Becca was appalled by the injustice of the question. 'I swear I did! He wouldn't believe me.'

'That's because you talk such overblown nonsense all the time.' The freedom to be bluntly honest was exhilarating.

'I said *just call her*. I told him to go round and see you.' But Charlie had insisted Becca take the note, saying he needed an honest answer, not a *yes* said in pity or in the heat of the moment. 'I accused him of being a coward.'

Both women were united for a moment in despising Charlie a little for his lack of courage and what it had caused.

'The moment he handed over the envelope, I knew I'd use it.' Becca scratched her head. Viciously, as if trying to claw at her thoughts. 'I wish I could tell you I had a long tussle with myself but I just couldn't resist the temptation.'

'Your feelings,' said Kate, 'had changed.'

'I'd begun to realise what you saw in Charlie. I'd always thought of "niceness" as boring, but he made me feel good. He *listened*. He thought before he spoke. Treated me as an equal. And he made me laugh.' Charlie lit a small flame that Becca hadn't wanted to douse. She hadn't planned to scupper anything. 'I hung on to the note. One day. Another day. Three days.' Becca grew scared of her own boldness. 'I couldn't believe I'd done it.' Like a plundered heart, the envelope throbbed beneath her bed, keeping her awake. 'I realised I *couldn't* give it to you, even though I was frightened by the consequences of what I'd done, because you'd both realise I'd kept it for a while.'

'Owning up is never an option with you, is it?'

'No,' replied Becca, as if glad that Kate understood. 'Charlie kept asking for news.' She fobbed him off until she had her brilliant idea. 'I realised I could reset everything.

Turn the clock back and re-start the process.' She returned the note. 'I told him you had no response.' Becca chewed her thumb nail. 'So it wasn't really a lie.'

'It was a huge dirty lie.' Kate forced herself to stay seated. She wanted to spring out of her seat. 'If you're going to rewrite history, there's no point in us doing this.'

'OK, OK. I lied.' Becca's chin puckered as she kept back tears.

'No response meant I'd read it and rejected it. That is *not* starting again. That is destroying.' Kate thought of his poetic words, falling – as Charlie thought – on deaf ears.

'You're right.' Becca had been whitewashing her duplicity to herself. 'The odd thing was that Charlie didn't seem shocked. As if he'd half expected it. Everybody knew he'd never felt good enough for you.'

*Everybody?* 'I didn't know it.'

'Growing up the way he did. With his mum the way she was . . .'

'I never made him feel he wasn't good enough. I loved him just the way he was. This is one of your smokescreens, Becca.'

Evidently terrified of being misconstrued, Becca flapped her hands. 'No! I'm not accusing you. Charlie did that to himself.'

'So, according to you, we're all fuck-ups and our individual hang-ups collided in some perfect storm? It was

257

nothing to do with your jealousy and greed and dishonesty and lack of love for the people who care about you?'

'I deserve that.'

'We agree on something at last!'

Taking a deep breath, Becca looked grateful to be on the final lap. 'When I gave him back the first note I forced him to sit and write another one. Straight away.' Clearly proud of her altruism, Becca recalled how she demanded that Charlie write exactly what was in his heart. 'It only took a few minutes so he obviously copied the original one, more or less. I called you and met you at the shoe shop and handed it over. I kept it for less than an hour this time. *No harm done*, I thought.' Becca looked carefully at the unusual look on Kate's face, before she chanced saying, 'And then you decided to go out with Julian instead, so . . .'

The whole farce had been so fine tuned. If Julian hadn't been hurtling towards Kate's house when she read that second note, maybe she would have found the wherewithal to confront Charlie. But he had, and she hadn't. 'Becca, that note was much shorter because it was final. It told me we were over.'

'He didn't say he wanted you back?' Hands flying to her face, Becca looked as if she was watching a car crash in slow motion. 'But I thought you decided against going back to Charlie because Julian asked you out?'

Becca hadn't been listening to Kate back then. Perhaps she never listened. Or more likely, she heard what she wanted to hear, sifting through the words until they were in tune with her own desires. 'You don't know me at all.' It was B-movie dialogue but it was true. 'Then again . . .' Kate spread her hands. 'Clearly, I don't know you either.' She would have defended Becca to the gates of Hell if anybody accused her of such treachery. Kate's outrage was hot and cleansing. She was right, she was righteous, but there was no pleasure in dismantling Becca's defence. She could justifiably roll over Becca in a tank, with full TV coverage and a specially composed theme tune, but Kate had no appetite for vengeance. More Dad than Mum, she wouldn't demand an eye for an eye.

Becca began to talk rapidly, as if channelling a spirit with much to say. 'It's taken me years to face what I did. I'm so used to feeling guilty it's normal to me.' She'd been looking over her shoulder for her nasty deeds to catch up with her, knowing they must. A drink, she said, helped. 'I've waited for this night. For when it would all come out. As the years went by I relaxed a bit. I couldn't believe you and Charlie didn't bring it up, work it out.' Fatalistic, she'd never kept them apart. 'You know how impulsive I am. I trusted to luck, put everything on black. Like I did on honeymoon in Vegas.'

The metaphor was insulting. 'You won that time, too, I recall.'

'Yup. Ten k.' Becca picked Jaffa up onto her lap and the dog yawned, closing his jaws with a small wet snap. 'I didn't ask too much about that second note. I should have, but I was frightened. The way I sold it to myself was . . . we all came out OK.'

Kate knew that Becca was referring to the penthouse, the long haul holidays. *As if I was paid off handsomely for losing out in love.* 'At least,' she said, stony, 'you and Charlie were in love, for a little while.'

'Well . . .' Becca stroked Jaffa's domed head a little too hard. 'The truth? My feelings never really changed. I thought Charlie was great, but he was always just Charlie to me.'

'We have something in common, then. My feelings never changed either. I'm still in love with him.'

'No you're not,' scoffed Becca, as if quashing a silly rumour. 'Not in that way.'

'I love Charlie. In that way.' Something fell into place inside Kate as she said it.

'But . . .' Becca was resistant. 'You fell in love with Julian. You *married* him.'

'Funny that you of all people can't believe a woman could marry a man she doesn't love.'

'You got over Charlie,' insisted Becca. 'You *chose* Julian.'

'Deep down,' said Kate, 'you know I didn't.'

They both needed a break at that point, like boxers retreating to their corners. Kate escaped to the newly decorated downstairs loo – out with shabby chic, in with minimalism. The smell of paint lingered and the soap was hidden.

When she emerged a mug of hot chocolate, made just the way she liked it, was at her place.

As Kate took her seat, Becca said, 'This'll make you laugh.'

'I doubt it, but go on.'

'When I'm snappy with you, when I'm a bitch, it's because I suddenly have an attack of guilt. And then I'm guilty about being snappy. And so on.' Becca slumped as the spirit retreated. 'How come you've never told Charlie about Flo?'

In no mood to change the subject, Kate shrugged.

'I was *so* drunk the night I told you. But I knew what I was doing.' Becca had handed Kate the weapons to fight back. 'I offered you my jaw so you could land a right hook.'

'If I hurt you like you hurt me, we'd be quits?'

'It sounds crazy when you put it like that.'

'It all sounds crazy! It did occur to me that I could tell Charlie he wasn't Flo's father.' This was an arena for honesty; Kate may as well admit her own sins. 'One word from me and your marriage would have been smashed to smithereens.'

It was almost an aside when Becca said, 'There wasn't much to shatter. We were in bad shape by then.'

'I thought you'd hang on to him forever.' Kate hesitated. 'I didn't think Charlie was a leaver.'

'You've always had more confidence in me than in yourself.'

261

Turning down the corners of her mouth at her own naivety, Kate admitted the delicious thoughts she had entertained that maybe Charlie would come to her if she blew the whistle on Flo's paternity. 'As if all those years were a dream and the damage could be plastered over, all lovely and smooth again.'

'That could still happen.' Becca snapped back to her usual gung-ho self. Even her matted bed hair perked up. 'Now you know it all, go and tell him the truth. How I tricked him. How you felt about him then. How you feel now.'

'Just because time's stood still for me . . .' Kate hung her head, suddenly exhausted. 'Charlie's a father. And he's in love with Lucy.' She tailed off. Kate knew how Charlie looked when he was in love because it was the way he used to look at her.

'You could chase away Lucy,' said Becca. 'Like *that*.' She clicked her fingers.

Kate slammed her palms on the table top. 'There you go again! Stage managing people! Lucy is a kind, intelligent woman who spends a lot of time with your daughter. Why not thank her instead of clicking your fingers as if she's a bluebottle you can swat? Thanking people isn't your style, is it? That would make Lucy more human and we can't have that. *You're* the only one allowed to have fears and desires.'

'There it is!' Becca pointed at Kate. No longer soggy with contrite fears, her eyes flashed. '*There's* the reason you and

Charlie aren't together. You're too busy being Mother Teresa. Fight, Kate! Get some blood on your hands!' Becca chewed her lips for a moment, a habit she'd lost when they were both eleven years old. 'If you don't, I will. I'm going to confess. I'll tell Charlie I kept his first note away from you.'

Kate's anger had ebbed and flowed throughout this tense tête à tête; hearing Becca's faltering step-by-step reconstruction had made it possible to understand. To a certain extent. Compassion and fury couldn't share the same space. This outburst, however, chased away all empathy and shot her through with hot rage. 'Don't you dare confess! I forbid it.'

'Or what?' Becca challenged her.

'Or I'll tell Charlie he's not Flo's father.'

'I don't believe you,' said Becca, slowly.

*Neither do I.* 'Look, me and Charlie aren't Taylor and Burton. Too much has happened. Charlie's in love and Lucy's good for him. I couldn't live with the storm you'd unleash if you rake up the past. The friendship I have with Charlie is the central one in my life.' Until this evening, Kate would have added *Along with yours*. 'I need him. When you play God you run the risk of demolishing what you meant to repair. As you should know.' She took a sip of the chocolate. It was perfect. Not too sweet. 'If you really want to atone, Becca, keep your mouth shut.' If Kate had to hear from Charlie's lips that he didn't want her, it would break her. Again.

An impatient huff from Becca made Kate bang down the mug. 'This isn't the playground, Becca. No more games. I resent being involved with your schemes and I want out. I need clarity. Not wide eyed hopes.'

'And me?' asked Becca, in a fearful voice. 'Do you need me?'

'No,' said Kate. 'I don't.'

'Happy Christmas.' Kate looked the newcomer up and down. She shouted over her shoulder. 'Angus! You didn't tell me you were letting *anybody* in this year!'

'Wouldn't be a party without this lovely lady.' Angus leaned over Kate and planted a smacker on Becca's lips.

In she bounded, heavier than ever, like a healthy animal. Leading with her magnificent breasts, her hair extensions curling to the fake fur over her shoulders, Becca embraced Kate, suffocating her with mingled perfume and conditioner and gel and God knows what else. This was Becca's fourth automatic invitation to Christmas lunch and she was every bit as star struck as she'd been at her first visit.

Kate watched her exclaim at the martini she was handed, and yelp her approval of each detail in the room, never relinquishing her host's arm.

The ostracism hadn't panned out.

Logic and kindness are a formidable team. Kate, who lacked the stamina necessary for feuds, saw Becca in focus at last. All her flaws and dangerous weaknesses, alongside the neediness, the wrong-headedness, the insecurity.

God knows she'd tried, but Kate could not hate Becca.

There were rules attached to the amnesty. *Otherwise*, thought Kate, *I'd be a sap*. Honesty at all times, no resentments and no amateurish evil, thank you very much.

The crux of it was Becca's remorse. It was real. After a week – a very dull week – Kate had called her and they'd negotiated their fresh start. After a long period of (rather exhausting) Best Behaviour, both women were back to their old selves.

This was Kate's favourite part of the day.

The remains of lunch on the table. Wine bottles emptied. Chocolate mint wrappers scattered everywhere. The staff on their way home with humungous tips in their pockets. Just the family.

Well, just the family and their pet celebs.

Kilian was asleep on a sofa, looking like a child beneath the blanket Angus laid over him. Over lunch, he'd displayed a bewilderment Kate had seen before in Angus's circle of luminaries.

For some, fame was uncomfortable, like a badly cut coat. Struggling to handle this side effect of their career, they retreated emotionally from others, unable to trust. In lieu of friendship they turned to what they could stick up their nose, in their veins or down their throats.

No such existential nonsense for Rosie, who'd taken to her outlandish life like a natural. Unfettered by self-doubt, confident that her every hackneyed opinion was fascinating, she flirted with both genders, snapped endless selfies and regaled them all through lunch with the wild flattery of her Instagram followers.

Becca fanned herself with a napkin from Kate's *Holly and Ivy* line. 'I couldn't eat another morsel. My appetite has shrunk since I've been on this strict diet.'

'But Mummy,' said Flo, 'you had thirds.' At nine, Flo's one concession to her mother's love of frippery was a sparkly bow clipped in her hair. Apart from that she was a mini goth, her dark hair and eyes matching, quite naturally, her dark leggings and tunic. Studious, funny, she was prone to leaning on her godmother like an awkward dog, as she was now.

'Hugh!' snapped Aunty Marjorie, and Uncle Hugh sat upright, shocked out of his sneaky nap.

'I wassenasleep,' he said, looking around him, sticky eyed.

'That man would sleep through World War Three,' said Aunty Marjorie, as if her husband's ability to doze was a moral failing. She covertly handed him the last chocolate truffle and he covertly patted her knee in thanks. Kate saw the undercover affection and wondered what had happened during her mother and her aunt's upbringing to render them so allergic to open displays of love.

Beneath the table the real dog, Jaffa, elderly and moth-eaten, stretched out like a well-trodden bath mat. He slept on Flo's bed, despite his distinctive bouquet. The child's take on it was *Jaffa can't help it if he stinks*.

At Becca's side, a cheerful man with a wide black face and beaded dreadlocks that clinked and chimed as he talked, said, 'I like a woman with meat on her bones!' Three years of being with Becca hadn't taught Leon what to say and what not to say in her presence.

'So I'm fat?' Becca rounded on him. 'You're saying I'm fat?'

Beaming, rubbing his hands, Leon giggled, 'I'm in for it now!' in imitation of his own mother's Ghanaian accent. He liked nothing better than being scolded in front of company.

'Becca, my love,' said Angus, his jacket missing, his shirt as tossed as an unmade bed. 'Go easy on Leon.'

Tartly, Becca said, 'I don't mind. It's good for a woman to know her husband thinks she's obese.'

Having gritted his teeth and hung on in there, Leon had been promoted from internet date to husband.

'She's off!' chuckled Leon. Having snaffled Becca he existed in a personal weather system of blue skies and sunshine. Her harsh words were balm, her incessant criticism muzak.

'Of course you're not fat, Becca, pet.' Mum prowled the room, opening up Christmas cards, hoping to find more autographs for the collection she browbeat her book group with.

'You're a *bit* fat, Mummy.' Flo's honesty earned herself a quelling *Flo-rence!* from Charlie, who made an *Oh my God* face at Kate above his daughter's head.

'It's my metabolism.' Becca's metabolism was often named and shamed: she refused to believe her extra poundage was anything to do with her constant eating. As she grew larger, so did her appeal. Becca was ripe, round, juicy: an eloquent retort to the fat-phobics who would round up all of womankind and herd them to the gym. Much of their income from Leon's career as a current affairs camera operator went on glossing, veneering and waxing Becca, as if she was a municipal building that required constant upkeep. 'If I even *look* at a cream cake I put on weight.'

'Then don't look at them.' Flo couldn't grasp the problem.

'Ooh.' Mum murmured happily to herself as she slipped an arty card into her bag. 'Michael Fassbender.'

The length of the table sat between Kate and Angus, but she still felt his paw prints on her body from their lazy morning in his disordered four poster up on the top floor.

Fancying Angus had stolen up on Kate. Just as falling in love was a journey, so was working through lust to find true lovemaking. Kate had always gone for sleeker models, but Angus excited her.

Always on the edge of his seat, primed to dash off, he never dashed too far from Kate. She was, he told her, a long drink of cool refreshing water after his long route march across his very own Sahara. 'My thirst for you,' he would say, kissing the top of her head, 'can never be slaked.'

His recognition of her had been instant; Kate took longer, but tumbling into bed with him had been inevitable after a few dates in low-lit rooms, with claret on tap and the air of debauchery that Angus disseminated even when in a green-grocer's. Nothing like Warren's stage-managed squalor, sex with Angus made a wench of her.

Lying together, his big hand on her hip, his hair on end like a dandelion, Angus would talk freely. Not the evasive gushing of his public persona, the way Angus spoke to Kate in bed was a compliment he bestowed on nobody else.

Mum waved a glittery card. 'Who's this Esther woman, Angus?' She was coquettish and it was not nice to look upon.

Kate couldn't be sure if her mother caught the discreet, distressed shake of her head. Mum was capable of ignoring such a warning. Of *enjoying* ignoring such a warning.

'All these kisses!' Mum pulled in her chin to underline the innuendo. 'She's certainly keen on you!' She peered through her glasses to read. 'Happy Christmas Big A kiss kiss kiss kiss.'

Not built for speed, Angus was at her side in a moment. Laughing, as ever, he spirited the card into his pocket as Kate felt Becca's quizzical look boring into the side of her face. Mum's thoughtlessness had set the ley lines of the table buzzing. She nodded; *Yes, that's her*; Becca's face softened in sympathy.

'Wish Lucy was here,' said Flo.

Another glance from Becca to Kate, this time checking that Kate had clocked her noble refusal to comment.

Leon, it would seem, couldn't resist cliff edges. 'Lovely girl, that Lucy,' he sighed.

'I wish she was here too, Flo,' said Charlie.

'To absent friends!' Angus held up his glass, winking at Kate as the others all found a vessel to raise. The toast wasn't just for Charlie, it was for Kate's dad, and for his own spectres.

It had taken a long while to open up to Angus but he'd sniffed out Kate's truths like a truffle hound. Kate felt older, larger, as if she added up to more than she did before. She felt like a woman. 'To Angus!' It was her turn to wink. He was the best, most un-looked for present she'd ever received.

'Party games!' shouted Angus.

Flo had begged. 'Charades! Please!'

As Mum toiled her way through a complicated mime of *When Harry Met Sally*, Kate crept out to join Charlie in the courtyard, home to a tiled fresco and some bins, and therefore as schizophrenic as the rest of Soho, blending high culture and sleaze.

'Had to get out,' said Charlie. 'To breathe.'

'I understand.' *Who better to understand?* thought Kate. When you're nursing a bruised heart, Christmas Day is long.

'Thanks for having me, Kate. It's not my year to have Flo, so I'd have been on my own.'

'You're not a charity case, idiot. You have a mandatory invitation to my life, you know that. Have you written anything today?' Kate knew all about Charlie's diligence.

'Nothing else to do.'

This despondency began when Lucy exited, stage right, three months earlier. Flo's inability to get her head around why one of her favourite people disappeared tore at the scab each time it formed.

Only some of Charlie's beans had been spilled; Kate wasn't sure why he and Lucy had broken up. She knew about a series of rows and stormings out. A tearful reconciliation. A final goodbye. Your average heartbreak.

Lucy had stonewalled his endless phone messages. *Charlie's modus operandi has evidently changed since he split up with me:* Kate did her best to keep that bitter thought at bay but sometimes it sneaked in by the back door.

She and Angus invited him to the club for long gossipy dinners: always room for one more at Angus's table and he knew what Charlie meant to her.

Kate wondered if Angus knew more than that. The buffoonery was a front; Angus could sum folk up in a flash.

When the right moment presented itself, Kate would fill him in on her backstory with Charlie. It would resign KateandCharlie to antiquity where they rightfully belonged.

A one man woman, Kate had found somebody else – somebody available, who loved her back – to be that one man.

'Did Lucy send you a Christmas card?'

'Nope. Too busy with her new bloke.'

'You don't know that.'

'She should be here. I feel all wrong.' Charlie grasped at his arm as if it was a phantom limb.

Lucy's defection had put a firework in Becca's Spanx. 'Now's your chance! Charlie's vulnerable,' she'd coached. 'Pounce.'

'Charlie is not a wounded gnu and I am not a lion.' Kate didn't see herself as a pouncer.

'He's lonely. He needs you. That silly girl was just a passing fancy. He was blinded by her thigh gap.'

'You never took the time to get to know Lucy. They were in love. He still is.'

'Bollocks.' Becca had been intransigent. 'You're the love of Charlie's life. Go get him.'

Again, the chess board. If Kate and Charlie were to reunite, it would exonerate Becca, put right the wrong she'd done them both. Playing devil's advocate, Kate had posited, 'So, I pounce. Charlie isn't appalled by my lack of sensitivity. No. Charlie takes me in his arms and it's happy ever after. What about Angus?' When Becca had made no answer, Kate had carried on. 'No more parties at the club. No more Christmas lunches.'

That had silenced Becca on the subject. A future where she couldn't casually name drop Ewan McGregor wasn't a future she relished.

Like a well-groomed Satan, Becca had tempted the poor sinner, Kate, with a vision of an alternative reality, where Kate and Charlie lived in harmony, together at last. When Charlie's masterpiece was published to great acclaim, he'd tell interviewers he couldn't have done it without Kate.

There were other alternative realities, however. Ones where, as in the current reality, Charlie was dropped by his agent and suffered a crisis of confidence. Alternative Charlie would lash out at alternative Kate, and she would snap back.

And somewhere out there, laughing and singing and lonely as hell, would be Angus.

Mature Kate wasn't convinced she could cohabit with the mature Charlie. He complained. A *lot*. He'd turned into a fussy eater. They argued about politics with genuine vehemence.

Whatever happened with Charlie, Kate believed she would have found her way to Angus.

'Becca's right,' said Charlie, in the here and now. 'Lucy's too young for me.'

'Becca's never right. Love just happens, Charlie.'

'Was it love?'

'It looked like it from where I stood.'

'What now?' Charlie looked hungrily at Kate, as if she might have the answer to it all.

Kate, who couldn't even remember the password to her own laptop, was glad to be Charlie's confessor and confidante, but lately she'd felt stretched. There were only so many times she could say *It's going to be all right*. He needed honesty from her. *I'll be there for you*: she could promise that. Dad's favourite Shakespearean nugget came to mind. *Thank you, Dad*, she thought. 'To thine own self be true, Charlie,' she said.

'Which self, though? The self that's moping around, writing a book nobody wants to read?' Charlie straightened up. Brightened. 'I could come to China with you!'

'Ah. Well.'

'Oh no, Kate you've—'

'Cancelled? Yes.' Kate shrugged. 'I know. *Again*.' Her focus on Yulan House had led, inevitably, to an aspiration to visit Jia Tang.

Charlie bent to interrogate her. His breath smelled of gravy. 'What's the reason this time?'

'I'm too busy with work.'

'Your company practically runs itself.'

'Only somebody who's never run a business would say that.'

'It's Angus, isn't it?'

'No! He loves Yulan House.'

The white building among the magnolia trees had captured Angus's imagination. The annual fundraiser at Astor House contributed to the cost of building a clinic in the grounds. Although they didn't recognise any of them, the children had reportedly loved the video of famous faces wishing them 'Good luck from London!' in stuttering Mandarin.

'It's a shrine,' Angus had laughed when he saw the photo of Kate's spare room she'd sent to Yulan House, the space where she hung photos and displayed the myriad trinkets the children sent her above ranks of files and folders. Spotting the prized 'Chinese teapot' snap of a tiny Kate with her dad, he'd asked, 'Do you think he'd approve of me?'

'He'd approve of anybody who made me happy.'

When Angus had asked, 'And I do, don't I, despite it all?' there'd been a plea in his voice that jarred with his physical bulk.

Charlie brought her back to him, tousling her hair as if she was Flo. 'I know Angus loves Yulan House. I meant you won't go without him. You two are tethered together.'

'I haven't had time to fix my place up properly.'

'Because you're always here.'

'I like it here.'

'And you like Angus, the lucky old lump. When are you both coming to mine? I'm fed up asking.'

'It's hard to drag him away from the club. Customers expect to see him.'

'Just you, then.' Charlie lifted his chin to look down at her knowingly. 'Or do you have to ask permission?'

Kate poked him hard, glad he'd found a lighter tone. 'I stay with Angus because I want to.' *And because I have to.*

'It's . . . how long since I cooked you dinner? My fish pie isn't as good as Lucy's but I do my best.' Charlie pushed hair that needed a cut out of his eyes. 'This,' he said, pointing first at her and then at himself, 'is *good*, isn't it?'

'What are you on about?' Kate felt something jump in her breast. Was it panic? Gladness? Through the glazed door she saw Angus lead a conga through the back bar.

'Friendship,' Charlie went on. 'You're my best friend in the world, Kate. I don't know what I'd do without you.'

A rush of feeling made Kate bow her head, lips pursed tight.

Charlie put a finger beneath her chin and lifted her face. A sense memory, at a deeper level than thought, silenced Kate. The younger Charlie had done that to her a thousand times and what came next was always a kiss.

'This,' said Charlie, 'is better than what we thought we had. This can't split up.'

'Friendship,' agreed Kate, 'trumps love every time.' She stood up, startling Charlie with the abruptness of the movement. 'Shall we get back to the others?'

Indoors, the party began to peter out. There were more defections.

Charlie slipped away.

Mum's driver – a female: 'very modern,' said Mum – had strict instructions to toot the horn as they entered the close, in case the neighbours hadn't noticed Mrs Minelli coming home in a Mercedes.

Kilian melted away at some point, and Rosie was picked up by a dubious-looking man.

Torn from her new Wii, Flo wore the scarf knitted for her by Kate as she hopped down the steps with her mother and stepdad, Leon guffawing at his own jokes about the dimensions of Becca's bottom.

'Kate, precious, I love your family . . .' Angus sank like a toppled oak to the sofa.

'But thank God they've gone?'

'Exactly.' Angus pulled Kate to him and together they jostled and fidgeted until they'd achieved maximum sofa comfiness.

Outside a lone drunkard sang a carol mash-up. Inside the old house creaked and ticked as the fire crackled. Kate assumed Astor House was haunted. By Ghosts of Piss Ups Past, perhaps. She'd grown accustomed to the odd merger of domesticity and trade, to the green glow of the fire exit sign and the glimpse of the cash register in the back bar.

Holding up her hand, she said, 'I love my new ring.'

'Your poor ma thought it was an engagement ring.'

'Becca put her right.'

Angus's impression was spot on. 'No way!' he flounced, à la Becca. 'If Angus proposed he'd get her a massive diamond not a stupid pearl.'

'No offence!' They mimicked her postscript together.

'Don't,' said Kate gently, staying his hand as Angus reached out for the decanter on a low table. 'We're too cosy to move.' She snuggled deeper, pinning him down. 'Another Christmas almost over. Today was a microcosm of our relationship.'

'Don't call it that. We're having a grand affair, not a relationship. A conveyor belt of hanky panky and profiteroles.'

'Whatever you call it, this morning was like our first dates.' Both of them fresh as daisies, she explained, exploring each other. By the time they put the turkey in the oven they were on to the later dates, sure this was something special, a festive feel in the air. 'And now, we're relaxed and languid, because we've seen each other at our worst and our best, we've shared our secrets and we still love one another.'

'But today's not over yet.' Angus shifted, the better to see Kate's face. 'Now you've compared today to our *relationship*, what does that make tomorrow? Our break-up?'

'Tomorrow is Boxing Day. Just Boxing Day.'

'How come my secrets haven't sent you screaming for the door?'

Kate knew he was remembering Mum reading out the Christmas card. *Kiss kiss kiss*. 'It was too late. I was already in love.'

'I'm going to try. Really *try*, darling.'

'Angus, don't promise if you—'

'I mean it.'

'Good.' Such understatement.

The gurglings of their tummies woke them up when they nodded off. Sitting up, sticky eyed, the room was still warm. The open fire, being gas, hadn't gone out.

'Almost midnight.' Kate yawned, her breath noxious enough to qualify as a weapon.

'Let's have one last snifter.' Almost toppling off the sofa, Angus leaned over and groped for the brandy.

'Darling. Remember what you said . . .' Kate laid her hand on Angus's arm.

'Kate, angel, don't be such a fucking killjoy.'

It was her own fault. Kate had set herself up. Comparing today to their affair meant that their recent past was mirrored in the dregs of Christmas Day.

The fire was out. The lights were turned up full. Kate collected discarded glasses and smeared plates, stepping around the rug.

From the rug, where he lay stranded like an upended turtle, Angus hollered, 'Look at you! You're turning into your mother!'

'Come on, you.' Kate knelt, carefully jocular. 'Time for bed.'

As she'd known he would, Angus lashed out, his legs pumping. The predictability of it all was one of the worst aspects of her situation. 'Unhand me!'

'It's late, darling.'

'The night is young.'

When Angus latched his arms about her neck, Kate used his ardour to heave him up until they both knelt, awkwardly facing each other. It was like a shambling Olympic Floor Exercise. Kate pulled at the much heavier Angus, who, limp and giggling, resisted her.

The four poster was three flights of stairs away. Kate persisted. She did this most nights, so she knew what it took to haul Angus to bed.

Convulsing, Angus broke free and scuttled through to the bar on all fours like a cockroach. 'Let's break out the rum!'

'I've had enough to drink,' said Kate. She added, tentatively, lightly, 'and so have you, sweetheart! Let's get you to bed.'

'Seductress!' Angus hauled himself to a standing position against the wooden bar counter. He slapped his tummy. 'You only want me for my body.' He grasped, like a baby grasps for a rusk, at the optics on the far side of the bar. 'Plenty of time for monkey business after a tot of rum.' There would be no monkey business in the four poster that night.

'OK! I'll be your barmaid.' Bright. Chipper. That way she could dilute the booze, although she ran the risk of him charging like a bull if she went too far with that trick. 'Here's your rum, kind sir.'

The kiss Angus blew was wet and grotesque.

Kate's analogy held; the end of their Christmas Day was tediously inevitable.

On a stool, Angus fulminated against imaginary foes. 'Fucking Kilian,' he spat, eyes blank. 'After all I've done for him.'

Kate didn't ask what Kilian had done because Kilian hadn't 'done' anything.

'Barmaid! I'm thirsty.'

Kate filled his glass, adding a surreptitious measure of water. She knew his thirst could never be satisfied. It was a need that had nothing to do with hydration, or partying. To the lame ducks he supported, the journalists he feted, being Angus looked like a heap of fun but Angus needed to stop being Angus at regular intervals, or he couldn't carry on.

'Smile, can't you?' Angus's machine gun had swivelled to find Kate, as she'd known it would. 'It's fucking Christmas.'

Lover and nursemaid was an uneasy mix. Prolonged exposure to Angus's alter ego resulted in a dimming of Kate's inner lights, a shrinking of her expectations of happiness. She'd been lured into intimacy by Angus's virtues, each as big and as bold as his faults. By the time she'd looked up *alcoholism* on Google, Kate was trapped.

Trapped by love, which throws the most unbreakable bonds of all around people. And, furthermore, trapped by Angus's potential.

*It doesn't have to be like this.* That truth nagged and fretted at Kate. Her lover was in the grip of a disease, but it was one that could be controlled. If he'd been one iota less fond and loving, Kate would have fled long ago. But somewhere inside the after-hours monster who roamed Astor House was the man she loved, who she would wake up with the next morning.

And when even the love grew thin, when it was sorely tested by Angus's crimes, there was duty.

*He needs me.*

'Hey, who's that texting at this bloody hour?'

'Mum. She says thank you for a wonderful day and the lady driver was lovely.' Kate could never admit to Mum that Angus hired chauffeurs because of his tendency to jump, pissed, into the driver's seat.

Eyes filled with tears, Angus said, 'God, I love your mother.'

It could have gone either way; last week Mum had been branded a 'Mesopotamian harlot'.

Patting his pockets, Angus seemed to have lost something.

Guessing what it was he searched for and hoping to distract him, Kate said, 'I had an email from Jia Tang today.

The children have finished painting the fresco in the dining hall. It looks amazing. She thinks February will be a good time to visit so should I—'

'Go whenever you like.' Angus's hand was stuck fast in his pocket. 'I couldn't give a stuff, as Rhett Butler almost said.' He wrenched his hand free and stopped, taken aback by the Christmas card he'd pulled out of his pocket. Kate was glad; Angus's drunken bile about Yulan House – the antithesis of his daytime attitude – was hard to absorb and forgive.

Forgive. That wasn't the word for what Kate did. Like much about Angus, there was no word for the feelings she went through. Midnight Angus was the opposite of the daylight man, a deformed caricature. The vile opinions he spouted weren't his own. Not really.

'Esther.' Angus's face melted with sadness as he straightened out the creases of the card. 'Where are you, Esther?'

Questions would be asked; Mum had sensed a secret when she mentioned the taboo name. If she'd had time to take in the handwritten date at the top of the card, she'd have seen that Esther had signed her name at Christmas 1999.

Gently, as if praying, Kate said, 'She'll come back. One day.'

The rest of the night hinged on what Angus did next. Kate was ready to duck, but instead she had to brace herself as Angus sobbed, his arms around her, burying his face in her as if he wanted to burrow through her body.

Kate almost toppled, but she held fast and she held him up.

Having refused to go to bed, Angus lay in state on the sofa. From the tilt of his head Kate reckoned he'd soon nod off. With enormous experience in the field, she was an authority on his behaviours.

When his voice dwindled and the story tailed off, Kate tucked a blanket around him and doused all the candles he insisted on. She lived in fear of hearing Angus had burned to death in this panelled house.

Creeping away, Kate let herself out. The chill of the courtyard garden was welcome on her burning skin after the claustrophobic building.

*I wish I smoked.* The bad habit would suit the moment. Kate longed to text Charlie, to wake him with a howl, but she would never 'out' Angus, not even to Charlie.

Pacing the small yard, Kate thought about Esther. Angus would flip if he knew Kate had tracked her down. Over a herbal tea in a Shoreditch café – so nearby! – Esther had finally said, 'Just *no*,' holding up paint stained hands as if to fend Kate off. 'I get it, really, you're doing this for the best but I won't see him.' She'd filled in a lot of gaps in the narrative.

Esther had been twelve when her mother had 'finally got her shit together' and left Angus. The divorce had been 'rough'. 'I went to Dad for weekends,' said Esther. She'd seemed ready to cry but Kate could tell the young woman was made of strong stuff. 'Sometimes it was funny but mostly it was . . .'

Kate had known the word she needed was 'sad'.

'When I was fifteen I said, right, you've got no more responsibilities, Big A. You're not my dad any more.' The girl's voice had cracked on that quote. 'He's not dad material. It's not his fault. But it's not mine either.'

'Just one more chance?' Kate had pleaded in a way she never would on her own behalf.

'This is what he does.' Esther had stood up in spattered overalls. 'He makes the people around him responsible when what he should do is stand up and face the mess he's made. That look on your face,' Esther had said, pointing. 'That's the look I remember on my mum's face. She was broken in the end, and for what?' She'd fiercely buttoned up her parka. 'So Big A can booze, that's what.'

That Angus put Esther's last card on the mantelpiece year after year, that he thought of her constantly when sober and cried for her when drunk didn't matter to Esther. She knew what a diamond her father was, but 'none of that means anything day to day when you're dealing with alcoholism and its power to spoil'.

The two note beep that heralded a text reminded Kate of the world beyond Astor House. A reassuringly normal place where people right now were setting their alarm clocks and brushing their teeth.

Book that trip to China with Angus. Make 2013 the year you finally do it. You made a promise to your dad, remember!
C xxx

All the lies, layered over each other, had solidified into a patina. Angus would never go to China. He barely went to the end of the street. He could tramp a path from society 'do' to PR bash and back to the club, to places where his endless drinking looked like high living and not low addiction.

Kate couldn't persuade Angus to her own house, never mind China.

Love never came without strings. Kate was more than old enough to know this. It brought duty, too; she loved Angus and therefore she looked after him. Twice he'd gone cold turkey. He'd meekly obeyed her (daytime) demand that he see a therapist. Every time that Angus drove Kate to an ultimatum, he vowed to turn over a new leaf.

Kate was stuck. As if the courtyard was paved not with Cornish slate but gum.

After one memorable abomination, Angus had hung his head and said, 'You should leave me. Everybody walks away backwards in the end.'

Instead of leaving, Kate had pledged herself anew. 'If you don't care enough about yourself to clean up, do it for *me*.'

There had followed a period of calm and stability, which had erupted one night into chaos. Still, Kate hoped for change.

When Angus was what Kate thought of as his real self, she needed nothing more than his jokes and his giggling and the smell of his skin and the clumsy way he held her, to get her through life. She fed off Angus, drawing energy from the light that surrounded him. There was always fun afoot, and after the fun there was the calm of their togetherness, when all was private and quiet and she could see that he – miracle of miracles – felt the same way about her.

Reading the signs, Kate guessed that this Christmas chaos was the start of an epic binge. With the club closed for three days, Angus could apply himself to drinking with the diligence of a professional, the shutters barred and a miasma of self-hate like a shawl about his shoulders.

*If I left* . . . The front door was ten steps away, whether Kate walked there backwards or not. The cold dark street would swallow her.

. . . *I could go to Charlie.* Charlie would take her in. He'd listen and expostulate and then he'd console. But he no longer loved Kate the way she wanted him to. The way Angus loved her.

Like the carved man and woman on a wooden cuckoo clock, Charlie and Kate constantly missed each other. One came out as the other went back in. When she was single, he was in love, and vice versa. They were obviously a pair but the mechanism that ruled their lives was implacable. Never together, eternally out of step, their segregation was pre-ordained . . . *Or I could just go home.* She imagined herself curled up in her own house, feeling it come back to life around her after months of neglect. She could be herself, not the person anybody else expected or wanted her to be.

The shout from indoors shocked Kate. She'd expected two, maybe three hours of respite as Angus slept, comatose.

'Damn her!'

Through the glazed door Kate saw Angus jigging about the back bar.

A flame soared. Kate leaped to her feet.

'Little bitch!' Like a pagan, Angus danced around the burning Christmas card in an ashtray on the counter.

Kate threw a glass of water over the small blaze. She hadn't meant to cry, but he'd punched through to one of her fears. 'Angus! You could have burned the house down.'

'I want to,' said Angus, his face florid. 'I want to burn down the world.'

You are cordially invited to

## Ms. Catherine Minellis

*Wicked*
*Hen Night!*

*Second time lucky!*

Corks Wine Bar
Wednesday 19th March 2014
8 o'clock

'Another round of shots, please.' Even as Kate said it, she regretted it. The 'reserved' booth in the corner was anything but; Aunty Marjorie had never tasted shots until an hour ago and now she was threatening to kiss the barman. 'Just a Coke for me.' Somebody had to keep their head. Becca, who was notionally the organiser of this hen night, was already giddy and Mum was gearing up for a rendition of *Danny Boy*.

'You've got another guest.' The barman gestured at a tall figure further down the bar, shrugging off a coat. 'Nice-looking bird.'

'But everybody's here.' The eleven hens were all present and correct. Kate peered at the well-built lass grinning at her, lipstick all over her teeth. 'Charlie?'

His legs supermodel long in thick tan tights, Charlie's little black dress clung on for dear life. Mincing towards her on stiletto heels, he grunted with pain at each step. 'You women deserve a medal,' he said, 'simply for being able to walk and talk at the same time.'

'You make an . . . interesting woman,' said Kate through her laughter. 'That's quite a cleavage.'

'Too much?'

'*Too much* he asks, standing there in a Dolly Parton wig and sparkly eye shadow. You look amazing. The hens will *die*.'

They almost did. The corner booth erupted as the giant-ess approached. Aunty Marjorie crossed herself over and over, and Mum had to dig out her glasses. 'You make a better-looking woman than Kate!'

'I don't understand.' Becca didn't join in with the jubila-tion. 'Charlie can't come, he's a bloke.'

'I had to be here,' said Charlie. 'Couldn't miss the hen night of one of my favourite women. Equality!' He punched the air and his bangles rattled.

'You're very welcome, Charlie,' said Mum, making space beside her.

'Why didn't you bring your girlfriend?' Becca was as

arch as somebody who'd been alternating shots with vodka jellies could be. 'Does she have to be up for school tomorrow?'

'She's picking me up later,' said Charlie, pretending the query was kindly meant.

'On her skateboard?'

'Shush, Becca!' Kate was determined to keep the peace.

'Don't shush me,' said Becca. 'You've told me you think it's daft. A thirty-seven-year-old man running around with a twenty-year-old girl.'

'We don't run around,' said Charlie. 'And I'm plainly a thirty-seven-year-old woman.'

'Easily the most terrifying thirty-seven-year-old woman I've ever seen,' said Kate, grateful that the barman took that moment to arrive with the shots. The combination of booze and an opportunity for sexual harassment distracted Becca from goading her ex-husband.

'Do you really think me and Anna are daft?' asked Charlie, discreetly.

'You know I do.' Kate saw no reason to pretend. Zipping around in his new camper van, hanging out at music festivals he hadn't even heard of before he met Anna, texting Kate snaps of himself bare-chested in love beads, Charlie was having lots of fun but it smacked of displacement activity. He and Anna never sat still; she wondered how well they actually knew each other.

'I love her, you know,' said Charlie, in a wounded voice at odds with the hell bent hedonism of the rest of the table.

That was the trouble: Charlie *always* loved them. He wasn't to know that his declarations cheapened Kate's memories of when he'd said the same about her. With Lucy she'd understood, but Anna was vapid and . . . there was no flowery way to put it, the woman wasn't *nice*.

'Flo likes her. Flo *loves* the camper van. I'm not an embarrassing dad.' Charlie made a noise in his throat. 'Not yet.' At eleven, Flo was nearing the tipping point whereafter *everything* Charlie said, did or thought would mortify her.

'I can't take anything you say seriously when you have eyeliner on. Oh my God.' Kate put her drink down. 'In drag, you look just like . . .'

'I know.'

Kate and Charlie both looked across the table at Becca, partway through some complex joke which would have no punchline, tossing back her blonde extensions and fixing her cantilevered black dress's neckline.

'It's uncanny.' Kate needed a shot, suddenly. 'It would take a troupe of Freudians to work that out.'

'Becca's *furious* with me,' said Charlie. 'I won't back down. I'll fight her on this.'

'This isn't the time or place to discuss that.' Kate didn't want the latest bone of contention to ruin the hen night.

'Has Jaffa . . .' Charlie didn't seem able to finish the sentence. The dog, an OAP, had been poorly.

'He's here tonight,' said Kate. She nodded cagily at an urn in the middle of the table.

Charlie's eyes widened. Kate knew he was sorely tempted to laugh. Instead he whispered, 'R.I.P. Jaffa.'

A man loomed over Kate. She jumped, startled, when she realised he was a policeman. 'We've had a serious complaint,' he said, silencing the cackling hens. 'About the bride to be.'

*His uniform's very tight*, thought Kate.

'The complaint is,' the officer continued, 'she's too SEXY!'

And with that he whipped off his trousers.

'Dear God no!' shouted Kate, who had a long-standing fear of male strippers.

'Yay!' shouted Becca who'd booked him and would book one for herself every evening if only Leon would allow it.

'Where's this naughty bride?' shouted the officer, who smelled strongly of self-tan.

All fingers pointed and, her hands on her head, screaming with mingled humiliation and excitement, Mum stood up and yelled, 'Arrest me, officer!'

The crowded wine bar clapped along to Right Said Fred's *I'm Too Sexy* while the stripper whittled Kate's mother's nose to a point with his groin.

'Jaffa's loving it,' said Becca, sentimental tears in her eyes as she cradled the urn.

'Why,' said Charlie, clapping out of time and avoiding the gyrating man on the table, 'did Jaffa have to shuffle off his mortal coil just when I need Becca to be rational? I wanted to discuss the situation this evening.'

It was all Seattle's fault. If that rainy city had sufficient home-grown camera operatives with a degree in media technology then Leon wouldn't have been offered a job in one of that city's cable channel newsrooms.

An opportunity for Leon, an adventure for Becca, the job spelled misery for Charlie. *I'd be relegated to part time dad*, he raged. *I'd only see Flo during school holidays.*

At loggerheads with Becca, Charlie stopped short of canvassing Flo. The girl remained silent as her parents raged behind her back, at the heart of the conundrum yet removed from it. Still a goth, Flo was sparing with words. Perhaps growing up with Becca, who spent them like a sailor on shore leave, had made her that way. Such a sensitive girl would see merit in both her parents' viewpoints – as did Kate – but would Flo, like Kate, believe that the need for a father and daughter to be close trumped everything else?

When the stripper had bared all – Kate tried not to stare; her mother let out a frank *Jayzus!* – Becca shouted, 'Speech!'

To wild applause and stamping of feet, Mum stood. The smile on her face, a rarity during Kate's childhood, was now a constant. 'I've found my Dodi,' she told the faces turned towards her. Kate could tell who among them were Princess Di fans from the reaction; only the women who remembered the unfortunate who died alongside Diana in the Parisian car crash understood. Mum had persevered in her belief that Dodi was the love of Diana's life, despite evidence to the contrary. It suited the myth. 'I was introduced to the love of my life . . .' She turned to Kate. 'By Angus.'

When Mum had arrived home after the 2012 Christmas lunch at Astor House, she'd invited the lady driver in for a cup of tea, as would any self-respecting Irish woman. 'Lovely woman, that Mary,' she'd told Kate the next morning. 'And a divil for country music!'

Mum's allegiance to Garth Brooks – inferior only to Princess Di and the baby Jesus in her personal pantheon – had driven Kate's father to distraction. At Mary's suggestion, Mum joined her line dancing club. Mary bought Mum a Stetson for her birthday. They popped out together to car boot sales and country pubs.

Kate and Becca discussed this new friendship. 'Has your mum, you know, *realised*?' Becca would ask.

With boyishly short hair, Mary was refreshingly free of make-up, just her ever-ready smile brightening her face. Always in jeans and plain shirt, Mary favoured a lace-up brogue. Kate concluded that Mary was either Amish or lesbian. 'And,' she added, 'she's not Amish.'

Sincere, sensible Mary was obviously fond of Mum, and that fondness was obviously reciprocated, but Mum wasn't noted for her broad mind. Kate feared what might happen when Mum finally woke up and smelled the coffee.

Unexpectedly manifesting one morning on Kate's doorstep, her face pale, her handbag gripped to her chest in consternation, Mum whispered, 'You'll never guess!'

'Oh, Mum, I think I will.'

Mary had told Mum that she loved her.

'What did you say, Mum?' Kate almost didn't want to hear.

'I told her the truth. That I've never really believed in lesbians.'

Leprechauns: yes. Lesbians: no.

Confused, querulous, Mum had spent the next few nights with Kate in her new house, an ordinary and proper suburban villa that sat comfortably in its plot alongside other similar homes. Red brick. White wood. Inside were rows of books, a magnificent freezer, whimsical cushions. In Kate's room there was just a bed and a work of art on the wall. The Yulan House 'shrine' was now just part of the decor, and her cherished photo of herself as a tot with Dad hung over the log burner in the sitting room.

It was a real home.

The spare room still smelled of paint, but Mum barely left it. Kate didn't want to meddle but Becca had no compunction about repaying the oldies for all their prying over the years. 'Love is love, Aunty,' she hectored. 'What's holding you back?'

When they were alone, watching *Antiques Roadshow* together, Kate would suggest that, if love comes from God, might it be a sin to ignore it? 'At least talk to Mary. She'll be feeling hurt and rejected. She's a good person and she doesn't deserve that.'

'Whisht, you.' Mum resorted to Dublinese when her daughter turned the generational tables. 'Don't lecture me. It's easy for you and Angus. Your love is . . . normal.' Mum would twist in the chair at saying such things about Mary.

There were things Mum didn't know about Kate's normal love affair. Locked out of Astor House at midnight by Angus, Kate had walked home in her slippers. Normal didn't mean easy. She tuned back into her mum's hen speech.

'I thought it was foolish to fall in love at my age,' said Mum. 'And I told her so.'

Sitting with Jaffa's ashes in her lap, Becca shook her head. 'You can't choose who you love. I mean, look at me and Jaffa.'

Kate caught Charlie's raised, pencilled eyebrow. Even by her own standards, Becca was very drunk.

'I didn't make it easy for Mary,' said Mum, implying that this was no bad thing. 'I told her to stay away. But one day she disobeyed me and . . .'

Kate remembered that day. Mum had moved back home at last, and Kate, worried about her mother's state of mind, had dropped around with a Battenburg to find Mary in the kitchen. The two women were planning a rambling holiday in the Peak District.

'And that was that!' crowed Mum.

So narrow-minded, so closed off, a dead end for philosophical thought of any hue, Mum's consciousness had been expanded by love. Beneath the permed helmet of strangely blue hair a radical change had taken place, a transformation of outlook and behaviour that made the elderly Irish lady every bit as much a revolutionary as Trotsky. She and Mary, sitting in adjacent armchairs and calling out crossword clues, had managed to make single sex love utterly ordinary.

When Mary smiled up at Mum – a perk of a same sex wedding is that both partners can attend the hen night – she didn't see what Kate saw: a clingy, carping woman who could never be satisfied. Mary saw the love of her life. In a cardigan.

The mention of her own name in Mum's speech caught Kate off guard.

'I wouldn't have taken this step without the support of my darling daughter, Kate.'

*Darling daughter?* Bemused, pleased, Kate bowed as everybody cheered.

'Kate loved Jaffa!' shouted Becca.

'Shut up,' said Aunty Marjorie, 'about the feckin' dog, Becca.' She was out of sorts and had been since Mary's arrival. It wasn't just that Mary was a lesbian and had turned Mum into one (Aunty Marjorie's take on events); Mary had usurped Aunty Marjorie as prime confidante. Uncle Hugh was still in shock at this turn of events, but he'd happily welcomed Mary into the family, proudly wearing the hand-knits she churned out for him at an impressive rate.

Charlie spoke into Kate's ear, his false eyelashes tickling her neck. 'Did you sign the paperwork?'

Kate nodded. 'I now own only one Party Games shop.' Kate had hung on to her first premises, a decision in equal parts sentimental and shrewd.

'Now for the next phase of your life, eh?' Charlie's physicality had altered with the application of a Wonderbra. Knees primly together, his shoulder touched hers as if they were gal pals sharing gossip.

'China here I come.' Kate hoped she sounded more excited than she felt. The scale of organisation necessary had surprised her. 'This time next month, I'll be at Yulan House.'

'Don't forget to come home, will you?'

Even if it was only lip service that was good to hear. 'I'm only going for a month.'

'Angus has been calling me.' Charlie dropped his voice so only she could hear in the hubbub. 'Late at night. Says he'll do anything if you let him go with you.'

'How does he sound?'

Charlie sighed and they said it together.

'Drunk.'

The trip didn't spell the end of the affair. That had happened months ago. As prophesied by Angus, Kate had walked away backwards, weeping at each step, unable to stand the demands on her time, her wits, her energy. And fearing for her safety; each time she'd swallowed Angus's bad behaviour he'd dug deeper until he was chasing her through Astor House's beautiful rooms, locking her in, locking her out, terrorising her.

Daytime Angus accepted his fate. Night-time Angus railed against it until Kate changed her number. Her sense of duty, a stolid beast, was pep talked daily by Becca who'd been a rock from the moment she'd heard the truth.

Charlie, this strange Charlie who smelled of hairspray, evidently wanted to chat about China but superstition – the sort she abhorred – held Kate back. To be thirty-seven and *still* planning a long-anticipated trip felt plain silly. To divert him she said the magic words – *Anna* and *camper van* – and Charlie was off.

'Did I tell you we booked a week in Ibiza?'

Two details sprang to mind whenever Kate thought of Anna. One was her breasts, two of the jauntiest little chaps one could hope to meet. Two was the fact that Anna was the same age as *Friends*.

'It'll be a riot,' said Charlie, the v-shaped hairline of his soldier-short dark hair showing under his wig. 'Unless Becca comes good on her threat. Then everything changes.'

'It's not a threat.' Kate saw both sides of this latest clash; Becca, with her customary disbelief that other people had inner lives, couldn't see the problem. 'Writers can write anywhere,' she stormed. 'Why can't Charlie move to Seattle and write there?' As for Flo: 'That child's smothered with love! She can see Charlie in the holidays!'

The Flo Charlie sketched in the air was a girl who needed both her parents however imperfect they might be, a girl who must be shielded from the fallout of divorce. The disabling guilt he carried around from the break-up was shared with nobody – least of all Flo – except Kate.

As the evening hit a lull, the hens catching their breath, retouching their make-up, checking their phones, two new arrivals joined the booth.

'Leon!' shouted Mum, her face sweaty beneath her face powder. 'And, um . . .'

'Anna,' said Anna.

'That's mine, thank *you*.' Becca unhooked Leon's arm from Anna's, as if the hot pant-wearing young woman was after Becca's fifty-year-old pot-bellied husband.

'Thought I'd better turn up when your texts stopped making sense!' Leon punched Becca playfully on the arm. In profile, his nose disappeared as if sliced off by a malicious giant; the rhinoplasty Becca insisted on had decimated his fleshy conk. 'You're sloshed, treacle.' Leon's eyes lit up at the sight of Charlie. 'Ooh, kinky!'

Not a trace of rancour. Kate loved Leon. Salt of the earth, his devotion to Becca was absolute and unexamined; he was as committed to his wife as an orphaned monkey is to a wooden spoon with a face drawn on it.

Anna settled on Charlie's lap, and stroked his left fake breast. 'This is kind of horny,' she said, causing Kate's mum to bless herself rapidly.

'Mmm,' said Charlie, looking very like a man trying to feel horny but only achieving embarrassed.

Anna's arrival in her sequinned shorts and strapless top had triggered spontaneous tummy-holding-in around the table. As the woman took the compulsory selfies, pouting duck-like, Kate wondered *Do I dislike Anna because I dislike her, full stop? Or is it outdated, irrelevant jealousy?* Anna's sense of entitlement made Becca look like a beginner.

Kate gave her tummy permission to flop. It was pointless. To rival Anna she'd need to build a time machine, return to 1990 and renounce chips.

'Where we going after this, babe?' Anna bounced on Charlie's lap. 'And don't say home. Don't be boring.'

When Kate had left Angus, Becca declared that surely the time had come to deal with unfinished business. 'You must tell Charlie about the mix-up with the notes!' (She'd rebranded the deception as a 'mix-up'.) Becca argued her case with the suave dexterity of a barrister and the bossy authority of a cousin, but Charlie had already met Anna. He and Kate were out of step again. She told Becca *I don't have your taste for drive-by shootings*.

That was the noble side of the coin. On the grimy flip side was Kate's fear of rebuff, of her friendship with Charlie being tainted. If he knew she still carried a torch – and Jesus, her wrist was *aching* – he might subtly withdraw and Kate couldn't bear that.

Pushing her point home, Becca had growled, 'You really *are* a daddy's girl. Your dad didn't insist on what he wanted so the poor man died without ever seeing China.' There had been fear of going too far in Becca's eyes but Kate understood she was whipping out the big guns. Furthermore, Becca was right.

'I can't put everything on black,' Kate had said. '*Never* go to Vegas with me.'

If Charlie wanted a fresh start with young flesh, that was his prerogative.

There was an exodus of hens. Mum, Mary and Aunty Marjorie were all on the move, shrugging on windcheaters and amassing handbags. Maximum fuss. Maximum disruption. The people in the next booth, hell bent on snogging each other's faces off, were roped into searching for Mum's bus pass among the cushions.

Kate realised something. *Dad was Mum's Julian.* Mum had settled for Kate's dad and now, in her sixties, Mum had discovered true love.

'Come here, little Mum.' It had been a relief to hand the baton to Mary but at times Kate missed the feel of it in her hand.

'Get away, you soppy piece!' Mum fought the hug before relaxing into it.

From the other side, Mary put her arms around them both.

'You have two mums now, Kate,' said Mary.

Love really did make everything easier.

'Kiss Jaffa!' Becca broke them up, brandishing the urn. 'Kiss poor Jaffa!'

'I didn't kiss that little feck when he was alive,' said Mum. 'I'm not starting now he's dead.'

When the older ladies and their friends had moved off, a solid mass of geriatric good times, Becca cried, 'More shots!' as she and the others retook their seats. At the counter, Leon ordered coffees all round.

*You brave, brave man,* thought Kate.

'Don't start,' said Becca to Charlie.

Charlie righted his wig. 'I didn't say anything.'

'You were thinking,' accused Becca. 'About Leon. And his amazing job offer. And you shouldn't because it's none of your business.'

Kate moved a glass from chucking range.

'It's very much my business,' said Charlie. He pinned his glossy red lips together and made a visible effort not to go on the attack. 'But let's not talk about it while you're . . . let's not talk about it tonight.'

Anna was gazing at the receptacle in Becca's grasp. 'I'm not a dog person myself,' she said, unaware of the death stare this provoked from the urn's owner. Anna often broadcast factoids about herself in this manner. 'I'm more of a cat person. Aren't I?' She nuzzled Charlie's neck.

'Urgh. Get a room,' said Becca.

'Actually,' said Anna, walking her fingers up her boyfriend's 40-DD chest, 'I'm a baby person.' She pouted and Charlie squirmed. 'A baby would suit me, wouldn't it, Charlie? An ickle baby of my own? Pweez. One day you'll gimme a baba, won't you?'

Lip curled, Becca hissed to Kate, 'Poor cow'll be waiting a looong time.'

'Time to go.' Kate stood, thankful that neither of the love-birds seemed to have heard. She stood on tiptoe and shot a warning look at Leon over the late night drinkers' heads.

'Not yet.' Becca shook off Kate's arm and leaned over the table. 'Don't hold your breath, Anna. You know that child whose life Charlie is ruining by not letting her go to America?' Becca had their attention now and she spoke over Kate's attempts to close her down. 'Flo's not even his. Yeah.

305

Good old *Chaz* shoots blanks. You could shag him for centuries and still have no need to buy a cot.'

Joining them, Leon banged down the tray of coffees and put his face in his hands.

'You're drunk, Becca. Shut up.' Kate turned to Charlie. 'She's off her head, Charlie.'

Charlie stared at Becca, sombre beneath the glam make-over. 'Wow,' he said. 'You really hate me.'

'Let's not do this now.' Kate wished somebody, one of them, would move, go. Anna gawped, motionless.

'Then when will we do it?' Becca hugged Jaffa's remains to her as if the charred dog was the only one who understood. 'Kate, you should have let me tell him years ago.'

'You knew?' Charlie's gaze moved to Kate and she shivered.

'Charlie, take off the wig,' said Kate. 'I can't talk to you all dragged up.'

Standing, Charlie took off the hairpiece. The sudden masculinity of his short hair rendered his perfect maquillage eerie. 'Anna. Let's go.'

'Stay.' Kate changed her mind; he mustn't leave. 'You can't just . . .' She groped for words. The surroundings and the personnel were all wrong for this conversation. 'Becca, what is *wrong* with you?'

Already on the road to regret, Becca was ashen. 'What's wrong with *him*? Why can't he just let Flo have an adventure instead of putting himself first? This job is important to Leon and—'

'There is no job,' said Leon. 'I didn't get the job.' Leon sounded bereaved. 'Sorry, princess, but we're not going to the States.' Awkwardly inserting himself into the booth, he put an arm around Becca.

Pushing him away, Becca knocked over the coffee cups in her haste to put some distance between herself, her husband and the scene she'd caused. Leon said to Charlie, 'This is all highly regrettable, mate. Believe me, if I'd known she was planning this I'd have done something.'

'Don't worry, Leon. I think it was spur of the moment.' Charlie was ready to fight or flee by the look of him, standing tense in his LBD.

'I'd better find the missus.' Leon slipped away.

Snatching up Jaffa who'd been left on the table, Kate rushed after him. 'Here. For God's sake don't go without this.'

'I prefer Jaffa dead,' said Leon sadly. 'He doesn't crap in my slippers any more.'

'Did the job really fall through?' asked Kate. This close, Leon's ever-cheery face was rugged, marked by a long life that surely wasn't all fun and games.

'Put it this way,' said Leon, after a pause. 'There's no way we're going after that little sideshow.'

'You're a hero,' said Kate.

'I'll get Jaffa thrown at my head if she ever finds out.'

'Your secret's safe with me.'

Back at the table Anna, her head on Charlie's shoulder, was working her way through her stock of insults. 'What a cow. What a bitch.'

Unable to disagree, Kate said, 'It's complicated,' hoping it translated as *You've only just arrived in our lives so please back off.* It was unfair to expect a girl – that's all Anna was – to comprehend the complexity of galling, glorious Becca. How could she empathise with the lengths Becca had gone to in her quest to feel valued? At times Kate herself had trouble scraping together sufficient empathy. Tonight was one of those times.

'So she, what? She had an affair?' Anna poked through the entrails, appalled but excited as if discussing the plot of a movie.

Beneath his false lashes, Charlie winced as if somebody had stuck a blade in his side. 'Can we get out of here?'

Kate knew that two's company, three's a crowd, but she had the excuse of Charlie's insistence that she go back to his flat with them.

Showered, changed into jeans, Charlie was himself again, apart from stray glitter in his eyebrows. He was thin, *too thin*, in Kate's opinion. The thinness was for Anna, who preferred the trendy, wasted silhouette of the archetypal hipster. The spare frame was easier to achieve for young guys; Charlie had ripped up his gym membership and now carried a well-thumbed carb counter in the back pocket of his – skinny – jeans. Kate found it ridiculous that anybody would alter their actual body shape for the sake of fashion; she was sitting it out until big bums were à la mode.

'At times like this, people drink whisky for the shock.' Charlie scratched his head. 'But I've only got tea. Will that do?'

'Bring me some, pweez!' called Anna in a baby voice from the other room. She'd gone to bed and called out occasionally, by turns grumpy and imploring, like some giant kid they were babysitting.

Kate wandered about the room, touching things as Charlie fussed with the kettle and dropped the sweeteners. Charlie's writing had commandeered the poky flat. Towers of lined pads tottered on the rug. Post-It notes snaked across the walls. A plot diagram was drawn in the dust on a window pane. None of the books leaning chummily against each other on the shelves were by Charles Garland: all that effort and nothing published.

'Charleeeee! Me want a cuddle!'

'In a min, darling.' Charlie fobbed off Anna as he joined Kate on the sofa, an aged behemoth only made bearable by a myriad of cushions.

*Sex doesn't cure everything, Anna.* Kate heard the tone of her own thoughts and wondered if she was finally turning into her mother. The old, pre-Mary model.

A welcome contrast to the wine bar, the quiet room, a catch-all cooking/eating/relaxing space, was pure Charlie: no order, all charm.

Having rehearsed and discarded a number of phrases, Kate chose to open with, 'I'm sorry you had to find out this way.'

'You silly sausage,' said Charlie. 'I already knew.' He leaned back, closed his eyes. 'Remember how bad things got between me and Lucy at the end?' He opened his eyes and glanced at the door: mention of the most recent Queen was outlawed by the present monarch. 'We tried for a baby. It wasn't like me and Anna, just silly talk. Lucy, God bless her, was desperate to be a mum.' Charlie looked into the middle distance. 'It was a sticking plaster, sure, a bad idea, but we both wanted it.'

The sigh made Kate suspect that not only Lucy was 'desperate' for a child.

'Weeks passed. Months. Nothing. Lucy was jittery because, of course, *I* was obviously fertile. Flo was proof of that. She wanted to get herself checked out and I said I would too because, well . . .'

'You're a nice guy,' said Kate, feeling intently how near he was. And how far away.

'Not really.' Charlie ducked the compliment. 'I just wanted to support her. You can imagine what happened next. Lucy got the all clear. I was told I was infertile.'

They were quiet for a moment, giving that memory the space it needed.

'She's got a little son now, did I tell you?' Charlie tried to smile. 'Lucy'll be a great mum.' He slapped his knees. 'Ah, well . . .'

'What was the problem? With you, I mean?' Kate thought of those miscarriages and didn't like the light it shed on Becca.

'You sure you want to know?' Charlie gave her a sideways look. 'None of the story is pretty, as you can imagine. I have ejaculatory duct obstruction.'

'Right,' said Kate, uncertainly.

'Don't worry. You're allowed to pull a face. I pulled a face for about a month when I first heard the term. Basically . . .' Charlie sighed, hating putting it into words. 'Me tubes are bunged up. I can make, you know . . .'

'Semen?' said Kate, helpfully. She hadn't expected the evening to end this way.

'Yeah, that stuff,' smiled Charlie. 'But there's very little sperm.' He rubbed the end of his nose, suddenly and viciously. 'Not something blokes like to admit.'

'Oh Charlie, it's only me.' Kate moved nearer. 'Can't the doctors do anything?'

311

'There are procedures. I won't explain. It'd put you off your dinner for life. It's very invasive, lots of possible side effects, and even then only a twenty per cent possibility of a natural pregnancy for the partner.' Charlie shrugged, understating. 'It wasn't the nicest afternoon of my life.'

'How did Lucy react?'

'She was shocked, like me. We couldn't speak about it, or anything else, until the next morning. And then we talked about nothing else. Lucy had had a ton of tests herself by this point, and she was sick of waiting rooms and statistics and bad news. She didn't want to make me go through the treatment if it might not make a difference. I told her I'd do it for her and that was . . .' He exhaled sadly. 'That did it, really. Lucy wanted me to do it for *us*.'

'I suppose,' said Kate, 'there's a world of difference between those two words.'

'I said I'd do it, said I'd do *anything*. I loved Lucy. You know that. But not enough, it turned out. The pressure pushed at the stress points in our relationship. We tried and we hung on but in the end we parted and we were right. It still feels right,' said Charlie, a lump in his throat strangling the words.

'Oh Charlie.' Kate felt for him, wanting to make it all better.

'As well as the implications for me and Lucy, there was, of course . . .'

'Flo,' said Kate.

'My Flo,' said Charlie.

'Is there any chance she *is* yours?'

'I'll tell you what the experts told me. Ejaculatory duct obstruction can be something you're born with, but in my case it was late onset. They pinpointed 2000 as the approximate year the problem began. They were sure it was no later than 2001.'

'Flo was conceived in . . .' Kate counted on her fingers. 'Summer 2002.' Her shoulders wilted.

'It's not like *CSI*. They can't be completely accurate.' Charlie had trawled back through his life, remembering a period when Becca had seemed elusive, when he hadn't always known where she was, when she'd been twitchy, touchy. 'Hiding something.'

Kate remembered how she'd done the same thing with Becca, retracing her steps, unpicking the betrayal.

'Obviously Becca was impatient to fall pregnant again. Whether she had a proper affair or just a drunken one night stand . . . It doesn't really matter. But the diagnosis plus Becca's behaviour plus my own sixth sense added up to the fact that, although the early babies, the children we lost, were mine, Flo very probably wasn't.' Charlie's demeanour changed. No longer reflective, he was almost angry. 'You didn't tell me.'

'It wasn't my job.' Kate was firm. Her decision to keep quiet hadn't been taken lightly. 'It would have blown your marriage apart. More importantly, it would have had repercussions between you and Flo.'

'Yeah. Me and Flo,' said Charlie slowly. 'Look, you and Becca, you like to thrash things out, go over things again and again. But me, I've done my thinking and it's this.' Charlie sat up, deaf to the yowled '*Chaz babes! Pleeease!*' from the bedroom. He stabbed a cushion with his finger as he made his points. 'I was the first to hold Flo. All that love can't go to waste. I rank her happiness and safety far above mine. That child needs me and I don't just *need* Flo. They haven't minted the word that covers how I feel about her. So I've done my thinking. Flo's my little girl. And I'm her daddy.'

Qīn'ài de kǎitè

wǒ zìjǐ, zhōu, xú cèng zǔ zhīle yīgè xǐ ǎ oxīng de júhuì
zhōng n ī de rongyù  shuō zàijiàn. qǐng lái dào shítǎng,
mingtiān xiàwǔ 5 diǎn.

Nǐ de
jiā tang

2014-11-04

Dear Kate

Myself, Chow and Xu have organised a small party in your honour to say goodbye. Please come to the canteen tomorrow at 5pm.

Your friend

Jia Tang

Every second word was a crackle.

'I *crackle* hate *crackle crackle* Skype,' said Charlie, as he flew apart into technicolour fragments and then came together again.

'Hang on, hang on. That's better.' Kate smiled as his face, grumpy and discombobulated, sharpened up.

'I only half believe you're getting on that plane tomorrow.'

'This time I mean it.'

'One month my arse. Seven months you've been there. What's it got that London hasn't got?'

'Stop teasing.' Charlie knew what Beijing had. It had challenge, it had promise, it needed her.

'Even with this crappy technology I can see in your face that you're already planning your next trip.'

'You could always come with me . . .'

'I can't see Anna swapping swinging London for Fangshang district.'

*I didn't invite Anna*, thought Kate. The girl had grit. Even Becca had to admit that. Anna had chewed up and digested the horrible scene in the wine bar, telling Charlie it didn't matter. Kate reminded herself that the girl was only twenty, that her earlier talk of wanting a baby and subsequent change of heart were probably just attitudes she was trying on for size. Anna had plenty of time to work out what she really wanted. *When I was that age I wasn't thinking about babies*. At thirty-eight, almost twice Anna's age – Kate gulped and shooed away that thought – Kate realised she'd spent almost two decades believing the cosmos had a little being with her name on it, waiting for the perfect moment to waft the child her way.

'So,' the fuzzy Charlie said, 'did you read it?'

'Every word.'

'And?'

'Charlie, I love your book.'

'Really?' The elation lasted all of a second. 'You have to say that, though.'

'True. But luckily I really do love your book.'

The four hundred pages and one hundred thousand words of *BLOKE* had engrossed Kate in her tidy single bed at the orphanage. Charlie's aim to write a story that enthralled on a human scale, without explosions or plagues or a plot to blow up the Eiffel Tower, had resulted in a beautifully detailed novel of the impact that ordinary love has on an ordinary man. 'I loved it. Every word.' She'd searched for herself in the pages, at first trepidatious, then disappointed. If not the love interest, couldn't he have included her as a villain? Or even a thumbnail sketch?

Desperate for detail, Charlie asked, 'And the scene where the hero gets together with the love of his life after all they went through? Did it ring true?'

'I wept. Actual tears.' In Kate's head Charlie had voiced the hero's lines and the heroine had sounded suspiciously like herself. 'It was my favourite chapter.'

'Mine too. Not my editor's, though. I have rewrites to plough through.' Charlie exhaled showily. 'Man, I feel as if I've been writing this book since I was born and it's still not finished.'

'Works of art are never finished,' said Kate, in the lofty tone she used for aphorisms. 'They're merely abandoned.'

'Very true. You're my personal guru. Can you believe that next May you'll actually be able to walk into a bookshop and buy a novel with my name on it?' Charlie looked the way Flo did on rollercoasters, just before she threw up.

'*Charles Garland.*' That person was a stranger to Kate; the book was pure Charlie, all the way through.

'You weren't here to celebrate the deal.' Charlie leaned in, his face suddenly enormous. 'You owe me a big night out.'

The stars had aligned above the last-gasp pitch by Charlie's disenchanted agent. The twentieth editor to read his manuscript had seen potential in it, renaming it on the spot. '*BLOKE*' ran contrary to all of Charlie's earnest suggestions, but he had to admit that in shiny black lettering on a plain white cover it was eye catching. After the publishers named a figure more than he earned in five years of consulting, Charlie would have let them call his book anything at all.

'And that's only the beginning,' his agent claimed. Charlie's life had gone up a gear overnight. His agent, now his bestest friend in all the world, had danced off to sell translation rights in over thirty territories and was currently standing by his phone waiting to hear from Sony about a possible movie version. Charlie and Kate had spent happy hours on Skype casting *BLOKE: THE MOVIE,* and fantasising about Charlie's Oscar acceptance speech. 'If you don't thank me,' Kate warned, 'I'll beat you senseless with your little gold statuette.'

As Charlie dissolved into fizzy lines, Kate said, 'You do know that Becca's only pretending she hasn't read it to annoy you, don't you? She thinks it's brilliant. She's sorry now that she nagged you so much about leaving your job to write. She had no idea you were so talented.'

The Charlie on the screen tried not to look chuffed. 'Does she realise the character of the horrific ex-wife who drowns in a speedboat accident is based on her?'

'Not. A. Clue.'

'Typical.' Charlie sat back in his chair and gazed at his ceiling, so far away in London. 'I love that woman. Even after all the crap she put me through. There's nobody quite like Becca. It's as if she's full of love she can't express and it all comes out sideways. Now I'm getting older I appreciate one-offs, people who really are *themselves* and make no bones about it.'

'I love her too. It's a life sentence.' Charlie had more to forgive than he knew. Kate would never squeal about the double-cross that split them up. Kate held up the top page from the pile. 'I bet Anna's enchanted by this!'

*BLOKE*'s dedication read *For Anna, this bloke's bird.*

'She doesn't know yet.'

'Funny that you dedicate your book to her but you won't give her a key to your flat.'

Hints, many of them heavy enough to break through to the flat below, had been dropped by Anna about taking their relationship to the next level but Charlie had misconstrued them all. 'Plenty of time for all that. Why get bogged down in domesticity when we're having so much fun? I want to chase her around in her underwear, not argue about whose turn it is to bleach the loo.'

'This is so you, Charlie. You make out it's just fun and games yet you dedicate your book to her. You're in love.' Again. *Charlie falls in love*, thought Kate, *with the same regularity I have a bikini wax*.

'I like being in love.' Since 'that' call from his agent it had been impossible to dent Charlie's good humour. 'You like being in love, too, madam. It's not just the dodgy connection that's making your face glow. You look different. You look ten years younger. Still not as young as Anna, but it's a start. And all because you're in love.'

Charlie was the only one who knew. 'Wish I *felt* ten years younger but yes, OK, you got me, it does feel amazing. I've never felt this way.' *Not even about you*. One day Kate would tot up how many of her sentences were finished off in her mind when she spoke to Charlie.

'When it's right, you know it.'

'Like you and Anna?'

'Naughty. Putting words in my mouth.'

'What's that I see behind you? Already spending your loot?' It had been an age since Charlie had disposable income; the majority of his earnings went straight to Becca and Flo.

Swivelling so Kate could appreciate every one of the widescreen TV's fifty glorious inches, Charlie said, 'Isn't it great? Now I can watch all the shit programmes I normally watch, only *huge*.'

'It makes your flat look tiny.'

Even Charlie's modest home looked like another, ostentatious planet after seven months at Yulan House. The squashy sofa, the pile rug, the old fireplace with quaint tiled surround, the framed Picasso print, the nostalgic lava lamp all added up to a busy opulence quite unlike the room Kate sat in.

It was a cell. Bare and clean and neat, her allotted bedroom affected the way Kate thought. When she sat on her iron bed, just wide enough for one and covered with a simple striped cover, Kate could focus. She had civilised her scampering wayward feelings between these cream walls.

It was easier to differentiate between the important and the trivial in this spartan environment. Answers became obvious, rising out of the fog. At first she'd found the room austere but now she knew the few items in it like friends. They all had an application and most had the patina of the second-hand and well used. Kate scrunched up her toes on the rag rug the children had made for her, appreciating its softness all the more for the contrast between it and the ubiquitous blue lino.

Happily isolated, Kate hadn't missed the constant stream of news and comment the internet had pumped into her brain back in the UK. The important events got through; Jia Tang wanted the children at Yulan House to grow up as world citizens. For the trivial, Kate relied on Becca, who had told her breathlessly about the leak of nude celebrity photos on the web. That had seemed inconsequential to Kate, who'd spent the day holding a traumatised, abandoned four year old, but the news of Robin Williams's death had saddened her. *The world needs its funnymen.*

'Charlie, can you hear that?' Kate cocked her head. A song Kate had taught the children about the English alphabet drifted in from a classroom across the courtyard. It sounded like small bells chiming.

'Nah. I can only hear the traffic outside my window. How're you going to cope with noisy old London after all that time down a dirt track in China?'

'Honestly? I'm not sure.'

The doorbell sounded at Charlie's end, a murky sound as if underwater. 'That'll be Anna. Gotta go. We're eating at some overpriced hipster shack she heard about on Twitter.'

'See you soon IRL.'

The screen died.

**From:** cathm392@hotmail.com
**To:** kateminelliparties@gmail.co.uk
**Subject:** Wedding snaps
5 Nov 2014 13.32

Jesus it's cold. I have icicles in me hair. Mary sends her love and says to tell you she's nearly finished the gloves she's knitting for you. She had to start again because she gave you an extra thumb.

I've attached more photos of the wedding. Mary says you'll be sick of them but sure you're not are you? Mary says I must have sent you a hundred by now but I counted and it's only seventy-two. I want you to feel as if you were there even though you weren't because you considered some kids in China more important than the wedding day of the woman who endured fourteen hours of labour for you. As you know I don't mind one little bit that you missed the wedding. In fact I never think about it.

Becca was over yesterday with Flo, who's nearly as tall as me now. Lovely manners but I wish she'd wear something that wasn't black now and again. Show off that pretty face. Becca has found a grand diet and is after losing a whole pound. She looks very different. Poor woman misses you terrible. Says it's like having her arm cut off. Mary says at least that way she'd have one less arm to eat biscuits with but Mary can be awful sharp and I've told her so.

Becca and Leon are off to THE BAHAMAS if you don't mind. Another holiday! Me and Mary have just put a deposit on a week in Wales.

Now, listen, don't shout but me and Mary and Becca want to throw you a little party to say 'welcome home'. Not on the night you touch down. We'll let you get over your lag jet or whatever it's called. The night after. Nothing fancy, now. Maybe a sausage and a Daniel O'Donnell CD. We'll save the glitter cannons for your four oh! You never know, you might even have a fella by then. As my granny used to say, for every old sock there's an old shoe.

I've cleaned your house from top to bottom. I know you didn't mean it when you turned down my offer. I must say I found a lot of grime in your nooks and crannies but it looks like a new pin now. I hate to interfere but you're going to love how I rearranged your furniture.

So, love, we'll see you in two days! Mary's making one of her special cakes for the party and we'll bring round the rest of the wedding photos.

Lots of love,

your Ma x

P.S. Daddy would be proud of you. I imagine him up there in heaven, looking down and protecting you as you help out with all his Chinese children.

P.P.S. I also believe he's forgiven me for being a secret lesbian all these years.

P.P.P.S. That was the first time I've ever typed lesbian. Ooh! That was the second!

Kate stood on tiptoe to see her face in the small framed mirror that hung on an awkwardly positioned nail. Her hair, uncut since her arrival, was scooped into a ponytail that tickled her back.

A pile of underwear awaited its turn to go into the open suitcase, along with some paperbacks, a wash bag and the photograph of Dad she loved so much, the one of him with a young Kate on his lap and a Chinese teapot in the background. It had sat on her chest of drawers in a smart leather travelling frame for the duration of Kate's stay at Yulan House.

Whipping a clean tee shirt out of the case, she pulled it over her head and that was her party prep accomplished. Fashion had fallen away, like other irrelevances. The kids found her foreignness interesting enough without any embellishment. Kate pulled out her make-up bag and peered at its tubs and brushes as if they were relics of a bygone civilisation whose peculiar ways were nothing like her own.

*Ping!* An email arrived. *I bet that's him.*

It was.

**From:** kingangus@astorhouse.com
**To:** kateminelliparties@gmail.co.uk
**Subject:** You'n'me
5 Nov 2014 8.34

Greetings my little China girl
Here are today's stats for your delectation:
Weight lost:    3st 3lbs
Days sober:    62
Hours spent pining for you:    Countless

I've made myself a name badge so you'll recognise me at Heathrow. *Who* you will ask *is that handsome blond devil? He looks like a younger slimmer sober version of my darling Angus!* PLUS I smell divine now i.e. not like the floor of a pub. PLUS I'll carry your cases without wheezing. PLUS I'll be driving myself there because I finally opened my ears and listened to a certain lady who kept telling me I had to stop hiding in Astor House. Oh, hang on! There's another important stat!

Days without ciggies    1

I finally kicked the habit. For my health. And for you. I only want to live longer if I can spend the extra years with Catherine Rose Minelli. A rose by any other name would smell only half as sweet.

Ax

As Kate lifted her hand to type a response, another email arrived.

**From:** bonkersbeccaoopboopadoop@leonlens.com
**To:** kateminelliparties@gmail.co.uk
**Subject:** YIPPEE!
5 Nov 2014 8.50

So much to tell you. SO MUCH. Can't wait to hear what you think of my new teeth. Cost 8k!! Leon hit the roof. One roast dinner and a good seeing to and he was fine.

I nipped over this morning and changed your furniture back the way you had it. Your mum made your house look like an old folks' home. I threw out the pot pourri she put on every surface and I opened the windows to get rid of that sickly air freshener she sprays everywhere. Tomorrow I'll pop over and put some essentials in your fridge. Milk. Tea. Sliced loaf. Tell me if there's anything specific you want. I suppose you eat your Shredded Wheat with chopsticks now . . .

There's a big parcel waiting in the hall for you. Can't make out what it is. The label's torn. Do you want me to open it and check it's OK? I don't mind. It's no bother.

Feeling a bit cry-y today. Had to take Flo out to buy her first bra. She's only 11! Still my little baby! It's not really a bra just a cropped thing with straps but she does need it. She went red as a berry every time I said 'bra'. I started saying it on purpose and she called me 'Mother' like she does when she's annoyed with me (99% of the time). She's grown up so much since you went away. God knows how but she's just like Charlie!!

On that subject your nagging/sound advice got through to me. I apologised. Not only about the way I misled him about Flo but also the way I let it slip out in public. There were many harsh words but I deserved them so I just listened. That was hard! You're good at listening but I would get an F in a listening exam. Finally he said he forgave me and it felt as if I'd lost a stone. Off my brain, if that makes sense. We're civil now. No, we're more than that. Charlie and me are cool.

Do you think I'm allowed to be proud of him and his book? Well, I don't care, I am. Apparently pictures of his gob are going to be on the sides of buses! Flo is BURSTING with pride about her famous dad. Well, not yet famous but he will be and then I'll be the ex-wife of Charles Garland who wrote *BLOKE*. I'll be very positive about him in interviews, I promise.

Right. I should bugger off and do something useful. Leon'll be home in a bit. I'm soooooo glad you've achieved your dream (and your dad's dream). But I'm gladder that you're coming home because you're family, Kate, and I need you close.

See you at the party!!!

Oodles of love

B xoxoxoxo

P.S. Don't forget to pick me up a massive bottle of Coco Mademoiselle in duty free or I'll wallop you.

Kylie Minogue is a blameless individual but Kate had had her fill of *Spinning Around*. The smaller children had learned the song phonetically; with no idea what they were saying they belted out the lyrics as they gyrated in the canteen.

'Xiao yi xiao!' Chow, the caretaker, aimed a camera at Kate and the various small individuals piled on her.

Kate's minimal Mandarin vocabulary recognised this as 'smile'. The kids shouted, 'Cheese!' just as she'd trained them.

They took countless photographs at Yulan House, but there was a poignant edge to these 'last opportunity' snaps. Little Fan wouldn't let go of Kate's leg, clinging on and having to be prised away by her friends.

There were fifty orphans or abandoned children in Jia Tang's care. A nice round number, it would grow or reduce as youngsters arrived or left, but right now each of them wanted to dance. Jerky, ecstatic, they seethed with uninhibited joy. Gao pumped the air with her tiny fists as her friends whirled her in her wheelchair. Even Song, recovering from an operation to fix her cleft palate, was present in the arms of a trusted older child, Sammi.

On the edge of the action, Sammi seemed immune to the lure of the music. He was quiet, as he generally was. Before Yulan House took over his care (Jia Tang had refused to take no for an answer when dealing with his parents) Sammi saw things he was just beginning to talk about. He put his face close to Song's and pulled the blanket over the baby's sleeping face.

Laughing as Rocky, the most flamboyant of Yulan House's office staff, spun her round – for a seventy year old he had moves – Kate fixed the scene in her mind. The low ceilinged canteen in the building's signature cream was the heart of the orphanage. Food happened here, and lessons and impromptu theatricals. Kate had already decided to apply the Yulan palette to her own home. Cream. Moss green. A dull, knocked back red. Accustomed now to fewer things around her, she would de-clutter; when Kate saw Charlie's home on Skype the fussy backgrounds sparked a fuzz of static in her head.

A scuffle broke out. High pitched screams in the corner. Egg tart on the floor. Kate dashed over to adjudicate. She made peace in pidgin Mandarin, exploiting her special status with the children. She was the foreigner, the strange one. And they loved her for it. Her funny-coloured skin. Her peculiar hair that kinked and waved. Her sky-coloured eyes. None of them stayed belligerent for long when she talked their language: natural gigglers, they fell about at her attempts to wrap her lips around their words. It was all in the intonation; each time she took off Kate wondered where she would land. She knew the word for *friends*, however. 'Pengyou?' she asked, squatting down to their level.

'Pengyou!' the abbreviated pugilists agreed.

With little experience around kids, apart from her time spent lolling with Flo, Kate had been stiff at first, unsure how to relate to the little characters pulling at her, chattering to her, ignoring her. Jia Tang had given her some advice which unlocked the door to each of their hearts. *Treat them like individuals*.

In the centre of the room, barely taller than her older charges and radiating warmth like a mobile sun, Jia Tang clapped and wriggled arthritically. Ageless – Kate never dared ask – she had the same combustible energy as the small fry. Jia Tang had confided that the children were the secret to her endlessly recycled zeal.

'When I tire,' Jia Tang said, 'I kneel down with the little ones, hold their hands, sing their songs with them, or just listen. And I am renewed.'

Massive, far too sweet, a celebration cake stood proud on a stand, obliterated with icing and held in the peripheral vision of every juvenile in the room. Kate could sense their anticipation. After months as an *ayi* – Yulan's term for a volunteer prepared to do anything and everything that was asked of them – Kate knew their quirks. She'd doled out dinner, shampooed their blue-black hair, tucked them up and shushed them in their long dormitories, woken them up, read to them, listened to them read to her. Mother, sister, friend, not only to the delightful dots like Dishi, who was sunny and sweet and as fat as a doughnut, but Li who stabbed her companions with a fork if their hands came too near her supper tray.

Each of them deserved love just for *being*, not for being good or kind or pretty; the ethos of Yulan House correlated with Kate's own. Each of them was a disparate thread Jia

Tang had gathered up and knitted into one unusual but warm garment.

'We'll miss you,' said the young teacher who'd travelled one and a half thousand miles from Guangzhou to offer her services for nothing. The cook, a paradoxically thin woman, said, with the help of the teacher to translate, 'Think of my Smacked Cucumber when you're eating horrible Yorkshire pudding and chips!'

Accepting so much carefully expressed goodwill was exhausting for a composite of Irish repression and English restraint like Kate. She felt herself fill up with complex emotion, feelings she'd been fending off. It was becoming real: tomorrow she would leave this place.

The magnolia tree in the courtyard offered consolation and peace, as it so often had. She settled into a spot at its base that knew her bottom so well they might have been made for each other. Kate had woken up to this tree every morning – shockingly early: Yulan House kept monastery hours – and fallen asleep in its shadow every night. It had taken her breath away when she'd first seen it, for real, after all the photographs.

The tree was where naughty children were sent to ponder their sins. Troubled children cried against the trunk. Happy ones ran round and round it. Kate had spent hours with the tree, sometimes with a baby on her knees, often alone, as she endeavoured to borrow some of the magnolia's patience.

Kate had been slow to admit what was happening. She'd fought it. The Kate who'd arrived at Yulan House had lost her belief in transformative love, love that made better people of those it touched. Watching the tree's abundant waxy blossoms bloom into cups, drop, get swept away, she felt her faith return.

'This tree is a good friend to us.' Jia Tang was at her side, dressed in her best, a neat navy uniform-style garment that Becca wouldn't wear to do housework. Her breath was scented with the chrysanthemum tea she favoured. 'As you know, we named our whole community after the Yulan, what you would call a magnolia. He always listens. Never interrupts.'

'Are you poetic because English is your second language?' Kate regarded the much smaller woman. 'Or are you poetic in Mandarin, too?'

'Actually, English is my *fourth* language.' Black teardrop eyes beneath smooth lids met Kate's slyly.

The formality of the English spoken by those of the staff who were multilingual had alienated Kate. She'd longed for slang, lazy pronunciation and less-than-respectful greetings. In time the decorous expressions felt soothing, just like the orphanage routines. Jia Tang insisted on structure, in order to reassure the children that, whatever their lives may have been like before, they could expect consistency from Yulan House.

During their late chats in Jia Tang's sparse office, Kate had asked how she dared to make the promise implicit in Yulan House's welcome. 'The children believe you'll look after them as long as they need you to. But this place is in continual need of money and resources. I see you holding your breath when you do the books.'

'Yes, we live hand to mouth,' admitted Jia Tang. Despite the solidity of the compound, the loud clang of the iron gates and the comforting smell of mu shu pork curling through the corridors, Yulan House got by on a wing and a prayer. 'We've kept going for thirty-six years. The orphanage works because it has to.'

Poetry again. Kate knew better. She'd witnessed the small hard-headed woman haggle with tradesmen until they were almost paying *her* to take their goods. She'd seen Jia Tang stare down shifty officials who stood between her and a little soul in need of her help.

That night, beneath the tree, Kate asked, with a note of anxiety in her voice she wouldn't allow anybody else to hear, 'Am I doing the right thing?'

Inside, Kylie had given way to Rihanna. Dishi gyrated on a trolley.

'You'll find the answer inside yourself.' Jai Tang rolled her eyes. 'Sorry. I can't seem to turn off the oriental whimsy.' She produced a small wrapped package from the folds of her outfit, like a conjuror. 'Open this,' she said, 'and think of me when you're back in rainy London.'

Reluctant to leave the tree, Kate went back to the party. Normally so rational, Kate had found herself entertaining notions that she'd offended some goddess of love. What other explanation could there be for a lifetime of near misses? The minxy goddess whisked Charlie away each time the music changed.

Now that Kate had duped the goddess and found a love without any divine help, perhaps she could accept Charlie's friendship as the prize it was, without wishing it was something other, something *more*. He, after all, had managed to convert his fervour for her into platonic love.

'Yam sing!' A fellow volunteer, Xu, touched her on the shoulder.

'What does that mean?' Kate touched her hair, wishing it was in better nick; Xu was dashing, with ripe lips and a slender, androgynous body.

'It means cheers,' said Jia Tang.

'But,' said Xu, in his dancing accent, 'it can also mean have a safe journey home.'

'Home,' said Kate, liking the shape of the soft word on her lips.

'Yam sing,' said Jia Tang. 'To you both.'

Mum, Mary, Becca, Leon, Charlie, Anna, Flo,
Aunty Marjorie & Uncle Hugh

You are cordially dis-invited

to the *Welcome Home Party*

that is *Not Happening*

at my house
8pm
7th November 2014

Seriously, guys, I love you all but
I'm too jet lagged to party.
Come to lunch on Sunday at 2pm
when I promise I'll be bright as a button.

Kx

Kate could imagine the disgruntled mutters, the tutting that she shouldn't be alone. She had no intention of being alone; if they knew the identity of her only guest it would cause a stampede. There would be disapproval and gratuitous advice, all of which could wait until Sunday, over a leg of lamb.

The house smelled all wrong. It felt neglected. Slowly, Kate reclaimed her home, lighting candles, roasting a chicken. The perfectly ordinary decor seemed opulent, the ensemble of texture and tone overwhelming her. As her first full day back in London went by, she became acclimatised and could see the beauty of it again. After all, she'd chosen every element herself. The house was hers, her footprint on the Earth. Yulan House had proved to Kate the value of home.

Jet lag made a mockery of routine. Energy peaks had to be utilised because dips followed close behind. Any minute now and Kate would be sleepy as a kitten, so she opened her laptop to bash out the email she'd been composing.

**From:** kateminelliparties@gmail.co.uk
**To:** kingangus@astorhouse.com
**Subject:** In Which I Explain Myself
7 Nov 2014 6.20

Angus,

You're right. I am an ungrateful and horrid harpy. Even though you were teasing when you said that, I know that most women would leap at the chance of a handsome chap collecting her from the airport. But I have my reasons.

(a) I wanted to do this whole trip under my own steam. So no limo. No chilled champers. No blond non-smoker carrying my bags.

(b) We needn't go into (b). You know why we can't pretend the last few months of our relationship didn't happen. I love you to bits, Angus, but I'm not able to come back to you. Dinner, yes. I've missed you. But on my terms, not yours. OK?

Much love,

Kx


P.S. I brought you back a panda in my suitcase.


Kate didn't quite trust Angus's rehabilitation. He flaunted his sobriety the way he used to flaunt his boozing. The recovery felt brittle.

She empathised with Angus's sense of being left behind by the tide, of knowing that what he most wanted was not going to happen, so she was gentle with him.

And firm. Life with an alcoholic had been grim. There had been laughs and luxury and real love, but mainly it had been a slog, a coal mining of the heart. Kate didn't regret her decision to scram.

Sometimes Kate asked herself *If Charlie and I were together, would I leave him if he was an alcoholic?* It was a rhetorical question: Kate would be at his shoulder throughout. She was full of such pointless self-knowledge.

A dense, damp November night had already closed in by seven o'clock. If Becca had had her way, the sitting room would be fizzing with music now. Flo would be refusing to dance; Becca would be refusing to stop.

Savouring the calm, Kate picked at something on a tray and eyed the undemanding pap on the television. After seven months with no blaring box she wanted to shout *Look at all the colours!*

Sleep began to steal over her. Kate felt obliged to fight it. She should get up, shake herself, and root around for the photograph of Dad. Kate was always careful with the treasured snap and she remembered, or thought she did, slipping it in the side pocket of her suitcase. It hadn't been there when she unpacked.

The missing photograph played on her mind. *It'll turn up.* Dread nibbled at her. She referred to – *deferred* to – the snap every day. *I need it.*

Sleep proved too seductive. Her eyelids closed, her limbs liquefied. Her head lolled back on the armchair.

A sudden noise.

Kate was alert. Dribble cooled on her chin. On the television screen a quiz show had been supplanted by a black and white movie.

That noise again. This time Kate was awake enough to recognise the doorbell.

The broken outline of the lone figure beyond the crazed glass in the front door drew nearer as Kate approached. She patted her hair, which was staging an eighties revival on her head.

'Welcome home, wanderer!' Charlie held up wine, choc-olates and a sheaf of roses; a cliché guest, but none the worse for that. 'Oh,' he said, deflated, taking in Kate's outfit of laundered-too-many-times hoodie and yoga pants. 'Why aren't you all trussed up in an uncomfortable dress?'

'Because the party was cancelled.'

'You're kidding.' The flowers and the bottle and the be-ribboned box went to his sides, as if Charlie was a knight dropping his shield.

'Didn't you get my email?' Kate didn't stand aside. Her house was her castle and nobody was getting over her drawbridge. There was much to do, not least finding the mislaid photo. Not even Charlie was welcome tonight.

'What email?' Charlie opened his pinstripe jacket to show off the lining. 'I bought this jacket especially. A tenner from Oxfam.'

'That book advance has gone to your head.' Kate rolled her eyes, giving in. Turning away she called over her shoul-der, 'Come in if you're coming, you gatecrasher.'

'Ah, that famous Irish hospitality.' Charlie followed her to the kitchen, where Kate was already plundering cupboards for glasses and a vase. 'Let's have an un-party.'

'Very *Alice in Wonderland*.' Kate kept the table between her and Charlie as she opened the chocolates, placing the box between them.

'You look well,' said Charlie, settling back on a kitchen chair. 'China agrees with you.'

'I look like a tramp, Charlie.' Kate wondered if she'd been institutionalised at the orphanage: this had all the requisites for a relaxing evening yet she was edgy. It was Charlie's fault for appearing without warning, like a genie. A genie with thick dark hair and soft eyes and a new chip in his front tooth.

Dismayed at such corn, Kate blamed the shock of being catapulted out of sleep. Charlie was just the same as he always was: untidy; in need of a haircut; in love with somebody else.

'I've missed you.' Charlie said it shyly, as if unsure how she would react.

'Me too. I mean, I've missed *you*. Obviously. Otherwise I'd be missing myself. Which would be a bit . . .'

They laughed together and it felt significant. One of those out-of-the-ordinary moments that stand out from the mundane, the way photographs emerge like silver ghosts in the chemicals of the darkroom. 'I did miss you, Charlie. Loads.'

'Good.' He said it again. 'Good.' He sat up and gently slapped away her hand hovering over the chocolates. 'Not that one. It's a raspberry creme.'

'Thank you,' said Kate. 'For saving me from the dreaded raspberry creme.'

'I couldn't take the fuss if you bit into it.'

Kate stretched her arms over her head, trying to wake up, trying to shake the presentiment she felt of something trying to happen if only she'd let it. *This is just me and Charlie in my kitchen.* It had happened dozens of times and would happen many times more. *If God spares us.* She parroted the phrase Mum compulsively murmured if any of them invoked the future. 'You know me so well,' she said.

As if to prove this, Charlie ticked off a list on his fingers. 'Praline, caramel, yes. Hazelnut, no. Yes, however, for its fellow nut, the almond. All cremes – raspberry, orange, whatever – are out. But you'd sell your soul for a fudge.' He held out a sweet cube between thumb and forefinger. 'Which is what I happen to have here.' Charlie put his head on one side. 'What will you swap me for it? Can I have your soul?'

*You can have all of me.* Kate coughed, as if she'd said it out loud. The techniques she relied on to jam the thoughts that assailed her around Charlie were malfunctioning. 'You wouldn't want my soul. It's a tatty old thing.'

'In that case, just take the fudge.' Charlie leaned over, as if to pop it into Kate's mouth, and Kate realised that he wasn't his usual self either. He hesitated, the chocolate in mid-air, before thinking better of the playful gesture and setting it down awkwardly in front of her. 'Eat up.'

They'd only been apart for seven months. There was no reason for this first-date stiffness. It was tense. It was stimulating.

Kate stood up. She'd deduced the reason for the atmosphere. 'Charlie,' she said. 'Come upstairs.'

Charlie rose. He asked no questions, just held out his hand.

Leading him upstairs, Charlie's fingers felt warm and strong in Kate's grasp.

The landing was dark. Kate heard him swallow. 'In here.' She pushed open a door.

The room was under-lit, intimate. Like a church. A mobile of fluffy clouds twirled.

'You *did* get my email cancelling tonight, didn't you?'

'Yeah,' said Charlie. 'But I couldn't stay away.' He seemed unsure what to do; if he'd had a cap he would have been wringing it in his hands.

Kate led him to the cot. 'Charlie, meet Song.'

'Hello, Song.' Charlie made a noise that could have passed for both a laugh and a sob, as if he was witnessing something glorious and hard to believe. As if Song was a unicorn and not a snuffling, sleepy baby with a quiff of jet black hair. 'I'm your Uncle Charlie.' He turned to Kate. 'That's OK to say, isn't it?'

'That's exactly who you are.'

Charlie knew Song's backstory. Kate had told him how the little girl was abandoned in Bawangfen bus station. Just a few weeks old and already alone. Perhaps Song's cleft palate was the reason her desperate mother had felt unable to care for her.

'The operation,' whispered Kate, 'was a success.' The scar would flatten and fade but never completely disappear.

'She's so cute,' said Charlie, getting close. 'She's, like, *super* cute.'

'Wait until she wakes up. Her eyes are like shiny buttons.' Kate could look at Song all day. Song liked to stare back, gurgling. Gurgling and staring. Staring and gurgling. The two of them wasted a lot of time that way. 'She took so long to drop off, let's leave her to sleep. You can get better acquainted on Sunday.'

The clouds above the cot trembled as they closed the door behind them.


As if sunbathing in the lamplit room, Charlie was stretched out on the rug, hands clasped behind his head, staring up at the ceiling as he listened to Kate, who was prostrate on the sofa, parallel to her guest but higher up.

'Why didn't you tell me what having a child is like?' Kate gesticulated and wine splashed on her hoodie. 'It's incredible, but a different sort of incredible every day. She's the same but different each morning. She changes in teeny tiny ways that nobody but me would notice.' Like a wholesome stalker, Kate was obsessed with the baby. She was Song's number one fan, her groupie, her disciple, a conscientious Boswell to Song's Dr Johnson.

Quelling a hiccup, Charlie said, 'Surely it was at the back of your mind when you volunteered at an orphanage that you might adopt? Not even a sneaky suspicion that you'd bring a baby home?'

'You make it sound as if I popped out to the supermarket for a pint of milk and came back with a pizza as well.' Drunk Kate couldn't be angry with drunk Charlie; he was only expressing what everybody else would surely think.

'Becca's been proph . . . prophes . . . saying you'd bring a child back from China.'

'I hate it when she's right.'

'Go on. Tell me how it happened.' Charlie fidgeted on the rug until he was comfortable, as if settling down for a bedtime story.

'I've never had a deep need for a baby.' Kate unpicked her thoughts as she went along, content for Charlie to hear the unalloyed truths about her attitude towards parenthood. 'I believe there's more than one way to live a life. Not just one proper way and all the other options are making do.'

'Damn right.' Charlie concurred from the floor. 'So no burning deshire?' he slurred.

'Exactly. Although I've always had this spooky feeling that a baby was in my stars. As if somewhere out there a tiny somebody was drawing closer and closer, at its own pace, in no hurry but determined.' Kate stole a glance down at Charlie to see how he was taking this whimsy. She chose the wrong moment; he was stealing a glance up at Kate.

'Go on.'

Kate's quiet belief in her own eventual motherhood had much in common with her philosophy about herself and Charlie. *Except* – she needed to be honest; the wine helped – *there's always been a futility mixed with my longing for Charlie.* The hushed confidence was entirely missing. Her belief in a love between herself and Charlie was exposed as something she'd concocted out of loneliness. Kate dragged herself back to her tale. 'I was drawn to Yulan House, not because of all the little babies I could kidnap, but because of Dad.' She felt a stab of fear about the missing photograph. 'And because I wanted to do something . . . *good.* That sounds revoltingly noble but—'

'Oh but you *are* noble.'

'Shut up. I didn't go there just to honour Dad, or whatever, but also to feel close to him. It's been hard, sometimes, to *feel* him . . .' She took a moment. Charlie allowed her the silence. 'When I got there, I loved the work. Just for its own sake. Nothing to do with Dad or giving something back or any of that. It was proper, hard work and it had *meaning.* I was needed.' She described her typical day as an *ayi,* waking the children, supervising splashy baths, feeding, cuddling, mopping up, telling off, consoling. Her smile as she spoke was unquashable.

347

Charlie said dreamily, 'Bet it put life back here in perspective.'

'It did.' Kate was looking forward to serving customers at the shop once more, but Jia Tang's example had illuminated the repetition of commerce. 'We do the same things over and over, for the purpose of . . . what? To buy a bigger house, a faster car, go on more expensive holidays? I had a bigger house and a faster car, and I got rid of them. I haven't flown first class since I left Julian.' That name brought Kate up short. It hadn't occurred to her to get in touch and tell him about Song. Kate wondered if he'd care. She hoped he would, although it wouldn't damage her if he didn't. *How odd to spend a chunk of my life with somebody and then neglect to involve him in something so profound.*

'Are you asleep? Don't be asleep,' begged Charlie from his spot below.

'I'm wide awake.' Kate drained her glass, not easy in a supine position. 'I got to know so many children out there. Caring for somebody, looking after them, means you get close.'

'It sounds bloody tough. But you're making me want to set off for China.'

'You don't have time. You'll be too busy being a rich and famous writer man. *BLOKE* needs a sequel.' Kate described some of the kids, each short musical name jabbing her with sadness at being so far away from them. 'I loved them. I really did. *Do*. But one morning . . .' Kate felt the day again in all her senses. Early September, it was the Mid-Autumn Festival. The skinny little cook had been making Moon Cakes all morning. The sky was a polished blue and the colours of summer were muted to browns and golds. 'A bus driver came to the compound. He was still in his military style uniform.' She digressed for a moment. 'Their bus drivers are *fancy*, Charlie. Epaulettes, and everything.'

'I like epaulettes,' said Charlie.

'It was just chance that I was by the gates when he drove up. He shouted through the bars. He was really agitated but I kept shaking my head, shrugging, trying to communicate that I'd fetch somebody to help him. He had something in his arms, a baby all wrapped up in blankets, and he was shouting the name of a big bus station in Beijing. People turned up like this occasionally, with babies they'd found just left on a bench.'

'Who could do something like that?'

'It's complicated, Charlie.' Jia Tang had taught Kate never to judge too hastily. The Chinese government's one child policy had created a culture of fear, where women were scared of their own fertility. 'It's hard to imagine living in a country where a second baby could mean ruin. The parents might lose their jobs, have their houses seized. There are hatches, you know, in each major city, for babies to be abandoned, no questions asked. The little boxes are heated and lit, and nobody chases down the adult who leaves the child.' Kate sighed. 'More girls than boys are abandoned.' She returned to her tale. 'I opened up the gates and asked him to come to the main house. At least, I tried to. My few words of Chinese are woeful; I might have asked him to marry me. I half turned . . .' Kate slowed down. The memory was glistening bright: probably because she buffed it every day. 'But he dodged forward, stuffed the bundle into my arms and stomped back to his bus. I stood there like an idiot, watching him. Then I teased back the blanket to look at the baby.' A fissure in the space between the lip and nose, a shocking absence where the flesh should have formed a tidy covering, registered. But Kate noticed something far more important. 'I recognised her,' said Kate, experiencing some of the wonder all over again. '*Hello*, I said. *You're mine.*'

'Bloody hell.' Charlie's voice was small. 'Bloody hell,' he repeated. 'You did it, Kate. You kept her. That's so brave. No, stop squawking. Let me say it. Brave *isn't* the wrong word.' He rebutted her rebuttal. 'You're brave and compassionate and independent and I'm proud of you. You're the bestest one-that-got-away a man could have.'

'Is that how you think of me?' A-tingle, as if tiny scorpions high-stepped up and down her body, Kate knew what she was doing and she knew it could go very wrong. This was sky diving. Bungee jumping. All without leaving the comfort of her own sofa and under the influence of alcohol. 'The one who got away?'

After a pause, Charlie said, 'You know it is.'

They lay still, like a Lord and his Lady on a medieval tomb. Kate didn't dare look down. The dedication to Anna on the front page of his manuscript reared up at her, only to be rinsed clean away by wine, adrenaline and lust.

Kate spoke without drawing breath. 'Sometimes I think we might still have something so I avoid touching you, like tonight when you came in and I should have hugged you, I would have hugged any other visitor but I didn't hug you because it felt like something explosive might happen if I put my arms around you.' She closed her eyes. 'Did you notice?'

As if responding via satellite link-up, there was a hiatus before Charlie said, 'Yeah, I noticed.'

*Is that a green light?* Kate felt the atmosphere thicken, as if they were both staying as still as possible. *Are we on a threshold?*

When Charlie spoke it was as if a cannon crashed. 'I knew you cancelled the party. I had to come here. I . . .' He hesitated. 'I just had to.'

There were so many questions. They crowded, demanding to be asked first. *What's going on with you and Anna? How long have you felt like this? Is it the drink talking? Or the jet lag? Am I so desperate you have no choice? Could we have a future? Is it happening for us at last?* She weighed them all up, feeling the clock ticking on this new and strange honesty, as if they were both enchanted by a fairy godmother and would turn back into pumpkins at midnight.

In the end, none of the questions won. They would only lead to more talk, and Kate didn't want to talk. She rolled over and dropped off the sofa, landing to kneel neatly astride Charlie. If she kissed him now and there was nothing, no fireworks, just a standard kiss, then she would, finally, know. They could shake hands, walk away.

'Kate, yes.' Charlie's whole body seemed to reach upwards for her and Kate bent, angling her head slightly, and her hair made a curtain around both their faces as she placed her mouth gently on Charlie's.

His lips were cushioned, soft, then busy as they responded to the feel of Kate's mouth. Charlie let out a soft groan and lifted his arms to embrace her, but Kate swiftly pinned them down. This was just a kiss.

Their lips ground together until Kate parted his with her tongue.

The experiment was an abject failure; the kiss was far more than the sum of its parts.

Intimate, familiar, Charlie's mouth was a drug. Kate collapsed onto him. They rolled and he was above her, his hands in her hair, his lips greedy.

Kate pulled away, just long enough to say, 'Not here.'

Glued together, a many limbed creature, Kate and Charlie grappled their way up the staircase, stumbling, staggering, devouring.

They crashed through her bedroom door. Charlie pulled down the zip of Kate's top with a gratifying *zzzp!*

'Cheeky!' Kate held the top together and darted into her en-suite. 'Hold that thought.'

'Hurry up, woman!'

Kate leaned against the back of the door, breathing hard. Her mind was popping candy. Her skin was thinking for her and it cried out for Charlie.

It was dicey to apply the handbrake to passion but the last time Charlie had seen Kate without clothes, she'd been nineteen years old and in the full glory of her youth. She needed to prepare herself.

Charlie would be confronted with the flesh of middle age. Kate's bra straps had dug into her shoulders. The mysterious rash by her belly button had spread. Since she'd realised her left breast was slightly larger than her right one she couldn't stop noticing the difference.

'Kate . . .' called Charlie in a low voice, through the crack of the door.

Ripping off her clothes as if they were soaked in acid, Kate threw them from her and confronted herself in the full length mirror.

There was her recognisable, mundane body, with its baffling colour scheme of palest lilywhite to purple. Kate took in her lopsided bosom, her footballers' knees and the hips where nineteen years of dessert congregated.

And she liked it. She knew that Charlie would like it too.

Tearing open the door, Kate launched herself at Charlie. He didn't miss a beat, his arms closing around her as if powered by a mechanism.

'Kate!' Charlie looked down at her nakedness. 'You're way ahead of me.'

Kate yanked so hard at his jeans that a button flew off. Soon they were equals, both pale and nude and warm and moving against each other, deliriously happy.

Or as happy as two people about to make love can be; desire has a knack of leaving no room for other sensations.

With Charlie hard against her in the chaos they'd made of the bed, Kate whispered, 'Are you sure?'

'Shut *up*,' growled Charlie.

'Language!' As punishment, Kate flipped him, hanging over him like a lovestruck bird of prey.

'If only you'd done this sooner,' said Charlie, his hands on her hips.

On the edge of Kate's vision, a tiny rectangle lit up – the screen of Charlie's mobile, a casualty of lust, fallen to the floorboards.

Charlie's mouth was on her neck as her breasts crowded him, and his erection waved a hectic *hello!* but Kate still managed to read the text.

Where r u babes? What's the point of moving in if you're not
here with me? Call me xXx

Kate pulled away from Charlie, from all of him, whether
soft or hard. 'Anna's moved in with you?'

Disoriented at the sudden disappearance of so many lovely
bits of Kate, Charlie managed to say, 'What?'

Kate scrabbled for the duvet to cover herself up. Her
nudity felt wrong. 'Anna, Charlie!' She tried not to shout.
'She's moved into your flat.'

'No.' Charlie looked insulted. He exhaled, passed a hand
over his features. 'Well, yes. Kind of.'

Her mouth numb from kissing, Kate demanded, 'Which is
it? Yes or no? Does she have a key? Are her possessions there?'

'She moved in today but—' Charlie sat up and covered
his groin with a pillow as Kate let out an infuriated grunt and
began to pace the room with the duvet trailing behind like
an ill fitting bridal gown. 'But, but, listen, it's not like it's,
you know, *official*. Most of her gear is still at her mum's.
She's kind of staying, yes.' Charlie evidently preferred that
term: his face, flustered and sweaty, lit up. 'That's all it is.
Anna's staying with me for a bit.'

'Is that what Anna would call it?'

Silence was an eloquent answer.

As if floodlights had blazed into life, Kate saw the evening
for what it was.

Her loins had billed it as a glorious, at-last moment just to get her head on board. The delirium wasn't suppressed love, it was good old horniness. Kate was desperate and as for Charlie . . . 'You're a sexual opportunist, Charlie Garland.'

'What? No I'm not.' As stung as if she'd accused him of murder, Charlie shook his head. 'This was as much you as it was me.' He was shouting now. 'It was *more* you!'

'Very gallant. What a gent.'

'I'm not an opportunist and I'm not a gentleman. I'm just me and you're just you and this just happened.' Charlie spoke more quietly now. Kate could hardly hear him when he held out his hand and said, 'It could still happen.'

'You're right.' Kate spun round, her hair on end and her eyes crazy. 'It could happen because this is exactly what I need. A drunken romp behind your girlfriend's back. What lady could refuse? It's my dream, Charlie, my dream, I tell you. Will you let me give you a blow job before you toddle off home? Pretty please?'

Face grim, Charlie stared. Kate was no longer interested in what was behind the pillow he clutched but she suspected there was nothing much to see. 'If you're just going to be a bitch . . .'

'I'm a bitch and you're a cheat. What a lovely couple we make.'

It had been perfect. Exciting and *right*. Now it was ruined, like a birthday cake upended on the floor.

Breathing hard, Charlie said, eyes cast down, 'Let's give each other a few minutes and then talk.'

'About what?'

'About *this*.' Charlie slapped the bed.

'Text Anna back.' Kate snatched up his phone and brandished it like a weapon. 'Go on. Tell her where you are. Tell her what's happening.'

'I can't do that.'

'Why not? Because it would be shitty?' Kate let the phone slip from her fingers, all her fight dried out. 'And you're not a shitty man. But this, Charlie . . .' She gestured around the room. 'This is shitty.'

Charlie didn't look as if he disagreed. They regarded each other with the same intensity of moments before, but this time it was laced with unhappiness and fear, not the prospect of wild lovemaking.

A small sound, nasal and snuffling, broke the spell.

*Song.* Kate wanted to fold down into herself, cringe until she was nothing. She'd forgotten Song.

Since Kate had brought her baby home they'd barely been out of each other's sight. Kate had only managed to cope with putting Song to bed in the new cot – the one whose delivery had piqued Becca's interest – by creeping up every twenty minutes to check her and admire her and find something new to adore in Song's hair or hands or knees.

Keeping her tread light, Kate sprinted to the spare room – or, rather, the nursery – as a high, thin wail started up.

Song was a quiet soul. She never grizzled or cried. When Jia Tang had helped Kate prepare Song for her cleft palate operation at Beijing Stomatological Hospital, she'd stroked the child's face, cooing, 'Express yourself, little one. Let it out.' Song's silence made her an 'easy' baby but Jia Tang had hated it; 'quiet babies have learned that nobody comes when they cry.'

'Let it out, Song!' Kate scooped up her little girl and gathered her to her chest.

Pristine in a white Babygro, Song roared.

'Me too, darling,' muttered Kate, rocking. 'Me too.'

Charlie, trousers on, shirt buttoned halfway up, was in the doorway. 'I should . . .'

'Yeah, you should.'

Song, calmed by Kate's heartbeat, lowered the volume of her protest.

'I want you to know, this isn't . . .' Tongue tied, Charlie stood, irresolute, the picture of confusion. 'This wasn't sordid, OK? I could never see you that way.'

'We had too much to drink.'

Clutching at this straw, Charlie nodded gratefully. 'Exactly. And Anna . . .'

*Be careful.* Kate fired a look his way from the pastel haven of the nursery.

'Anna moving in really was an ad hoc thing. It wasn't planned. She's been having problems with her landlord. She caught me off guard. I said *why not?*' Charlie was frowning, as if reprimanding himself. 'Maybe it was a mistake. I don't know.' He scratched his head violently, as if his scalp had offended him. 'Damn. This is such a mess.'

*For Anna, this bloke's bird.*

'There you go. Rationalising again.' Kate kissed Song's head, revelling in the heavy warmth of the baby against her. Charlie seemed unable to concede the truth whenever he was in love. 'Isn't it time you got behind your romantic decisions? It can't always be the woman's fault. Becca. Anna.' She hesitated, before plunging on. '*This.*'

Charlie sucked his lips. 'This wasn't anybody's *fault.*' He didn't seem to have anything more to say.

'This is the part where you go home to your girlfriend,' said Kate.

Shaking his head sadly – a gesture Kate couldn't decipher – Charlie looked at the floor as he said, 'Goodnight, Kate.' He put his hands over his face, muffling his words as he said, 'And goodnight little Song. Sorry about upsetting your mummy.'

By the time the front door was pulled to, Song was asleep.


Even the birds were still in bed when Kate woke up. She envied Song asleep in her crib next door, a plush toy cat alongside her. Puss Cat had been in the package Jia Tang told her to open in London; some of his whiskers had been lost – loved off, by Song – but he never left the baby's side.

Sleep eluded Kate, leaving her to relive the previous night's feverish highs and guilty lows. A quotation bobbed to the surface of her teeming mind. When she'd been wakeful in her childhood bed, Dad used to tell her about Macbeth.

'He had trouble sleeping too, and he longed for *Sleep, that knits up the ravell'd sleave of care.*'

Alight with purpose, Kate jumped out of bed, glad to leave the clammy sheets behind. Crossing to the suitcase standing open on the floor, Kate began to search. Methodical at first, she grew extra thumbs as panic set in. *It's really not here.* The teapot photo, as she thought of the snap of herself and her father, was gone.

'You'd have liked your granddad,' whispered Kate as she gave Song her first bottle of the day. Dawn woke the colours of the house around them. 'And he would have adored you.'

The arrival of Song would change the family's roles, forcing them all to budge up and make room. Mum didn't know it yet but she was a grandma. Becca was now an aunt, of sorts. Poor old Marjorie wouldn't like the title 'Great Aunt'; more excellent fodder for Great Uncle Hugh's teasing. Flo had a longed-for cousin; the girls would get along just fine. Not caring to contemplate Charlie's uncle-hood, Kate confronted her own title.

'I'm your mummy.' She said that dozens of times a day to Song, who stared back levelly with her deep set eyes. Kate imagined the baby thinking *That's old news*, but, in truth, she had no idea what Song was thinking and that was turning out to be part of the fun.

Song burped. 'Who's a windy little lass?' asked Kate, manipulating the small solid body until Song looked over Kate's shoulder, resting against her, a cosy bolster.

Patting Song's narrow back, Kate spoke into the baby's hair as she wandered about the kitchen, the early sun making the mundane utensils and pans gleam like amulets. 'We don't need photos, Song,' she said as the baby finished a thunderous burp. 'I've got your granddad up here.' Kate tapped her forehead. 'You'll know him through my stories and funny little sayings. It's only a photograph that got lost. He left all the love behind, more than enough to keep us both going. You can't drop love out of a suitcase, can you, Song, my pet?'

The child didn't settle in her cot, with its new bedding and its array of soft animals lined up for her pleasure. She kicked and gurned until Kate picked her up again. 'If I'm not careful I'll spoil you rotten, young lady.' Kate padded downstairs with the now content baby.

The new playpen with a multicoloured mat was laid out in the sitting room. Song lived in a world of new things, fresh out of the box. Trips back to Yulan House would help keep her grounded, and would do the same for Kate, who keenly felt the responsibility of caring for this malleable little person. It didn't frighten her; on the contrary, it was exhilarating.

Setting down Puss Cat within mauling distance – Song loved to bite the poor thing's ears – Kate reviewed her use of *malleable*. Song was fully formed, all there, a magnolia bud waiting to blossom.

'What have you got there, naughty pants?' Kate gently retrieved the cardboard square Song was sucking.

A little creased, a little damp, Kate's mustachioed father stared out at Kate, who looked from the snap to Song, to Song from the snap.

**Merrion Books**

are proud to invite you to
the launch of 'the decade's most
profound and provocative novel a
bout modern masculinity'

## «BLOKE»

«Come and meet the author
**Charles Garland**
Governor Magazine's
Writer of the Year»

7pm
Yellow Hand Gallery, WC1
13 May 2015
rsvp: gary@finklehoffpr.co.uk

'Relax!' snapped Becca. 'Imagine I'm not here.'

Easier said than done. Each of Becca's diets had added a few more pounds to her frame, and her blonde hair was so subsidised with hair extensions she was a trendy version of the Cowardly Lion.

'I've never been filmed before,' said Kate, straight backed on a hard chair, facing the single silver eye of a camera on a tripod. She didn't know what to do with her hands; suddenly they were the size of table tennis bats.

Becca tutted. 'You're not a Masai tribeswoman. You've seen a camera before. It's not going to eat your soul.'

Accustomed to subjects' nerves, Leon was gentler than his wife. 'Look over at Becca,' he advised. 'Not into the lens. Stand up and sit down again, casually, like you usually sit. And separate those hands.'

'You look as if you're strangling a chicken,' added Becca.

'And ignore my wife. Just cos she loves being filmed she thinks everybody else does too.' Leon rolled his eyes at Becca's eruption and his dreadlocks danced to the rhythm of his laughter.

'Shut up, Leon,' said Becca. It was without rancour; she said it four times an hour and never meant it. 'Look, Kate, even though we've pinned a sheet up over the cabinets to make a neutral backdrop this is still just my kitchen diner.' She always referred to it in that way, in case somebody might miss its splendour. Becca bent down to Song, who was playing with the laces on Becca's boots, as focused as if splitting the atom. 'Your mummy is nice and relaxed when she comes here for supper, isn't she, Song?'

*Your mummy.* After six months back in Blighty, Kate still got goose bumps when she heard her title. Maybe the thrill would never wear off and the rest of her life would be a long succession of Christmas mornings.

'Actually,' said Leon, squinting at a light meter on a cord around his neck, 'this is *more* relaxing than supper at our house because there's no spare man sitting next to you, Kate.'

'You mean . . .' Kate feigned incredulity. 'All those last minute unattached male guests are a *set up*?'

'Mock me all you like,' said Becca. 'I won't apologise for trying to fix up my pretty, clever, single mother, cousin. You'll thank me one day.' Becca was as unrepentant about her quest to marry Kate off as she was about smoking, or having cake for breakfast.

'Is that what I am? A single mother?' Kate was amused. She sounded like a statistic, something that would crop up in an earnest BBC documentary about broken Britain.

'Yes,' said Becca, happy to put her straight. 'I was one and it was lonely and it was hard and I worried I'd die alone and the police could only identify me by my dental records.'

'Surely,' said Leon mildly as he bent to peer through his viewfinder, 'they'd identify you by your silicone implants, love?'

'I'm not alone,' said Kate. 'I've got Song, like you had Flo.'

'It's not the same.' Becca was dismissive, as if this was Life 101. 'I was a mess until this hunk of burning love came along.' She slapped her husband lovingly (if extremely hard) on the bottom. 'You need your own Leon, Kate.'

'First, though,' said Leon, accustomed to speeding matters along, 'you need to contribute your soundbite to the video for Charlie's launch party. So chop chop, ladies.'

'Don't chop chop me, Leon,' said Becca, ramming glasses onto the bridge of her nose. A new nose, it was neither better nor worse than the perfectly nice original. 'Right. Like I said, we're getting a load of people, some well known, others nobodies like you, to talk about Charlie's book. We'll edit them all together and it'll be projected on a big screen at the party.' She winced. 'Couldn't you at least put a bit of lipstick on?'

'Just start talking,' said Leon to Kate.

'*BLOKE*,' said Kate, recognising Song's bottom wiggle as a signifier that her nappy was full, 'is a book I could read again and again.' She had done exactly that, alone in bed, with Song in the next room. 'It's wise without being preachy. It's a great story but that's not all it is. I find something new each time I flick through the pages.'

Leon nodded, happy, encouraging, and Becca tried to look interested, even though Kate knew she was planning what to have for dinner.

'Despite the title, it's not just about blokes. It's about people and how they find each other and what they do to hang on to one another.' Which was, when she stopped to think about it, ironic. *Better not stop to think about it then.* 'I've never read anything quite like it before and I can't wait for his next book.' Kate shrugged. 'Is that enough?'

Satisfied, Leon had left for a night shoot. Sharing a bottle of wine and an indifferent mezze Becca put together from the contents of the fridge, the women chatted about this and that. And Charlie.

Becca, who had a bloodhound's nose for sniffing out intrigue, had easily broken down Kate's defences about the sexual close call on the night of the un-party. When the wine came out, so did her insistence that Kate must 'do something' about Charlie.

'I know I interfere, I know I'm a pain in the arse,' said Becca, rifling the fridge for more foodstuffs to tip into bowls. 'But I can see what you're going through. You still love the silly git.'

'So what?' Kate pushed her glass out of Song's reach. 'It's like the weather. It's always there but I can't affect it. There's nothing I can do.'

'There's *always* something you can do.' Becca sniffed at some olives in a plastic tub before slinging them into the bin. 'Always.'

The last few months would have been very different without Becca's support and enthusiasm and unhinged love for Song. All the vices which made her impossible were, turned on their heads, the virtues which made her invaluable. Her nosiness was concern. Her bossiness cleared a path when Kate was unsure what to do. Her rampaging ego mutated into ironclad self-confidence when dealing with the doctor who saw 'no cause for concern' at Song's symptoms the time it transpired that the little girl had developed a hernia. Kate, cold with fear, had stood beside Becca in A&E while her cousin demanded a second opinion. Everything about Becca was turned up to eleven; these days Kate revelled in the amplified love more than she quailed at the volume.

'Charlie and me,' said Becca, 'get along fine now.'

'I noticed.' Kate pushed a lock of hair out of Song's eyes as she settled the sleepy child in a padded carrycot, on the floor between her mum and her aunt. 'About time. Flo's chuffed.'

'It took me a long time to get over the death of my marriage. I was climbing out of the wreckage and I didn't even know it was wreckage.'

Kate remembered Becca's insistence on 'partying' and 'girl power'. 'We get through life the best way we can.'

'And *your* way,' said Becca with distaste, 'is suffering in silence. Like some Renaissance saint on a tapestry.'

'I'm not suffering,' said Kate. That was true. 'I have Song. Not only that,' she rushed on, before Becca could interject, 'but I have the time to enjoy her, now that I have only one shop. I have a decent income.' Not as decent as she'd hoped; Kate, accustomed to healthy cash flow, found that even her non-Becca standard of living had suffered a little. 'I'm busy every minute of every day. I'm full of plans for this little one and myself. We're off to Beijing in a couple of months. And then I'll have to pick out a nursery school. I'm already investigating junior schools.' She looked down at Song, sleeping sweetly as if acting the part of an ideal baby in a TV commercial. 'I don't have time to sit around and ponder on what might have been. Not any more.'

'I'm sure all of that's true,' said Becca, who didn't look as if she found a mere bauble like the truth particularly compelling. 'But it's all about Song.' Becca dipped a carrot stick into some hummus. 'Look at Song,' she ordered.

'I am,' said Kate, sensing a lecture.

'Is she or is she not the best cared for ten month old you've ever seen? I thought I fussed over Flo but you make me look like an unfit mother.' Becca lowered her voice, a family tradition when touching on 'difficult' topics. 'I know the scar hasn't healed as well as you hoped, but Song will take that in her stride.'

Mention of the legacy left by Song's cleft palate made Kate shift on her seat. The weal on Song's face in the tiny space between her squat nose and her pout had faded in colour as the surgeons had prophesied, but it hadn't flattened out. Nothing could mar the perfection of Song – she was herself, everything about her was as it should be – but Kate projected herself into her daughter's future and saw curious stares or worse. These morbid daydreams set a bonfire in her stomach, so she wanted to snatch Song up and hold her to her, counteracting prejudice and ridicule with the ferocity of her love.

'The fortress you've built,' said Becca, licking her fingers, 'isn't necessary.' Her hand hovered hawkishly over the various dishes, before swooping on a sad chunk of cheese. 'Song has a smitten community of adults all looking out for her. She's got a cousin in Flo who thinks the sun shines out of her bum. She has *you*: Joan of Arc and Earth Mother all rolled into one.' Becca put down the cheese to make her final point all the more emphatically. 'And most importantly she's got herself. Song is going to be kick-ass.'

It should have been absurd, describing a pudgy baby in a nightdress embroidered with butterflies as kick-ass, but Kate agreed. Song had been born with a full quiver of arrows.

'So who is the fortress really for?' asked Becca. 'Are those thick walls for you?'

'I'm bored,' said Kate suddenly, as if thumbscrews had been applied to drag this confession out of her. Her hand shot to her mouth at her own blasphemy.

Becca sat up.

'Not with Song,' said Kate, hastily. It was impossible to be bored of Song. Of the countless, tedious, repetitive jobs that keeping her alive/fed/warm entailed maybe, but Song was a pearl whose iridescence threw up new colours each time Kate looked at her.

'I know what you mean.' Becca absolved her from being that dreaded ogre, the Bad Mother. 'It's a slog. Everything is ten times more complicated than it should be. I remember how settling Flo in her car seat used to feel like scaling the Matterhorn. And as for getting her to eat vegetables . . .' She shook herself, chasing away memories of the long broccoli war. 'I had Charlie to help and I was *still* exhausted. And yes, I can read your mind, I know I'm a demanding bitch but my exhaustion was real. How you do it on your own I can't imagine.'

Mummy + daddy + baby. Kate had never shared Becca's belief that this was the only equation for happiness. She perceived different paths through the forest. A subtle change had crept over her recently, slowly, relentlessly. The way the intense colour had faded from Song's scar.

*I'm ready.* Kate hadn't lunged at Charlie just because of the oddly fervid atmosphere, or the drink, or even her feelings about him. Her body had told her something her brain had been slow to compute. Kate needed a partner. A.N. Other. Somebody to hold her hand, to talk to her and make love to her, to make her laugh and irritate the living hell out of her. She needed somebody who needed these things from her in return. 'I do it on my own,' said Kate, in answer to Becca's speculation, 'because I have to.'

'What if you didn't have to?' Becca was keen, sharp, despite her curves and lack of angles. She leaned forward: a point was about to be drummed home. Again. 'What if you and Charlie could bring up Song together?' She leaned back, arms folded, triumphant. 'Do you really think Charlie would have kissed you, undressed you if he didn't mean it? He's not a womaniser, our Charles. He believes there's a contract made in every bed. And you . . . he wouldn't take *you* lightly. Ever.' Becca's voice went up as she made light of something Kate knew had had a massive effect on Becca's life. 'All through our marriage, he never stopped thinking about you. Not really. There were two levels, you know.' Becca put her hands out stiffly, parallel to each other. 'There was the top level.' She shook her left hand, replete with rings of varying magnificence and Cruella de Vil nails. 'He jogged along, being my hubby and your mate. But there was also *this* level.' Becca waggled her lower hand. 'The love was still there, bubbling along. You,' said Becca, letting her hands drop, 'are his favourite person. End of.'

'It's time to stop all this,' said Kate. As she drew breath to go on, Becca interrupted.

'I agree,' she said.

Mouth partly open, Kate regarded Becca, saying, 'You do?'

'Yes. You're right. I wish you weren't, but it's too late for you and Charlie. There'd be too many . . . what's that word you always use?'

'Casualties.'

'Exactly. Charlie and Anna seem to be making a go of it. You need to break free of his testicles.'

'You mean tentacles. At least, I hope you do.'

'Yes, them. The great KateandCharlie show is finally at an end and thank God!'

Kate imagined a striped marquee fluttering inwards and collapsing. Becca's capitulation after decades as Head Cheerleader gave Kate nothing to push against, nobody to argue with. The idea of herself and Charlie as a viable, achievable partnership must stand on its own merits and she found herself scrabbling to remember what they were. Remove the devil's advocate and the case collapsed. 'Indeed,' she murmured, '*thank God.*' It did feel refreshing. Or was that health-giving breeze a touch frosty?

'That's why you should reply to his letter.'

'Which . . .' Kate was befuddled for a moment. 'Do you mean the original note he sent me, the one you—'

'Yes, yes, the one I hung on to,' said Becca peevishly, as if it was time everybody got over this infinitesimal moral slip of hers. 'Answer it fully and frankly, telling Charlie how you felt, how you *feel.*'

'How is that letting go?'

'Because, silly, you won't send it.' Becca tossed her hair, pleased with herself. 'You just let it all out. Get it all said once and for all. Don't make your mind up right now. Just think about it.' Becca looked down at her nails, turning her hand over, then lifted her head. 'OK. Enough thinking time.'

'It does make sense.' Kate felt herself slump. 'Therapists suggest this kind of thing, don't they? Writing out your feelings but not sending them.' Song stirred, a baby dream forcing a clogged sound from her. 'She'll need changing soon.'

'When she does,' said Becca, sternly, 'we'll change her. Stop thinking about Song for a couple of minutes and focus on yourself.'

Words, phrases, images that had been walled up alive clamoured to be free. It would be purging. It would be a full stop. It would be right and proper to finally speak the truth without fear of repercussion. Kate could talk frankly on the subject that had towered above her since her teens, without the need to obfuscate or double talk. 'Paper, Becca!' she hissed. 'And a pen!'

It took five minutes. Kate wrote as if possessed, the pen careering away from her across the lined notepad. Finished, she went limp. The words had come from everywhere, from her brain, her heart, from her subconscious. Inside she was washed clean. She was empty, but she was clean.

'Can I read it out to you?' It seemed wrong that the letter would reach nobody's ears at all.

Becca nodded.

'Dear Charlie,' said Kate, from her seat on the hard chair, in a nice clear 'reading' voice she hadn't used since school.

'Thank you for your letter. I'm sorry for taking twenty years to reply but there were a few problems with the delivery service. When the letter was handed back to you by Becca, in 1995, I had never seen it. The only letter I read was your second one – which Becca *did* deliver – telling me it was all over between us. Next time, Charlie, put a stamp on an envelope and pop it in a post box.

'I eventually read the lovely words you wrote to me in 2009. They set me on fire. They made me want to jump out of my seat and run through the streets until I found you. But I didn't. I just reread it over and over, relieved that I hadn't been wrong about us, that we had shared a great love.

'It was too late to wave the letter and shout *Stop the game!* A piece of paper, tatty and old, couldn't change the facts. You were a father, and a divorcee in the first throes of a new relationship which, we all knew, was going to be an important one. There was Flo to consider.

'And me. I couldn't have coped with a rejection, Charlie. So I slunk away, clutching your words to my heart. I could recite it now. Don't worry, I won't. It warms me to think you once felt that way about me, that I inspired such love.

'Because I still feel that way.'

Kate felt a tear make its way down her cheek. She didn't wipe it away. It was part of the letter.

'Oh Kate . . .' murmured Becca.

375

'It's time to be honest. I love you, Charlie Garland. I can't see that ever ending. You told me you loved me at my fifth birthday party; do you remember? And do you remember how I pushed your face in the cake? I only did that because I was embarrassed and confused. Plus I was five: five year olds are like that. But the truth is I loved you back, even then. I could sense you were different. That you weren't going to grow up a copy of anybody. That you knew what it meant to suffer. And that it had made you kind, instead of beastly.

'So I've been constant, in my own quiet way, behind the scenes. Loving you and loving you and loving you. And wanting you so badly that sometimes the need would bring me to my knees in the midst of an ordinary day.

'So, to recap. We loved each other when we were five. We broke up when we were nineteen. We moved on, as they say. But I still love you, Charlie.'

Kate hesitated. She hadn't got any further with her thinking. It felt both forbidden and liberating to air these taboo feelings. Loving Charlie wasn't a crime, even though it felt that way sometimes. Perhaps this exercise would help her to derive some warmth from that love, even if she'd stopped hoping it could be reciprocated. 'So, um,' she continued, 'best wishes, Kate kiss kiss kiss.' She laughed and Becca laughed and Song's nappy emitted an un-spellable noise.

★   ★   ★

The ruse of writing a response to Charlie had worked like a charm. Perhaps Becca was a witch. Kate, struggling out of a black taxi with Song and all the attendant paraphernalia (babies travel in full pomp like Tudor monarchs), felt as if her soul had gone through the delicates cycle in her washing machine.

More than that, Kate felt open. Her love for Charlie hadn't diminished, but it had found its place. She could see past him now – *because I have to!* – and the fortress walls had crumbled to dust and the view was breathtaking.

The view, right then, was Mum and Mary, bearing down on her from the steps of the Yellow Hand Gallery.

'Isn't it grand?' Mum was overawed by the black doors and the brass knobs and the marble steps.

'Tickets,' said Mary, handing Mum her invitation. She'd taken over Dad's responsibility for all things practical. 'But first . . .' She looked pleadingly at Kate.

'Here she is.' Kate handed over Song, who had a sneaky preference for Mary. *Sensible girl*, thought Kate. The baby's two grandmothers doted on Song, but it was Mary who volunteered to babysit, and mopped up regurgitated din-dins as readily as she sang nursery rhymes. 'Quite a crowd.' Kate looked around her, at the chatting knots of people filing in, at the banner above the door. '*BLOKE*,' she read aloud, with a smile. She still hated that title.

'We saw Angus go in just now,' said Mum. 'We could have all gone in together if you weren't late.'

'Kate's not late, dear,' said Mary. 'We were early.'

'Same difference.'

'Yoo hoo!' Aunty Marjorie bore down on them, shampoo-and-set bristling with excitement. Uncle Hugh brought up the rear, as ever; Kate noticed a stoop to his shoulders she hadn't spotted before and felt a stab of pain. At some point these members of her personal cast list would leave the stage. *Have I ever told Uncle Hugh I love him?* It wasn't a throbbing, purple love; it was a quiet steady affection made up of nine parts proximity and one part appreciation. Hugh was a good, old-fashioned man. She remembered the fifty pence pieces he used to slip her. 'For sweets!' he'd wink. Impulsively, Kate reached up and kissed her uncle on the cheek.

He looked surprised. And touched. She was glad she'd done it. He held out his arm and she took it to mount the steps.

'This music is too bloody loud,' was Mum's opening gambit as she swiped a glass from a passing waiter. At odds with the Regency exterior, the gallery's interior was an austere cube. Charlie's face, ten feet tall, covered a projector screen. 'I can see right up his nose,' said Mum.

They found Becca 'testing' the buffet, bouncing on vertiginous heels. 'This is a big night,' she said. 'Big. *Big.*' She seemed more flustered than the occasion merited, and Kate gave her a searching look, which was ignored.

'Dad's nervous,' said Flo. 'He's gone all sweaty.'

'Nice.' Kate hugged the girl, who seemed to have borrowed some nerves from Charlie. 'Do you think you'll write books like your dad when you grow up?'

As Flo nodded, liking the comparison, Becca said, 'She'll be a top model.'

'No I won't,' said Flo. 'Unless I model *brains*.'

A tide of incomers filled the room. Anna, leading a gaggle of stork-legged friends, waved in their direction. She'd never cultivated Charlie's circle. *Thank God*, thought Kate. She wasn't sure how much Anna knew. There was a possibility she saw Kate not as Valued Old Chum but as Rapacious Hag Who Seduced My Boyfriend the Night I Moved in with Him.

The 'temporary' living arrangement had endured. The bathroom had been painted purple and its cupboards stuffed with toners, BB creams, hydrating serums and all the apparatus of the beauty black arts.

'That Anna's pissed already,' said Becca.

Kate looked deliberately at the glass in Becca's hand. 'Is that your first?'

'That's different. Listen!' Becca put her head close to Kate's. 'You know how you forgave me? About not handing the note to Charlie?'

'Yes,' said Kate slowly.

'You didn't use up all your forgiveness, did you? There's some left, isn't there?'

'What have you said to Anna?'

Charlie joined them just as Becca opened and closed her mouth wordlessly like a landed carp. Turning to him, Becca launched into an extended gush about his genius, his success, his tie.

As jittery as a bridegroom, Charlie was in modish black from head to toe. Sleek, sketchy, there was no quibbling about how good he looked, but Kate hid a smile at the artful tailoring of his outfit. Heads swivelled as he greeted her, his hair newly styled and held with product.

'This,' said Charlie, careful to focus on the two women and block out the interest being shown in him, 'is the exact opposite of writing a novel. You spend years and years in solitary confinement and then they make you come to *this*.'

'Your overnight success has taken two decades,' said Kate.

'True,' laughed Charlie. And there it was. That hateful transparent plane of civility that had slid into place between them every time they'd spoken since 'that' night. Charlie was punctilious about observing the rules of friendship, but his behaviour lacked the warmth that made friendship worthwhile.

'I keep having this dream,' said Charlie, 'about making my speech.' He held up a disintegrating piece of paper. 'Everyone points and laughs and it turns out that they're not publishing my book at all. It's a massive practical joke. Anna says I'm pathetic and she's right.'

Kate looked at Becca. They'd both noticed how his hands trembled.

Seeing Song in Mary's arms, Charlie asked the little child, 'Is that a new dress for the party?' He took delivery of Song and his shaking stopped. 'Thanks for coming, Mary. Cath.' Kisses. Arm squeezes. This landmark night was flying by.

'It's your night. Make the most of it,' said Kate, hating the polite smile he gave her in answer.

There were still emails, just fewer of them, and not so rambling. Kate and Charlie saw each other on the treadmill of family gatherings: *do other clans celebrate* everything *the way we do?*

Song was now the nucleus of these parties, the small, self-possessed, farting heart of it all. Charlie's relationship with Song was solid, but there was something robotic about his dealings with her mother. The vitality of true connection was missing.

This rupture didn't have the texture of their other ups and downs, which had only needed time to heal. This was complete, condemning Kate to a cordial purgatory.

'She wants a book!' laughed Charlie as Song lunged at a pile of hardbacks.

'No, Charlie,' said Mum, disapproving. 'She won't be able to hold it.'

'Let her have one,' said Charlie as Song sucked the binding of *BLOKE*. 'Song can do whatever she wants.'

'Hear hear!' said Kate, the phrase dwindling on her lips as Charlie evaded eye contact, making himself smaller, as if trying to erase himself in her presence.

'Girl power!' said Flo. From her, the saying felt right: it had nothing to do with the right to wear a short skirt past fifty and everything to do with equality.

'Where are your shoes, darling?'

At Charlie's question they all looked down at Flo's bare feet. 'Mum chose horrific tarty shoes for me to wear,' said Flo. 'I said no way.'

'So I end up carrying them,' said Becca, moving away to snaffle a bruschetta.

As Becca moved, Flo moved, keeping the distance between them constant. She needed her mum, the woman she fought on every detail no matter how trivial. Their bond was strong; no need for it to be pretty.

The screen brightened, music played, heads turned upwards to an image of *BLOKE*'s cover. High above them, Leon gave a thumbs up from his precarious eyrie in the rigging.

A voice boomed, and the image on the screen changed. An *Ah!* of recognition floated from the couple of hundred assembled book lovers/canapé fans as the head and shoulders of a well-known author appeared. 'This book doesn't read like a debut,' he began, earnest, confident.

Mum was disgruntled. 'Why amn't I on first?'

A glittering woman with a waist Song could have fitted her hands around grasped Charlie's arm. '*Love* the book.'

'Ta.' Charlie's ineptness at identifying flirtation hadn't improved.

A hand raised out of the crowd. 'Kate!' Angus pushed towards them through the room, which was filling up with a crackling urgency, as if they were all well-dressed refugees from some calamity out on the streets.

Just as Charlie was spirited away by his succubus, Kate leaned in to say, 'Break a leg!'

Ducking his head, Charlie winced, gave a tight smile. With a lightning bolt of insight, Kate recognised that look. She knew what lay between them: hurt.

*I hurt him.*

'You,' said Angus, 'look utterly delicious.' He kissed her cheek, tentative, but with a hint of ownership as if he could go further but chose not to.

'Fibber.' The floral wrap dress which looked so good on the mannequin bit into soft parts of Kate. 'I look every second of my thirty-eight years and ten months but I appreciate the compliment.'

Thin-ness, the holy grail of modern life, is not for everybody. The new look, pared down Angus was diminished and hungry looking. Even his outrageous hair had calmed down to a tidy shape as if too busy fantasising about sausage rolls to party.

This close, Angus smelled of shampoo and raw good health. Kate couldn't shake the notion that he was in fancy dress, that he would unzip his pale suit and the real Angus would step out, belly wobbling, cigar ash all over an inherited waistcoat.

'Dinner?' With his Santa cheeks trimmed away, Angus was handsome in the pink and white English manner. He still had the power to move Kate, to shrink the rest of the room. 'Later?'

'I'd love that, but only if I choose the venue. That whole-food establishment felt a little too like church for my liking.' Angus didn't laugh. Angus didn't laugh as often or as heartily as he used to. But Kate liked him and desired him and she nurtured hopes that this pious macrobiotic Angus was a transitional phase. The raw material was still the same; at some point the 'true' Angus must break free and grab a doughnut. 'I'll ask Mum and Mary to babysit.' Kate was in need of a beginning and Angus had been dangling just that for months.

Up on the screen, a terrifying apparition with a perm and an arch expression spoke with Mum's voice. Or, rather, how Mum would sound if she was English and upper class. And bonkers. 'I didn't actually read Charlie's, Charles's, Charlie's book. It's terrible long and I'm a busy woman. It's probably ever so good.'

Laughter rose tinnily from the room. Leon, pressing buttons, blew a kiss down at Becca. Mum, pleased with her contribution, hoisted a blini to her lips.

'No, darling contessa, I won't let you do that to yourself.' Angus tugged at Mum's wrist. 'Those are sheer useless calories you are contemplating.'

'Feck *off*,' growled Mum. 'The useless ones are me favourites.' Angus removed his hand, smartly. He turned to Kate, gesturing at her champagne. 'For my sake, for your liver's sake, darling, make that your last one, yes?' He bent to eye her, nose to nose. 'I want the real Kate. I want authenticity.'

*Please*, thought Kate, *don't start talking about your juice business.*

'When my new juice business is up and running, I'll make sobriety trendy. Imagine that.'

Becca, who didn't seem to like what she was imagining, sighed. She was still unable to forgive Angus for confiscating her crackling when she cooked him roast pork. 'Just because you're the poster boy for clean living doesn't mean we'll all become puritans.'

'Although,' said Flo, 'you *should* give up smoking, Mummy.'

'You *smoke*?' said Mum and Aunty Marjorie in horrified unison.

'The child is correct,' intoned Angus sadly. 'Your body deserves respect, Becca,' said the man Kate had once found asleep in a skip. 'Once I get you reprobates juicing, we'll all live an extra ten years.'

'And what bloody tedious years they'll be.' Becca raised her glass with mock solemnity.

'Your health isn't something to joke about.' Angus sounded more saddened than annoyed.

'What you need, Angus,' said Becca, 'is a nice cheese-burger.'

'I'm practically vegan.' Angus was pious, as if announcing a new pope.

Mum scoffed, with the timbre of an expert; she'd been scoffing at fads since the sixties. 'You'll be raving about anti-ageing superfoods next. They say broccoli is a superfood. Broccoli!' Mum seemed outraged by broccoli's promotion. 'It's just feckin' broccoli.'

'Allow me,' said Angus, 'to explain the science behind it.'

'There's no science to broccoli.' Mum was robust. 'It's like saying there's a philosophy to carrots.'

Over their heads, a gigantic Flo was shyly saying, 'It's, like, the best book ever. Definitely better than Shakespeare.'

Leon's skilfully edited compilation was warming up the room as Charlie stood at the podium, raking through his notes and knocking back a glass of wine provided by his PR handmaidens.

Taking Song, complete with her copy of *BLOKE*, Kate moved to gain a better view of an actor she vaguely recognised saying, 'Books are the new rock 'n'roll.' Through the ether, she sensed Charlie's sphincter tightening at that comment.

Resting her lips on Song's head, Kate closed her eyes, the better to evoke the jolt of recognition that had shaken her earlier. The specific tilt of Charlie's head, the air of being forced at gunpoint to speak to her, the soft bruised look in his eye – it all whisked her down a wormhole to her fifth birthday party.

Charlie had exhibited these same behaviours then, when he overheard the mums' stage whispers about his torn shorts and his odd socks.

Charlie had been hurt, then. He was hurt now. *I hurt him*.

Replaying 'that' night, words stood out in her memory. Cheat. Shitty.

*But they're true*. Kate defended herself to herself. Charlie was another woman's boyfriend yet he'd been naked in her bed.

Song slapped the book. 'Boo!'

'Yes, sweetie. Boo! Book. Book. Can you say *book*?'

Burning to communicate, Song brought her palm down again on Charlie's author photo. 'Boo!' she yelled.

The congregation shifted. Through an avenue of backs, Anna caught Kate's eye and began to move towards her. If she hadn't been hemmed in by bodies Kate would have fled. Anna, sinewy in a jumpsuit, brought out a guilt so intense that Kate feared it was visible on her face.

As Anna glided through the crush, glass aloft, Kate faced that guilt squarely; *I went into that bedroom in full knowledge of Anna's existence*. She was as much to blame as Charlie. It took two, as the saying went, to tango.

'Hey you!' Anna showed all her teeth as Mary, way over their heads, said, 'You'll want to read it again the minute you finish the last page.' 'This is unreal! There's fucking *celebs* here!'

'Is Charlie OK? He seems a bit shredded.'

'Oh, *him*. He's been shitting himself all week. I said it's a party, babes. What's so scary about a party?'

'Well . . .' *Lots.* 'Are you chuffed with the dedication?'

'What's a dedication?' Anna put her shoulders up to her ears, in a parody of embarrassment. 'To be honest, babes, I haven't read the book.' She shook her head, eyes lazily closing. 'It's too long.'

'And there are no pictures.'

'Exactly.' Anna guffawed, then looked Kate up and down. 'I never realised you and Charlie . . .'

'What?' Blood rushed to Kate's face.

'You know,' said Anna. 'You were together. Back in caveman days.' She paused. 'Before I was born.'

'We went out for a while,' said Kate. 'Before he married Becca.' Reduced, it sounded so trivial.

'I can't imagine it.' Anna held Kate's gaze.

'Me neither,' said Kate.

*That's all it takes for me to deny him.* Kate's need for Charlie hadn't diminished but, since Dad's death, she was practised at needing people whom she couldn't have.

Her own clumsiness appalled her: she'd shamed Charlie,

thrown him out like a degenerate for doing something she'd wanted too.

As Anna dived back into the melee, Kate hugged Song so hard the baby squeaked. Song made everything bearable. Not that it was the child's job to 'cure' Kate's loneliness: Song's only job was to be Song.

'We're ready,' said Kate, into Song's circle of a face. 'Aren't we, baby?'

Kate was ready for a man to tread dirt on her hoovered carpets, disarrange the towels in her bathroom and muss up her bedclothes.

Above all, he must muss up Kate.

That it couldn't be Charlie was a caveat she accepted. *I embrace it!* she told herself. This felt unlike the other times she'd indoctrinated herself to face facts. She was ready for second best.

Second best could be good enough. Second best was the dress Kate could afford, not the one-off couture piece she slavered over in *Vogue*. It was the tasty, satisfying slice of Victoria Sponge ordered after somebody else bought the last towering wedge of gateau. Kate's best shoes pinched; her second best leather ballet pumps were as comfortable as slippers on her feet.

Finding – or being found by – Song had used up all Kate's cosmic luck. Nobody wins the lottery twice. Time for the understudy to step up.

An actress shook her bracelets on the screen. 'This book should be a movie!'

'Angus!' Kate saw him scanning the room for her. As he closed in, she said, excited, 'Fish and chips! After the party. Yeah?'

'But, darling, the batter is made with—' Angus bit his tongue. 'Just this once, you rascal. We do have something to celebrate. I had an offer. For Astor House.'

Kate laughed, then stared. 'Seriously?'

'It's time.'

Even though slimline, teetotal Angus was out of step with the club's core values, Kate couldn't imagine the place without him. Or he without the club.

'Running a members' club isn't the best lifestyle if a man wants to settle down.'

Kate saw Flo approaching through the scrum, her face at elbow height. 'Is that what you want? To settle down, I mean.'

'I do.' Angus was so intent he looked sad. 'If you do. I cleaned up for you, Kate.'

'You cleaned up for *you*, Angus.'

'It's all for you.' Angus opened his arms and let them drop again. 'All of it.'

Kate was Angus's best; Angus was Kate's second best. Could it work with such imbalance at the centre? She imagined a vegan wedding reception.

'I know,' she whispered.

A tug at her sleeve and Flo said rapidly, 'Mum said to say she's really sorry.'

'What for?' frowned Kate.

Uninterested now she'd discharged her duty, Flo shrugged.

Kate turned to Angus to say, 'I *really* don't like the sound of that,' but he was stooping to check his pedometer.

On a raised dais, Charlie was ready at the lectern, a secular priest about to address his flock, as behind him on the screen Kate's face loomed, a giant moon, hair uncombed, pink with discomfort.

*Is that what I look like?* Kate wondered why nobody had ever told her the end of her nose wiggled when she spoke. *My voice sounds like a squeaky supermarket trolley.* Thankfully, nobody seemed to be taking much notice of her platitudes, least of all Charlie.

From the foot of the dais, Becca's stare cut through the party.

Holding Song like a shield, Kate felt a nibble of foreboding. Angus nudged her. 'Fame at last.'

The gigantic Kate, nose wobbling, was finishing up. 'I've never read anything quite like it before and I can't wait for his next book.'

'How do famous people cope with seeing themselves all the time?' giggled Kate, relieved that her turn was over.

But giant Kate was still talking, still *booming*.

'Dear Charlie.'

'Ooh,' said Angus. 'There's more.'

Outlined dark against the brightness of the screen, Charlie turned to stare at it.

'Thank you for your letter. I'm sorry for taking twenty years to reply but there were a few problems with the delivery service.'

The room swelled and shrank in Kate's vision. She blinked and steadied herself.

'The only letter I read was your second one.' The lips on the screen kept moving. The words kept tumbling. Kate found Becca's beseeching eyes.

*So this is what Becca's sorry for.*

The chatter in the room barely slackened, although a few puzzled looks were exchanged. A figure sitting on the edge of the podium, legs dangling, leaned over to poke Charlie in the calf. Kate saw Anna's face; it was confused, ready to be either mollified or to explode.

'It's time to be honest. I love you, Charlie Garland. I can't see that ever ending.'

As if struck, Kate closed her eyes and turned her face away.

Her alter ego had its audience in the palm of her hand. There were stifled giggles, a hissed *Is this a stunt?* but the gathering grew quiet.

'Darling,' said Angus. He was tense, quick. 'Listen.' He wasn't angry. *Angus* should *be angry!* All this wasted love flying around, landing in the wrong laps. Kate had been about to saddle Angus with a ready made family just to assuage her feelings of isolation. She'd been prepared to sacrifice him on the altar of 'fitting in'. 'I'm sorry, Angus,' said Kate as she turned to hurtle through the press of bodies.

'Is that her?' she heard.

'Kate!' Angus grabbed her arm.

'No! Just no.' Kate shook him off, unable to look at his face. More hurt. With the smell of burning bridges in her nostrils she propelled herself and Song through the double doors and down the steps she'd tripped up so thoughtlessly an hour earlier.

Before the doors swung shut behind her, Kate heard herself say, from the screen, 'We moved on, as they say. But I still love you, Charlie.'

Hard practicalities nipped at Kate's heels. She had no cash. Song's bag was with Mary. A taxi turned the corner of the street. Throwing out her hand, Kate hoped the driver wouldn't mind stopping at a cashpoint. *Even if he does mind*, she thought, *we'll be a few streets away from this apocalypse before he chucks me out.*

Song buckled in, they pulled away from the kerb, only to stop at traffic lights. Kate hunched down in her seat, refusing to look back at the gallery. She tried to curate the new anxieties all hatching at once. Her mother would have a thousand questions. Anna would be mortified. And Flo . . . the thought of what Flo would think of her forced the first tear.

A sharp rap at the window yanked Kate out of her painful reverie. Charlie's face was at the window, tormented, like a mask.

The driver, just a pair of ears beneath a flat cap, said, 'D'you want—'

'Just drive on. Please.'

'You're the boss, lady.'

The lights changed and the taxi accelerated.

'Boo!' *BLOKE*, open beside Song on the seat, was a drum for the baby. She thumped out an erratic beat of her own composition on the dedication page and the book slid to the floor of the cab.

Leaning over to rescue the book, Kate yelled, 'Stop! Please stop!'

'For gawd's sake . . .' The cabbie swung them deftly out of the traffic, setting off a rude tooting of horns.

Swinging open the taxi door, Kate looked back along the street. Arranged on the steps were all the cast members of her life. Becca. Flo. Mum. Mary. Aunty Marjorie. Uncle Hugh. Leon. In front of them stood Angus, watching Charlie fly over the paving stones to reach the cab.

'Get in!' shouted Kate.

First, Charlie kissed her, leaning over her, blocking out the light, his foot on the signed copy of *BLOKE*, tracking mud all over the dedication.

*For my K, because sometimes what looks like love is love.*

'Anna,' was Kate's first word as they drew apart.

'Over. Long ago.' Charlie looked bewildered. 'She won't move out!'

'Where are we going?' snapped the driver.

'Anywhere!' cried Charlie as he bundled into the seat beside Song. 'Anywhere at all, mate. I hate parties.'

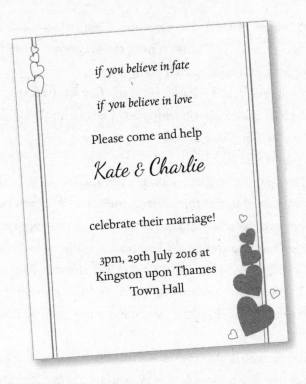

*if you believe in fate*

*if you believe in love*

Please come and help

*Kate & Charlie*

celebrate their marriage!

3pm, 29th July 2016 at
Kingston upon Thames
Town Hall

Now, Kate replaced the dress in the wardrobe, where it effort-lessly outranked its denim and cotton peers. She stroked it regretfully, as if it was an exotic pet that had to be put down. *Pity I'll never get to wear you.* Kate shut the door on the wonderful confection, its skirt puffing out and resisting. Even if she dyed it or took up the hem, a dress like that could never be anything but a wedding dress, which rendered it quite useless to Kate.

She wheeled at the unmistakable sound of a foot on the stairs. Kate crossed to the door. 'Who's there?' she called, certain now that she was not alone. Charlie had taken Song to the restaurant, to double check the seating plan and place a disposable camera at each place setting.

'Only us!' yelled Charlie from the foot of the stairs. Kate heard his keys land in the china bowl where he always threw them when he came home.

'You were quick!'

'No I wasn't.' Charlie sounded bemused. 'Get your skates on, woman.' His feet thumped on the stairs. 'We can't be late for our own wedding and the traffic's bumper to bumper.' He popped his head around the bedroom door, Song in his arms.

*Oh no, his wedding haircut is too radical*, thought Kate.

'You're still in your underwear!' said Charlie, dismayed. 'Get dressed, quick, while I wrestle this tiny woman into her new frock.'

Refusing to buy a new suit, Charlie had declared he wanted to get married as himself 'this time around'. Flashbacks to his top hat still woke him in the middle of the night, he said.

The couple had compromised; Charlie was going as a version of himself, wearing his old faithful pinstripe jacket from Oxfam over a crisp new white shirt, chosen by Kate. Biased, she would have thought him gorgeous if Charlie turned up at the registry office in his dressing gown.

Not many brides could get ready for their Big Day in twenty minutes, but Charlie was unimpressed by Kate's haste. As she clattered down the stairs in new shoes, bouquet in hand, she heard the frustrated honk of their car horn. Despite this, Kate lingered in the hall for a moment, taking her leave of the framed photo hanging by the door.

'See you later, Dad,' she said, and kissed his image, wishing, with a fervour that shook her entire body, that he could be there to give her away.

Diving into the car like a bank robber making a getaway, Kate buckled up her seat belt, twisting round to establish that Song was secure.

'What the hell,' said Charlie, 'are you wearing?'

'Last minute change of plan,' said Kate. 'You know you had to whizz out and buy a replacement cake because Song found the original one and ate half of it?'

'Ye-es.' Charlie sounded as if he knew what was coming.

'Well, the cake made a reappearance. Song staggered into our bedroom and threw up all over my dress.' Kate was brisk. 'Drive, man, *drive!* Are you sure we have time, Charlie, to stop on the way?'

'We'll *make* time.' He smiled across at her as they pulled away from the kerb, both of them knowing that was the only possible answer.

When they reached the long low building set back in bland gardens, Kate pointed out a parking space. 'Here, Charlie.' All three of them left the car at a trot; Kate thought wryly of bridal magazines advocating a serene atmosphere on the Big Day.

The family of three raced through beige corridors, Kate scooping up Song when her little legs flagged. The room they sought was a long glass extension at the back, bright and stiflingly warm.

Aunty Marjorie sat in a high backed armchair, eating toffees and glaring suspiciously at her visitors.

'She recognises you,' said Uncle Hugh. 'I can tell.' His wife had her good days and her bad days; to Kate this looked like one of the latter. She saw nothing of her aunt in the woman's gaze, as if the lights had gone out in a much loved house.

They sat for a while, making conversation, until the implacable clock couldn't be ignored any longer.

'You're sure you won't come to the wedding?' Kate embraced Uncle Hugh and held on for longer than necessary. She'd heard her mother tut that he spent too much time at the care home, but he would shrug and say, *What else would I do with myself?*

'Quite sure, love. We'll think of you at three o'clock.'

Song refused, point blank, to kiss the stony faced woman; Kate realised that her daughter would remember only this Marjorie and not the bubbly, snobby, kind and sarcastic aunt who'd been a stalwart of Kate's life. 'Goodbye, Aunty.' She bent and embraced her. 'This is for you.' Kate pulled a peony from her bouquet and popped it into a glass of water.

'Right,' said Charlie, as they retraced their steps through the institution. 'Let's get married!'

The room was functional and without charm, but it exploded with emotion as Kate and Charlie bounced in, Song between them, holding hands and beaming.

*Things Can Only Get Better* blared from a terrible sound system as Kate, Charlie and Song walked up the abbreviated, cheaply carpeted 'aisle' between rows of utilitarian chairs. The assembled family and friends sang the chorus, none of them knowing it was the song that reminded Kate and Charlie of the night they gifted their virginity to one another.

The short journey to the registrar was time travelling for Kate. All – almost all – the important players of her life were there.

At the very back Julian was no doubt already plotting his escape. Kate had been gratified by his 'yes' when she'd tracked him down; it felt mature and oh-so-modern to have her first husband at her second wedding. Julian caught her eye and smiled, still a golden boy, although these days he was a bald golden boy. Beside him his wife, a petite Japanese lady half his height and age, gave Kate a frosty once-over.

Newlywed Angus stood in the next row of seats, his hair tamed, his attire conservative, and his arm around his new wife. Anna, leaning on her hubby, surreptitiously checked her phone. Already estranged from Charlie by the time of the infamous book launch, she'd been philosophical when he chased after Kate. She'd turned around and there was Angus; mutual consolation had turned to love, or something very like it. *They're both too thin*, thought Kate, pulling in her tummy as she passed. Mr and Mrs Walker-Smith looked like x-rays of themselves.

Holding hands in matching dresses, Mum and Mary dabbed their streaming eyes as Kate passed them. Mum nodded a blessing.

*Don't cry*, mouthed Kate. *You'll start me off!*

Becca wasn't crying. She looked too stunned to cry, horrified by the striped chain-store sundress Kate had yanked from the wardrobe. Long forgiven for her meddling at the book launch – Becca's chess playing had ultimately made her hapless pawns happy – she'd helped Kate choose the lace wedding dress and looked incensed by the last minute substitution. Beside her, Leon wept unashamedly as he jiggled one-month-old Clinton, a child the colour of coffee, who had his father's flair for happiness and his mother's way with a well-timed tantrum.

'Flo!' squeaked Song, spotting her favourite person.

Flo's wave was a jerky gesture. The thirteen year old was nervous about her ring bearing duties. Pink with self-consciousness, Flo would much rather be reading. Kate blew her a kiss, just for being Flo.

As they reached the registrar, a small, beaming woman in a suit, Kate *went*. Tears claimed her, spoiling her hastily done make-up, clouding her vision.

*Aww!* said the room.

Fumbling in his pockets, Charlie found a tissue and handed it to her, as the registrar waited patiently for the bride to compose herself.

'Don't cry, Mummy,' said Song, tugging on her hand. 'Everything's OK.'

'I know, sweetheart,' said Kate. 'Everything is much much better than OK.'

Later, much much later, after the three course meal in their favourite bistro and the sentimental, disrespectful speeches, and Song eating so much of the replacement wedding cake that she vomited over her mother's replacement wedding dress, Kate and Charlie were back on their own sofa.

Lying facing each other, feet companionably muddled, their shoes were off, the lamps were low, and Song was sound asleep in the new toddler bed she was so proud of.

'That was quite a day,' said Kate, head back, remembering. 'Much better than any fortieth party.' Her birthday had been lost in the mix.

'The best and the last wedding ever,' said Charlie. 'Agreed?'

'Agreed. I couldn't face all that admin again.' Kate saw Charlie's lip wobble in a comedy way. 'Plus I married the man of my dreams. Should I have said that first?'

'Ideally, yes. Sorry about the dress, love. You handled it magnificently. My first wife,' Charlie enjoyed saying that; he said it again. 'My *first* wife would have cancelled the entire wedding.'

'You mean sorry about the *dresses*. Plural.' Kate looked down at the brittle blot on her sundress. 'Good old Song, managing to ruin them both. I didn't care a bit. The lace dress is gorgeous but this comfy old thing is more *me*. Like that ten quid jacket is *you*. The real Kate married the real Charlie today,' she said. 'Spattered with their daughter's vomit.' Kate prodded Charlie's chest lovingly with her big toe. She had goose bumps, as she did every time she recalled that morning, six months into their proper, at-long-last relationship, when Charlie had woken her with a cup of tea and an urgent, *I want to adopt Song*. 'So, groom-boy, are you going to carry me up the stairs and ravish me, as just-marrieds are contractually obliged to do?'

'With my back? You know I can't lift heavy loads.'

Kate prodded him again, not so lovingly this time. 'Oi!'

'Ow!' Charlie took her foot in his hands and rubbed it the way she loved. 'You're forgetting my deadline, Mrs Garland.'

'Ah. Yes.'

The sequel to *BLOKE* was overdue. Charlie was working around the clock in his study, rising before Kate and joining her in bed long after she'd fallen asleep.

'So,' she said, 'it's another all-night session at the laptop for Mr Minelli?'

'Afraid so. We have the rest of our lives to ravish one another.'

'True.' Kate thought of Uncle Hugh, sitting beside Aunty Marjorie in a room that smelled of canteen food. She thought of her dad, his lovely face frozen in time and framed in her hallway.

*The rest of our lives.*

The phrase didn't oppress or constrict Kate. Just the opposite. It signified freedom, an adventure constantly unfurling.

Clumsily, kneeing him in his tender parts, Kate clambered over her new husband. *My first* real *husband.* Lying against him, her head on his chest, she savoured him. Charlie was an endless luxury, a well of contentment that never ran dry.

'This is nice,' murmured Charlie, once he'd recovered from her knee. 'This so nearly didn't happen. Imagine that. Imagine we hadn't finally got it together.'

'I don't want to.' Kate had lived that very scenario for long enough.

'I don't want to work tonight.' Charlie wriggled until he was in a position to kiss Kate on the lips. 'I want to take my wife upstairs.'

They stood, clinging to each other, two middle-aged folk in their untidy, ordinary, perfect sitting room. Charlie whispered into Kate's hair. 'Hear my soul speak.'

They recited the next couplet in unison.

'The very instant that I saw you, did my heart fly to your service.'

'Come on, Kate.' Charlie switched off the lamp and led her out of the room, his eyes on hers. 'The party's over.'

*You're wrong*, thought Kate. *The party's just begun.*

# Acknowledgements

Every book needs a champion and the people who helped me believe in this one were Sara-Jade Virtue, Jo Dickinson and Ditta Friedrich. Thank you all.

And thank *you*, Clare Hey, for being both picky and charming as you edited the manuscript. That's a hard act to pull off, but you do it with aplomb.

It's traditional to thank your other half and your children at this juncture and I don't intend to break with tradition. The reason authors thank their families is that they're the poor sods who have to put up with us as we career towards our deadlines. So thank you, Matthew and Niamh, for the love and the understanding and the eating of burned fish fingers without comment.

# GROSVENOR HOUSE
## A JW MARRIOTT. HOTEL
### LONDON

## *Experience Luxury*

Grosvenor House, A JW Marriott Hotel is one of London's most historic hotels, centrally located in the heart of London in one of the capitals most desirable addresses; 'Park Lane'. Elegant and British in style, Grosvenor House has been frequented by royalty and celebrities since opening in 1929.

Grosvenor House is delighted to offer one lucky reader and a guest, an overnight stay, Afternoon Tea for two in the newly opened Park Room plus a Benefit Cosmetics goodie bag worth over £100.

For further details please visit www.simonandschuster.co.uk/competitions

## *Literati events*
### at GROSVENOR HOUSE

Taking the traditional book club a step further, Literati at Grosvenor House, A JW Marriott Hotel, is an elegant event that hosts authors to lead an intimate discussion of their latest book with hotel residents and guests. Champagne and canapés are served, guests are encouraged to interact and ask questions and receive a signed copy of the book.

Literati authors have included 'first lady' of broadcast journalism, Kate Adie, Lord Michael Dobbs of international bestseller, *House of Cards*, Royal Correspondent, Hugo Vickers, number one bestseller, Santa Montefiore, author, journalist & TV personality, Richard Madeley, and iconic novelist, the late Jackie Collins.

To hear about future Literati events, email literati@marriott.com or visit the website www.grosvenorhouseliterati.co.uk